Snowfall at Willow Lake

Center Point
Large Print

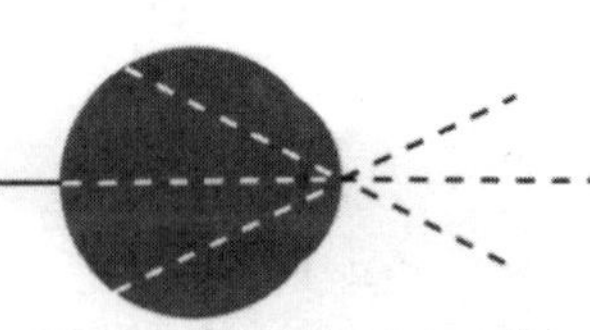

This Large Print Book carries the
Seal of Approval of N.A.V.H.

Snowfall at Willow Lake

SUSAN WIGGS

CENTER POINT PUBLISHING
THORNDIKE, MAINE

This Center Point Large Print edition
is published in the year 2008 by arrangement with
Harlequin Books S.A.

The text of this Large Print edition is unabridged. In other
aspects, this book may vary from the original edition.
Printed in the United States of America.
Set in 16-point Times New Roman type.

ISBN: 978-1-60285-123-8

Library of Congress Cataloging-in-Publication Data

Wiggs, Susan.
Snowfall at Willow Lake / Susan Wiggs.--Center Point large print ed.
p. cm.
ISBN 978-1-60285-123-8 (lib. bdg. : alk. paper)
1. Large type books. I. Title.

PS3573.I38616S85 2008
813'.54--dc22

2007049014

To Rose Marie Harris,
who owned and operated Paperbacks Plus, the best little bookstore in Washington State for the past twenty-seven years. She's the kind of bookseller every writer dreams about—well-read, enthusiastic, caring and helpful, with an uncanny knack for putting the right book into the hands of the reader who is sure to love it. A book signing at Paperbacks Plus always involved plenty of food, friends and fun, making for unforgettable events, year in and year out.

To Rose Marie, Kate, Lois and the rest of the staff—it was a great run, ladies.

Thanks for everything.

ACKNOWLEDGMENTS

The daily work of a writer involves spending many hours alone with a roomful of fictional characters, and it takes a lot of love and understanding from the real people in my life to put up with that.

Thanks to the real Momzillas, who are nothing like the ones in this book.

I am truly blessed by the women writers in my life. Their moral support and brain power enrich the entire experience of making stories and art, and their talents keep me in awe—Anjali Banerjee, Carol Cassella, Sheila Rabe, Suzanne Selfors, Elsa Watson, Kate Breslin, Lois Faye Dyer, Rose Marie Harris, Patty Jough-Haan, Susan Plunkett and Krysteen Seelen.

Thanks also to Margaret O'Neill Marbury, my ever-patient editor, Meg Ruley, my agent, and her associate Annelise Robey, for invaluable advice and input. Thanks to my publisher and readers for turning the Lakeshore Chronicles into a great success. The books came from me, but the success from you.

I'm so very grateful for my family, including our newest arrival, Barkis the wonderdog. Special thanks to my wonderful mom and dad—I only wish I could be as good as you think I am.

Part One

February

Lake Effect

Each winter, when cold arctic air sweeps across North America, snow squalls may form along the lee shores of lakes. These squalls, known as lake-effect snowstorms, bring locally heavy snowfalls to a relatively small area. Often, while squalls hit one area, brilliant blue skies prevail only a short distance away.

One

Avalon, Ulster County, New York

Every station on Noah Shepherd's truck radio was broadcasting the incessant warning. The National Weather Service had issued an advisory—a prediction of snow, ice and wind—whiteout conditions in a lake-effect snowstorm. Authorities were urging people to stay home tonight, to keep the roads clear for emergency vehicles only. The county airport had closed hours ago. Even the heaviest snow-removal equipment was having trouble lumbering along the highway. Only madmen and fools would be out in this.

Well, madmen, fools and large-animal vets. Noah wished his windshield wipers had a faster setting. The wind-driven snow was coming so hard and fast it was like a solid wall of white. He could barely tell whether or not he was on an actual road.

Legend had it that during lake effect, magic happened. Right, he thought. If this was magic, he'd stick with reality.

After delivering the Osmonds' foal, he should have taken them up on their offer to stay the night, waiting until the weather and roads cleared before making his way back to his home and adjacent clinic miles away. However, according to reports, it could be days before the storm played itself out and it was likely to get worse before it got better. He had the Palmquists' geriatric beagle in the clinic, a cat recovering from spinal surgery and his own animals, which currently included an abandoned pup. He knew he could always call his neighbor, Gayle, to look in on them, but he hated to bother her. With her husband serving overseas and three kids underfoot, she sure as hell didn't need to go traipsing over to his place to check on the animals.

Besides, his scrubs were covered in birth blood and fluid. He needed a shower, bad. He was wearing his favorite hat, a wool cap with earflaps. It was from his "early dork" phase, as one of his former girlfriends had called it. Noah had quite a few former girlfriends. Women his age tended to want something other than life with a country vet.

He leaned forward over the steering wheel, squinting at the road ahead. Illuminated by his headlamps, the snowflakes appeared to be flying straight at him in a movie-like special effect. He thought of *Star Wars,* when the Millennium Falcon went into warp speed. And that thought, of course, inspired him to whistle the *Star Wars* theme between his teeth. Bored with crawling along, he imagined his windshield was a window to a galaxy far, far away. He was Han Solo, and the snowflakes flying at him were stars. He issued orders to his copilot, who perked up at the sound of his master's voice. "Prepare for throttle up. Chewie, do you read? Go at throttle up."

Rudy, a mutt in the passenger seat, gave a huff in response, fogging the window.

Noah's last girlfriend, Daphne, used to accuse him of being a kid who would never grow up. And Noah, who had the subtlety of a jackhammer, suggested only half-jokingly that they make a few kids of their own so he'd have someone to play with.

That had been the last he'd seen of Daphne.

Yeah, he had a real way with the ladies. No wonder he worked exclusively with animals.

"General Kenobi, target sighted, a thermal detonator," he said. In his mind, Noah pictured a galaxy slave clad in a chain mail bikini. If only the universe would actually send him someone like that.

Then he changed his voice to a wise baritone with a bad English accent. "I trust you will find what you seek. And . . . shit." A pale shadow glimmered in the road right in front of him. He turned the wheel and eased off the accelerator. The truck fishtailed. Rudy scrabbled around on his seat, trying to stay put. In the middle of the road stood a big-eyed doe, ribs showing through its thick winter coat.

He leaned on the horn. The doe sprang into action, sprinting across the road, leaping the ditch and disappearing into darkness. Midwinter was the worst time of year for the wildlife. The starving season.

The radio station played its usual test of the emergency broadcast system. He turned it off.

Almost home. There were no landmarks visible to tell him so, just an inner sense that he was nearing home. Other than college and vet school at Cornell, he'd never lived anywhere else. Each rural mailbox was supposed to be marked by a tall segment of rebar, but the snowdrifts were too deep and the rebar and mailboxes were buried.

He sensed but could not see Willow Lake, which lay to the left of the road. Willow Lake was the prettiest in the county, a natural beauty fringed by the Catskills wilderness. At the moment it was invisible behind the curtain of snowfall. Noah's place was across the road from the lake and slightly uphill. Along the lakefront itself were several old summer cottages, unoccupied in winter.

"General Azkanabi, we need reinforcements," he said, hearing the imaginary music swell in his ears. "Send me someone without delay!"

In that instant, he noticed . . . something. A glimmer of red in the snowy shadows. The whistled theme song died between his teeth. He eased off the accelerator and kept his eyes on the crimson glow, eventually making out a matching light. Taillights, which seemed to belong to a car stuck in a snowbank.

He stopped the truck in the middle of the road. The car was still running; he could see a plume of exhaust coming from its unnaturally angled pipe. The taillights poured an eerie red light into the night. One of the headlights was buried in the snow-bank. The other illuminated the deer that had been hit.

"Stay, boy," Noah ordered Rudy. He grabbed his kit,

which contained enough tranquilizer to put down the deer. He lit his flashlight, an elastic headlamp.

Switching on his hazard lights, he emerged into the stormy night. The flying snow and howling wind sliced at him like blades of ice. He hurried over to the car, spying a single occupant inside, a woman. She seemed to be fumbling with a cell phone.

She lowered the window. "Thank God you came," she said, and got out of the car.

She was inadequately dressed for the weather, that was for sure. A high-fashion coat and thin leather boots with tall, skinny heels. No hat. No gloves. Blond hair, blowing wildly in the wind, partially obscured her face.

"You got here so quickly," she yelled.

He figured she thought he was from roadside assistance or the highway department. No time to explain.

She seemed to share his urgency as she grabbed his sleeve and pulled him to the front of the car, wobbling a little on her boots. "Please," she said, her voice strained with distress. "I can't believe this happened. Do you think it can be saved?"

He aimed the beam of the headlamp at the deer. It wasn't the doe he'd spotted earlier, but a young buck with a broken antler on one side, three points on the other. Its eyes were glassy and it panted in a way Noah recognized—the panicked breaths of an animal in shock. He saw no blood, but so often, the injuries that killed were internal.

Damn. He hated putting animals down. Hated it.

"Please," the stranger said again, "you have to save it."

"Hold this," he said, handing her a flashlight from his kit to supplement the headlamp. He eased himself down next to the animal, making a soothing sound in his throat. "Easy, fella." He took off his gloves, stuffed them in a pocket of his parka. The rough coat of the deer warmed his fingers as he palpated its belly, finding no sign of fluid, no abnormal softening or heat. Maybe—

Without warning, the deer scrambled into action, legs flailing for traction in the deep, soft snow. Noah caught a sharp blow to the arm and backed off. The animal lurched to its feet and leaped over a snowbank; Noah instinctively moved in front of the woman to shield her from the hooves as the animal clambered off into the woods.

"I didn't kill it," the woman said. "You saved it."

No, he thought, although it must have looked impressive, what with the deer jumping up as soon as he placed his hands on it. He didn't say so, but there was still a good chance the buck might collapse somewhere in the forest, and die.

He turned off the headlamp and straightened up. She shone the flashlight into his face, blinding him. When he flinched, she lowered the beam. "I'm sorry," she said.

Pulling on his gloves, he asked her, "Where are you headed?"

"Twelve forty-seven Lakeshore Road. The Wilson place. Do you know it?"

He squinted, getting his bearings. She had run her car off the road right by his driveway. “Another few hundred yards down toward the lake and you’re there,” he said. “I can give you a lift.”

“Thank you.” Snowflakes caught in her eyelashes, and she blinked them away. He caught a glimpse of her face—startlingly pretty, but pale and strained. “I’ll get my things.” She handed him the flashlight, then fetched a purse and a big tote bag from her car. There was also a roll-aboard, fluttering with tags. In the glow of the dome light, he could see words in some foreign language—’s-Gravenhage? He had no idea what that was. And another with an official-looking seal, like from the State Department or something. Whoa, he thought. International woman of mystery.

She turned off the ignition and the lights. “I don’t suppose there’s anything to be done about the car,” she said.

“Not tonight, anyway.”

“I’ve got a few more bags in the trunk,” she said. “Do you think it’s safe to leave them?”

“Probably not a huge night for thieves.” He led the way to his truck and opened the passenger-side door. “Get in the back,” he ordered Rudy, and the dog leaped into the jump seat behind.

The woman hesitated, clutching the purse to her chest and staring up at him. Even in the dim light from the truck’s cab, he could tell her eyes were blue. And she was no longer regarding him as the Deer Whisperer. Now she was looking at him as though he were an ax murderer.

"You're looking at me as if I'm an ax murderer."

"How do I know you're not one?"

"Noah Shepherd," he said. "I live right here. This is my driveway." He gestured. The drive leading up to the house, flanked by pine trees weighted with snow, now lay beneath knee-deep drifts. A glimmer shone from the front window, and the porch light created a misty yellow aura around the front door. The entranceway to the clinic, kennels and stables lay off to the left, the security lights barely visible.

She paused, touched her teeth to her lower lip. "Even ax murderers have to live somewhere."

"Right. So how do I know *you're* not an ax murderer?"

She seemed completely unperturbed by the question. "You don't," she said simply, and got in the truck.

As he walked around the front to the driver's side, Noah wondered if strange forces were at work. He wasn't given to thinking of such things, but hadn't he just been wishing for someone? Was the universe listening after all?

Of course, he didn't know anything about his unexpected passenger. As she'd aptly pointed out, he didn't even know whether or not she was an ax murderer.

Like that mattered. With those looks, she could be Lizzie Borden and he probably wouldn't care. She was gorgeous, and she was sitting in his pickup truck. Why look a gift horse in the mouth? A gift horse. Ha-ha.

He hoped the smell of snow-wet dog and birth fluid wouldn't bother her too much. Don't blow this, he cautioned himself as he climbed into the driver's seat. And quit jumping the gun. He didn't know if she was seeing someone, married, engaged, gay or psychotic. The only thing he knew for sure was—

"Damn," he said before he could stop himself, "Why didn't you tell me you were wounded?" Grabbing the flashlight, he shone the beam on her, following a viscous crimson stain up her leg to the ripped knee of her trousers.

She made a sound in her throat, a wheeze of fright so intense that Noah cringed. Then she began to tremble, her breath coming in panicked little gasps. She said something in a foreign language, like a German dialect, maybe. It sounded like a prayer. She looked up at him with wild fear in her eyes, as though he were her worst nightmare.

So much for not blowing it, Noah thought.

"Hey, no need to freak out," he said, but she was lost somewhere, drowning in panic, and then . . . nothing. She simply melted against the truck seat, her head tilting to one side.

"Hey," he said again, louder now. Shit, had the woman passed out? He ripped off his glove and felt her carotid artery for a pulse. She had one, thank God. "Come on, miss," he urged her, gently cupping her cheek in his hand. "Snap out of it."

Behind him, Rudy scrambled to and fro, whimpering. He could probably smell her terror and her blood. Then he paused, put back his head and howled.

That'll teach me, Noah thought. When he asked the stars to send him someone, he should be a little more specific. "Send me a Hooters waitress" was what he should have said, not some crazy-ass stranger who fainted at the sight of her own blood.

As far as Noah could tell, this was a loss of consciousness brought on by injury, fear and anxiety. In animals, it was sometimes a defense mechanism. In humans . . . he wasn't quite sure what it meant. Regardless, he needed to check her blood pressure, tend to her wound.

He made sure the truck was still in four-wheel drive, then eased it up the driveway. He passed the house and continued to the next building, which was his clinic. The property had once been his family's dairy, and this building had housed the company offices. When he set up his practice three years ago, he had transformed it into his veterinary clinic.

He got out of the truck and motioned to Rudy. With a yelp, the agile mutt cleared the front seat and bounded away, racing across a snowy field. Clearly he was eager to flee the stranger.

Noah jumped out and ran to the passenger side. "Miss? Can you hear me, miss?"

The woman was still unresponsive. He rechecked her pulse, then awkwardly pulled her from the cab, staggering backward in the knee-deep snow. She wasn't a large woman, but her deadweight dragged at him as he carried her to the clinic. He shouldered open the door and stepped inside, pausing to disarm the alarm system, which he managed to do without dropping the woman. Then he crossed the dimly lit reception area to an exam room. He lowered her to the stainless steel table, extending it to accommodate her length. It wasn't designed for humans, but he had no other choice. "Miss," he said yet again. Damn. He wondered if he should start CPR.

"Come on, come on, come on," he said, jiggling her with one hand, pulling out an oxygen mask with the other. The cone-shaped mask was designed to fit over a muzzle, but by pressing down hard, he made it work.

Her eyes flew open. Wide awake, she struggled and cried out. Noah backed away, holding his hands palms out. "Yo, calm down, okay?" he practically pleaded, thinking about the horse tranquilizer in his kit. He wondered what she would do if he said, *Don't make me get out the horse tranquilizer* . . . Bad idea. He was at a loss here. Should he touch her? Soothe her? Or throw water in her face? Touch her, definitely.

"Miss . . ." He put a gentle hand on her wrist, intending to check her pulse.

Big mistake. She jerked away as though he'd burned her, scrambling to a sitting position and regarding him as though he were Jack the Ripper.

"Miss," he said again, planting himself in front of her so she wouldn't fall off the table if she passed out again, "you're going to be all right, I swear. Please, look at me. I can help, but you need to focus."

Finally, his words seemed to penetrate. He could see the glaze of fear in her eyes begin to soften. She took a deep breath in a visible effort to calm herself.

"Hey," he said, resisting the urge to take her hand. "Calm down. It's going to be all right." He used his most soothing tone, the one he reserved for feral cats and skunks with distemper. "We're in my clinic. I'm a—I have training." Best to hold off explaining he was a vet. "I need to check you out, okay? I swear, that's all I want to do. Please?"

She began to shake, her face as white as the moon. "Yes," she said. "Yes, thank you. I . . . I don't know what came over me."

No shit, he thought.

"My guess is you experienced a vasovagal syncope," he said. "In layman's terms, you fainted from the sight of your own blood. There's been some physical trauma, so I need to ask you some questions, check your pulse and blood pressure."

This time, finally, his words seemed to penetrate. He took a risk, touched his fingers to her chin and studied her pupils. Her skin was velvet smooth, but chilled and clammy. He felt her effort to stop trembling, saw the resolution on her face. "I'm sorry," she said, her voice still slightly tremulous. "That was unforgivable of me." She squared her shoulders and tipped up her chin. She seemed to grow in confidence, transforming herself into a different person. The cowering victim disappeared. In her place was a controlled—though clearly shaken—young woman.

"No apology necessary," he said. "Lots of people freak out when they're hurt and bleeding." He shrugged. "Proves you're only human."

"What is this place?"

"My clinic," he said.

"I crashed my car in front of your clinic? That was good planning." She offered a weak smile.

"Has this happened before?" he asked her. "The syncope—fainting."

"No. Good heavens, no, never."

"Before the episode, do you recall experiencing headache, back pain, chest pain, shortness of breath?"

"No. I was right beside you. I felt fine up until . . . I don't recall."

He took off his parka, then remembered his scrubs were stained with blood and fluid from the foaling. He quickly turned away so she wouldn't see, peeled off his shirt, stuffed it into a hamper for the service, then grabbed a clean lab coat.

His patient was extremely quiet now. He turned to find her staring at his naked torso. Her mouth—a beautiful mouth, even for a crazy lady—formed a perfectly round O of surprise. Her face was still pale though; she was probably still at risk for syncope. And despite his fond wish, it was not over his physique. Something had spooked her, and he hoped it wasn't him.

"Just need to put on a clean shirt," he said.

Her gaze flicked away from him and darted around the clinic.

He felt her trust in him draining away. At vet school, they didn't teach you not to take your shirt off in front of a patient, because as a general rule, the patient didn't care.

"Sorry," he muttered to her, and quickly slung a stethoscope around his neck, hoping that might reassure her. "I swear, I just want to help."

"And I appreciate it," she said, bracing her hands on the waist-high stainless steel table, the array of supplies and instruments on the counter. "I won't go into a panic again. That was . . . it wasn't like me. And this is all very . . . *Rocky Horror Picture Show.*"

Noah instantly flashed on Susan Sarandon in her bra and panties. *I wish.*

He used a foot pump to lower the table. "You're still bleeding—no, don't look." He didn't want another fainting episode. "I really need to check out that leg." He scrubbed his hands at the sink, then plucked a pair of latex-free gloves from a dispenser, eyeing her leg as he drew them on. "I might need to cut your trousers off," he said, then couldn't suppress a grin.

"Is something funny?" she asked.

"It's just that I've never said that to a patient before. Have a seat on the table, okay? And scoot back so your leg's stretched out."

To his surprise, she obliged, propping herself on her hands as she looked around the exam room, focusing on canine growth charts and a calendar from a veterinary drug company. “You’re not a real doctor, are you?”

“That’s pretty much my favorite question,” he said. “See, if I were a *real* doctor, I’d only know the anatomy and pathology of one species, not six. I’d only have one specialty instead of nine.”

“I guess you must get that a lot.”

“Just enough to annoy me.” He took a step back, holding his gloved hands up. “Listen, I’m fine with not doing this.”

“If you don’t mind, I’d like you to go for it.”

So much for playing hard to get. “I’ll need to check you out, see where else you’re injured.”

“It’s just my knee.”

“You might have an internal injury.”

“And you can tell this.”

“You’re exhibiting signs of shock. I need to examine your chest and belly for bruising and palpate your abdomen.”

“You’re not kidding, are you?” She stiffened, folding her arms tightly. “I’ll pass. I didn’t hit myself on anything. I don’t hurt anywhere. It’s just the knee.”

He wasn’t about to push her. The situation was already bizarre enough. “I could call EMS, but on a night like tonight, I’d hate to call them for anything less than a life-threatening emergency,” he said.

“This isn’t life threatening,” the woman said. “Believe me, I know the difference.”

“Okay. Just the knee for the time being. But if you feel anything—double vision, dizziness, anything—you need to let me know.” He checked her blood pressure. It was in the normal range, a good sign. An internal bleed caused the pressure to drop. "Okay," he said. "Let's have a look at that knee."

She lay back and covered her eyes with her forearm. "You'll understand if I don't watch."

"I noticed you're not fond of blood." He selected a pair of bandage cutters and started at the hem of the dark wool trousers, cutting upward. The thin, expensive-looking leather of her boot was drenched in blood. He kept cutting upward, hoping he didn't have to go so far that he'd look like a complete perv. The cut was arc shaped; she must have sliced it on something under the dashboard. "You've got a gash here, just above the knee." The laceration probably hurt like hell. It wasn't a bad cut, but it appeared to be a bleeder. "You need sutures," he said.

"Can you do it?"

"I'm no plastic surgeon. Whatever I do is bound to leave a scar."

"Then can you stop the bleeding and I'll find a surgeon in the morning?"

"It can't wait that long. The risk of infection is too high. The maximum any doc would allow is seven hours. Roads'll still be closed in the morning."

"Then stitch it up, and I'll live with the scar."

For a woman this good-looking, it was an unexpected remark. "All right. I can numb the area . . . it'll probably need a dozen stitches. If I make them really small, it'll minimize the scarring." He considered offering her a tranquilizer to calm her down, but wasn't sure of the dosage. She probably weighed about the same as a Rottweiler, so 80mg should do it. Then again, maybe not. He'd stick with a local anesthetic.

"I'll hold still for the novocaine," she said.

"It's lidocaine, one percent." And he hoped it didn't take much to numb the area. It was strange, having a patient that didn't need restraining. He injected the local and she didn't flinch.

"That'll go numb in a couple of minutes," he said.

"I'm counting on it." She took her forearm away from her eyes, turned her head and stared at the counter. "If I'm really good, do I get one of those biscuits from the jar?"

"You can have as many as you want," he said, making a slit in the sterile wrap of a suture tray. "They give you minty-fresh breath and whiter teeth."

"We can all use that," she murmured.

He changed gloves and got busy with the cleansing and suturing. Many animals had skin that was more delicate than humans. He chose 3-0 nylon with a skin-cutting needle, standard equine external suture material.

He put on a pair of magnifying glasses and angled a task light at the site, working with as much delicate precision as he could to avoid a zipperlike scar on her pale, delicate skin. He felt her starting to tremble again and wondered if he should be making small talk to ease her nerves a little and, please God, make her hold still. With his regular patients, a few sympathetic clucks usually did the trick.

"I didn't get your name," he said.

"It's Sophie. Sophie Bellamy."

"Any relation to the Bellamys that have the resort up at the north end of the lake?"

"Sort of. I was married to Greg Bellamy. We're divorced now."

But she still used the guy's name, Noah observed.

"I've got two kids here in Avalon," she continued.

That probably explained the name, then. What it didn't explain was why the kids didn't live with her. Noah reminded himself that it was none of his business. People were complicated, with a mind-boggling array of emotions and issues. Nothing was simple with this species. He found working with animals to be much more straightforward. Dealing with humans was like crossing a minefield. You never knew when something might blow up in your face.

Small talk, he thought. Distract her with small talk. "So are you here for a visit? Or just getting back from a trip?"

She paused, as though considering what to say, which was odd, since it was not a challenging question. She said, "I landed at JFK this afternoon. There were no commuter flights to Kingston-Ulster Airport because of the weather, so I rented a car and drove up. I suppose I could've taken the train, but I was just so anxious to get here."

Landed at JFK from where? He didn't ask, expecting her to fill him in. When she didn't, he focused on his task. Human skin was remarkably similar to canine or equine, he noted. "And you're staying with the Wilsons across the road?" he prompted.

"Not exactly. I'm using their house. It's a summer place. Alberta—Bertie—Wilson and I have known each other since law school."

"Oh." His hands stilled. "You're a lawyer?"

"Yes."

"A *real* lawyer?"

"Okay, I deserved that," she said.

"You couldn't have told me this before I stitched you up with equine sutures?"

"Would you have treated me any differently?"

"I don't know," he said honestly. "I might not have treated you at all. Or I might have asked you to sign a treatment waiver."

"That's never stopped a good lawyer." She quickly added, "But you don't have a thing to worry about. You rescued me and made the bleeding stop. The last thing in the world I'd do is sue you."

"Good to know." Noah removed the surgical draping from her leg and gave the wound a final washing with povidone iodine topical solution. "Although you should probably take a look. It's not real pretty."

She braced her hands behind her and sat up. The stitching formed a thin black curve in her pale flesh, now painted amber with the disinfectant. "You stopped the bleeding," she said again.

"It appears so." He laid a gauze patch over the

wound. “I have to bandage this. You’ll need to be careful, not mess with the stitches or let them pull. If you were one of my usual patients, I’d fit you with a lamp-shade collar to keep you from chewing at the bandage.”

“That won’t be necessary.”

“You need to keep this area dry if possible.”

“I think I can handle that.” She held still while he finished bandaging her. He checked her blood pressure a second time. He studied the meter. “No change,” he said. “That’s good.”

“Thank you. Really, I can’t thank you enough.”

He held both her hands as she gingerly let herself down off the table. She swayed a little, and he slipped his arm around her. “Easy now,” he said. “You’re going to need to keep that leg elevated as much as possible tonight.”

“All right.”

The shock of holding her in his arms struck him. His chin brushed over her silky hair. She smelled like crisp winter wind, and she felt both soft and light.

She seemed equally startled by his touch, and a small shudder went through her. Fear? Relief? He couldn’t tell. Then, very gently, she extracted herself from his arms. He led the way to the reception area. Mildred’s workstation was as meticulously neat as his assistant herself was. Noah’s desk was cluttered with journals and reference books, toys and little figurines, cards from patients’ owners. There was a small bulletin board entirely devoted to notes from kids and photos of them with their pets. Noah was a complete sucker for kids.

"Thank you again," she said. "You need to let me know what I owe you."

"You're kidding, right?"

"I never kid. You performed a professional service. You're entitled to charge for that."

"Right." Spoken like a true lawyer. If he'd performed the same procedure on a Doberman, he would've charged a few hundred bucks. "It's on the house. You should be seen by a doctor as soon as possible."

"Well. You've gone above and beyond the call of duty," she said. "My hero."

He still detected a subtle vibrato of fear in her voice, so he suspected she was just trying to show him some bravado—or irony. "No one's ever called me that before."

"I bet some of your patients would if they could talk." She looked away, and he was glad to see a bit of color in her face. And damn, she was one good-looking woman. "Anyway. I should get down to the cottage now—"

"That's not going to happen," he said. "Not tonight."

"But—"

"The roads are worse than ever. I know there's a driveway down to the Wilsons', but it's buried under feet of snow. The place is probably freezing. Tonight, you're staying here."

She looked around the clinic. "So you're going to put me in a crate in the back?"

"Right next to Mrs. Levinson's Manx cat." He gestured at the Naugahyde bench in the waiting area. "Have a seat and put your leg up. I need to check on my patients, and then we'll go over to the house. It's not the Ritz, but I'll give you something to eat and a place to sleep. I've got tons of room."

"I've already troubled you far too much—"

"Then a little more won't matter."

"But—"

"Seriously, it's no trouble." He went in the back, where dim bluish night-lights illuminated the area. Toby the cat was alert but seemed content in her crate. She had plenty of water. Brutus, the beagle, was sound asleep and snoring loudly. The other cat, Clementine, sat methodically grooming itself.

Noah detached its nearly empty water bottle. "Did you see her, Clem?" he whispered. "Can you believe my luck? I won the girl-stuck-in-the-ditch lottery."

The cat blinked at him, then lifted a forepaw and started grooming it.

"Yeah, high fives to you, too," Noah said. Sure, an accident had brought Sophie to him. But maybe fate had a hand in it, too. The most gorgeous woman in the galaxy, a woman who called him "my hero," was going to be moving in across the road from him.

All right, so he was probably reading too much into a chance encounter. But what the hey. Han Solo wouldn't hesitate to make the most of the situation. She was beautiful and had made a point of telling him she was single. And she had kids. Noah loved kids.

He'd always wanted a houseful. His last girlfriend had left him over the issue of wanting kids. Now here was a woman who already had some.

He washed up at the sink, reminding himself not to get ahead of himself, something he had a habit of doing. Fate had dropped a golden opportunity in his hands. Now it was up to him to see what this might become.

Noah was pretty sure he'd never met anyone like Sophie Bellamy. He wondered who she really was, besides some guy's ex-wife. He wondered where she had come from and what had driven her here in the dark, in the middle of a snowstorm, and if the desperation he glimpsed in her eyes was something that should worry him.

Part Two

One month earlier

Epiphany

An epiphany is a sudden realization, insight or rebirth, often brought on by a life-altering event.

Originally from the Greek for “appearance” or “manifestation,” Epiphany is a Christian feast, also know as Twelfth Day, as it is the twelfth day after Christmas. Traditionally, this coincides with the visit of the Magi. The day is marked by feasting and celebration.

Gougères

Gougères are airy French cheese puffs that originated in France, and are traditionally served this time of year with champagne dry, not brut.

1 cup water
1 stick unsalted butter, cut into small pieces
½ teaspoon salt
1 cup flour

4 large eggs
1½ cups coarsely grated Gruyère cheese

Preheat oven to 375°F. Line a baking sheet with parchment paper. Place the water, butter and salt in a saucepan and bring to a boil, then reduce heat to moderate. Add flour all at once and beat with a wooden spoon until the mixture pulls away from side of pan.

Transfer mixture—known as *pâte à choux*—to a bowl and use an electric mixer to beat in the eggs, one at a time. If the batter is too stiff, add another egg.

Stir the Gruyère into the *pâte à choux* and drop by tablespoons, about one inch apart, on the baking sheet. Bake for about twenty-five minutes, or until golden brown. Serve warm.

Two

The Peace Palace
The Hague, Holland
6 January – Epiphany

The shiny black limousine glided to a stop in front of the carved-stone Gothic building, its blocky silhouette cutting into the false glow of yellow fog lights. A hard rain peppered the roof of the Citroën with the tinny sound of birdshot.

Behind the bulletproof glass windows of the passenger compartment, Sophie Bellamy performed one final check of her hair and makeup and snapped her compact shut. She tucked her evening bag into a cubby in the armrest. With security so tight at the palace these days, it was just simpler to enter the building with nothing but her prescreened credential card and the clothes on her back.

When she'd first started attending functions at the Peace Palace, she used to feel naked without an evening bag. Now she'd grown used to spending a formal evening without lipstick or comb, a set of keys or a mobile phone. Such things were forbidden in the interest of security.

Tonight, cautious measures were warranted. The recent decision rendered by the International Criminal Court on war crimes, a case that had consumed two years of her life, was controversial and apt to incite violence.

The limo took its place in a line behind a few others and waited its turn. Sophie used to be consumed by excitement when she attended ceremonial events, but now they had become routine. It was amazing how accustomed to this she had grown. Drivers and security agents, a couture wardrobe and smiling dignitaries, translations whispered into an earpiece—all were commonplace to her these days.

Guests were being shuttled to the outer guard gate under black umbrellas, their corrugated shadows reflecting silver-black on the cut-stone surface of the Paleisplein. She'd been told to expect media coverage of the event, but she only saw one windowless news van, its bedraggled crew setting up the requisite thirty meters from the building. Despite the historic significance of tonight's event, despite the fact that Queen Beatrix herself would be in attendance, the occasion would go unnoticed by the world at large. In America, people were too busy watching the latest Internet video to tune in to the fact that the geography of Africa had just changed, thanks, in large part, to Sophie herself.

Her phone vibrated—a photo and text message from her son, Max: white sand beach and turquoise sea with the caption "St Croix awesome. Dad & Nina getting ready 2 tie the knot. Xoxo!"

Sophie stared at the words from her twelve-year-old. She'd known today was the day, though she'd been trying not to think about it. Her ex was on a tropical island, about to marry the woman who had stepped into the shoes Sophie had left vacant. She gently closed the phone and held it against her chest, trying to quiet the feelings churning inside her and gnawing a hole in her heart. Not possible. Not even tonight.

André, her driver, turned on the hazard lights to signal that he was about to exit the vehicle. He adjusted the flat cap of his uniform. His shoulders lifted as he took a deep breath. A native of Senegal, André had never been a fan of the weather in Northern Europe, particularly in January.

A sudden squeal of tires and a sound like a gunshot erupted. Without a single beat of hesitation, Sophie dropped to the floorboards, at the same time grabbing for the car phone. In the front seat, André did the same. Then came a honking horn and a voice over the loudspeaker, giving the all-clear in Dutch, French and English.

André lowered the shield between the driver and passenger compartment. *"C'est rien,"* he said. "A car backfired, that is all. *Merde.* Always some reason to be on edge."

For the past week, the city had been on special alert due to gang violence, and foreign service drivers were often targets for robbery, since they tended to park for hours in public places, sleeping in their cars.

Sophie reached for the compact mirror to check herself again. She'd undergone hours of crisis training and she dealt with some of the most dangerous people in the world, yet she never really feared for her own safety. There were so many security measures in place that the risk was extremely low.

André held up a gloved hand to ask her wordlessly if she was ready. She abandoned vanity and nodded, clutching the laminated *carte d'identité* in her hand. The passenger door opened and a dark umbrella bloomed overhead, held by a liveried palace attendant.

"On y va, alors," she said to André. Here we go.

"Assurément, madame," he said in his lilting French-African accent. *"J'attends."*

Of course he would be waiting, she thought. He always did. And thank God for that. She was going to be high as a kite by the end of the evening, on champagne and a soaring sense of accomplishment, with no one to babble her news to. André was a good listener. During the short drive tonight from Sophie's residence to the palace, she had confessed to him how much she missed her children.

She would have loved to have Max and her daughter Daisy by her side tonight, to bear witness to the honors that would be bestowed upon her. But they were an ocean away, with their father who on this very day was getting married. *Married.* Perhaps at this very moment, her ex-husband was getting remarried.

The knowledge sat like a stone in her shoe. The dull truth of it stole some of the glitter from the evening.

Stop it, she admonished herself. This is *your* night.

She emerged from the car. Her foot slipped on the wet cobblestones and, for a nightmarish second, she nearly went down. A strong arm caught her around the waist, propping her up. "André," she said a little breathlessly, "you just averted a disaster."

"Rien du tout, madame," he replied, hovering close. The light glimmered over his solemn, kindly face.

It occurred to her that this was the closest she'd come to being held in a man's arms in . . . far too long. She shut down the entirely inappropriate thought, steadied her footing and stepped away from him. The cold drilled into her. Her long cashmere coat wasn't enough, not tonight. There were predictions of snow. It would be a rare occurrence for The Hague, but already, the rain was hardening to sleet. Under the broad umbrella, she hurried past the guardhouse to the first checkpoint. A walkway circled the eternal peace flame monument, shielded from the weather by a hammered metal hood. It was another twenty meters to the portico, which had been fitted with an awning and red carpet for the occasion. Once she was safely under the shelter of the arched awning, her attendant murmured, *"Bonsoir, madame. Et bienvenue."* Most of the personnel spoke in French which, along with English, was the common language of the international courts.

"Merci."

The attendant with the umbrella ducked back out into the rain to collect the next guest.

The line to the main entrance moved slowly, as there was a cloakroom to pass through, and another security checkpoint. Sophie didn't know any of the people in line, but she recognized many of them—black-clad dignitaries and their families, Africans in ceremonial garb, diplomats from all over the globe. They had come to pay homage to a new day for Umoja, the nation the court had just liberated from a warlord financed by a corrupt diamond syndicate operating outside the law.

There was an American family ahead of her. The uniformed husband had the effortless good posture of a career military man. The wife and teenage daughters surrounded him like satellite nations. Sophie vaguely recognized the husband, an attaché from Supreme Headquarters Allied Powers Europe in Belgium. She didn't greet them, not wanting to interrupt what appeared to be a delightful family outing.

The attaché's wife pressed close to him as though shielding herself from the cold. She was plump and easy in her confidence; like Sophie, she wore plain gold earrings unadorned by gemstones. To wear stones, especially diamonds, to an event like this would be the height of insensitivity.

The American family looked safe and secure in their little world of four. In that moment, Sophie missed her own children so much it felt like a stab wound.

A searingly cold wind swept across the plaza, stinging her eyes. She blinked fast, not wanting her mascara to run. She lifted the collar of her coat and turned her back to the wind. At a side entrance to the palace was a caterer's van. Haagsche Voedsel Dienst, S.A. Good, thought Sophie. The best caterer in town.

They must be running late, though. The white-coated waiters were rushing about with a frantic air, shoving heavy carts into a service entrance to the building and speaking in agitated fashion to one another.

Sophie was shivering when she reached the cloak-room. There were few places that felt as cold as The Hague did during a winter storm. The city lay below sea level, built on land reclaimed from the frigid North Sea, walled off by dikes. During a storm, it felt as though nature was trying to wrest back its own. The wind sliced like a knife, cutting to the bone. In The Hague there was a saying: If I can stand up in it, I can go out in it.

Reluctantly, she peeled off her butter-soft deerskin gloves and surrendered her long cashmere coat, handing them over to an attendant and making a note of the numbered card: 47. She slipped it into the pocket of her dress. As she smoothed the front of her outfit and turned toward the entranceway, she noticed the attaché's wife watching her, a hint of both envy and admiration in her eyes.

Sophie had spent half the day getting ready. She was wearing a couture gown and shoes that cost more than a piece of furniture. The gown fit her beautifully. She'd been a distance swimmer in college and still competed at the master's level, an endeavor that kept her in shape. Her every blond hair was in place, pulled sleekly back into a chignon. Bijou, her stylist, claimed she looked exactly like a latter-day Grace Kelly. An actress, which was appropriate. A big part of this job had to do with image and theatrics. Smoke and mirrors.

She smiled at the attaché's wife and felt a twinge of irony. *Don't envy me,* she wanted to say. *You have your family with you. What more could you want?*

After walking through a metal detector, she proceeded unaccompanied down an open, colonnaded walkway toward the grand ballroom. She waited amid a milling crowd in the doorway for her turn to be announced.

Standing on tiptoe, she craned her neck to see. So much of her work took place in the glass-and-steel high-rise of the International Criminal Court that she often forgot the romantic ideals that had driven her career to this point. But here in the ornate palace, built by Andrew Carnegie with no regard for expense, she remembered that this was a job most people only dreamed of. She was Cinderella, but without the prince.

The majordomo, resplendent in palace livery, bent toward her to study her identity card. He was wired with an interpreter's mike, a tiny coil into his ear. "Have you an escort, *madame?*"

"No," Sophie said. "I'm by myself." In this job, who had time for a prince?

"Madame Sophie Lindstrom Bellamy," he proclaimed in ringing tones, *"au Canada et aux États-Unis."*

From Canada and the United States—she had dual citizenship, thanks to her Canadian mother and American father. Although the U.S. wasn't a member of the ICC, the rest of the world concurred with the need for a vehicle to prosecute war criminals, so it was as a Canadian citizen that Sophie served the court. Fixing a camera-ready smile on her lips, she entered the ballroom, brilliant with golden light beaming from chandeliers and wall sconces, the air ringing with greetings from other guests. Despite the warm welcome, she understood that she would face tonight the way she had faced nearly all the greatest moments of her life—alone.

She chased away the thought with a flute of champagne served by a tall, awkward waiter. She was not about to spoil this with regrets and second thoughts. After all, it wasn't every night you got to meet an actual queen and accept a medal of freedom from a grateful nation.

The Hague was a royal city, the seat of the Dutch government, and Queen Beatrix was tireless when it came to performing her official duties. Britain's royals might have their scandals, but the Oranje-Nassau family of Holland had a monarch who was as hard-working as any salaried official. Security agents in street clothes discreetly patrolled the periphery of the room, their restless eyes scanning the crowd. It was an international, festive group. There was a woman in a head scarf, her tiered dress a bright flare of color, and another in a kimono, several men in colorful dashikis, as well as the Westerners in their tailored suits and evening gowns. For these few moments Sophie felt vibrant and alive, letting herself forget what was happening with her family. In their crisp, starched school uniforms, smiles displaying the gaps of lost teeth, a children's choir performed with contagious joy, their bright voices filling the cavernous Gothic hall. The music was a mix of cultural offerings—traditional songs for Epiphany, such as *"Il Est Né, Le Divin Enfant"* and *"Ça Bergers,"* as well as native dance songs and the throaty humming of a ceremonial chant.

The choir launched into *"Impuka Nekati,"* an action chant dramatizing the chase of a cat and mouse. They were still able to sing, these orphans of war. Sophie wished she could take every single one home with her. She recognized some of them from earlier in the week when a group of them had come to deliver flowers to the prosecution team.

Her fight to stop transnational crimes against children took all her time and attention, and the ones who paid the price for that were her own kids. How many of Max and Daisy's recitals and performances had she missed because of work? Had her son and daughter ever sung with their faces filled with joy, or had they scanned the audience, their eyes dimming when they failed to spot their mom? Dear Lord, how she wished they could be here to see the results of their sacrifice. Maybe then, they would understand. Maybe they'd forgive her.

There was a girl, all knobby legs and big white teeth, who sang as though singing was the same as breathing for her—necessary to sustain life. When the song ended, Sophie sought out the show-stealing girl. "Your singing is beautiful," she said.

Oh, that smile. "Thank you, *madame,*" said the girl. She bashfully added, "My name is Fatou. I come from the village of Kuumba."

She didn't have to explain further. The militia's attack on that village had rivaled the worst of wartime atrocities. Remembering the reports of Kuumba, Sophie felt a new surge of rage at the men who committed their inhuman acts upon children like Fatou.

Imagining what those velvety brown eyes had seen, what this child had endured, made Sophie wonder how Fatou was still standing, how she could face the world. How she could open her mouth and sing.

"I'm so happy you're here now," Sophie said, "and that you're safe."

"Yes, *madame.* Thank you, *madame.*" She smiled again.

And that smile reflected all the reasons Sophie did what she did, living far from her family and working more hours than a day actually had, or so it seemed, sometimes.

Just then, a murmur rippled through the crowd. The girl looked apprehensive, but Sophie overheard someone whispering. There was a rumor of snow.

"Come," Sophie said, taking Fatou by the hand. "Look out the window." She led the way to a tall Gothic window and pushed aside the velvet drapes. "Look," she said again.

Fatou cupped her hands around her eyes and leaned

forward. The snow was coming down in thick flakes now, turning the palace gardens into a winter wonderland, bathed in a glow from the sodium vapor lights. "I have never seen such a thing before. It is magic, *madame,*" Fatou said.

Outside, on a small cobble-paved driveway, shadows flickered across the fast-whitening ground. Sophie leaned in for a closer look, noting that the courtyard was deserted and peaceful. She wished Max and Daisy could see this, the splendor and the gravitas of this night. She was glad, at least, that the friendly girl beside her was sharing the moment. She turned to her with a smile.

Fatou didn't notice but kept looking out the window, seemingly mesmerized by the snowfall.

Three

Once everyone had marveled over the snow, the performance resumed. Sophie went to a long serving table to peruse the offerings. Like the music, the food would represent the community of nations gathered here tonight. A tray of buttery gougères, cheese pastries baked to a light golden-brown, made her mouth water, but she resisted the temptation to sample them. She couldn't allow herself to eat anything. She needed to look her best for tonight's presentation. Pastry crumbs or faded lip color would never do.

To her surprise, the culinary display, usually so

meticulous, appeared haphazard tonight, the food and flowers artlessly displayed. The head waiter, a big-boned blond man, snapped his fingers and issued an order into the mouthpiece of his headset. As he reached to replenish the chilled prawns, he managed to break an ice sculpture, and Sophie was certain she heard him swear under his breath. *Enjoy your evening,* she thought as she took a flute of champagne from the end table. You won't be back. Here at the most powerful court in the world, the catering had to be impeccable. One false move and the caterer was toast.

She made her way to a group of people gathered around Momoh Sanni Momoh, Premier of Umoja, resplendent in his robe of saffron silk and tall, intricately wound headdress. While waiting to greet him, she encountered a colleague, Bibi Lateef. A native of Umoja, Mme Lateef was decked out tonight in native garb, a startling contrast to her usual somber court robes.

"You are staring, *madame,*" she said to Sophie, offering a smile as bright and wide as the moon. Victory and joy danced in her eyes.

They embraced, and Sophie stepped back to regard her friend. "I'm dazzled. This is a good look for you."

"I am glad to hear it," Mme Lateef said, "because I will no longer be needing the robes."

Sophie beamed with pride. Her colleague was as accomplished and educated as any of the jurists of the court, and she would be given a major role in the new government. “You have a new title, then? Can you share?”

“How do you like ‘Minister of Social Welfare’?” Mme Lateef said.

Sophie took her hand. Bibi Lateef had lost family members in the fighting; her struggle had been personal. Returning to her native land was bound to be bittersweet. “It sounds perfect for you,” Sophie said. “Congratulations. I’ll miss you, though. No one wanted to see the conclusion of this case more than I, but I’ll miss working with you.”

“There is much work to be done. Displaced families and children orphaned by war will be my most urgent concerns. You must promise to visit.”

“Of course.” Sophie had been to Umoja several times. It was a land of heartbreaking beauty, even in the wake of war. The fighting and encroachment by mining had decimated its cities, but there were vast regions that lay untouched—high red plains and mountain rain forests, and the river-fed regions where towns were already recovering.

“I will hold you to that promise,” said Mme Lateef. The genuine gratitude in her eyes touched Sophie’s heart. “I’m grateful to have known you.”

“It’s been an honor to serve the cause of justice, truly,” she said, watching her colleague’s face even as she stepped away to speak with the children in their native tongue. This was what Sophie lived for, this moment when she was absolutely certain that what she did mattered. That it was worth all the pain and sacrifices she'd made. But always the question remained—would her own children agree?

As she hung back, still waiting to greet the premier, a man with a press badge appeared. "Brooks Fordham, *New York Times*. Please, tell us what tonight is about."

Sophie offered a restrained smile. "Mr. Fordham, if you really want the story, it would take hours to tell."

"I really want the story. Why don't you give me the digest version. And please, call me Brooks."

Sophie knew his type—spoiled, ambitious, overeducated, handsome, and he knew it. But she obliged, summarizing the situation that had brought them to this night. Umoja had been a nation enslaved, oppressed by a semi-legal syndicate of European diamond merchants and their African collaborators, led by a notorious war criminal named General Timi Abacha. For two decades, the nation had been run by a ruthless militia funded by the blood diamond trade. In time, the atrocities became so severe that finally the world took notice.

Then came the photograph, the one that finally put Umoja on the map and in the public consciousness. The picture showed a young native boy, missing a hand and an ear, glaring at the camera with eyes that had lost all innocence. He had been ripped from his family, forced to work and punished by mutilation, all because he was small enough to fit into a mine shaft. The photograph made the front page of newspapers and journals and galvanized the world community to take action. A team of international investigators verified incidents of slavery and abuse, of child conscription and rape. The case was built with meticulous care, imperiling many of the key players. "Accidents" befell those who questioned the wrong people or found themselves in the wrong place at the wrong time.

Sophie knew the tale by heart, perhaps better than anyone in the room. In preparing for the case, she had sunk herself deep into the red clay earth of the landlocked nation. On a map, it was shaped like a pitcher, its spout tipping down into the top of South Africa.

And that, of course, was what made it such a rich prize. In its borderlands were some of the most prolific diamond mines in the world, yielding up rough stones of exceptional quality. For untold generations, the native tribes had defended themselves from European colonists and rival tribes. Finally, ten years before, a rogue tribe, armed and financed by diamond interests, took over the nation in a bloody coup.

Its people suffered tortures beyond imagining—rape, ethnic cleansing, genocide. Little boys were conscripted as soldiers; young girls were used and discarded, or forced to bear the children of their rapists. In preparing the case against the dictator and warlord, Sophie and her team had interviewed victims of every possible crime. There were so many stories of unspeakable brutality that some members of the staff had resigned, traumatized. Others turned numb as a defense, desensitized by an overload of horror.

Every time Sophie heard of a boy, no older than her

own son, brainwashed and forced into drug addiction, and turned into a killing machine, she bled a little. When she heard of a young woman, a teenager perhaps her daughter's age, raped within an inch of her life, she bled a little more. Every story ripped at her heart, and very early on in the case it became personal.

Protests and calls for international sanctions were insufficient. Calculating as coldly as the diamond lords who called all the shots, she set about building a case against the regime, ousting the government and restoring the natives to power.

The process had taken two years. Sophie had worked herself into exhaustion. She'd lost her marriage and now lived an ocean away from her children. But tonight she reminded herself that the battle had been won. Tonight was about recognizing those who had restored a nation to its rightful keepers. No longer did villagers flee before armies of thugs. No longer were people forced to work in the mines, suffering abuse and starvation until they died at the hands of the inhuman jackals who had stolen their country.

She felt Brooks watching her. She tried not to look at him because she was afraid he would distract her. Though they'd only just met, she sensed he had the sort of easy charm and witty insouciance that would bring a smile to her face. Emerging from the emotional pain of divorce, she was discovering she had a great liking for men. And as soon as that thought crossed her mind, she felt a blush creep upward through her cheeks.

Sophie served as assistant deputy counsel for the prosecution. When illness struck two of her superiors, she found herself directly addressing the fifteen judges of the International Criminal Court. It was said that her relentless and passionate arguments were key to attaining a conviction. After that, UN troops moved in, ousted the corrupt government and restored the exiled premier to his rightful place.

"Anyway," she concluded, addressing Brooks, "that's the digest version, and I can already see your eyes glazing over."

"Jet lag," he said, taking out a hand-size notepad and wooden pencil. "Phone number?" He flashed her a grin.

She gave him her second assistant's mobile number. That was close enough.

He wrote it down and added some notes, then gave her his own number. "Don't you want to write it down?" he asked.

"I already have it," she said. It was a gift of hers. She had a near-photographic memory for phone numbers. She could remember the number of the arbitrator who had handled her divorce more than a year before. The number of her son's hockey coach, whom she'd never met in person. The number of Greg's new wife, Nina, though Sophie would never call it. She looked up at Brooks and repeated his phone number back to him.

"A woman of many talents," he said. "Really, it's an incredible story—"

"That will be reduced to a one-inch blurb under 'Around the Globe' and buried on page 19-A," she finished for him.

"I'll try for more space," he said. "Another question."

"Go ahead." She folded her arms in front of her.

"Is it true you gained access to the syndicate's banking records by using the same methods as the Nigerian banking scam?"

Sophie felt her mouth twitch with a smile. "We finally found a use for e-mail spam. The investigative team did the technical work, but it did amount to duping the syndicate's chief treasurer. It's not the oldest trick in the book, but close. And it made them look incredibly foolish."

In the tradition of the Nigerian banking spammers whose scam was so notorious it was known as a 419, they had targeted the dictator's top treasury official, Mr. Femi Gidado. He was known to be an ambitious, greedy man whose high-risk investments had brought high returns to the regime.

Having learned this about him, Sophie's team had sent him a "phishing" e-mail, posing as an innocent government official in charge of a staggering fortune. They had "begged his worthy indulgence" on a "matter of utmost financial urgency," promising a sum of $3.5 million if he would simply provide his banking information to be used in a simple, clandestine transaction.

After a relatively short exchange of e-mail information, Sophie and her staff found themselves in possession of the regime's fortune. Since it was obtained through illegal means, they couldn't use the money at all—but the insanely simple ploy gave them leverage. They offered the dishonest treasurer a choice. He could serve as the key witness in the case against the dictator, or his participation in the banking scam would be revealed to his superiors. Since the punishment for betrayal was excruciating torture followed by a beheading, he chose to throw in his lot with the Umojan people. His cooperation had proved to be the undoing of the regime.

"What became of General Timi Abacha? And the head of the diamond syndicate, Serge Henger?"

Great. He would ask her that. "They're still at large. But since everything was seized, they have no staff or assets. It's only a matter of time before they are hunted down." She paused, then added, "And I hope you'll include that in your article."

"Are you kidding? We should make a video to run on the paper's Web site. You're great, by the way."

"Thank you."

"Are you worried about retaliation? Attacks? Before the army was disbanded, they were one of the most heavily armed militias in the region. It's said a number of them have gone into hiding right here in The Netherlands."

"Cowards who are motivated by greed will always be with us. I'm not going to live in fear because of them."

He wrote that down—a good sound byte. "You're very young to hold this position," he remarked.

"Age has nothing to do with it," Sophie told him. "It's dedication and experience, and I have plenty of that." She knew he could discover her age with a few clicks on his BlackBerry; it was a matter of public record, as were her blood type, passport numbers, rank in class at her law school and the fact that she'd set collegiate records in distance swimming. She decided to end his suspense. "Thirty-nine," she said. "Divorced. Two kids who live in Avalon, New York." Summed up like that, so nice and neat, she sounded like a professional, career-minded international lawyer. The nonchalance of her "They live in Avalon, New York" comment did not begin to cover the agony of her shattered family in the aftermath of divorce. And she wasn't about to go there with him, though she lived with the pain of it every day. She was a mother without kids to raise. Her mothering was carried out by phone, e-mail, text message and IMs. But the things that happened in her absence were legion. She might find that Daisy had turned into a brunette or Max had started drum lessons . . . She might find that her ex-husband was getting married. That Max was still begging for a dog, and that Daisy was about to start college. Sophie was forever torn between her simultaneous yearning to be involved in their lives and her abject fear that she'd make more of a mess of her kids than she already had.

Brooks was asking her something, and she realized

she hadn't been listening at all. "You have a whole room full of dignitaries here," she told him, gesturing at the milling guests. "Why me?"

"Because you make good copy," he told her bluntly. "I write about you, and I've got half a chance of getting it placed somewhere other than in the footnotes."

"And I should help you because . . ."

"Look," he said, "this is a big deal, what's happening here—a sovereign nation was saved from being erased off the map. But we both know John Q. Public doesn't give a rat's ass about that. He's too busy texting his vote for *American Idol* to worry about the state of some third-world country he's never heard of."

"Don't think writing about me is going to change that."

"It will if you do something outrageous that'll play well on YouTube."

"What, like drive across Europe wearing Depends? I can see you're completely tuned into the solemnity of the occasion," she said.

"Seriously," he said, "how does a nice girl like you wind up toppling warlords and dictators?"

"Just lucky, I guess."

"When people think of world court personnel, they think of seventy-year-old guys in musty robes. Not . . ." He gave her a meaningful look.

She forced herself not to respond. One of the strictest rules of this job was to increase public perception of the court's mission. "First of all, you could clarify the trial was through the International Criminal Court, which was created only six years ago, so it's not some venerable, old institution. And honestly, the only reason I served as a prosecutor is that the lead counsel and his deputy got sick right before the first hearing." Willem De Groot was an older man who shared her passion for a just cause. Hooked up to a dialysis machine, he had guided her and his staff through the case, week after week.

"So it was a matter of luck meeting opportunity," Brooks said.

"Bad luck meeting necessity," she clarified. "I'd give anything if he could be here tonight."

"You really don't want to be the star of this, do you? What a waste of looks and talent."

"You seem preoccupied with my looks."

"It's the dress. You had to have known it would affect men this way, even without jewelry. I assume you're making a statement."

"I'm opposed to diamonds for obvious reasons. And so many other stones are questionable that it's simpler to wear none. But pearls! They're produced by oysters and hunted by happy divers, right? I should take to wearing pearls."

"You could wear pearls in the video," he said.

Sophie was about two sips of champagne away from ditching this guy. "You're obnoxious, Mr. Fordham. And I'm leaving. Everything is about to start."

"One final question and I'll leave you alone," he added.

"Go ahead."

"Will you let me take you to dinner tomorrow night?"

"That doesn't sound like leaving me alone."

"But does it sound . . . like a plan?"

She hesitated. He probably had a degree from an Ivy League school, a pedigree back to the *Mayflower* and a brazen sense of entitlement. Still, going to dinner with him meant not eating alone. "I'll have my assistant call you to arrange things."

"It's a dinner date, not an international summit."

"My assistants are excellent at arranging things," she assured him. A date with this man might be a diversion. Her romantic past was . . . undistinguished. Perhaps that was the word for it. Forgettable teenage gropings in high school had given way to slightly more sophisticated dating in college—frat parties and raves. And then there was Greg. They'd married before they even knew who they were. It was like grafting together two incompatible trees—tolerable at first but eventually the differences could not be ignored. Had she loved him? Everyone loved Greg. He was the adorable, charming, indulged youngest of the four Bellamy siblings. How could anyone not love him? This sense that she *should* love him had sustained the marriage over sixteen years, long enough for her to be absolutely certain the love was gone. Afterward she had walked around shell-shocked for several months.

Only last fall had she dared to stick her toe into the dating pool. The first time a man had asked her out, she had regarded him as if he'd spoken in a dead language. Go out? On a date? What a novel idea.

Thus began the dating phase, which was infinitely preferable to the post-divorce shell-shocked phase. Her first prospect was a diplomatic protection agent who was more interested in showing off his 007 trappings—an alert device hidden in his lapel, a cigarette pack that could dispense cyanide gas—than in discovering who Sophie actually was. Despite her disenchantment, she'd tried to move seamlessly into the sleeping-around phase during which a newly divorced woman indulged her every fantasy. Women who slept around always seemed as though they were having such fun. Yet Sophie found it disappointing and stressful and quickly retreated to the benign safety of casual dating. She told herself she would stay open to the possibility that one day one of the attachés or diplomats or Georgian nationals she was dating would unexpectedly inflame her passions. So far, it hadn't happened.

She regarded Brooks and wondered if he might be the one to make her drop her natural reserve. To make her remember what it felt like to be held in someone's arms. *Not tonight,* she thought.

"You'll have to excuse me," she said, and headed for the dais.

She looked around for a place to set down her champagne flute, and approached a passing waiter. He didn't seem to see her.

"Pardon," she said.

The man jumped, and a glass fell from his tray, shattering on the marble floor. In the immediate area, people fell silent and turned to stare. At the periphery of the room, the security agents tensed, prepared to take action.

"I'm sorry," Sophie murmured. "I didn't mean to startle you."

"It's nothing, *madame,*" he murmured, his accent very thick. She was about to ask him where he was from when she caught the look in his eyes. It was a glittering, burning fury all out of proportion with a broken glass.

Sophie lifted her eyebrows, wordlessly conveying a warning, the way she might to a key witness. He moved slightly, and the light fell on his face, illuminating ebony skin highlighted by twin rows of shiny scars, a pattern of ritual scarring that looked vaguely familiar to her. He was Umojan, she surmised. Employing him was a nice touch by the caterer, and it explained his inexperience.

The waiter started to move away.

"Pardon me," Sophie said to him.

He turned back, seeming more agitated than ever.

You're a waiter, she thought, *get over yourself.* She held out the champagne glass. "Can you please take this? They're about to begin."

He all but snatched it from her and stalked away. *Touchy fellow,* she thought. *We just liberated your country. You ought to be happier about that.* She dismissed the incident from her mind. Focus, Sophie, she told herself. You're about to meet a queen.

Four

The group on the raised dais at the end of the ballroom consisted of three of the justices from the International Criminal Court, another from the Court of Justice, a liaison from the United Nations and the queen of the Netherlands herself, whose bloodlines went back through seventeen generations of Dutch royalty. Sophie joined the rest of the prosecution team on a lower tier, where the event producer's assistant had instructed them to wait. This group included Sophie's best friend and colleague, Tariq Abdul-Hakeem. Like her, he was an assistant deputy to the ICC and they'd worked together on the case. She'd known Tariq from their intern days in London, years ago, and he was one of her favorite people in the world. He was also one of the most attractive, with the kind of looks found in high-fashion spreads—creamy skin and intense eyes, and features that appeared to have been shaped by an idealistic sculptor. He was a gifted linguist and had the most delicious English accent. While working together, they'd become more than colleagues. He was one of the few people in the world she'd opened up to, telling him about the situation with Greg and her children.

"Are you all right, Petal?" Tariq whispered to her.

"Of course, I'm all right. Why wouldn't I be?"

"Quite possibly, you're somewhat *bouleversée* by

the fact that your ex-husband is getting married today."

She waved her hand in a dismissive gesture, even though she knew Tariq would not be fooled. "So he's getting married. We knew it was coming. He's a guy. It's what they do. They remarry." She gave a small, soft laugh. "Somebody's got to finish raising them." Despite her sarcasm, she remembered Max's text message with a twinge, along with the perennial unanswerable question—was this career worth the price she'd paid?

"Such a generous opinion of the male sex," Tariq said. "After tonight's ceremony, I'm taking you out and getting you so drunk you'll forget your own name."

"Sounds delightful."

"Isn't that what you Yanks do, go out and get—what's the term?—shitfaced?"

She sniffed. "You have no idea what you're talking about. You don't even drink."

"But I *buy* drinks. I'll take you to Club Sillies after this."

Sophie knew she would go, and she'd be the envy of every woman there, at the hottest nightclub in The Hague, a place frequented by the European elite. Tariq never failed to turn heads; he was elegant, with a subtle layer of sadness in his regard. The sadness was real, but few people knew the reason for it. Oxford-educated, one of the top jurists in the free world, he dedicated his every waking moment to the law. Yet as a gay man, and a Saudi, he struggled every day; in his native country, same-sex relations carried a penalty of death.

"Anyway," she said, "thank you for the offer. I really should get home afterward. I have work—"

"Yes, Allah forbid that you should have anything resembling a life."

"I have a life."

"You have work—at court, and at the office, and in the field—and then you have sleep. Oh, yes. You also have that entirely dreadful sport you do."

"It's not dreadful. Distance swimming is good for me." She was always in training for some kind of extreme race or another. She never placed first. Ever. But she always finished. Every time.

For Tariq, whose only athletic activity was a dash for the elevator, her sport seemed madly dangerous.

"Paddling about in a wet suit in freezing waters is mad. You need to have some fun, Petal. You need a life beyond work. And don't think I don't know why you refuse to unbend a little. Because if you were actually to have fun and enjoy something, that would interfere with your penance."

"You don't know the first thing about doing penance."

"Guilt is not the exclusive domain of Christians," he pointed out. "You feel guilty about your kids, so you refuse to allow yourself to enjoy anything. Simple as that. And clearly it doesn't do a bit of good. Whether you're in court prosecuting terrorists or riding a bicycle along Hogeweg during tourist season doesn't matter."

"True. I'm still separated from my kids."

"Here is what you're giving your kids—a mother who cares enough about the world to make it a better place for them. Do you really think they'd rather have you driving carpool to soccer practice and the mall?"

"Sometimes, yes." She knew it was unproductive, but couldn't help wondering if things would have turned out differently for Daisy if she had been more present.

"My dear mum was there every day, and look at me. A quivering mess."

"A well-adjusted person."

"An outcast. A heretic." He spoke jokingly, but she sensed his underlying pain, different from her own yet somehow familiar.

"Stop," she said in an undertone. She and Tariq were both career-focused. Trying to escape the person he really was, he had made this court his life. "It's all I have," he'd told her many times in the past. "Fortunately, it's all I want."

Sophie couldn't say the same, so she said nothing. She saw the premier and queen moving toward them, and cleared her throat to warn Tariq. The queen of the Netherlands looked like everyone's favorite aunt, displaying an abundance of personal charm twinkling in her eyes as she went about her duties, treating each person as though, in that moment, they were the most important person in the world.

"Thank you very much for your service," she murmured as the line of dignitaries passed.

I'm a dignitary, thought Sophie. *What do you know, I'm a dignitary.*

When she was presented, she responded with a poise she'd been practicing for days, dipping slightly into a curtsy, addressing the queen as *Uwe Majesteit.* It was all very solemn and ritualized, no surprises. No one would ever know that deep down, her Inner Girl was exulting. She was meeting a queen, a real live queen.

Queen Beatrix was a lawyer like Sophie. Maybe the two of them would have talked, compared shoe-shopping experiences, swapped gossip like girlfriends.

She imagined the conversation. "Have you seen the new George Clooney movie? I like your earrings. Which museum did they come from? What's it like having an airport named after you? And tell me about your family. How do you make it work?"

Yes, that was the burning question. The thing Sophie wanted to ask other working women. Here they were watching the rebirth of a nation, and she was fixated on domestic troubles. All she wanted to know was how Beatrix managed to run a country and still keep her marriage intact, her family together.

Some things, said a quiet inner voice, you sacrifice.

The queen was a widow now, her children grown. Sophie wondered if she had regrets, if she wished she'd done something differently, spent more time with them, had more parent-teacher conferences, restricted their TV, read them more good-night stories.

Color guards presented the flags of the UN and the court of the Netherlands and finally, with grave ceremony, the flag of Umoja, planting it like a tree behind the dais. The newly appointed ambassador, Mr. Bensouda, took his place at the microphone. Behind him stood six attendants, each holding a ceremonial medal of honor. By the end of the night, one of them would belong to Sophie.

"Mesdames et messieurs," the ambassador said, *"bienvenue, les visiteurs distingues. . . ."* He launched into the saga of his country.

The medals were bestowed and praises sung. Her black dress perfectly showed off the token of thanks from a grateful people. Interesting notion for a line of clothing, she thought, her mind wandering. Garments for dignitaries, with hidden credential pockets and necklines fashioned to display medals to advantage. Then she realized what she was doing—trying to detach herself from this huge moment. She couldn't help it. Something was missing from her life and she could not pretend otherwise. How could she have a triumph like this without her family to witness it? The thought brought about a flash of resentment toward Greg. This was a big day for him, as well, though she wished she could stop dwelling on that. Still, it wasn't every day the man who had once been your husband married someone else.

A podium and microphone transformed normal people into long-winded bombasts, and Sophie was trapped on stage with the crowd of dignitaries.

Tonight, she'd foolishly, recklessly had two and a half glasses of champagne. As a result, she listened to speeches about the historic event in a state of supreme discomfort, with a bladder so full that her back teeth were floating.

No one seemed to be in a hurry to leave the dais. She couldn't wait another moment. She had to decide which was the bigger diplomatic faux pas—leaving the dais before she was dismissed, or wetting herself in front of the queen.

Sophie made her move. She took a step back, slipping behind the line of people as she followed the black snakes of electrical cables that connected the lighting and sound. At the back of the dais, she stepped down and slipped out through a side door to an empty corridor.

She rounded a corner and encountered a pair of men in dark clothing, their shoulders dampened by melting snow. They stiffened and whirled on her, and Sophie froze, holding her hands with the palms facing out. Security agents, she thought. They were suspicious of everything. "Sorry," she murmured. "I'm trying to find the lavatory."

She followed signs to the ladies' room. Passing through the antechamber, she smiled briefly at the attendant, a sleepy-looking older woman reading a copy of a Dutch gossip magazine.

Sophie used the restroom, then went to a sink to freshen up. From one of the stalls came the unmistakable sound of someone being sick. Lovely. What idiot would get drunk at an event like this? Sophie wondered. She had no evening bag, so she had to pat her hair with a damp hand and dab at her makeup with a tissue.

A girl came out of the stall. It was Fatou, the girl who had sung so beautifully earlier. Despite her dark skin, she looked pallid, yet her eyes were clear, not bleary from drinking or drugs. She stood at one of the sinks, hands braced on the countertop, her hair falling forward. She turned on the water and rinsed her face and mouth but somehow looked even worse when she finished.

"You seem ill," Sophie said to her in French. "Should I try to get some help for you?"

"No thank you, *madame,*" Fatou replied. "I'm not ill." She touched her stomach.

Sophie wasn't sure what to say to that. The girl was clearly too young to be starting a family, yet there was something about her that Sophie recognized. A tiny gleam of excitement mingling with desperation. Sophie recognized it because she had been there, too, and so had her own daughter, Daisy, for that matter. "You're expecting a baby," she said quietly.

Fatou stared at the floor.

"Do you have someone to look after you?" Sophie asked.

She nodded. "I am a student intern. I live with a family in Lilles. I suppose, under the circumstances, that is fortunate. But my hosts are not going to be happy about this."

"They will be. Not right away, but . . . perhaps eventually." Sophie spoke from experience. At the same time, she felt a welling of sadness and regret. She hadn't been there for Daisy, the way her own mother hadn't been there for her.

Fatou stepped back and straightened her dress, a traditional garment made beautiful by the girl's youth.

"Better?" Sophie asked.

"For now."

Sophie placed two euros on the attendant's tip plate and stepped out into the colonnaded hallway. Through a window in the high-ceilinged corridor, she caught a glimpse of fat white snowflakes coming down fast and thick, illuminated by the floodlights outside. Soon, the courtyard and gardens would be a panorama of winter white.

"What does it feel like?" Fatou asked softly over her shoulder.

"The snow?" Sophie made a snap decision. A very un-Sophie-like decision. She took Fatou by the hand and tugged her toward the exit to the courtyard. "Come. You can find out now."

Sophie was aware that it was risky to disappear even for a few minutes from a professional event. But she was feeling strange and reckless tonight. The case that had consumed her was officially over. Her children were half a world away in the sunny Caribbean, watching their father remarry. Never had she felt so disconnected yet also aware of how fleeting and tenuous some things were, such as snowfall in coastal

Holland. A greeting from a queen. An anthem sung by war orphans. Or the youth of a girl who was pregnant before she was done with childhood herself.

The arched doorway, shadowed by a pair of brooding security cameras, framed a world transformed. Fatou gasped and said something in her native tongue. Then she balked under the dagged canvas awning. Sophie stepped out into the fast-falling snow, turning her face up to feel the soft flakes on her cheeks.

"See, it's harmless," she said. "Much more pleasant than rain."

Fatou joined her in the stone-paved courtyard. Her face lit up with pure wonder, reflecting the glow of the sodium vapor floodlights. She laughed in amazement at the sensation of snow. It now covered everything in a pristine layer of white. "It is, *madame,*" she said. "It is a wondrous thing."

Sophie took a mental snapshot of the girl with her face tilted up to the sky, laughing as snowflakes caught in her eyelashes. The moment with Fatou was a reminder that there was beauty and joy in the world, even in the most unlikely of places. She pointed out the individual snowflakes landing on a low garden wall, each one a tiny miracle of perfection.

"They look like the smallest of flowers," Fatou said.

"Yes." Sophie took her hand again. Both she and the girl were freezing by now. "We should go back inside."

She heard something then, a footfall and a breathy voice, and turned to see a hulking shadow coming toward her. "Go inside," she said more urgently to Fatou. "Quickly. I'll join you in a moment."

Sophie recognized the set of his shoulders, silhouetted by the exterior lights. André? She frowned at him. Staggering, he lurched around the side of the building, his dark footprints marking a sinuous path behind him. She wondered what had gotten into him. André was an observant Muslim. He didn't drink. Sophie hurried forward.

"André," she said, *"qu'est-ce qui ce passe?* What happened?"

"Madame," he mumbled, and sank to his knees, right there in the snow. Then he toppled sideways, resembling a bear felled by a hunter.

At some moment, between the time he spoke and the time his head hit the ground, Sophie's confusion turned to ice-cold clarity. *No,* she thought, even though she knew the denial was in vain. *Oh, no.*

She landed on her knees beside André, scarcely feeling the bite of the cold through her dress and her stockings. "Please, oh, please be all right."

Yet even as the words left her mouth, Sophie knew it was already too late. She had never seen a person die before, yet when it happened, she recognized the event on some horrible gut level. He emitted an eerie rattle; then there was a shutting down. A slackening. A release. She clung to a moment of disbelief. She had just spoken with her driver, a man who was dedicated to keeping her safe. Now some violence had been done to him.

The hot, meaty odor of blood was so strong she couldn't believe she hadn't smelled it earlier.

He was wounded in the chest, the gut. Probably more places than that. She couldn't tell whether they were stab or gunshot wounds. She had never seen such a thing up close. As she knelt next to him, feeling the amazing speed with which the heat left his body, she felt as though her own blood had stopped circulating and she simply dropped to the ground. He lay so still, his bulky form limned by the yellowish lights.

Sophie looked around the area, finding it eerily deserted. She screamed for help, her voice echoing through the courtyard. She was edging toward panic as she tried to pat his torn and bloody overcoat back into its proper place. "Please," she said, over and over again, with no idea what she was pleading for. "Please." She pressed herself down on top of him, pressed her face to his as though she could somehow infuse her own life back into him. This was André, her friend, a gentle giant who had never done anything but good in the world, who was dedicated to Sophie, devoted to keeping her safe, wherever she went.

Keeping her safe.

Her rational mind pushed past the terrible sense of loss. André had come to find her. Not to seek help or to bid her a sentimental farewell. That wouldn't be like him. No, he had forced himself to survive his wounds long enough to find Sophie for only one reason she could imagine—to warn her.

Five

Sophie had occasionally wondered how she would react in a crisis. Would she be helpless? She didn't know. She did not disappoint herself by flying into hysterics or folding herself into a whimpering fetal position. Instead, she froze inside, her emotions barricaded behind a stone-cold facade. She felt as if a thick layer of ice insulated her from all feeling. It had to be that way. If she allowed herself to feel one single thing, she would fall apart. She would be lost.

She heard a sound behind her and jumped up, terror surging through her. "Fatou. You startled me. I told you to go inside." In spite of herself, she was glad for the girl's presence.

Fatou wore an expression of quiet resignation. Apparently none of this was new to her, or even shocking.

"I am very sorry, *madame,*" the girl said. "Did you know him?"

"He was my driver." He was more than that, a man whose loyalty and dedication she possessed but was never quite sure she deserved. She knew he had emigrated to Holland with nothing and now lived alone in a flat on the outskirts of the Statenkwartier district, though she had never visited him there. Now she wished she had. These were matters she would grieve in private, when she allowed herself to thaw out and feel something.

She grabbed Fatou by the hand and drew her to the shadows of the palace. It was still snowing, the thick wet flakes already settling on André's unmoving form. "We'll find a security agent," she said, leading the way back into the building. They hesitated in the hallway and stood for a moment, listening. The light trill of singing drifted from the grand hall. Her first impulse was to burst in and sound an alarm, to babble that someone had murdered her driver. Then a feeling, like a breath of cold air on the back of her neck, made her hesitate.

She felt certain the murder of André was not an isolated incident. She looked around, saw no one. "We mustn't go back in there," she whispered. "We'll go to the security office." There were cameras everywhere, though they'd done André no good at all. She knocked at the door. Getting no response, she pushed at it, expecting to find it locked. But the door opened.

Sophie hesitated. There was this thing that happened to her sometimes, a cold clutch of awareness in the center of her stomach. It told her when someone was lying, when something didn't add up—like now. The lights were off, the room illuminated by the bluish haze of monitors and electronic equipment. There were three men inside; at first she thought they might be passed out, drunk. Then she noticed a faint odor of bitter almond.

"Gas," she hissed at Fatou. "Stay outside."

Sophie held her breath. She could probably hold it longer than anyone she knew, thanks to her years of swim training. The men wore the uniforms of the Diplomatic Protection Group. She went to the nearest victim, who lay on the floor, and touched his shoulder, finding his body disconcertingly stiff and resistant. She tried not to look at his face—still-wet blood streaming from his nose—as she found the tiny alert device on his lapel and depressed the button, praying it worked as it was supposed to, instantly alerting the team in the ballroom downstairs, as well as deploying an antiterrorist squad from their remote headquarters in Rotterdam. She had no idea how long it would take for help to arrive, though.

The array of monitors, still glowing dully, showed nothing amiss anywhere in the building. The reception was still going on. She caught sight of a security agent in his dark suit in the ballroom. He showed no outward sign of having received the alert, yet to Sophie he seemed to move with a briskness of purpose that was reassuring. His hand rested on the front button of his suit coat, and he was murmuring into his mouthpiece.

She ducked out of the room, nearly bursting from holding her breath. Shutting the door behind her, she told Fatou, "I think it worked. They'll evacuate everyone and—" Fatou was looking not at her, but at a point somewhere past her shoulder.

"Ne bougez pas," said a low voice in a thick accent, *"ou je tire."*

The words made no sense to Sophie for approximately two beats of her heart. Then something was shoved against the underside of her jaw. *Don't move, or I'll shoot.*

A second man appeared behind Fatou, and Sophie realized he'd been there, in the shadows, all along. Dressed as a security agent, he had a big, bony Dutchman's face and a pistol of some sort with its barrel pressed up under the girl's jaw.

"Oh, please, no, she's only a child. Don't harm her," Sophie said.

A third man, an African also disguised as an agent, stepped forward, kicking open the door to the security office, crossing the room to crank open the windows. So she'd been right about the gas.

It was too soon to feel afraid. Too surreal to grasp the idea that with one squeeze of a stranger's finger, she would be gone. She said nothing, though her heart pounded so loudly she was certain it could be heard. Two thoughts filled her mind—*Max* and *Daisy.* Her children. She might never see them again. In her mind, she reviewed the last time she had seen them, talked to them. Her phone conversation yesterday with Max. Had she spoken with kindness, respect, love? Or had she been in a rush? Had she been demanding? Daisy always accused her of being demanding. Maybe *exacting* was the word. She was too exacting.

"Merde," said one of the men—the French African—leaning on the counter to study an image of the main hall. The security agents at the ceremony were taking action, their weapons drawn as they gave

orders to evacuate. "The alert went through." As he spoke, he straightened up and turned and, with a curious grace, smacked Sophie across the face with the back of his hand.

She had never been touched with violence before, and the shock of the attack preceded the pain. Then it felt like the time she'd been hit in the face with a field hockey ball. She saw a flash of white followed by multiple images, the monitor screens floating in front of her. The blow jostled her against the man with the gun. She shut her eyes, terrified he'd panic and pull the trigger.

"Stop," ordered one of the other men. "An alert's been sounded. We may need her."

For what? Sophie wondered. She caught a whiff of something emanating from the man holding the gun on her. It was the sweat of fear. She didn't know how she knew this, but she somehow recognized the reek of terror, sharp and bitter, more dangerous than cold determination. Perhaps he would obey orders, perhaps not. She could be gone in an instant.

Just like that.

She made herself focus on the monitors. The agents in the room were already in control of the situation, with the white-coated waiters on the floor and the room being swiftly evacuated. *Thank God,* thought Sophie. Thank—

"Vite," said the Frenchman. "Bring the girl, also."

Sophie was all but thrown down the stairs, then dragged along the corridor to the service bay. A crowd of agents moved toward them. Sophie flinched at the dull gleam of a gun. The men held Sophie and Fatou in front of them like shields.

"Drop your weapons or the women die," shouted the Frenchman as they forced their way into the ballroom.

Four of the security agents instantly complied. A fifth hesitated, made a move toward the Frenchman. The hiss of a silenced shot quivered through the room, and Fatou crumpled to the floor. *No,* Sophie thought. *Please, God, she's only a child.*

A woman screamed, and the fifth agent dropped his gun and raised his hands.

Many of the guests had been evacuated to safety, probably due to the alert sent by Sophie. The queen and prime minister were nowhere in sight. Those who remained were now herded to the center of the room and made to lie facedown on the floor. Sophie nearly cried out when she spied Tariq, his black eyes on fire as he caught her gaze. Instinct told her not to focus on anyone in particular lest she single him out. She noticed the reporter, Brooks Fordham, staring dully at her, and prayed he would stay silent. Also remaining was the military attaché, his arms around his family, his angular face alert with bitter rage. And vigilance.

Some of the children remained in the room. They should have been the first evacuated, yet four of them lay on the floor. Everyone was eerily silent, even the little ones. They were from a war-torn place. They had probably endured worse than this.

The Frenchman quickly took control of the situation, issuing orders to the men in the catering jackets. They jumped up, seized the agents' weapons and, just like that, the tables were turned. The men dressed as caterers brought out guns they'd smuggled in on serving carts, concealed by crisp white linen tablecloths. And the massacre took place in silence. Sophie knew that no matter how long she lived, she would always remember the eerie, unexpected silence of these moments as the five agents were executed with swift and chilling dispatch. Instead of mayhem, the killings proceeded in orderly fashion, which was somehow even more horrifying.

For the first time, Sophie got a look at her captor's face. He was African and young, his cheeks boyishly rounded, his eyes feverish, probably with narcotics. She could only pray an anti-terrorist squad was now racing through the city, en route to the palace.

Sophie looked at Fatou on the floor, motionless, bleeding. The girl made a sound, a whisper for help. Sophie took a step toward her but a barked order froze her in her tracks.

Only for a moment, though.

"This is absurd," Sophie declared. "This is the Peace Palace. We don't leave children to die on the floor here." She dropped to her knees beside the fallen girl. Fatou was bleeding, but she was conscious, blinking, and moaning in pain.

"Stop," said the Frenchman. "Do not touch her. Get away."

Sophie ignored him. She found that it was possible

to ignore everything, including the fact that a murderer had a gun pointed at her. She kept her focus, pressing a wad of linen napkins to the wound. Somehow, the close-range shot had failed to kill her. Perhaps it wasn't meant to.

"Get away now," the man ordered.

Sophie didn't look up. Something possessed her. Not courage or some high sense of compassion or outrage. Instead it was the absolute conviction that she could not abide one more killing. Even if they shot her.

They didn't shoot her, but the African boy pulled her away from Fatou. The men issued orders for everyone to stay on the floor. Some of the others were closing doors, locking them from within. *We're hostages,* she thought. *We've been taken hostage.* The big Frenchman and the blond man who had been serving champagne earlier got into an argument over whether to stay and negotiate or flee with a human shield.

Sophie had undergone mandatory violence-prevention training, and the class had addressed hostage taking. Like everything else in her field of work, there was an acronym. The trouble was, she couldn't remember it. E-I-S . . . something. E-evaluate the situation. That was easy. The situation was bad. Extremely bad. I-isolate. As in, isolate the perpetrator. After that, she drew a blank.

She did recall learning that while it was politically popular to declare you didn't bargain with terrorists or extremists, it was also extremely risky. In a hostage situation, one of the key strategies was to buy time, and another was to foster divisiveness among the hostage takers. They were already doing this on their own, which she took as a good sign. She alone was still standing, with the fearful, dangerous boy holding her. Brooks Fordham appeared to be on the verge of saying something. The moment he glanced her way, she gave the barest shake of her head. *No.*

One of the caterers noticed the reporter looking around the room, and delivered a kick to the head with emotionless dispatch. Brooks made no sound as he fell still. Tariq exhorted the thugs in Arabic, earning the same response, his beautiful face shattered by the toe of a large boot. Sophie felt dizzy with the urge to throw up.

At the same time, she felt a crushing, overwhelming sense of futility. She and dozens of others had given everything they had to restoring peace and justice, but ultimately, people were still being bullied and killed. André lay dead in the courtyard. Staring numbly at Fatou, Sophie realized she'd been fooling herself thinking she was making a difference in the world. Greed and evil were tireless enemies. The larger truth was that nothing—no amount of sacrifice or diplomacy—could stop the killing and rid the world of people like this.

She guessed that the French-speaking African was a cohort of General Timi Abacha who, with the diamond merchant Serge Henger, had fled the prosecution of the ICC. So, although the media would probably see these men as terrorists, fanatically devoted to a cause, Sophie knew better. This wasn't about anyone's ideals or sense of justice. It was not even about revenge. It was about money. Not a belief system or family or patriotism. Their "cause" was simple greed. The action of the court and the enforcement of UN troops had deprived them of their fortune, and they wanted it back.

In a way, this made the situation simple. A transaction.

"Taking children hostage is only going to make you hated and hunted by the world. You don't want the world to hate you," she said. Her jaw ached from the blow she'd taken, making it hard to speak. "You just want what was taken from you."

"We are clear on what we want." The blond Dutchman checked the chamber of the pistol he'd taken from a security agent.

"Then be clear on how to get it," Sophie stated. Was this her speaking up? Negotiating with terrorists? "You're not stupid. You've gotten this far. You can leave now without incident."

The man stared at her. Then his eyes glittered and he smiled at her, his mouth curving like a cold slice of moon. "And Madame Bellamy, we are familiar with you."

Dear Lord. They knew who she was. They probably knew she was a member of the prosecution team. She felt the color drop from her face, though she struggled to show no reaction. "As familiar as you are with the

Kuumba Mine case," he added, "and with the process of setting up accounting in a country with no laws of extradition." Faintly, from a distance, the two-toned sound of sirens drifted into the room. Their predicament flashed through her mind like lightning. If they stayed here, there would be a standoff—until it deteriorated into a shoot-out.

"None of this will matter," she told him, "if you allow yourselves to be trapped here."

The ring of a cell phone sounded, causing Sophie's captor to tense, reminding her that she was a trigger-squeeze between life and death. One of the men she had noticed earlier—the name Karl stitched on his catering livery—rifled through the jacket of a fallen security agent and took out a mobile phone. He glanced at the Dutchman, then answered. She strained to hear, but he was speaking Dutch in a low, rapid voice.

"You don't need a group of hostages," she said to the men with her. "In fact, you should go now, while you still can. If you try to stay here and bargain for your fortune, you'll fail." She looked from one man to the other. "These things always end badly."

The next rapid exchange took place in the Umojan dialect. Sophie was nominally familiar with it but she couldn't catch what was being said. The African gave an order and the men dressed as caterers made for the door. The Dutchman went to the attaché, handed him a mobile phone. The shiny-eyed boy with Sophie kept hold of her upper arm, yanking her forward.

She balked, tried to pull away, but the boy held her fast. The African turned to her. "*Madame,* you must come with me."

She looked up into his face and saw no humanity there. Only cold determination. It dawned on Sophie that she made the ideal hostage. She was easily outmatched, unarmed, defenseless. Yet she spoke multiple languages and was known in diplomatic circles, thus adding to her value as a bargaining chip.

She briefly considered putting up a fight here and now. She could feel the attaché urging her, and knew he would take action. She also knew that would get him killed.

Seconds later, she found herself in a haze of numbness, being shoved into one of the catering vans. *I'm so sorry,* she thought, wishing there was a way to beam the silent message to her children. She was in the hands of murderers. She had all but guaranteed she would be taken from her children. They would survive. Despite her faults as a mother, she knew they were smart and sturdy—survivors. Perhaps she hadn't been much of a mother, but at least she'd given them that.

It was still snowing outside. She was crammed into the front seat of the van with the Dutchman and the African boy. Her legs were awkwardly canted to one side of the stick shift. Her captors didn't bother restraining her, no doubt—and correctly—deeming her no physical threat.

Four more conspirators crowded into the back,

protesting in French and Dutch. The entire operation had gone awry, Sophie gathered, because she had alerted security. From their agitated talk, she gleaned that their plan had been to barricade themselves in the building, demanding the restoration of their impounded fortune and their safe transit to Africa. "We leave with nothing, *nothing,*" groused a reedy voice.

"You leave with your life," the driver snapped. "That is something."

"And a life insurance policy," said someone else.

To her horror, Sophie felt a touch at the nape of her neck. It made her skin crawl. She drew her shoulders up and leaned forward to draw away, eliciting nervous laughter from some of the men. She tried not to think about what they were capable of, but her mind filled with images of torture, rape and murder. She had spent two years building a case of such crimes, but until this very moment, they had been merely legal concepts. Now they were very, very real.

The Dutchman drove, taking corners too fast in the snow and heading for the port with the confidence of someone familiar with the city. The vehicle sped down the roadway that ran alongside the Verversingskanaal that flowed into the Voorhaven, a lock-controlled waterway of the North Sea.

A bridge rose in a high arc over the locks station. Snow flew at the windshield. The tires slipped and spun on the slick roadway. The bridge was entirely deserted of traffic, aglow with amber lights on tall poles, which turned the covering of snow to pure gold.

From the rear of the van, someone said, "There's a helicopter. We're being followed."

"Not to worry," said the Dutchman, accelerating past 130 kilometers per hour. "I left instructions."

Sophie realized then what the man's exchange with the attaché had been about. They had promised to kill their hostage if their needs were not met. She also realized that, at some point, they would kill her anyway. Why give them that chance, then? She had lived her life trying to do everything right, yet things so often turned out wrong anyway.

Her hands seemed to belong to someone else as she moved with a speed and strength she didn't know she possessed. She grabbed for the steering wheel and dragged it into a sharp turn.

The Dutchman cursed and tried to wrestle back control of the van. But it was too late. The bridge was too slippery, the guardrail too flimsy to stop the van from hurdling over the side of the bridge and plunging into the ink-black water.

Part Three

St. Croix, U.S. Virgin Islands

Three Kings Day

Three Kings Day, or Epiphany, is the culmination of a month of celebration on the Caribbean island of St. Croix, a place famed for its sugar, molasses and rum. Wedding fruit cake is so dense and richly flavored that it must be served in small pieces as a memento of the event.

Wedding Fruit Cake

Place five pounds of mixed dried fruit (currants, raisins, dates, figs, prunes) in a very large bowl, and cover it with about three cups of Cruzan rum. Set this aside to macerate for two days or up to a week.

To make the cake, you will need the macerated fruit, plus:

2½ cups flour
1½ teaspoons baking powder
1 pound brown sugar

1 teaspoon cinnamon
1 teaspoon vanilla
1 cup molasses
½ pound butter at room temperature
6 eggs

Beat the butter in a large bowl and add the sugar, cinnamon, vanilla and molasses. Add the eggs one at a time. Beat in flour and baking powder and then stir in the fruit mixture.

Pour into two or three well-greased 13”x9” baking pans. Bake in a 350ºF oven for about one hour.

Six

St. Croix, U.S. Virgin Islands
6 January – Epiphany

Max Bellamy couldn't stand weddings. In his family, weddings seemed to crop up on a regular basis, like flu season. Since he was just a kid, he wasn't allowed to check off "regrets" on the invitation reply card and stay home. But boy, did he regret having to sit through a wedding.

Sometimes they even made him participate. Twice, when he was really little, he'd been a ring bearer. At age four, he'd thought it was cool until he realized they wanted him to dress up and stay clean and stand still through a ceremony that wouldn't end.

At twelve, he was way too old for such an indignity, but his family managed to find a new one. Last summer, he'd been upgraded to usher for his cousin Olivia, who married Connor Davis at Camp Kioga on Willow Lake. That was when he knew for sure all weddings were pretty much the same. Same level of discomfort, in starched clothes and shoes that pinched, same droning ceremony and sappy songs, different couple at the altar.

His take on weddings—they were long and boring and everyone talked about love and promises, and it was pretty much all a load of crap, as far as he was concerned.

Today the discomfort came from a different source. Since the ceremony was on the beach, everybody got to wear beach clothes. They looked like a reunion of Hawaiian punch guys, as far as Max was concerned. Which was a lot more comfortable than tuxedos and tight shoes, but that didn't mean he was having a great time.

How could he, when the groom was his dad?

Okay, so Max liked Nina Romano. A lot. She was going to do fine as a stepmother. He wanted her to marry his dad. He wanted them to be married. But he didn't want to have to sit through all the endless vows and recitations. He didn't want to have to listen to his dad say stuff like "I offer you my heart" to *anyone.*

That kind of stuff just skeezed him out. He wished they had sneaked off somewhere to do it instead of involving families. There were like a gazillion Romanos milling around. Nina had eight brothers and sisters, and most of them had kids, so between the Romanos and the Bellamys, this had turned into some huge deal.

Cheerful, Italian-American strangers had been coming up to him all week, thumping him on the back and acting like his best friend. They weren't all strangers. Two of them—who by the end of the day would be step-cousins—were in his grade at Avalon Middle School. Angelica Romano was in his pre-algebra class and Ricky Pastorini was on his hockey team. Ricky's mom was Nina's sister, Maria. She was the team mother. Although he was Max's age, Ricky was already shaving and his voice had changed. *Big deal,* thought Max.

He tried not to grind his teeth in disgust as another lame song was sung about two hearts beating as one, while most of the women cried. It was just too sweet. He was going to slip into a diabetic coma if they didn't end this soon.

He cast a restless eye through the gathering on the beach. Everyone was seated in white folding chairs, their feet in flip-flops, sifting through the white-sugar sand. Max's hand stole into the pocket of his cargo shorts. He palmed his phone, checked the screen. His mom hadn't texted him back after he sent her the picture earlier. He'd tried to put a positive spin on it, because his mom was all about trying to act like everything was fine, all the time, even when you had to sit through your own father's wedding. Max's message had been that St. Croix was awesome.

He couldn't exactly say the same for today's ceremony. It seemed as though everybody but him was really into it, though. He stuck the phone away, endured another reading. Finally the ceremony was winding down. There was a moment—a split second, really—when Max's dad looked so happy that Max caught himself smiling in spite of himself.

During the kissing, he stared at the ground—*enough's enough*—and at last, it was over. The ensemble played a reggae rendition of "What a Wonderful World" as Dad and Nina came down the aisle formed by the rows of chairs.

All the wedding guests filed out behind them to the pavilion with the banquet and dance floor. As they made their way to the feast, Max found himself surrounded by Romanos. Nina sure had a big family. The sun had just begun to set, turning everything in sight a livid sunburned pink.

His phone rang. He looked at the screen, seeing an international number he didn't recognize. "I think this might be my mom," he said.

Nina's sister, Maria—the bossy one—gave a sniff. "Unbelievable. On today, of all days."

He pretended he hadn't heard her, and flipped open the phone.

"Hello?"

"Hey, Max." It was his mom. She sounded . . . different. Her voice was thin. "Max, I know this probably isn't the best timing—"

"It's all right." He stepped aside and moved to the shade of a large tree where it was quiet. "I'm glad you called, Mom," he said.

"Are you, Max?" She sounded so tired, more tired than he'd ever heard her. He wondered what time it was, over in Holland. The middle of the night. "I'm glad, too," she said.

Daisy Bellamy loved weddings. She always had, ever since she was little and got to be the flower girl in her aunt Helen's wedding. She still remembered the lacy dress, the flowers twining through her hair, the shiny patent-leather Mary Janes, the feeling that she had a critically important role to play.

Taking a break from her dad's wedding festivities, she sat on the balcony of her hotel room, looking down at the pavilion that had been set up on the beach for the reception. Sunset painted the sky every color of the rainbow. In a few minutes, she'd take out her camera to get some candid shots of the party.

All her life, she had fantasized about the day it would be her turn to be the bride. She had actually planned the entire event, right down to the seed pearls on her gown. She could perfectly picture every moment of her special day, from the delivery of the flowers—daisies, what else?—to the roaring send-off, to the Parisian honeymoon.

The only detail she couldn't picture was the face of the groom.

At nineteen, she still couldn't help dreaming about her own wedding, but there was a difference now. It was only a dream, not an eventuality. That option had been taken off the table last August.

She glanced down at the infant nursing at her breast and knew that the fantasy wedding simply wasn't going to happen. Unless Prince Charming was willing to take on Daisy and Charlie both.

Logan O'Donnell, the baby's father, kept trying to convince her that he was the one. There was one problem with that. Logan wasn't Prince Charming. Oh, he looked like a prince, which was what had landed Daisy in trouble in the first place. But now that reality had hit Daisy like a brick to the head, she knew it took a lot more than looks to make a prince.

She lifted Charlie against her and draped a cloth over her shoulder to catch the spit-up, which was his custom after every meal. Thanks to Charlie, she had missed the very tail end of the wedding. He'd been great right up until the final reading. She'd promised her dad and Nina that she wouldn't let him interrupt and, true to her word, she'd whisked him away at the first squawk.

Now she rubbed the baby's back, standing up and swaying back and forth on the balcony. "We don't need a prince, do we?" she whispered in his ear. "We just need to fantasize about something different. I've been meaning to talk to you about that. I mean, I know you're really little, but I wonder if you'd mind staying with a babysitter for a few hours a week while I take a photography course at the college."

He rewarded her with a gentle belch.

Daisy smiled. "That's right, I got in. My portfolio was approved for the class, and it all starts in a few weeks. I'm going to feel totally guilty about leaving you, though. Mom left Max and me a lot when we were little. She had to, because of her work. I wonder if she felt like this, too. Just totally guilty—"

"Hey, Daisy!" Standing two stories below, Sonnet Romano waved at her. "Come on down. They're about to cut the cake."

"Don't let them start without me," Daisy called.

“You want some help?”

“That’s okay. We’ll be right there.”

Nina’s daughter Sonnet was the first friend Daisy had made in Avalon, New York, where they’d moved after Daisy’s parents divorced. She was the first person Daisy had told, after her dad, about being pregnant. Now Sonnet and Daisy were stepsisters. She hoped that didn’t mean the end of a beautiful friendship.

“You hear that?” Daisy said to Charlie as she put her camera into the ever-present diaper bag. “Cake! I love cake.” One of the best things about breastfeeding was that you could eat anything you wanted—cake, peanut butter, cookie dough, you name it—and you didn’t gain weight, because it took a lot of calories to be a milk factory.

She buckled the baby into his carrier and headed out the door. The hotel had open-air hallways and stairwells, and a warm breeze flowed through, carrying the scent of exotic flowers. Here in the tropics, winter seemed a million miles away.

At the bottom of the stairs, she headed toward the reception, but stopped when she saw Max running toward her.

She took one look at her brother’s face and knew something was wrong. Well, whatever it was, they weren’t going to bug Dad about it. Not today, of all days.

Part Four

Three weeks later

Decision

Every act you have ever performed since the day you were born was performed because you wanted something.
—Andrew Carnegie, founding contributor of the Peace Palace

Seven

The Hague, Holland
Three weeks later

While waiting for Tariq in the courtyard of the Peace Palace, Sophie turned in a slow circle, waiting for the flashbacks to hit like a bolt from the sky. She'd been told by her post-trauma treatment team to expect unsettling reminders of the ordeal she'd suffered here. But nothing happened, not even when she thought about André staggering toward her, bleeding into the snow. She felt a wave of grief, but no panic, no insanity. The sky remained its usual brooding gray. The neo-Gothic walls of the palace, stained by age and pollution, looked the same as they always had, coldly beautiful and impenetrable.

This was not the first time she'd come here in the past few weeks. She'd been brought here several times, as her doctors wanted to be sure the location did not trigger any sort of trauma-induced reaction. On the contrary, she felt nothing but the usual bone-deep dampness of a typical winter day.

The screen of her PDA displayed a text message from Max sent the day before. *Dad taking us skiing at Saddle Mt 2day. Wish U were here xoxo.* She checked her watch, which was always set at her children's time zone, and deemed it too early to phone the States.

There would be time to call after her meeting today to tell them her plans.

A moment later, Tariq joined her, his Burberry greatcoat swirling fashionably in the wind. Like Sophie, he was shadowed by security agents, whose constant presence was a given these days.

"You look remarkably calm," said Tariq.

They set off together to a meeting at the supreme chamber. Sophie eyed him with a slight frown. "Why do you say 'remarkably calm'? Why not just calm?"

"No one would blame you for not wanting to set foot in this place. After what happened to you—"

"I swear, if I hear that phrase one more time . . . And what about you? It happened to you, too."

He waved away her comment. "I've survived worse than a bloodied nose. Besides, being unconscious is my preferred way of enduring an attack." He paused in the colonnaded hallway and touched her arm. "I wish you'd been spared as I was."

Three weeks had passed since the incident. That was how the events on the night of Epiphany had come to be known—the incident. Or, The Incident. The Epiphany Incident, referred to in somber tones by foreign correspondents. *The London Times* had called it the Twelfth Night Massacre. But there was no term that could encompass the terror and powerlessness of that night until it became a code word—The Incident.

She had walked away from death that night, soaked to the skin but feeling nothing. Hypothermia created such symptoms, the doctors later told her. The body went numb to protect itself from damage. So, in a way, had her mind. Her memory of the ordeal was fragmented. Sometimes, in her nightmares, she relived the ordeal in terrifying bursts. There was the weightlessness of her free fall as the van hurtled through the night. The impact when it hit the water thundered up through the vehicle, jarring her teeth so that she bit her tongue, snapping her head back. The air was filled with screams and howls that sounded almost animal-like. Water flooded the van from front to back, and she felt herself swept backward; her captors hadn't bothered to fasten her seat belt.

The investigative team speculated that she'd exited via a broken window, as evidenced by the pattern of scratches on her arms and legs. She'd survived thanks to a combination of luck and skill at swimming. She had a vague recollection of swimming—icy water, aiming at a dull flicker of light shimmering on the surface above her, battling her way free of the vortex created by the sinking van. Oil-tainted seawater rushed into her nose and mouth, causing her to choke while she clung to an iron loop set into the cut-stone side of the canal.

Another gap of memory. Somehow, she hoisted herself out amid wailing sirens and the pulsating roar of a helicopter's rotor blades beating the air and churning up the water. Emergency vehicles swarmed the bridge, but no one seemed to notice her. It was as though she were invisible. Maybe she was. She remembered thinking maybe this was death, and no one could see her as she wandered among squad cars and emergency vehicles. One great mercy of working for such a powerful organization was the strict control of information. Only a few people knew Sophie had been taken; fewer still were aware of her mode of escape. And no one knew she had caused the van to go off the bridge. No one, except the terrorists who had been pulled alive from the Voorhaven. And they weren't talking.

To avoid retaliation, her name was kept out of accounts released to the public.

"I *was* spared," she told Tariq, her tone edged by an unreasoning anger. "I'm here, aren't I?"

"Sorry," Tariq said. "Honestly, Petal, I want to know you're all right."

Sophie's decisive action in the van had effectively ended The Incident. Three of her captors had drowned. Three others, like Sophie, had survived—just barely—and were recovering under heavy guard in the hospital.

People looked at her and marveled that she'd escaped "unscathed." She bore no outward sign of her ordeal.

She'd suffered only minor scratches, contusions and a touch of hypothermia. The treatment team at Bronovo Hospital had warned her that she was at risk for posttraumatic stress disorder, though tests revealed that her psyche appeared to have survived, as well. Certainly she didn't consider herself a casualty of the event. Casualties were André, her driver. And the security agents who had been murdered. And, it had to be said, the men in the van. Fatou had lost the baby and now faced a third surgery, and Brooks Fordham was still recovering from a coma. Sophie had walked away, dripping wet, a survivor. And, she was soon to discover, a stranger to herself. She was willing to let everyone believe nothing about her had changed. She certainly was not comfortable allowing people to look into her heart and mind. Still, it left her feeling adrift. Misunderstood.

Immediately following the incident, she had called her children in St. Croix and her parents in Seattle, on the off chance that the news would somehow creep into the American or Canadian media. No danger of that, as it turned out. She'd told her family simply that there had been a "security situation" at the Peace Palace but she was fine and in no danger. The incident was no big secret, but she didn't want to worry her family. She hadn't cried on the phone. She'd felt displaced from herself, as though she were watching her own actions.

As she told the two psychiatrists who had treated her, "If I let this be a big deal, it won't leave room for the things that are important." Through hours and hours of intensive therapy, she had come to realize exactly what those things were.

She had not spoken of what had happened during the ordeal, not even to the medical and psychological team that had cared for her during the aftermath. Dr. Maarten had tried to persuade her that exploring every moment in exhaustive detail was the key to defeating the demons.

"You don't understand," she had told him. "There are no demons. They went away the moment I survived."

"Are you sure?" He clearly thought she was either lying or fooling herself.

"Of course I'm sure. I've studied every item on your post-trauma assessment lists. I'm not suffering from any such symptoms, and I don't plan to in the future."

Now she glanced over at Tariq. He knew as well as she did what was going to happen here today. They had offered her an appointment most jurists only dreamed about and today she was expected to give her answer.

She was used to the bodyguards by now. In a very short time, she'd become accustomed to the safety precautions. It all felt very surreal. Did she want this to be her normal life, to be crushed by scrutiny, to walk among armed strangers who were utterly focused on her safety?

"Off we go, then," Tariq muttered.

"Off to see the wizard," she said.

The double doors of the lead justice's office opened, and she and Tariq went inside. There was a heartbeat of panic—not because of The Incident but because of something much deeper-reaching than that. Willem De Groot, Esquire, sat at a carved Gothic desk in front of an array of stained-glass windows. Illuminated from behind by jewel-toned light, he looked imposing, otherworldly and intimidating. The wizard.

Actually, he looked like Sophie's father. Yet unlike

Sophie's father, the redoubtable Ragnar Lindstrom, a partner in a Seattle firm, Judge De Groot displayed an array of family photos in his office. There were shots of him with children and grandchildren of all ages, incongruous amid the ponderous legal tomes. Yet at the moment, he was all business. He wanted to see her strive and achieve. He wanted greatness for her.

His version of greatness.

She and Tariq stood together across from him. De Groot's assistants were stationed discreetly to one side, silently pressing the keys of their mobile devices.

"Thank you for seeing me," she said. "And for the honor of this offer."

"It's an offer we didn't make lightly," Willem De Groot said. "A seat on the Permanent Court of Arbitration is not a reward for your actions. It's an acknowledgment of your potential as a jurist." He steepled his fingers. "This vacancy comes at an opportune time. I'm pleased to be able to offer you the position."

Sophie nodded, even as she felt a chill of skepticism in her bones. This promotion was the ultimate prize. As a jurist of the PCA, she would be on track to one day become a justice of the World Court. That marked the pinnacle of any career in international law, the Olympic gold medal of achievements. She would earn not just the accolades but maybe even a place in history. Her influence would come to bear on great matters of the day.

There was a ring of triumph in her ears. She had reached the apex of her career, and it was higher than she'd ever dreamed. From this seat, she could change the world. She could help whole populations of people. Her policies and decisions would become a part of history.

Sophie could feel Tariq beside her, practically growing taller out of sheer pride. This was not just her achievement, and they both knew that. With her elevation to the Permanent Court of Arbitration, her staff and associates would all advance, like train cars hooked to the same engine. This appointment would change not only her life and her career, but also the careers of everyone she worked with. De Groot was speaking to Tariq now, explaining his role as deputy.

Her spirit flared up like a fire splashed with accelerant. Yet, just as quickly, the feeling was doused by the cold damper of memory. She had been taken hostage. She'd seen people murdered, inches from her. She'd held a bleeding child in her arms. She'd caused people to plunge to their death.

That was her reality. She'd worked long and hard with the treatment team whose mission had been to heal her spirit, even though she swore her spirit didn't need healing. Still, the counselors persisted. They worked every day to show her that although she could never escape or outrun what had happened to her, she could live her life with purpose and deliberation, not in spite of what had happened but, perhaps, because of it.

"Thank you," she said to De Groot. "I'm honored." She took a deep breath, squared her shoulders, made steady eye contact with the chief jurist. "But I can't."

The words dropped like cold stones into the office, echoing off the neo-Gothic walls. *I can't.*

Those two words had been banished by Sophie's father from her vocabulary, long ago. She'd been raised to embrace the concept of "I can."

I can bring down a corrupt dictator. (But only if I move an ocean away from my children and work eighteen-hour days.)

I can escape when captured by terrorists. (But only if I force myself to do something that will haunt me for the rest of my life.)

I can be the youngest jurist ever appointed to the PCA. (But only if I turn myself into a robot, starting now.)

That was what her parents failed to see, that for every "I can" statement proclaiming her invincibility, there was a huge and terrible hidden sacrifice.

Sophie felt utterly calm and focused. "I've given this a lot of thought," she said, then reiterated her statement. "I won't be accepting the post." She heard Tariq pull in a breath and didn't let herself look at him, knowing he'd be staring at her, aghast, as though she had sprouted antlers.

The old Sophie would have leaped at this chance, the brass ring of judgeships. Now the new Sophie, the one who had been melted down and remade during the hostage ordeal, knew that the prestige and excitement of this once-in-a-lifetime opportunity was no longer her calling.

In the aftermath of the intensive treatment and counseling she had received, she felt like a different person. Perhaps the goal of all the interventions she had undergone was to bring her back to her normal, ordinary life. If so, Sophie's treatment had failed. Instead, The Incident and fallout had proved to her that a life lived without family was meaningless.

Judge De Groot was old and unflappable. Unlike Tariq, he was matter-of-fact when Sophie explained about her family. "If you walk away from this opportunity, it won't be here when you come back. I cannot hold it open for you."

"I understand that, Your Honor," Sophie said.

"Your children are your children. They will always be there. This appointment will not. I am certain your family would support a decision to stay and work on behalf of world justice."

Would they? she wondered. Had she ever given them a choice? "I'm sure that's true, but I'm moving back to the United States," she said. There. Spoken aloud, it was simple and direct. She had to go back to her children.

She allowed herself a quick glance at Tariq, who looked as though his head was about to explode. She didn't let herself veer from a decision made in those moments when the van had hit the water. If she survived this, she would go home to her children. It had been a powerful, clear moment. Her psychiatric intervention team had encouraged her to focus on the present moment, a strategy encouraged to prevent post-trauma symptoms. "Their job was to get me ready to come back to work. But the plan backfired."

Then she faced the man who had been her mentor for the past year. "What happened at the Peace Palace changed my focus," she explained. "I thought I knew what I should be doing with my life, but that night forced me to examine my priorities." Her gaze wandered to De Groot's display of photos. "I'm ashamed to say it took a brush with death to show me the things that matter most. And with all due respect, it's not this mission, not in my case, anyway. It's not prestige. It's not even saving people from the cruelties of the world. That's a job, and in my job, I am replaceable. In my life, my family, I'm not. I have a family I don't see nearly enough of. I have a lot to answer for. I need to do that, starting now."

The recriminations, when they came, were from Tariq. "You're mad," he accused as she bustled around her apartment, filling up pieces of luggage and moving boxes. "You've gone utterly bonkers. I'm begging you, Sophie. Don't throw this away."

"I'm not. I'm giving it to you. They'll offer you the position and you'll be brilliant."

"This is your prize for the taking," he insisted. "Your children have grown beyond needing a mum at home all day." He waved a hand, dismissing her retort before she made it. "I'm only stating the obvious,

Petal. Max is half grown, and Daisy has a baby of her own to raise."

"They need me more than ever," she insisted. "The fact that they're older only means I have even less time. And then there's Charlie. A baby, Tariq. I can't imagine what I was thinking, not being there for Daisy and Charlie."

"You were there for the birth, and Daisy will be fine. I'm certain she's her mother's daughter. You were a young mum yourself. You coped beautifully."

Sophie had done nothing of the sort, although she was the only one who seemed to know that. She'd lived her life on the surface, going through the motions of a successful education and career. There was a whole rich world of possibilities beneath that surface, something she hadn't realized until she'd nearly lost it all.

She taped a label on a plastic shipping box. Her personal possessions took up remarkably little space. The apartment had come furnished, so all she really had was her wardrobe, a few books, framed pictures of her kids. Looking around, she suddenly felt less sure of herself. This was a different sort of fear from being taken hostage. What if she failed? What if it was too late?

She took the portrait down from a shelf and studied their faces. "When Greg and I divorced, I begged them to live here with me," she said. "I wish we could have made that work."

"They scarcely gave it a chance," Tariq reminded her.

She remembered the two miserable weeks, her kids in a high-rise looking out over the Dutch flatlands, where the rain never quite stopped altogether. The sun hadn't come out, not once. "I saw no reason to prolong the inevitable," she said. "Nor did I want to sacrifice even more of their happiness so I could have this career. They wanted to go with their father. It was really a no-brainer. On the one hand there was me, rushing off to court in a foreign country. And then there was Greg, who decided to go all Andy-of-Mayberry—"

"Andy of who?"

"One of America's biggest TV icons. He's a single dad, actually, on an old classic show. He lives in a small American town and takes his kid fishing and has this idyllic, picture-perfect life in a town where autumn leaves always seem to be falling and it never, ever rains. No wonder Max and Daisy wanted to stay with their dad." She carefully and methodically folded a sweater, lining up the seams of the sleeves just so.

"What about what you wanted?" Tariq challenged her.

"Right after the divorce, I was so confused I didn't even know what I wanted. You remember what a mess I was. The divorce made me question everything about myself, especially my parenting. I didn't exactly have the world's best role models, you'll recall. I finally have a clear idea of what I want, and that's what this is about. I'm giving myself a second chance to do better." She folded three more sweaters.

Where she was going, she would need them.

"But why there? Why that town in the wilderness?"

"My kids are there. I also need to deal with the fact that my ex is living happily ever after with a woman who is my polar opposite."

He gave a fatalistic shrug. "It happens."

"You're a big help."

"You don't want my help. You want to go prostrate yourself on an altar of shame and flagellate yourself until you're bloody. And, by the way, I know a few blokes who would pay to see such a thing."

"Don't be obnoxious." She finished filling a section of her garment bag. "You're going to get your dream job because I'm leaving," she told him.

"I'd rather have you," he said simply, opening his arms.

"You're not obnoxious," she said as he closed her into a hug. "You're the best. You're the one person I'm going to miss, desperately."

"I know."

She pressed her cheek to the soft Scottish cashmere of his sweater. "I'm scared," she whispered, thinking about what awaited her in Avalon—the failed marriage to Greg and her inadequate mothering.

"I don't blame you, Petal." He stroked her hair in a soothing gesture. "I'd be scared of a small town in America, too. I keep thinking about plaid hunting jackets and open-bed lorries on gigantic tires."

She pulled back, gently slapped him on the shoulder. "Oh, come on. It's not that bad."

But it might be, she conceded. She was no expert, having always lived in big, bustling cities—Seattle, Boston, Tokyo, New York, The Hague. She had no idea how she would manage in a town like Avalon. But she had to get back to her family. She felt a keen sense of mission about it, the way she used to feel about an important case. She needed to reclaim the things she had lost to her career. She needed to find a new direction for her life.

"I haven't said anything to them yet. Just that I'm fine and I'll be coming home. They don't know I'm staying."

"You are mad. Certifiable." Tariq started to pitch in, folding trousers and stacking them precisely in the oversize Louis Vuitton bag.

"If I tell them I'm moving to Avalon, they'll think something's wrong."

"Something is wrong. You've lost your mind."

"No, listen, I do have a plan. Some friends of mine from New York—the Wilsons—have a lake house they only use in the summer. They've offered it to me for the entire winter. So I have a place to live."

"In Mayberry."

"Avalon, but that's the idea."

"And do . . . what, exactly? You need to reconnect with your kids. I get that. Is that a full-time occupation?"

She zipped her jewelry into a side pocket of her case. The small pouch of tasteful baubles made her remember the conversation with Brooks Fordham that night about her refusal to own anything produced by exploitation of labor. "I don't know," she said to Tariq. "I've never done it before."

"And why would you even want this?" he asked her without a hint of irony.

"Because I've never had it," she replied. "Because being part of a community has never happened to me and I think it's about time. Because underneath this legal robot you see, I have a heart."

She and Tariq went to the tiny nook of the main room, which served as her study. This, too, was devoid of personal items except her laptop and a corkboard to which she'd pinned a few items. "My rogues' gallery," she told Tariq. "And it's all yours now."

The faces of the warlords had been her motivation for the past two years. The plan was to prosecute each one in turn at the International Criminal Court. The people on her corkboard represented the very worst of humankind—men who practiced child conscription, sexual torture, slavery. She took down each picture in turn, making a small ceremony of handing them to Tariq.

"That's it, then," she said, slipping the laptop into its case. "You're going to do great things."

"And you're walking away from doing great things."

She shook her head. "I walked away from my marriage and family. I can't ever go back to the marriage, but my family still needs me." She thought they did, anyway. She hoped. They had certainly taught themselves to get along without her. Maybe the truth was that *she* needed them.

"I've never seen you run away from anything," Tariq said. "This isn't like you."

"Oh, it's exactly like me. When it comes to my professional life, to cases involving genocidal murderers, you're absolutely right. I've been like a dog with a bone since I was in high school. But in my personal life, I've done exactly the opposite. Here's the thing. You can't run from yourself. It only took twenty years and a few hours with a team of terrorists for me to figure that out."

She took a deep breath, looked around the apartment with her things packed in boxes. The place was as impersonal and anonymous as a hotel room.

She was off, then, to make things right with her family. It was insane, going to a place where the Bellamy family had been entrenched for generations, where her ex-husband was living happily ever after with his new wife. Yet this was the place her children lived, and she intended to be their full-time mother. She hoped with all her heart that it wasn't too late.

Part Five

February

A cheer for the snow—the drifting snow;
Smoother and purer than Beauty's brow;
The creature of thought scarce likes to tread
On the delicate carpet so richly spread.
—Eliza Cook, English poet

Morning Muffins from the Sky River Bakery

1½ cups flour
¾ cup ground flax seed
¾ cup oat bran
1½ cups brown sugar
2 teaspoons baking soda
1 teaspoon baking powder
1 teaspoon salt
1 tablespoon ground cinnamon
¾ cup milk
2 eggs, beaten
1 teaspoon vanilla extract
½ cup vegetable oil

2 cups peeled and shredded carrots
2 apples, peeled and shredded
½ cup raisins or currants
1 cup chopped walnuts

Preheat oven to 350°F. Mix flour, flax seed, bran, brown sugar, baking soda, baking powder, salt and cinnamon. In a separate bowl, combine the milk, eggs, vanilla and oil. Add to the dry ingredients. Fold in the carrots, apples, raisins and nuts. Fill prepared muffin cups two-thirds full with batter.

Bake for fifteen to twenty minutes.

Eight

Sophie woke up hugging a warm teddy bear in a strange bed. Hovering in the zone between full alert and dreams, she lay very still, waiting for the customary nightmares to fade. She'd learned that they would, eventually. But she wondered if she would ever stop seeing the faces of the dead or feeling the desperation and panic that had seized her in the moments before the accident.

Yet this morning, the memories seemed curiously distant. Simply lying adrift felt so good that she held still, hugged the teddy bear closer and kept her eyes shut, prolonging a completely unjustified sensation of well-being.

When it came to jet lag, she was a champ at dealing with it. Besides, with her frequent trips back to the States, she had enough miles for an upgrade every time. She'd schooled herself to sleep with the self-discipline of a yoga master. But it was never a restful sleep. Therefore, feeling warm, comfortable and rested was simply wrong.

Finally, like drips of water through a slow leak, little awarenesses pried her awake.

Landing at JFK, making the drive upstate through ever-thickening snowfall. A deer leaping out of nowhere, the swinging glare of her headlights as she swerved to avoid hitting it. Then came the terrible thud and a bone-jarring jolt as she came to rest in the ditch. And then . . . someone had arrived. She remembered looking up and seeing him outside her window, a man . . .

Encountering a large, strange man, when she was alone, stuck in a snowbank in the middle of nowhere, should have set off alarm bells. However, she experienced nothing of the sort. After his imposing height and big shoulders, the first things she'd noticed about him were his kindly eyes and boyish grin. She and Dr. Maarten had talked about this in her therapy sessions, the gut sense of danger that she must learn to distinguish normal caution from trauma-induced anxiety. When she'd looked at the stranger, standing in the snow, the only thing she felt in her gut was a wave of sturdy trust.

He'd rescued her. He had somehow healed the fallen deer. He'd sewn up her wound. He was heart-thumpingly, shatteringly attractive in an unexpected way. Big and broad, like a working-class hero or farmer, a far cry from the sort of men she knew.

And now, having succumbed to the multiple fatigues of jet lag, exhaustion and injury, she lay in a comfy bed in a guest room of his house.

The teddy bear yawned and stretched.

Sophie gave a gasp and scrambled out of bed, clutching the blankets to her chest. There was a heated tug of pain in her knee, but she ignored it and stared at the small, furry thing on the bed.

"Oh, my God," she whispered on a breath of panic. "Oh, my God."

She was ordinarily more articulate than this, but all she could do was stare. Then she opened the drapes to reveal the cold white glare of the winter morning, and stated the obvious. “You’re a puppy. I slept with a puppy.”

It stared at her, alert and seemingly unperturbed by her erratic behavior. Its tiny spike of a tail quivered, and it let out a series of yips, sounding like a windup toy at FAO Schwarz.

Sophie didn’t do puppies. She’d never had a dog, growing up, and raising her children in Manhattan had made it completely impractical.

The pup went to the edge of the bed and gazed fearfully at the floor, then worriedly at Sophie.

“Just jump,” she said. “It’s not that far.”

It skittered back and forth, gave a nervous whimper.

“You managed to climb up, so you should be able to find a way down.”

The dog responded with a pitiful whine.

“Oh,” Sophie said, feeling a curious flood of sentiment. She reached out with her hand, and the puppy sniffed it delicately, gave her a lick of approval with its tiny pink tongue, then yipped at her. Awkwardly, she scooped the little thing up, holding it at arm’s length. The puppy squirmed and she nearly dropped it, so she quickly gathered it against her chest. Its coat was a yellow fluff of down—half dog, half Easter chick. It had a milky-new smell, and it wriggled somewhat frantically, trying to lick her face. Then, like a newborn, it snuggled against her shoulder.

“So this is a puppy,” she whispered, brushing her lips over its velveteen ear. “How did I live so long without a puppy?”

Like all kids, Max and Daisy had of course begged her for a dog. Their friends all had dogs, they pointed out with age-old kid logic. She fired back that their friends all had dog walkers or stay-at-home moms. She explained that it would be cruel to the dog. Left alone during the day, its outside would consist of controlled visits to the postage-stamp-size park where you were required to pick up its poop. Did either Max or Daisy feel like walking around behind a dog in the rain, picking up its poop? That effectively shut down the arguments.

“Max and Daisy,” she said aloud, setting down the puppy and snatching up her phone. Her thumb was hovering over the keypad when she noticed the time—6:47 a.m. Too early to call. Setting aside the phone, she caught a glimpse of herself in the mirror on the back of the door.

“Lovely,” she muttered. “I’m channeling Blanche Dubois.” It was a combination of her negligee and the fact that she had just rolled out of bed. After a night of hard sleep, even the Dior negligee looked cheap. And skimpy. Sophie’s salon-pampered hair was rumpled, her eyes still blurred with sleep. She had long favored skimpy nightgowns, a secret, decadent indulgence.

It wasn’t as if she bought them to impress a man. She and Greg had been in college when they met. College boys tended to like anything with boobs, so she didn't need lingerie—a team T-shirt would do. She loved the luxurious feel of lace and silks, though. The lingerie was the last bastion of femininity and youth. Giving in to flannel granny gowns would be an admission of defeat.

She refused to become a flannel granny.

But good heavens. It was cold this morning. Shivering, she looked around the room. This was an older house with tall ceilings and braided rugs on wood floors. She was in an old-fashioned bedroom with fading quilts on the bed, a marble-topped washstand, chintz curtains on the windows. Everything here had a sense of permanence, yet there was an ineffable air of neglect, as well. The faint cedary smell of the bed linens suggested that this room didn't get much use.

She had a luxurious cashmere robe, but it was in her other bag, still in the trunk of the rental car. So were her slippers. She examined her boots, finding one of them stained with dried blood. She wiped it as best she could with some damp tissues. Then she zipped on her high-heeled boots, which made a bold statement combined with her skimpy nightgown. *Just give me a whip and a chain,* she thought, *and I'll be the dominatrix you've always dreamed of.* She tugged a soft, hand-crocheted throw from a rocking chair and drew it around her.

The puppy let out a yip and peed on the floor.

"Oh, for heaven's sake." Sophie regarded the dark wetness spreading on the braided throw rug in the doorway. Now she remembered why she didn't do puppies. She loosely rolled up the throw rug. Holding it gingerly, she made her way downstairs, passing faded cabbage-rose wallpaper and a leaded-glass window at the landing. The puppy loyally followed, jumping from step to step down the stairs and nearly crash-landing at the bottom. It seemed completely unhurt, though, and stayed focused on Sophie, as though imprinted like a duck. She couldn't help smiling, despite the rug. The accident was her fault, really. The dog was a baby. Its bladder was tiny. She should have taken it out immediately to do its business.

She guessed her way to the kitchen by following a hallway with hardwood floors and framed pictures on the walls. An arched doorway led her to a big country kitchen, filled with the deep aroma of freshly brewed coffee.

Beyond the kitchen was a mudroom surrounded by windows that offered a view of nothing but white, miles and miles of white.

"Morning," said a deep, cheerful voice. Noah Shepherd came in through the back door, covered in fresh, powdery snow.

She nearly dropped the rolled rug. "Oh! I, er . . ." Her words evaporated as she stared at him. In a thick plaid mackinaw jacket, faded jeans and snow boots, he looked like a character from a storybook—the noble woodsman. A prince in disguise. *I'm in a Disney movie,* she thought.

Judging by the look on his face, he was thinking

something quite different about her. His expression hid nothing. He checked out the almost-translucent bodice of the negligee. She tugged the shawl closer around her. Then he looked at her legs, revealed by the short gown. Even with her bandaged knee, the fashion boots probably made her look like a pole dancer. Noah's expression was almost adolescent in its intensity, revealing a fundamental truth—a man hadn't been born who didn't like a pole dancer.

Finally, she found her voice and broke the tension. "The dog peed on the rug."

"I'll take it." He reached out with a gloved hand and stepped into a room adjacent to the mudroom. A moment later, she heard the swish of the washing machine. She was washing her hands at the kitchen sink when he returned.

"I guess you met Opal, then," he said. "I call that one Opal."

"Why?"

"No idea. Do I need a reason?"

"I guess not. So she must be a new addition to your house."

"Temporarily," he said. "She was born to a big litter and her mother rejected her."

Sophie felt a little beat of shock. "That's terrible."

"It happens. I've been bottle-feeding her."

"You're kidding me."

"About the bottle-feeding?" He shrugged and washed up at the sink. "Wouldn't be the first time. Is that so shocking?"

"I've never met anyone who bottle-feeds baby animals," she said.

"Just weaned her." The puppy had found a stainless steel food bowl on the floor and was busily chowing down.

Sophie had never heard a man say "wean" before, either. "She seems to be doing well."

He nodded. "Next project is to find her a home."

"She slept with me last night."

The words "slept with me" seemed to inflame his imagination, because he checked her out again with that relentless, teenager-like intensity. She felt exposed yet curiously bold. In all the drama of the divorce and its aftermath, her femininity had hardened into a stiff armor of propriety, an armor that seemed to be melting under the heat of his regard. There were few good things to be said for being thirty-nine going on forty. Having a man look at her the way Noah Shepherd was looking at her was unexpectedly empowering.

Still.

She adjusted the shawl and cleared her throat. Did she explain the boots and the negligee or let him assume whatever he would? "Thank you for last night," she said, belatedly catching the double entendre.

"It was my pleasure." His voice was all bedroom smoky, as though he perfectly grasped the double meaning.

She felt a flush bloom in her cheeks, supremely self-conscious now. “Anyway, I’ll just go get dressed and be out of your way.”

His smile exuded a sexy sweetness that made her feel foolish and young. “You’re not in my way,” he stated.

“Yes, well, I do have things to do. . . .”

He flicked a glance out the window where the world was a glare of light reflected off acres of thick snow. “What kind of things?”

He could have no idea that was such a loaded question. *Reinvent my life,* she thought. *Reconnect with my kids. Redefine the way I see the world. Redeem myself for mistakes in the past.* And that was just for starters.

He studied her with a keen intensity that almost made her want to tell him. But no. She was still working things out for herself, and at the moment her plan felt very fragile, as though it needed protection from other people’s skepticism. Her colleagues at the ICC already thought she was insane. She didn’t need to expose herself to a stranger’s doubts.

“For starters, I’ll need to call my son and daughter, let them know I’ve arrived.”

He nodded at a wall phone by the breakfast nook. “Help yourself. But I should tell you, the roads haven’t been cleared yet. It’s a lake-effect snowstorm, and it’s not over yet. The school district has declared a snow day, and most of the roads—including this one—are closed to all but emergency vehicles, so I wouldn’t count on going anywhere.”

“I guess I can’t do anything about the weather.” She

felt a wave of anxiety. Max and Daisy knew she was due to arrive, but they assumed it was for a visit, not for keeps. She had no idea what their reaction would be when she explained the move was permanent. The fact was, she hadn't quite worked out what she would say, how she would explain her presence in Avalon. This was the domain of the Bellamys, her ex-husband's family. They had deep roots in the region, while Sophie would be regarded as an outsider. An intruder. She suddenly felt very alone.

"I want to pull myself together and get organized first," she said, seized by cowardice.

"Okay," he said agreeably enough. "How's the knee? I should probably check it out."

Haven't you done that already? she wondered wryly. "No need. I'm all right. I haven't looked under the bandage, but it's not painful or itchy, nothing like that."

"You should probably take another antibiotic."

"More Rottweiler pills?" She shrugged. "Sure, why not? Can it wait until after I get dressed?"

"I'm tempted to say no, but that's just because of that nightgown." He grinned, and instead of feeling offended, Sophie almost smiled back. "Seriously," he said, "you should probably eat something, so the antibiotic doesn't upset your stomach."

She nodded. "Listen," she said, "I'm sorry I panicked last night, you know, when I saw all the blood."

"Don't worry about it. Lots of people can't stand the sight of blood."

She teetered on the verge of saying more, that the sight and smell of blood had brought back a rush of horror so intense she'd forgotten where she was. She didn't tell him, though. Here in this peaceful, snowed-in setting, it was hard to imagine the violence and mayhem she'd survived. He'd probably think she was making it up.

"I might need a few of my things. Is the rest of my luggage still in the trunk of the rental car?"

"I'll get it and bring it up to your room."

"I can manage."

"Not with that knee. It's no trouble."

"Well, then . . . thank you."

With that, she fled from the kitchen and hurried up the stairs. She phoned Daisy and then Max, in both cases getting voice mail on the first ring. She hung up without leaving a message. No doubt they assumed she had stayed in the city because of the weather.

The upstairs bathroom had an old-fashioned charm, with its vintage lighting and plumbing fixtures. She drew a bath in the deep, claw-foot bathtub and sank in with a heavy sigh of gratitude. She kept her bandaged knee out of the water as she lay back, covering her eyes with a damp cloth.

It felt quite strange, having no agenda for the day. To Sophie, this was a concept she had never explored—simply doing nothing. The moment her first child was born, she had stepped onto a treadmill, convinced she could have it all—marriage and family, career and success. She hadn't allowed herself to stop or even slow down.

It had taken a group of terrorists to do what no one else in Sophie's life had ever accomplished—to make her come up for air. The irony of this did not escape her.

Using techniques she had learned in the aftermath of the incident, she guided her thoughts away from planning, examining, regrets, anything that would take her out of the moment. She had yet to master the yoga-esque concept of completely emptying her mind of all thought. To her, that just felt wrong, brain-dead. Instead, she directed her wandering thoughts to this moment—right here, right now. And right now, she was curious about the stranger who had rescued her. Noah Shepherd, a veterinarian. He seemed to fit in this big, rambling farmhouse. He had a gentle, healing touch, and in the middle of disaster, she had trusted him completely. She didn't know why. Maybe it was his bear-like strength and the fact that he opted not to wield it. Or perhaps it was the expression of concern on his face—an uncommonly masculine face, square jawed, shadowed by a hint of beard, gorgeously sculpted cheekbones and an easy smile.

"You're projecting, Sophie," she said, levering herself up out of the tub. "You want him to be a hero, because you want to be rescued. Cared for. Looked after." She'd been told she was still at risk for Stockholm syndrome—the bizarre tendency for hostages to sympathize with their captors. Maybe Noah Shepherd had captured her. Maybe she was his hostage, and didn't even know it.

Pondering the twisted idea of being Noah Shepherd's hostage, she dried off, wound her hair in a towel and dressed. One of the first things she was going to have to do was buy clothes more appropriate for the weather. Her trousers had been ruined last night. She had one other pair of slacks with her, of soft camel hair lined with satin, the sort she might wear to take a statement from a monarch or statesman. Or, she thought, to have breakfast with a country vet.

She drew the slacks on carefully and donned the same black sweater she'd worn last night. Then she put on her boots, already anticipating Noah Shepherd's silent disapproval. The boots weren't warm and the heels made them a hazard. *Too bad,* she thought. She certainly hadn't come here expecting to find herself snowed in. She combed out her hair, put on a bit of lip gloss and at last felt vaguely human. She tried calling her children yet again and still got no answer. Perhaps they were taking advantage of the snow day by sleeping in.

She stepped out into the upstairs hallway, giving the place a cursory exploration. All right, she was snooping. This appeared to be a classic upstate farmhouse, with bright, boxy rooms and lots of figured woodwork. There were several rooms that looked as though no one had been in them in years—a wall calendar opened to April 2005 was a clue. This was a lot of house for one guy.

She headed downstairs, taking her time, studying the framed photographs lining the stairwell. They ranged from sepia-toned, soft-focused portraits from the 1920s to modern-day school pictures of smiling strangers. A strong family resemblance threaded through the generations, though she couldn't quite work out how Noah was placed in the group.

At the bottom of the stairs, she paused to peek into the front room. Judging by the decor, he was a man who didn't bother to hide the things that were important to him—an oversize sofa, a big fancy stereo, a wide-screen TV and a stack of electronic games. The place might have been furnished by a fourteen-year-old. In one corner of the living room was a complete drum set, a keyboard, two microphones and a bewildering array of speakers. It was a cross between a farmhouse and a frat house.

On the opposite side of the front vestibule was a formal parlor that didn't appear to get much use. A bay window afforded a magnificent view of a broad, sloping lawn and a tree-lined driveway. At least, she assumed it was a driveway. At the moment, everything was covered in a uniform blanket of snow.

Beyond the sloping yard was the road, which now bore no resemblance to a road. Somewhere down there, her rental car was in a ditch.

From this vantage point, she could make out two cottages in the distance, both of them all but buried in snow. The Wilson house was the one with the riverstone walls and gabled roof. Beyond that was Willow

Lake, as vast and magnificent in winter as it was in summer. It was completely frozen over.

Warm air from the furnace blew gently through a vent in the floor. She felt like standing here all day long, just gazing out at the white world and imagining her future here. Then a movement caught her eye as a group of people came into the front yard. A family, she thought, and then with an odd jolt she recognized Noah Shepherd. He was walking beside a woman in a blue ski jacket and they were towing three small children on a sled.

Oh, she thought. And then, *of course.* Of course he was married. Of course he was a family man. He was simply too appealing not to be taken. She must have been too confused by her eventful night to realize that.

As she watched, he scooped up the largest of the children, a boy of perhaps six. He swung the kid in the air, eliciting laughter. The two younger ones laughed and clapped their mittened hands. A grown dog and the yellow puppy cavorted together, completing the picture. They made an idyllic-looking family, Sophie observed, the kind depicted on sentimental Christmas cards. As he played with the kids, Noah seemed to be a man completely in his element, the kind of guy who was born to be a dad. He just had that energy about him.

Something didn't fit, though, Sophie thought as she took her coat from the hall tree and slipped it on. It was the way Noah had looked at her when she'd come down to the kitchen in her negligee. That, and the fact that no woman ever born would have a living room like the one across the hall, with its garage-band setup, neon beer clock on the wall and a display of old license tags and hubcaps on the chair rail.

Stepping out onto the front porch, she paused while the cold air shocked her lungs. Then she waved to get their attention.

Noah spied her and waved back. "Sophie, this is Gayle," he said. "And these are Henry, Mandy, and the little one's name is George, but everyone calls him Bear."

Sophie greeted them, mustering all her best skills of diplomacy. "It's nice to meet you. It was so good of Noah to help me out last night."

"Noah's good to everyone," Gayle assured her.

Meaning, *you're not so special,* thought Sophie.

Then Gayle said, "Well, we'd better get on home. I've got something in the oven. See you around, Noah. Nice to meet you, Sophie."

Each of the children insisted on a big hug from Noah. Then Gayle walked away, towing the sled behind her. Noah stomped the snow from his boots and held open the front door. Sophie went inside, the yellow puppy trotting at her heels. The larger dog went racing up into the woods.

She was feeling . . . she didn't know what she was feeling. Mostly a sense of relief that they weren't his family, after all.

"Gayle lives next door," Noah was saying, as if she'd asked the question aloud. "She and her kids have cabin fever so they went out for a walk."

The neighbor, thought Sophie. Not the wife. She shouldn't feel so relieved, but she did. She wanted Noah to be a good guy, and it turned out he was. So far.

She followed him back to the bright country kitchen.

"Coffee?" Noah offered.

"Yes, please. I'll help myself." She didn't want to feel like a guest here, but he seemed completely at ease with the situation.

Looking around the kitchen, she said, "This is a lot of house for one guy." Then she realized how that sounded. "I mean, assuming you live alone."

"I do. This is my family's house," he said. "Used to be a dairy farm on the property. My folks closed it down and retired to Florida. When I finished vet school, I decided to set up the practice right here."

She looked around the old-fashioned kitchen. In contrast to the scrubbed pine table, barn glass cabinets and farm sink, there was an iPod connected to a set of speakers, playing some kind of ska or hip-hop music she didn't recognize. It was the sort of thing Daisy might like.

"That's so nice, living in the place you grew up," Sophie said.

"I guess. Where are you from?" he asked.

"Seattle, but we moved a lot." Every few years, it seemed, her parents decided to upgrade their lifestyle. Each successive house was more luxurious, each neighborhood more exclusive as her parents' shared practice became more lucrative. The outward appearance of success and prosperity was important in the Lindstrom family, far more important than Sophie's attachment to a particular neighborhood or school.

"I used to envy kids like you," she told him. "Kids who called one place home."

"Good thing I didn't hate it here or I would have been shit out of luck." His smile was edged with mischief.

Sophie turned her thick china coffee mug between her hands. It was imprinted with a picture of a cow at the end of a rainbow and the logo "The Shepherd Dairy, Avalon, New York."

"This is authentic," she remarked. "Not one of those faux-vintage things you find in gift shops."

"It's the real thing." He topped off her cup. "So you've been living overseas?"

All right, he was curious. She didn't blame him. The question was, how much should she tell him? "I've been living in The Hague. In Holland." She didn't know whether or not he'd be familiar with it. "I was an assistant deputy counsel for the International Criminal Court. In the last case I worked on, we prosecuted a warlord who was aligned with a corrupt diamond syndicate."

"I didn't realize an American could work there, since the U.S. isn't a member of that particular court."

She blinked in surprise. "How did you know?"

"Let's see, it was in the paper? I do read something besides *Large Animal Digest.*"

"Sorry. And you're right, the U.S. is not a member. Neither are China, Iraq or North Korea but we keep hoping . . ." She let her voice trail off, deciding to keep her politics to herself. "Anyway, yes, there are Americans at the ICC. Besides, my mother is Canadian, so I have dual citizenship."

He got up and placed a jug of milk and a large white cardboard box on the table. "I stopped by the bakery yesterday before the storm," he said. "Help yourself."

Inside she found four perfect, glistening cinnamon rolls. They were from the Sky River Bakery, an institution in Avalon. "Maybe just a half," she said.

"Come on, live dangerously. Have a whole one."

"If I stick with my anti-jet-lag diet, I'm supposed to be eating protein this morning—ham and eggs, that sort of thing."

"I can fix you some eggs but no ham," he said. "I don't eat meat. I spent four years learning to heal animals, not cook them and eat them. Meat doesn't look too appetizing to someone who makes a living keeping animals alive and healthy. Some stuff, I'll eat," he added. "Like seafood. I've never had a patient who was a shrimp or a trout."

"I understand," Sophie said. "That's . . . commendable."

"But weird. Go ahead and say it, you think it's weird."

"I don't think that." Sophie had sampled everything from steak tartare to whole-roasted cabrito. She'd eaten sheep's eye in Asia and consumed a traditional

Masai concoction of cow's blood mixed with milk. "My diet's been adventurous at times," she said.

"Are you here on vacation, or . . . ?"

She felt the strangest urge to tell him about The Incident, the night she had been dismantled and turned into a different person. But she didn't, of course. This man was a stranger. A friendly, uncommonly appealing stranger, yes, but she wasn't about to bare her soul to him.

"I decided to make some changes. I loved my job, but . . ."

"But now you're here."

"Working in The Hague took me away from the things that are most important in life." So much for not baring her soul. He was just so easy to talk to. "Namely, my family. I realized I couldn't do both the job and the family. Something had to give. Working at the ICC is a big deal, but any lawyer with the right training and background can do it."

Her colleagues told her she was crazy, that what she did was worth any sacrifice, but she didn't believe that anymore. And she wasn't sure why, but she suspected Noah Shepherd would understand. "I wanted to live close to my kids. And to my grandson."

He stopped chewing, stared at her. Then he slugged back a gulp of milk. "I'm sorry. Did you say grandson?"

Sophie smiled. "His name's Emile Charles Bellamy—Charlie. He's almost six months old."

He didn't bother, as some did, to cover his astonishment. "You sure as hell don't look old enough to have a grandchild."

"I get that a lot." She looked down at her plate and was surprised to see that she'd devoured the entire cinnamon roll.

"Well," he said, "he's going to be glad you're here. My grandmother practically raised me, since my parents were so busy with the dairy. We're still close. We have lunch together every Sunday. She and her husband live over in Indian Wells."

Sophie said, "I barely knew any of my grandparents, growing up," she said. "My mother's parents lived on the Sunshine Coast of British Columbia, my father's in Palm Springs. Sometimes when I see pictures of them, I have the sensation that I'm looking at strangers. Makes me wish I'd known them better. My Canadian grandmother spoke with a slight English accent, and I never had a chance to ask her about herself—her girlhood and how she ended up in Canada."

"Then it's cool that you're here for little . . ."

"Charlie." And to be honest, Sophie didn't know if her being there was cool or not, given the way things were between her and Daisy.

"Did I say something wrong?" Noah asked.

"Why do you ask?"

"You're looking at me as if I said something wrong. I have sisters. I know what a girl's face does when a guy says something wrong."

"And what's that?"

He reached across the table and gently skimmed his

thumb across her brow, eliciting an unexpected shiver of feeling. "It's the frown, mainly."

His touch had unsettled her, but in a good way. "You didn't say anything wrong. I just haven't had someone actually tell me coming here was a good idea. You didn't point out the important work I left behind. I got a lot of that from my colleagues at the court."

"Then you don't need to hear it from me. Besides, choosing between a job and family is a no-brainer."

A curious warmth rushed through her. She was amazed to find her throat thick with emotion. She had an uncanny urge to grab his hand, ask him to touch her again. Her wild attraction to this man came as a complete surprise, out of the blue. She found herself studying his lips, his eyes, everything about him. Yet despite the physical attraction, he touched her in a way that was more unexpected—with the way he looked at her and the things he said.

"Okay, *now* what's the matter?"

She smiled despite an overwhelming feeling of sadness. "I was just thinking, if someone had said that to me a long time ago, my life would've been completely different."

"And that bums you out."

"I suppose it does."

"Then don't look back. It's pointless."

The remark was possibly more therapeutic than hours with her shrink, but Sophie had no idea how to keep misgivings at bay. She had worked so hard to stop herself from drowning in regrets. She couldn't regret the injustices that had been addressed, thanks to her work. But the harsh reality was, she couldn't be in two places at one time. She'd made a choice, and her most frequent pastime lately seemed to be tallying up the price her family had paid for that choice. "It's not that simple."

He shrugged, got up from the table and put their dishes in the sink. "I figure it's about as complicated as you make it."

"Spoken like someone who's never had children," she snapped, angered by a feeling of utter vulnerability.

His back was turned, but somehow she knew the verbal barb had hurt him. There was something in his posture, a tightening of his shoulders, perhaps. A defense mechanism? Dear heaven, maybe he did have kids somewhere. Or maybe she was just imagining his reaction. "I'm sorry," she said. "You struck a nerve, and I struck back."

He turned to face her. "No prob. What size shoe do you wear?"

"I beg your pardon?"

"Your shoe size. I was going to find you a better pair of boots."

"I'm a seven."

He went to the mudroom and returned with some thick-soled boots, setting them by a furnace register. "My younger sister used to wear these snowmobiling. You can borrow them until you get better equipped for this weather."

The boots were far from fashionable, but they looked perfectly suited for the snow. “Thanks,” Sophie said. “And thank you for breakfast. It was delicious.”

“No problem.”

“I’ll hike down to the Wilsons’ house,” she suggested. “At least I can get settled.”

“You’re not going anywhere in this by yourself.”

“I’ve survived worse,” she murmured.

“Yeah? Like what?”

“Like being taken hostage at gunpoint and plunging off a bridge in a speeding van.”

He laughed heartily at that. “I’ll have to start calling you Xena.”

Good. She wanted him to think she was pulling his leg. Here in this homey farmhouse in the middle of nowhere, it did sound preposterous.

“Tell you what,” he said, “I’ve got some chores to take care of, and then we’ll go down together.”

“I feel as though I should pay you,” she said. “I’ve been a lot of trouble. It seems I’ve taken ‘high maintenance’ to a new level.”

“You know I’m not going to take your money,” he said.

This came as no surprise to her. “Then I’ll find some other way to repay you.”

“Deal,” he said. “I’ll be back in half an hour.”

He went out to do his chores. Sophie had never lived in a place where people did chores. Or visited their neighbors before eight in the morning. Or bottle-fed puppies. Or gave beds to complete strangers.

And she *was* a stranger. A stranger in a strange land. A stranger to herself. She didn't recognize her own life anymore. The urban, apartment-dwelling, career-focused Sophie had changed overnight to an unemployed, snowed-in woman in borrowed boots, being looked after by Dr. Doolittle. Her colleagues in The Hague would never believe their eyes if they could see her now.

Nine

Daisy Bellamy worked out her day like a battle commander planning a siege. With the weather so bad and a baby to keep safe, she had to consider each and every detail. She went to the front window and looked out. The snow was still coming down, but lightly now, turning the wide, tree-lined street of wooden houses into a picture postcard. Empty of traffic, it could have been a place from a far-distant time, when people lived their lives at an unhurried pace, and when having a baby at eighteen was considered perfectly normal.

Of course, in the "good old days," she reminded herself, you had to marry the baby's father. You didn't have a choice.

She was totally glad she had a choice.

She stood for a few minutes, watching the scene outside. Clearly she wasn't the only one in the neighborhood with cabin fever. People were out—guys shoveling their walks, kids in snowsuits building forts or pulling sleds, whip-thin cross-country skiers gliding along, couples heading toward the lake with ice skates slung over their shoulders, others simply out walking, because, despite the cold, the snow was incredibly beautiful.

Daisy planned to go out today, too, although she had a purpose. She and Charlie were meeting with a prospective babysitter. Irma's house was only a few blocks away, and the walk would do her good. She was starting to feel cooped up in the small, cluttered and overheated house. It would have been perfectly reasonable to call Irma and cancel due to weather, but Daisy really wanted Charlie to spend some time there before he had to go to a sitter regularly. As soon as winter classes started at the state college, Charlie was going to stay with Irma for four hours a day, three days a week.

On paper, it didn't seem like such a big deal. Now that she was going to actually do it, the hours seemed cruelly long.

Chin up, Daisy told herself. This wasn't supposed to be easy. She'd done things that were much harder.

Preparing for her trek down the road, she bundled Charlie into his snowsuit and then painstakingly threaded his legs through the carrier, following each step as she strapped it to herself. At six months of age, Charlie was usually up for anything, and the carrier was no exception. Now they were face-to-face and

Daisy's hands were free. She adjusted the straps and put on her oversize down parka, zipping it over the carrier.

"I refuse to go near a mirror," she said, pulling on her hat and gloves. "I know I look ginormous."

Finally ready, she stepped out onto the front porch. The cold sweet air tasted like freedom. Before she started walking, she went through a mental checklist, which was part of the routine. Wallet, check. Keys, check. Diaper bag with enough supplies to outfit a day care center, check. Cell phone . . . oops. It was still stuck in its charger on the kitchen counter. The small oversight created a major dilemma. Her keys were in a pocket that was only accessible if she unzipped, exposing Charlie to the cold. Not only was that bad for him, he'd probably start crying, and she didn't want to arrive at Irma's with a crying baby.

Okay, forget the phone. People got along fine before such things. And she didn't need it going off, anyway. Half the time, she couldn't find it in all her pockets, and besides, Irma lived right down the street. Still, as she set out along a just-cleared sidewalk, a knot of guilt formed in her stomach. She hoped that lump she felt in the unreachable pocket really was a wad of keys. Locking herself out had been last month's screwup. She seemed to make every mistake in the book, but at least each mistake came around only once.

"You know," she said to the bundle strapped to her chest, "I used to be a spontaneous person. Now I plan every move I make as though I'm crossing a minefield."

From deep within the confines of her jacket, Charlie made a noise. She couldn't see his expression, but judging by the happy gurgles emanating from him, he was contented enough to last for the short walk.

"And I have to tell you," she concluded, "you're worth every bit of trouble and more."

Daisy allowed herself to breathe a sigh of relief, to relax a little and enjoy being outside in the bright glare of the winter day. It was hard to believe someone so small could have such a huge impact on her life. Even when he was little more than a ball of undifferentiated cells, he had turned her world upside down. She was a teenager, for God's sake. She hadn't pictured a future like this. Yet here she was.

And she didn't hate it. Most days, anyway. She adored Charlie, so that was good. But he did tend to complicate things. Like, everything.

And yet, there was this thing that happened with Charlie. Sure, she knew she would love her baby despite the fact that he was totally unplanned. Yet even during the months of waiting for his birth, she hadn't anticipated what that love would actually feel like. Nothing had prepared her for this kind of love, how deep it ran, so deep it hurt, but in a good way. In a way that reminded her that here was the one person on earth who owned every bit of her heart.

No wonder the kid was so high maintenance.

"It's true," she said to him, trudging along the block

at a leaden pace. "I used to do things at the drop of a hat, no planning involved, you know? I'd jump on the subway and off I'd go, with nothing but a wad of cash and my fake ID." She patted the bundle in her jacket. "I swear, if you ever try to pull anything like that, you'll be in such trouble." She wondered if everyone did this—if they all swore they would be better parents than the parents who had raised them. She'd be willing to bet her own mother had felt that way when Daisy was little. Her mom always strove to be the best at everything.

And then, of course, it had become Daisy's mission to prove her wrong.

Mom was supposed to have landed at JFK last night. Daisy figured the storm had kept her in the city, so they wouldn't see each other for several more days. Daisy was used to her mom's long absences so it was no big deal, though this time was a little different.

Since they'd last seen each other, Daisy's dad had married Nina, which had to be weird for her mom. Also, Mom had been involved in that horrible incident in The Hague. She'd assured Daisy she was fine, but that could mean anything. Mom was always "fine." It covered everything from breaking a nail to breaking a leg. Knowing Mom, she probably told everyone her marriage was "fine," right up until the divorce.

"I won't keep stuff from you," Daisy said to Charlie. "Because I'll know that when something isn't fine, you'll see right through me."

Daisy squinted through the snow flurries. "Almost

there," she said, heading for the sitter's front walk, which bore the fresh tracks of a snowblower. The main thoroughfare had been plowed, she could see. A few intrepid vehicles trolled slowly along, dwarfed by the huge dikes of snow left by the plows.

"People are idiots, driving in this," she murmured, feeling virtuous for having walked. "What kind of idiot—oh, tell me he's not here."

But he was, of course. She recognized Logan O'Donnell's BMW X3 with the SUNY decal on the back window. Although Logan was the baby's father, he'd never even been her boyfriend, not really. They'd been two stupid kids in high school, partying with careless abandon. Nine months later, they were parents. Daisy had insisted she wanted nothing from Logan, but he wouldn't take no for an answer. He wanted to be Charlie's father. She'd expected Logan to lose interest once he realized what it meant to be a parent. But he kept showing up like a bad penny.

Out of a sense of duty, Daisy had informed him about the meeting with the babysitter. She hadn't thought he would actually show up, though, not today. In these conditions, it was a short but treacherous drive from New Paltz to Avalon. A person would have to be crazy to try it.

However, she'd found out a long time ago that it took more than a snowstorm to stop Logan.

"All right," she said, standing on the porch of the babysitter's house. "Deep breath." She knocked at the door.

Irma greeted her with an effusive welcome. "There you are," she said. "I'm glad you could make it."

"It's nice to get out," Daisy said, unzipping her parka. "Hey, you," she said to Charlie.

He gurgled at her and pedaled his arms and legs as though he hadn't seen her in weeks.

"Yeah, back atcha," Daisy said, sitting down to extract the fleecy blue bundle from the carrier. His sweet, milky scent lingered in the fibers of her sweater.

The baby sounded off happily as Irma hoisted him into her arms with reassuring confidence. "Come here, you little cherub." Rounded and soft as a marshmallow, Irma held the baby while Daisy took off her jacket and snow boots. "Come in and make yourself at home. The others are down for a nap." Irma looked after a brother and sister, aged one and two.

"Thank you." Daisy followed her into the living room. It was a plain little house, child-proofed, with one room equipped as a play area, a basket of toys in the corner. It looked exactly like the sort of place you could picture leaving your baby.

Assuming you were okay with leaving your baby. *Oh, God,* thought Daisy. *Am I becoming my mother? Am I leaving my baby so I can go after something I want, just for me?*

The thought hung over her as she stood in the doorway. "Hello, Logan," she said.

"Hey." He strode across the room and took the baby from Irma. "Hey, buddy," he said. And Logan O'Donnell, the bad boy of New York City's exclusive Dalton School, whose fiery red hair and screw-you attitude tended to scare most people, turned into a grinning, adoring guy, just like that. A baby's smile was a powerful thing.

Charlie jabbered away, lying in his lap while Logan extracted him from his snowsuit. Charlie clearly knew Logan, who visited at least once a week, his devotion to the baby a total surprise to Daisy. This was definitely not the Logan she had known in high school. Of course, Logan had gone through a lot of changes since then.

She watched him with his son, feeling an uninvited tug of emotion as he tickled the baby. Logan looked incredible, with the kind of smile that made a girl stupid enough to sleep with him. Charlie had inherited Logan's red hair, and was beginning to look alarmingly like him. This did not please Daisy. Being that handsome never did a guy a lick of good—not for long, anyway.

Irma sat on the sofa next to Daisy and adjusted her smock apron in her lap. "So," she said, "there's good news and bad news."

"Oh?" Daisy braced herself. Since Charlie's birth, her life had grown quite complicated. She'd taught herself to wait and see what happened.

"So the good news is, my license for infants has been approved. I knew it would be, and I was just waiting for final approval."

"That's good. What's the other news?"

"I have to get my feet done this winter." She held out her feet, clad in quilted scuffs. "Bunions," she explained. "Really painful. Runs in the family."

"Oh. I'm sorry." Daisy wasn't sure what else to say.

"It's going to be fine. The trouble is, I won't be able to work for about three months. They have to do one foot at a time and the recovery takes several weeks. It'll be impossible to look after kids."

Logan seemed completely unconcerned. He fished a gel-filled teething toy from a pocket of the diaper bag and handed it to Charlie.

"Anyway, I'm sorry. I know this changes your plans," Irma said.

"I'll figure something out." Daisy's heart sank. She should have known Irma was too good to be true.

A small cry came from down the hall. "Somebody just woke up," Irma said. "Excuse me."

"Well." Logan looked over Charlie's head at Daisy. "Bummer."

She nodded. "I'm going to have to figure out some other arrangement." Her mind was already working the problem. "My dad and Nina would totally watch him for me, if I asked."

"But you don't want to ask."

"No kidding. I mean, they're great, but they just got married. Besides, it would feel like a step backward for me. I just got my own place, and I don't want to go running back to them."

"It would only be temporary," Logan pointed out.

"Temporary has a way of stretching out to indefinitely," she said. "I'd rather solve this myself." Truth be told, it had been a battle to leave home in search of her own life. Her father and Nina ran a historic inn on the lake, and they had plenty of room. Living with them had been easy, perhaps too easy. Right after the baby was born, Daisy had felt herself getting comfortable and disappearing into the fabric of a life that was not her own. She was deeply afraid that if she grew to depend on her dad too much, she'd never learn to be independent.

"There's no crime in asking your family for help," Logan said.

"It's complicated."

"Family stuff usually is." He grinned at Charlie. "Right, buddy?"

He would know, Daisy conceded. He came from a wealthy Manhattan family, and they had not made things easy for him. His workaholic father had big plans for Logan. His socially ambitious mother fantasized about her son being the toast of the town. Their expectations for him were enormous. The O'Donnells had wanted Logan to go to Boston College, their alma mater. He was supposed to study management and finance, take over the family shipping business. Instead, he'd opted to attend SUNY New Paltz, where he could be closer to Charlie.

Daisy could only imagine what the O'Donnells had had to say about that. Logan's parents had never come to see the baby. They were in total denial, and believed Logan should simply cut all ties with Daisy, counting himself lucky that she wasn't demanding a fortune in child support. They blamed her, of course, for the entire situation.

"I suppose I could put off school for another semester," she said.

"You don't want to do that," he remarked. "I can tell."

She hated that he knew her as well as he did. "I'll figure something out."

"I want to help," Logan said. He'd been saying that ever since he discovered she was pregnant. At first, she thought he'd quickly get past the initial surge of manly responsibility. Instead, he had surprised her and probably everyone who knew him, and stuck around.

"I can figure this out on my own."

"Damn it, Daisy. Why are you so set against letting me help?"

"Because I don't trust you, okay?" She saw no point in trying to spare his feelings, not when it came to her son. Despite being the American Prince Charming, Logan had his dark side. He was—and by definition always would be—an addict. He'd done cocaine all through high school, somehow managing to keep disaster at bay until senior year. After a weekend of partying—the same weekend he'd gotten Daisy pregnant, he'd been arrested for possession and ordered into rehab. Defying the odds, he'd stayed clean ever since, going to meetings and, as far as Daisy could tell, living a life of sobriety.

She was proud of him for sticking with his program.

She was gratified that he was so determined to be part of Charlie's life. But sometimes she wondered if he came around because he wanted to or if it was part of his twelve-step program and he felt obligated.

"I don't know what else I can do to make you trust me," he said, his jaw working in agitation. "And I don't know what you're so afraid of."

She felt bad, being so cautious with Logan. But Charlie was her child. She couldn't take chances. "I'm afraid he's going to get attached to you, and one day you'll just quit coming around."

"Hey, don't you get it? I'm here to stay, Daze. I'm in Charlie's life to stay and I deserve to be here. So get used to it."

Another thing she was afraid of—that he would keep his promise. And then she just might find herself having to deal with the fact that, because of all that had happened between them, he was going to be a part of her life forever.

All right, so that was admirable, but it was also . . . she didn't know quite how to deal with it. At their age, how could they be certain of anything? Would having Logan in her life leave room for anyone else?

Not that there *was* anyone else, but one day there might be. Two summers ago, before Daisy's family had fallen apart and everything had changed, she'd met someone. Sure, they were kids and nothing had happened, but it was one of those meetings when you knew in an instant that this person might be important. A freeze-frame moment. As a photographer, Daisy knew how the camera could freeze a particular moment for its beauty or importance. That was how she felt meeting Julian Gastineaux, and he was . . . wonderful. She barely knew him but she knew he was important in her life.

And then there was Logan. Meeting him had not been a freeze-frame moment. They'd been in kindergarten in Manhattan, and he had dabbed blue paint on her pigtail and had to do a time-out as punishment. As teenagers, they'd had wild times together. She used to fantasize that he *was* Prince Charming, and that she was in love with him. It wasn't real, though. It was beyond bizarre to think the two of them now had a baby together.

Correction, she reminded herself. They now had a baby. They weren't together.

Ten

Sophie stood at the window of her borrowed house on the lake, watching Noah Shepherd finish shoveling off the front steps. She was finding her neighbor a remarkably pleasant diversion. Earlier, he had attached a snowplow blade to the front of his truck and cleared her driveway. She'd followed him in the rental car, which he'd pulled from the ditch with his pickup truck. He'd insisted on giving her a few basic groceries from his own pantry, since the roads were still impassable and probably wouldn't be plowed for another day or two. He had also made a fire for her in the wood-burning stove and promised to bring more split wood tomorrow.

The man was one-stop shopping, she thought, watching the way his breath came in rhythmic, frosty plumes as he worked.

"I can't thank you enough," she said when he finished and came inside, shaking the snow from his jacket.

"Sure you can," he said over his shoulder. "I'm easy."

You are, she thought. *So easy to like.*

"Did you get hold of your kids?" he asked, adjusting the vent of the wood-burning stove.

"I left voice mails. I'll try again later." She refused to let her worry and uncertainty show. Her children had become so casual about her absences. Her comings and goings were routine by now. Dear Lord, how was she ever going to fix this?

"So they live in town," Noah said.

She nodded. "Daisy recently got her own place on Orchard Avenue, and Max lives with his father at the Inn at Willow Lake."

He straightened up, gave her his full attention.

She twined her hands together until her fingers knotted tightly—a sign that the witness was nervous and about to crack. "And I have to tell you, this part of the conversation never gets easier, the part where I say my children live with their father. I'd find it easier to say I have an STD or a felony record." Did Noah—

did anyone—get how deeply humiliating this admission was?

"Man, you really like beating yourself up," Noah observed.

"I don't."

"Then why do it?"

"Because—" She broke off. She wasn't used to simply blurting out everything to a virtual stranger. "No one's ever asked me that." She narrowed her eyes at him, feeling a mixture of resentment and distrust. "Do you have an answer?"

"I'm going to have to think about it."

"You think too hard, you'll lose the truth."

"Thank you, Dr. Freud." She sent him a sideways glance. "Are we done with the ugly, personal stuff?"

"Up to you. If you want to talk, I'm all ears," he said with a grin. "Don't want to pry about your family situation. I figure you'll explain when you're ready."

She narrowed her eyes. "Or not."

"You shouldn't feel lousy about the way you're raising your kids," he said.

"Again, thank you."

"And guess what? There are women who stay home with their kids every day, and the kids are still wrecked. Then there are kids who chill in day care every day, and they're fine. Whether you stay home or go to work is not the determining factor. It's how you love them."

"I didn't know they taught human psychology in vet school."

"Nice, Sophie."

"I mean—"

"Figuring you out is not that hard," he said. "Believe me, feline distemper is a lot harder. Anyway, no offense meant."

"None taken," she assured him. She found herself studying him, and wondered why she found him so wildly attractive. He wasn't conventionally handsome, but big and hearty, with an openness that was uncommonly appealing. And he had the most incredible eyes, brown, with long thick lashes. And his lips . . . *Oh, Lord,* she thought. She already had a crush on her neighbor. A crush? Yes. That was exactly what this felt like, a too-pleasant inner fluttering, the sort of thing a high-school girl might feel. Sophie had nearly forgotten the sensation, but meeting Noah reminded her that a person never outgrew some things.

"I'd better be going—"

"I won't keep you—"

They both spoke at once, and both stopped at once. "Thanks for everything, Noah," Sophie said, blushing as though he'd read her thoughts. "I really do appreciate it."

"I'll see you tomorrow." He took her mobile phone from the counter and keyed in his number. "Call me if you need anything, anything at all."

There was a moment, a heartbeat of time, when it would have been the most natural thing in the world for her to lean into him, lift her face for a kiss. A kiss?

Where had that thought come from? It wouldn't leave her alone. She pictured it so clearly that she felt foolish. At the same time, she wondered if he'd felt it, too, that same momentary connection, an urge that came out of nowhere.

"You take care now," he said. "I'll drop off some firewood in the morning."

He was an exceedingly nice man, she thought, watching from the doorway as he got in his truck. Some kind of crazy luck had been with her when she'd driven into the ditch in front of his house.

A chill wind blew across the surface of the lake, gusting drifts of snow up against the house. She shivered and turned on the heat, then went to familiarize herself with the place and unpack her things.

The stick-built house had a simple layout, with every room oriented toward the lake. There were two bedrooms and two baths, and a main room that incorporated the kitchen, dining and living areas. The furnishings were simple, too. Rustic tables, overstuffed chairs, lamps with painted shades. There was a closet with a selection of snowshoes and ice skates. At one time, the inhabitant of the house must have had a dog or cat. There was a padded mat on the floor near the stove, and in the pantry, she'd noticed a set of feeding bowls.

She spent some time setting up her laptop and synchronizing it with her mobile device so she would have an Internet connection. She sent a quick e-mail to a few friends, including Bertie, to let them know she'd arrived and all was well. No need to mention the car versus deer incident.

Then she unpacked her suitcases, shaking her head at the inappropriateness of her wardrobe. The tailored suits, with their creased slacks and skirts, the designer shoes and silk stockings were not going to work in this environment.

Good, thought Sophie. This would give her an excuse to invite Daisy to go shopping, help her find some clothes for the snow. Assuming Daisy wanted to do anything at all with her.

That was completely the wrong attitude, Sophie told herself. Almost defiantly, she grabbed her phone, scrolled to Daisy's number and hit Send.

This time, Daisy picked up right away. "Mom," she said. "Hi. I saw you'd called earlier, but I didn't have my phone with me." As always, she sounded cautious. Pleasant, but cautious. That tone, Sophie realized, was her own doing. She had trained Daisy to be cautious around her, to expect to hear that, once again, Sophie was going to be delayed or not show up at all, to miss a field hockey game or swim meet, an art show or teacher conference. To miss her entire childhood. Sophie's children had learned to expect nothing of their mother. She'd told herself that with the proper nannies and household help, the kids would not even miss her. It had taken many years, a painful divorce and finally an international incident for Sophie to realize just how much she had truly missed.

"Hi, honey," Sophie said. "I just got into town. I'm in Avalon."

"I didn't realize you were coming so soon, Mom," Daisy said. "I figured you'd stay in the city until the storm is over."

"I didn't feel like waiting. I'd come see you right this minute if the roads were better."

"Don't go out. It's not safe. Are you staying at the Apple Tree?"

Sophie visited Avalon frequently and usually stayed at the Apple Tree Inn, a luxury B and B near the historic center of town. "Actually, I have news. I'm at the Wilsons' cabin, up on Lakeshore Road."

A pause. "I don't get it, Mom."

"I have so much to tell you, Daisy. And I can't wait to see the baby." Charlie had been born last summer. Sophie had been present for the birth, thank God. To see her child give birth had been overwhelming, to hold her grandchild even more so. Since then, she had visited four times, but it wasn't enough. She'd found out that night in The Hague that it was not enough.

With the phone pressed to her ear, Sophie went to the window. She looked out across the lake, a picture of cold white magnificence. It was a scene out of a fairy tale, of ice palaces and frozen estates, a separate world of glittering splendor, as inhospitable as it was beautiful.

"I actually arrived last night," she said. "I drove up from JFK."

"That's nuts, Mom. You could've been killed."

Sophie's lips twitched at the irony. "I'm fine. But I would have waited if I'd known I was going to be snowed in."

"Are you all right?" Daisy asked. "Do you have food? Heat?"

"I have everything I need here, but I'm dying to see you. The roads on this side of the water are terrible, though."

"That's the lake effect."

"Right," Sophie said. "As soon as the roads are clear, I'll come see you."

"It's a date."

Sophie detected an edge in her daughter's voice. "Is this a bad time?"

"Um, no. But . . . I've got company."

"Oh! I'll let you go, then. Call me later. I want to hear all about Charlie and your new place . . ." In the background, she heard a murmur of male laughter followed by a baby's squeals.

All right, thought Sophie. *I get it. I've got company* was code for *my boyfriend's here.* "Is that . . . ?"

"Logan's here," Daisy said.

Logan O'Donnell. Sophie wasn't sure if he was the boyfriend or not, though she definitely had a preference for *not.* Spoiled, rich, an alumnus of an expensive rehab school. Not her favorite person.

"Call me later," she said.

"I will, Mom. Promise."

Well, thought Sophie. *How about that?*

She checked the time and tried Max's number. He

had his own mobile phone, which seemed a bit much for a twelve-year-old, except Sophie insisted on it. Once again he didn't answer, so she left a brief voice mail and said she'd call him later. For good measure, she also sent him a text message. Today's phones and gadgets allowed a person to keep in touch with everyone. You could download your kid's schedule. You could run your whole family. You could be in touch and out of reach. She wasn't sure this was such a good thing.

Sophie knew she could always call Greg's house and ask for her son, but the idea didn't appeal to her in the least. There were few things she despised more than calling Greg. It wasn't that she hated her ex-husband. Not at all. In fact, there was a small, pathetic part of her that loved him still, would always love him. Theirs had not been a bitter divorce. It had simply been inevitable and sad, and they both understood that.

Still, she hated having to call him, hated it more than anything.

Except, perhaps, talking to his wife, Nina. She hated that most of all.

She didn't hate Nina, either.

But she sure as heck didn't like talking to her.

Sophie spent her first night in the lake house alone, almost wishing she still had that warm puppy in bed with her. When she awakened, she flashed on haunting memories of The Hague, but they instantly dissolved in a flood of white light. She got up to see that more snow had fallen. A lot more snow. On the lake side of the cabin, it had drifted up to the windowpanes.

To her surprise, it was midmorning. Never had jet lag affected her like this. She attributed it to being snowed in. She'd quit keeping track of time—why bother, when she couldn't go anywhere? She checked for messages. Max had IMed her that there would be a half day of school today and he had hockey practice this afternoon. She digested the information, feeling her nerves burn with apprehension. Her son had his own life, his own schedule—and she wasn't a part of it.

Yet, she reminded herself. She wasn't a part of it *yet.* She wanted—needed—to matter to her kids. Not just for her, but for them. Max surely had the usual kid problems, and not having his mother around couldn't make life any easier. Now that she was here, would he be glad? Resentful? Indifferent? He would be glad to have her back, surely. Even though she'd been busy with work all of Max's life, she still remembered the funny little boy he'd been, the way his face would light up when she got home from the office, the stolen time they'd spent together on weekends. She prayed he remembered those times, too. She wanted to know both her children better, wanted to see who they were becoming as they grew up and hoped it wasn't too late to do that.

She took a bath, awkwardly keeping her stitches dry,

and found a thick terry robe to put on as she dried her hair. Standing at the window, she gazed out at the lake, an endless, windswept field of white. A flicker of color in the distance caught her eye. One of the neighbors a few houses over was clearing an area on the ice, she assumed for skating.

She lived on a lake you could skate on. If she told Tariq, he would never believe her. Sophie's closest friends knew her as a sophisticate, a city dweller. A rustic cabin on a skating lake—they'd think she had lost her marbles.

Which, depending on how you looked at it, she had.

A bubbling agitation always accompanied memories of The Incident. She needed to get out. This might be a good time to introduce herself to the guy clearing off the ice.

She tried to dress for the weather, layering wool trousers over panty hose and topping it with a cashmere twin set. She donned the borrowed snowmobile boots, found a Sherpa-style wool hat on a hall tree by the door and pulled it on, then headed outside. As soon as she stepped into the yard, she sank to her thighs in the soft snow.

All right, she thought. Maybe not such a good idea. She struggled to lever herself up, unable to get a purchase in the fresh snow. By the time she reached the edge of the lake, she was dusted in white and breathing heavily. There was no pain in her knee but a pulling sensation warned her to take it easy. She carefully made her way to the neighbor's.

He wore a black-and-red plaid hunting jacket, thick gloves and enormous boots, and he didn't notice her as she approached, so focused was he on working back and forth on the ice.

"Hello!" Sophie called, waving her arm.

The neighbor looked over, stuck the big orange-bladed shovel in a snowbank and came to greet her. "Hello yourself." The voice was melodic and decidedly feminine.

Taken aback, Sophie regrouped. "My name's Sophie Bellamy," she said. "I'm going to be staying at the Wilsons', so I thought I'd stop and introduce myself."

The woman—it was most definitely a woman—smiled. Cold air and exertion had whipped high color into her cheeks, adding cheer to her smile. "Tina Calloway," she said. "Nice to meet you."

Sophie couldn't quite tell if Tina thought it was nice or not. She gestured at the ice. "So is this for skating?"

Tina nodded. "It's perfectly safe. I grew up here, skating on the lake every winter."

"It looks just beautiful, like something out of a picture book."

"Do you skate?"

"A bit. I can manage to get around without falling. Or at least I used to." Although she had been living in the land of Hans Brinker, Sophie had never done much for fun in Holland, as Tariq was so fond of pointing out. She worked, and she worked some more. She worked at home every night, and the next morning she went to work. This was one reason she'd advanced so quickly in the ICC. She had no life. She was a machine.

"So you're a friend of the Wilsons?" Tina said.

"I am. Bertie Wilson and I were pretty much inseparable in law school. We're still close."

"You're a lawyer, then."

"That's right. I'm . . . well, for the time being, I'm on hiatus. I was working overseas." She paused, and thankfully, Tina didn't push for further details.

"I'm a women's hockey coach at SUNY New Paltz," Tina said. "My folks own this place."

"My daughter is just about to start there," Sophie said.

"You sure don't look old enough to have a daughter in college." She unzipped her jacket and fanned herself. "Sorry, I worked up a sweat, shoveling this." Underneath the hunting jacket, she was dressed like a snowboarder, in cargo pants with Ride Or Die in flaming letters on the pocket.

The chainsaw snarl of a motor filled the air, growing louder. A snowmobile burst into view and, without warning, Sophie's heart sped up.

"Hey, Noah." Brushing back her hood, Tina bloomed like a flower in the snow. *He's a little old for you,* Sophie thought, although she didn't actually know how old Noah Shepherd was.

He turned off the motor. "I brought some wood," he said, pointing at the pole-handled sled behind the snowmobile. "Wanted to make sure you're all right."

"Are you kidding? I live for this." Tina gestured at the endless white snowscape.

"So the two of you have met," he said.

Sophie nodded. "I wanted to let the neighbors know I'm not a squatter."

"How's your knee?"

"It's fine." She became acutely conscious of the warm but aggressively ugly hat, the earflaps crushing whatever was left of her hairstyle. Noah Shepherd, she noticed, had on a simple heather-green hat that had probably been knitted by a woman's loving hands. He just had that air about him, the look of a man for whom women made things.

He and Tina busied themselves, stacking the firewood on the porch. Sophie tried to pitch in, but he shooed her away. "You've got a bad knee," he reminded her. "She cut her knee," he explained to Tina, "and I stitched it up."

"Get out of town."

"Swear to God, I did."

"He did," Sophie verified.

"Way to go, Doc." Tina gave him a high five, and they went back to work. Sophie caught herself watching Noah's movements, his easy strength and the way he seemed so sure of himself. Good heavens, he was wonderful to watch. She couldn't recall the last time simply looking at a man had inspired such a flood of lust.

"I really appreciate this," Tina said as they finished up with the wood. "You want to come in for a cup of hot chocolate?" She glanced over at Sophie. "You, too, of course."

"No, thanks," said Noah.

"You want to go skating?"

"Maybe later," he said. "After chores."

She shrugged. "Whatev."

"I'd better be going," Sophie said. "Tina, it was nice to meet you."

Noah turned to Sophie. "I'll give you a ride back to your place." It wasn't a question.

Right, she thought, eyeing the snowmobile. Still, she didn't want him to think she was a spoiled city slicker, ill prepared for living in a rustic winter cabin.

"See you around, Tina," he said.

"Bye, Noah." The young woman sent him a worshipful look.

"You'll have to tell me what to do," said Sophie, following him to the snowmobile.

"Just have a seat on the back, and hold on."

She awkwardly straddled the long black saddle of the snowmobile, putting her feet on the narrow running boards. He mounted in front of her and fired up the engine. "Hang on," he yelled over his shoulder.

She put her hands on the edge of the seat, trying to find a purchase.

"To me," he said, "hang on to me."

She clutched the sides of his parka.

"Hold on harder," he said.

She hesitated, then tightened her fists.

"Like this." He disengaged her hands and pulled her arms clear around his middle, linking her hands together. He felt like a tree to her. She was a tree hugger. Then he laid into the throttle and the snowmobile jerked forward.

Sophie was glad he'd made her hold on hard. She turned her head, pressing her cheek to his back. And it struck her that she had not embraced a man in a hundred years, not like this. Never had physical closeness felt this way to her.

The snowmobile was fast and loud. Despite the bone-drilling cold of the wind rushing over her, she loved the feeling of freedom and speed. The thought crossed her mind that if Max could see her now, he would be impressed. Maybe when Max came to see her, Noah would—

She put aside the thought. It was too soon to make any sort of presumption, about her son and most certainly about her neighbor.

During the few minutes of the wild ride, she didn't have to do anything but hold on and enjoy the rush of speed. A feeling rose in her chest, along with a sound she hadn't heard in a long time—her own laughter. The wind snatched it away so that it trailed in their wake, an invisible ribbon of sound. For these few minutes, life was pure, uncomplicated fun. After the hell she'd been through, it was a huge relief to simply fly across the churning snow.

She felt slightly let down when they came to a stop at her place. At the same time, she felt completely exhilarated.

"My face is frozen," she said to Noah when they pulled up in front of her house and he killed the engine.

"At least you're smiling."

"Am I?" She put her hands to her cheeks. "I can't feel it."

"Well, you're showing it. And smiling looks good on you."

"Would you like to come in?"

She expected him to turn her down for the same reason he had turned down Tina earlier. He surprised her by saying, "Great. Thanks."

As they stomped the snow from their boots and headed inside, she mentioned it. "She's sweet on you."

"She?"

"Tina. Don't say you haven't noticed." She led the way inside and pointed to the boot tray.

"I like to think I don't miss these things. She's not my type, though."

Sophie felt stupidly gratified to hear it. "I barely remember what I was like at her age, you know?"

"Her old man's Sockeye Calloway," Noah said. "He played on the 1980 U.S. hockey team in Lake Placid."

The gold medal team. The miracle team. "I wish you hadn't called him an old man," Sophie said. "I vividly remember being on the edge of my seat, watching the Olympics that year. Tina must be a very good skater."

"Yeah. Your fire's low," he said, clearly done with the topic of Tina. "I'll stoke it up for you."

She stood back and watched him work, and was amazed to realize the feelings she'd had earlier still lingered and had, in fact, intensified. There was no mistaking it. She was turned-on.

Okay, Sophie, she told herself. *Deep breath.*

She held herself very still and quiet, waiting for the feeling to pass, like a wave of nausea or dizziness. Instead, as she watched Noah her fascination with him grew. Everything felt warm already, even before he added a seasoned log to the fire and gently blew upon the coals beneath it to coax a row of tiny flames licking along its underside.

The surface of her skin felt superheated. Her face, which only moments ago had been frozen, now flushed, and her limbs and eyelids seemed pleasantly heavy. This was no mere case of jet lag.

She tried to rationalize the feelings away. Honestly, how dumb did she have to be, falling for all this Naked Ape-style primal behavior? So a guy stoked the fire in her stove, so what? That didn't mean she wanted to rip his clothes off and jump his bones.

Except that she did.

Noah straightened up, turning to her as long fluttering ribbons of flame engulfed the logs. "That ought to do you for a while."

Sophie didn't stop to analyze or think through her actions. She went to him and grabbed the front of his sweatshirt and yanked him close, planting upon his surprised mouth a kiss of shameless, aggressive desire.

He tasted exactly the way she wanted him to taste, of some kind of sweetness that had no name. He smelled like the winter air, the woods and faintly of exhaust, a combination she found impossibly sexy. Within seconds, she lost herself in the texture of his mouth, the slight growth of beard on his face, the fall of dark, wavy hair brushing against her cheeks.

As though he had known this was coming, he deepened the kiss with a hunger he didn't bother to hide. Did he know how much of a turn-on his frank lust was? It was like lighting a match to a pool of kerosene. His hands found the shape of her, and she realized with a thrum of excitement that he was exploring the quickest way to get her out of her clothes.

Which was how, approximately thirty seconds after she attacked him with a kiss, she found herself standing on the braided rug in front of the roaring fire, wearing nothing but silk tap pants and a camisole.

So far neither of them had said a word, yet when she looked at his face, she felt such a pure understanding and affinity that any speech would be redundant. There were so many reasons this was a bad idea, yet it felt absolutely right. Maybe her need to be with him like this was part of the lingering post-trauma madness.

Still. She felt compelled to speak up while there was still time to put an end to this. She said, "I'm sorry."

"Don't be," he said. "Don't you dare be sorry." He yanked his red Cornell sweatshirt one-handed over his head, revealing his bare chest, banded with muscle, a patch of dark hair adorning the middle, another line of hair arrowing downward. His jeans hung low, seeming to be casually perched on his hipbones. The top button of the faded blue jeans had already been undone. She stopped short of fanning herself.

She forced herself to say, "You should go. Please."

"You want me to stay."

For someone she'd just met, he seemed to know her too well. "The feeling will pass, I'm sure."

"Why would you want that?" He took something out of his pocket. "Just so you know, I have protection."

Sophie couldn't get pregnant. She'd had her tubes tied after Max, but she didn't say anything. Too much information. "Having protection isn't the same as being safe. This is just so insane," she said, knowing her argument was weak. "Look, if we're going to do this, then we should honestly discuss it."

"Why? So you can talk yourself out of it? No way."

She froze, willing herself to object, to stop herself, to stop them both. The moment passed, and she hadn't spoken up. There were no objections to be made that he couldn't counter. There were no kisses she could resist. He made her feel like a hormone-crazed teenager again, discovering sex as though for the first time. He was marvelously spontaneous, uninhibited, and when Sophie was with him, she found it easy to step into a moment where absolutely nothing else mattered. Her brush with death in The Hague had changed her. In the past, she'd always favored putting off gratification for the future. Then when she was a hostage, she'd regretted the many times she hadn't acted on desire, the times she'd put something off, thinking she had all the time in the world.

She didn't have all the time in the world. She only had this moment. This had never happened to her before. She found it both powerful and liberating to simply sink into a moment with him. To not have to plan ahead or map out logical consequences—it was a first for her. She had forgotten the deep comfort of sleeping in a man's arms, or perhaps she had never known it. Not like this.

Eleven

Noah lay in a tangle of quilts and blankets, eyes shut, arms around Sophie Bellamy. He felt as though his whole body was smiling. This was something he had not felt in far too long—that warm, slack-limbed, postsex bliss, a feeling that made you want to stop the world and just float along for a while.

The last thing he'd expected from someone like Sophie Bellamy was that they'd wind up making love so soon. Yet from the moment he'd met her, she had managed to surprise him. There was a lot he didn't know about her, but the things he recognized were far more powerful—the loneliness in her eyes, a mirror of his own. The undeniable heat of mutual attraction, which neither of them bothered to hide. So maybe it wasn't surprising that they'd leapfrogged over the usual dating rituals.

He opened his eyes to discover it was still light out, though the afternoon shadows lay long across the hillocks of snow. He also discovered the most amazing sense of well-being, even more than the usual satisfaction of just getting laid. Why was that? What was going on? He studied the woman lying on the bed, sound asleep.

He'd held other women, sure. He'd drifted with them in a postcoital haze. But Sophie felt . . . different in his arms in a way he couldn't quite explain to himself. Her head lay just so in the slight hollow between his shoulder and collarbone. Her silky blond hair spilled over his chest and her slender arm lay in gentle possession across his bare torso.

Never had delivering a stack of firewood been so rewarding. Taking care not to disturb her, he got up to take a leak and stoke the fire. The flickering flames painted the homey room, and late-afternoon light streamed in through the windows. He hoped she liked it here. He hoped she was planning to stay for a long time. Sophie Bellamy. Who the hell was she, anyway? He knew virtually nothing about her, except that an afternoon with her blew the doors off every other encounter he'd ever had.

He was drawn to her bag, which lay open on the table. Beside that were two passports, one from the U.S., the other from Canada. Flipping through the watermarked pages, he saw exotic seals and stamps from all over. He wondered what it was like, that life of travel. He'd never been anywhere, though he'd always meant to get a passport, just in case. She was so beautiful even a passport photo couldn't make her homely. Born in Vancouver, British Columbia. June 9, 1969.

That made her quite a bit older than Noah. Hell, a *lot* older. He was momentarily startled, but then decided he had absolutely no problem with the difference in their ages, hell no. She was incredible. She sure didn't look thirty-nine. She had to know that, but Noah strongly suspected the age difference would not thrill her.

Fine, he wouldn't tell her. That wasn't a lie. It was just . . . not telling her. She didn't need to know her former law school classmate, Bertie Wilson, used to be his babysitter. If this wasn't going to amount to anything, then there would be no harm, no foul. If it turned out—please, God—to be something important, then he'd tell Sophie after she got to know him better, and she'd realize it was a nonissue.

He felt so damned good that he nearly woke her up to tell her so. He wouldn't, though. He kind of wished she would sleep forever; Sleeping Beauty, as relaxed and flawless as a dream.

Of course, when she was awake, she was pretty fun, too. Yet despite the fact that he had only just met her, he knew on some gut level that she probably wouldn't wake up as happy as she had drifted off in his arms. She seemed to be the type to think things through and analyze them to death, and he figured if she thought about the fact that they'd fallen into bed together a few seconds after *hello,* she'd come up with some serious objections.

He preferred to focus on the positive. There was a lot to be said for going for broke, which they had, all afternoon long. For a small house, the place had yielded a good variety of places to make love. They had started in a clothes-ripping frenzy on the oval braided rug in front of the wood-burning stove, with a few sofa pillows and an Afghan thrown in for comfort. After that they'd moved to the large, deep, claw-foot bathtub, making creative use of soaps and oils that smelled like evergreen and spearmint, somehow managing to keep her stitches dry. And finally they'd ended up here, in the high bed with a hand-hewn frame of unpeeled birch, piled high with quilts and fluffy pillows.

He slid back under the covers with her. She smelled incredible. Even the sound of her breathing turned him on. A few minutes later, he felt her waking up. He was freakishly attentive to her every nuance. She didn't really move or change the cadence of her breathing—it was more subtle than that. He simply felt a shift from sleeping Sophie to waking Sophie. He lay still, waiting for her to take in the fact that she was in bed with him.

It started with her hand, which lay palm down across his chest. Her fingertips slipped over the ridges of his ribs as though there was a message on him written in Braille.

This was pretty much all it took to turn him on

again. It was the simplest of formulas—Sophie's touch equaled instant erection.

Her wandering hands slid downward, and he heard her sigh lightly. Then she gave a loud gasp and rolled away from him on the bed, clutching the sheet against her.

He stopped himself from groaning aloud as he propped up on one elbow and turned to her.

"What time is it?" she asked.

"I don't know," he said. "Want me to check?"

She stumbled out of bed, pulling a blanket with her. Noah heard a dull thud followed by a hiss of pain and the softest of swearwords.

"You okay?" he asked.

"I stubbed my toe."

"Take it easy," he advised. "If I have to fix you up again I might have to start charging you."

A light snapped on. She was across the room, wearing the blanket like a toga. Her silky blond hair spilled down over her shoulders. This was the first time he'd seen it unbound. It was longer than he'd expected and it made her look young and vulnerable. Her eyes darted around the room, settling on a clock on a shelf.

"Nearly five," he said.

"A.m. or p.m.?"

He smiled at her expression, which was endearingly confused. "In the evening. And we're still snowed in. So you might as well come back to bed."

She gasped again, an echo of the surprised sound

she had made when she came. Agitated, she pulled the blanket tighter around her. "I'm sorry," she said. "I can't . . . I mean, we're not . . ."

She was awash with regrets. He could see that. She was drowning in mortification. Rather than letting her squirm, he intervened. "Hey, take it easy," he said, offering a reassuring smile.

"I'm not upset," she said. "Just . . . disappointed in myself."

"You didn't disappoint me." He reached for her; she stepped out of range. "Sorry," he said, palms out.

"You needn't apologize. I take full responsibility for my actions. It's just that I'm used to being on my own."

"Don't worry," he said, "I won't be that guy."

"What guy?"

"That scary guy who won't leave you alone."

Her lips twitched as though she wanted to smile. "That's not what I'm worried about."

He got out of bed, making no effort to cover himself. "Good. Because there's nothing scary about me."

She practically gave herself whiplash, looking away from him. He grinned and shook his head, taking his time as he put on his boxers and jeans.

"Okay, I'm half-decent," he informed her.

She cleared her throat, looked at him. Her gaze skimmed over his bare chest, and he felt turned-on all over again.

"You should go," she said softly.

There was something about her stance, so still and

stiff with anxiety, that moved him. He crossed the room, brushed his knuckles lightly across her collarbone. "I'd rather stay."

"That's not going to work for me."

Even as she was gently rejecting him, she made him smile. He didn't know why that was, but she did. Yet as she spoke, she looked as though she needed to go to confession or something.

To distract her, he checked her knee. "Looks okay. It's healing nicely."

"You did a good job." Despite her words, she still seemed uncomfortable.

"Listen," he said, "don't feel bad. And for what it's worth, I didn't come here for this, I swear."

"And I didn't mean to . . . grab you. Attack you."

"So that was just sort of a bonus."

"Honestly," she said, "that's not me."

"Well, then, I guess I should get to know you. Tell me about yourself."

"Trust me, I'm not that interesting."

Right, he thought, thinking of all the stamps from exotic places in her passport. "Sophie, you reading the phone book would be interesting. Suppose I Google you on the Internet."

"Please don't Google me. I hate when people Google me." She shot him a look of warning. All right, then. She wasn't going to level with him about whatever it was she'd left behind. Not yet, anyway. She then bent down and picked up her clothes one-handed, still holding the blanket in place. As if he didn't know what her body looked like underneath, as if he hadn't traced its curves, drawn cries of pleasure from her, held her next to him for hours. "I've never done this before."

"Never done what before?" He wanted to hear her say it.

She straightened up and looked him in the eye. "Sex with a . . . stranger. That's what I've never done before."

He grinned. "Me, neither. It was great. I'm glad we went for it. I like you, Sophie. I really like you."

She could probably tell from the expression on his face what he was going to say next. "I really do think you should go," she repeated.

He picked up his sweatshirt but didn't put it on. Instead, he stretched, folding his arms behind his head, flexing his biceps. "You already said that."

"And yet you're still here." Judging by her expression, he figured she liked the biceps, but then she seemed to shake herself and marched into the bathroom. "I thought you weren't going to be that guy," she called through the door.

"I'm not."

"Then what's with all the posing and flexing?"

He laughed. "I'm going," he said. He had to check on the animals, anyway.

She came out of the bathroom before he got his shirt on. For one unguarded second, she eyed his bare chest with an expression of pure lust and he wanted her all over again. It was crazy. In one afternoon she had accomplished what a half a year of his family's clucking sympathy, his friends' beer-fueled commiseration and a half-dozen awkward setup dates had failed to do. Sophie Bellamy had made him forget he was emotional roadkill. She didn't know any of that, though, and he knew he wouldn't tell her, not now, anyway. She was skittish as hell when she wasn't lost in sex.

With an effort, he looked away from her and she left while he finished dressing. A few minutes later he found her in the next room, checking for messages on a handheld device.

"Everything all right?" he asked.

She nodded. "But I missed a call from my son. I can't believe I did that."

Beating herself up again, Noah observed. "You're jetlagged. Wounded. Not to mention snowed in. Call him now."

She dialed her cell phone, listened for a minute. "No answer."

"It's a snow day. He's probably out playing in it." Noah sat down on a bench by the door to pull on his boots. "I played hockey all through school," he said. "I still do, sometimes. There's a men's rec league in town."

"Max loves it. Half the year, he's a baseball fanatic, and the other half, it's hockey."

"What about you?" he asked. "Do you skate?"

"Used to. I haven't in a long time. I'd like to try it sometime."

"We'll go as soon as your knee's better."

He zipped and fastened his jacket, pulled on his helmet and gloves. She peered through the sidelight by the door. "It's really dark," she said. "Does that thing have a light?"

"Yep."

"Well, then. Thanks . . . for the firewood. I really appreciate it."

"No problem. And thank you." He instantly realized that was totally the wrong thing to say. "I mean, I had a—" He stopped. A good time? An amazing time? A possibly life-altering time? He quit talking and did something he knew he was better at. He kissed her, pressing her back against the wall and himself against her. "I'm not so good at talking," he whispered, his mouth still close to hers. "Most of my patients don't need it. But listen, come have dinner with me."

"No." But she didn't push him away. Instead, she wound her arms around his neck.

"You've got no food in this house. Give me about an hour to fix something."

"I'm not—"

"If I don't see you then, I'm coming back." He wanted to kiss her one more time but decided against it. She wanted his kiss. He sensed that from the way her lips softened and parted just a little, the way her eyelids lowered.

With an effort of will, he pulled back. Not a bad strategy, to leave her wanting more. "See you in an hour."

Twelve

For several minutes after Noah Shepherd left, Sophie stayed pressed against the wall as though he still held her there, imprisoned by her own desire to keep him close. The room seemed instantly dimmer, the popping sounds in the wood-burning stove louder. What on earth had come over her, falling into bed with this guy, the two of them acting like a couple of overheated teenagers? Was this living spontaneously? Letting go of control?

"Snap out of it," she said aloud to the empty house, willfully pushing herself away from the wall. She was restless, but in a way that felt far too pleasant. She moved aimlessly through the house, perusing the books on the shelves, spying a number of fat, enticing novels of the sort she'd always intended to read but never seemed to have the time for. Now she had nothing but time. She picked one and set it on the nightstand.

Then she stopped and just stood there by the bed, regarding the mussed covers and rumpled sheets while everything she'd done with Noah replayed in her mind.

She bent down to tug the quilt back in place and make the bed. As she did so, she was inundated again with memories—every kiss, every touch, every word he'd whispered in her ear, every gasp of pleasure.

When was the last time she'd been that happy making love? When had she ever been?

She dropped the quilt. To hell with making the bed. Tonight she would sleep amid the rumpled mess and remember everything all over again. She hugged herself and threw back her head and laughed aloud. Laughed. It was a rusty, incongruous sound in the quiet cottage.

Still smiling, she checked her e-mail and was surprised to see a note from Brooks Fordham, the reporter.

"Hello," she said, clicking it open, "welcome back."

The note was brief, just one line: *What about that dinner you promised me?* followed by a phone number with a New York area code. She went to get her phone, eager to hear his voice, hoping this meant he was fully recovered.

Before she had a chance to dial, her phone jangled to life with Max's ringtone, and she snatched it up. "Hey, there," she said. "I've been waiting to hear from you."

"Hiya, Mom. I got your messages."

His deepening, nearly grown-up voice startled her. "I'm snowed in," she said. "I'm dying to see you, and I can't because I'm snowed in."

"Everybody's snowed in. It's awesome."

"An enforced time-out," she said. "Everyone can use one of those now and then. How have you been, Max? How is school going?"

"Okay."

"And hockey?"

"Okay."

"And life in general and the world at large?"

"Okay." A note of humor sneaked into his voice. "So what's the deal, Mom? Daisy said you're staying at some house on the lake."

"That's right. I am."

"For how long?"

It upset her that he would instantly assume her status to be temporary. But it didn't surprise her. This was what she had led her son to expect from her. When he was very small—still nursing, in fact—she had given more milk to the breast pump than she had to her child, leaving bottles behind for others to feed him. Because, she had told herself, her work was so important. Because she wanted to make the world a better place for her own children. Everyone said it was all right to do that because she was serving a greater purpose. Everyone thought it was fine except the one person who really mattered—Max himself. He never got a vote.

"For good," Sophie heard herself saying now, and the sound of the words coming out of her own mouth shocked her. She never did anything on a permanent basis. Even her marriage had reached an expiration date. She flinched from the thought, as though she'd touched a hot coal. At some point she would need to deal with what had happened in her marriage, but she wasn't there yet. One crisis at a time, wasn't that what Dr. Maarten advised?

"Seriously?" Max asked. "Come on, Mom."

"Seriously. I'm really excited about this. I can't wait to see you. Maybe the roads will be clear tomorrow."

"What's going on? Is this about that thing that happened in The Hague? Dad said—"

"Your father talked to you about it?" Her back stiffened, the way it always did when the subject of her ex came up. The thought of him talking to her son about *her* only added starch to the stiffness. She had talked to her kids; why did they need their father's input? She took a deep breath and forced herself to relax. "Like I said, Max, I have a lot to tell you. What's your schedule tomorrow? And the rest of the week?"

As he gave her a rundown on his daily life, it struck her that for the first time, she was going to be fitting herself into his world rather than the other way around. The notion both worried and excited her. She prayed she would measure up. She'd been a mother for nearly two decades. Now, for the first time ever, she was going to be a *mom*.

Later that evening, the snow finally stopped. The snowplows still hadn't made it out to Lakeshore Road, but they would be working all night. Sophie went to Noah's for supper. The puppy was ecstatic to see her, its whole fluffy body wriggling in a dance of joy.

"She needs a home, you know," he said, taking Sophie's coat.

"Ooh, that sounds like a hint." She expected to feel awkward, and yet she didn't. Given the shockingly intimate things they had done together, she thought she might have trouble facing him. Instead, she felt deliciously excited. And . . . happy. Pleased to be in his company.

"It's an offer."

"I don't do puppies. And I know I lack credibility with you now . . ."

"How so?"

"I said I didn't do one-night stands, either, yet I fell right into bed with you." She gave a nervous laugh. "I'm seizing the day. You know, carpe diem and all that."

"You just slept with me in order to carpe the diem? Or because you like me?" He paused. "So we're talking about this. I didn't know whether or not to bring it up."

"It would be silly to avoid it."

He nodded. "I was hoping for an encore."

She couldn't help herself. She felt an unbidden tug of concurrence. "That's why we should talk."

"Okay." He led the way to the kitchen. "Over dinner." He fixed macaroni and cheese, salad from a bag. "I'm not much of a cook," he said, not by way of apology, just explanation.

"Neither am I. This is comfort food." She couldn't help smiling at the way the dogs, Rudy and Opal, sat back and watched, their eyes following his every move. Then she realized she was stalling, so she took a deep breath. "So. As I mentioned earlier . . . a one-night stand isn't exactly my style."

"If we do it again, then it's no longer a one-night stand."

"That's not the point. The point is, we hardly know each other. We don't even know if we *like* each other. It makes no sense to start something."

He placed two wineglasses on the counter and opened a bottle of white wine. "Look, I don't know you as well as I want to. But I can safely say, I definitely like you. And today made perfect sense to me."

She opened the wine and poured while he put dinner on the table. "You're being incredibly matter-of-fact about all this. Is that because you do this all the time, or is it simply your nature to take things as they come?"

"I pick door number two." He lifted his glass in her direction and took a sip of the wine. "Seriously, I don't do this all the time."

"Do you do it sometimes?"

"Nope. But you . . . there's something about you."

He was just so great. Too great, actually, to be some single guy living alone among the animals like Dr. Doolittle. "Have you ever been married?" she asked him.

"Nope," he said again.

"That surprises me. You're a great guy, Noah. You have to know that." *Commitment-phobe,* she thought. He wouldn't be the first.

"I'm not a commitment-phobe," he said. "Counsellor."

Only then did Sophie realize she'd spoken aloud. "Sorry. Am I being too nosy? Too lawyerly?"

He folded his arms on the table. "I want to get to know you, too, but playing twenty questions feels kind of phony."

"Then what do you suggest?"

"How about we just hang out? See what happens?"

"Because—" She stopped, unable to think of a reason. "I've never done much of that. Hanging out. I'm not sure I know how."

He refilled her wine and offered her dessert. "Mystic Mints," he said, pushing a dangerous-looking package toward her. "They'll change your life."

"No, thank you."

"Tell you what. Why don't we head out and talk some more while I feed?"

She regarded the empty dishes. "Didn't you just do that?"

"The horses, I mean," he said. "I have to feed the horses."

"You have horses."

"I've always had them. I never actually meant to keep some of the animals that have ended up with me. Most are adopted out to permanent homes. Some, though, aren't really adoptable. And some, okay, nearly all—they steal my heart." He flushed, probably uncomfortable with getting sentimental, then asked. "Do you ride?"

"I used to ride. A long time ago." As a girl, Sophie had adored horses. Until the age of seventeen, her best friend in the world was Misty, a beautiful Warmblood she kept at a barn and rode every single day, even when the weather was foul and no one else was around. Those, perhaps, had been her favorite times, when she put aside everything else in the world. However, when Misty died, Sophie was inconsolable, crying so much from the agony of loss that she made herself ill. Her parents sympathized, yet they didn't understand her attachment to Misty who was, after all, "only" an animal. They advised Sophie not to get so emotionally attached, warning her that everything came to an end. Sophie took the lesson to heart, and took up swimming instead, a solitary sport. There was danger in loving something with its own mortality, a factor completely out of her control. She never went near a horse—or any other pet—again.

To her relief, he didn't question her further. He insisted that she borrow a pair of warm ski gloves and his sister's barn jacket and they ventured outside just as twilight was edging into purple darkness. It was one of those rare, perfect winter scenes, with a crystal-clear sky filled with stars and a full moon that lit the landscape like a huge, celestial floodlight. The contours of the light on the snow created a scene of beautiful mystery, enveloped by a deep cushion of quiet. The dogs came along, Rudy kicking up a flurry of fresh snow while the puppy tumbled along in his wake. When she stepped inside the barn, Sophie was folded into a warm, familiar atmosphere that brought back unexpected, far-off memories of the girl she had once been. She thought she'd forgotten that girl, someone who laughed and dreamed with abandon, who loved the view of the world from astride her horse. She was unprepared for this wave of nostalgia, evoking a past she hadn't thought about in ages, a rare happiness that was pure and unconditional, and dreams that belonged solely to her.

Even the ritual of caring for the animals—four horses of varying ages—felt familiar. They stuck their heads out of their stalls, ears pricked and nostrils flaring in anticipation of their evening meal. Sophie loved the smell of their feed and their breath, the dry scent of hay and even the earthy odor of manure that pervaded the barn. She took off her gloves and stroked the long nose of a bewhiskered mare, reveling in the warm velvet texture against her hand.

"That's Alice. The others are Jemma, Shamrock and Moe," Noah said. "I've had Moe for years, and the other three, I rescued."

Sophie smiled. "I'm seeing a pattern here—you rescuing things."

"I have a hard time turning my back on an animal. I lost one last month. He was old, and I had to put him down."

She shut her eyes briefly, trying to imagine what that was like, actually being the one giving the injection. She could remember exactly how the loss of her own horse had felt—like a sledgehammer pounding at her until she was numb. In the aftermath, her heart had turned, cell by cell, to stone. "How can you bear to lose an animal?"

"Because it would be worse than never having them in the first place. I just enjoy the time I'm given with the animals." He peeled a generous flake of hay from a bale and put it in the stall. "Shamrock's the newest. The idiots who owned him had no clue how to take care of a horse."

He moved on to the next horse. "Jemma was abandoned, and too mean to put up for adoption," he said as the horse nuzzled him gently.

"She looks very happy now."

"It took a long time to teach her to trust me, but all that work and patience paid off," Noah said.

"I guess finding yourself in charge of abandoned animals is one of the hazards of your profession," Sophie observed.

"It's one of the perks. Even the worst cases of abandonment will get better eventually."

Are you really this wonderful? she asked silently. Maybe she was blinded by the fact that she'd recently had some of the best sex of her life. She worked beside him at an unhurried pace, falling into the comfortable rhythm of the chores.

"You're good at this," he remarked.

"I had my horse for a long time." She felt shockingly close to tears, her emotions hovering just beneath the surface.

Noah whistled between his teeth as he finished up. They went outside again, where the shadows lay in sharp relief across the fields of snow. Sophie felt somewhat vulnerable, but grateful at the same time.

"How's your knee?" he asked.

"It's fine. It was minor, Noah, and you took good care of me."

"We've got a full moon and no cloud cover tonight. Let's go for a ride."

She balked. The idea of riding with him on a moonlit night just seemed so romantic. She didn't do romantic things. "It's the middle of winter."

"We won't go far." He was already taking down blankets, saddles, bridles. "Give me a hand with this, will you?"

"You're crazy, you know that?" Yet she found herself opening a stall, leading one of the mares out and clipping on the cross ties.

He flashed her a boyish grin, then brought out another horse. Sophie again fell into a rhythm her hands and heart remembered—blanket, saddle, cinch, leaving the correct breathing space between horse and leather. The tacking up, gently pressing downward to get the horse to drop her head. Slipping on the headstall, gently inserting the bit. She was amazed by the way simply being in this atmosphere took her back. Every day after school, she used to ride her bike through the hilly streets of her neighborhood, to the barn where Misty was kept. Sophie had loved every aspect of owning a horse, from feeding and caring for her to riding her in the arena or along the forest and bridle paths.

"You're good," Noah observed. "I'm guessing that saying you used to ride is an understatement."

"There was nothing more important to me in the world than my horse." She found it easier to talk if she focused on the task at hand. The mare—Alice—appeared to be well trained, mouthing the bit a little but then accepting it.

Sophie found herself talking about growing up in Seattle, moving from neighborhood to neighborhood as her parents climbed the social ladder. Misty had been the one constant. Sophie had loved the horse with every inch of her heart. She dreamed about her, created stories in her head about the mare, smiled at the very thought of an afternoon ride.

With Noah in the lead, they rode out of the barn and into the most perfect winter night Sophie had ever seen. At the sight of the smooth hillocks, deeply carved by moonlight and shadow, she caught her breath and turned to Noah. "This is another first for me, riding at night, in all this snow."

"Your knee still okay?" Noah asked.

"It's fine."

He headed across a pristine pasture, his horse churning a trail through the deep snow. She pressed her heels into the horse's sides and followed. There was that momentary jolt of pure exhilaration, bringing on a flood of sensation so intense that tears sprang to her eyes again. The cold air on her face, the warmth and strength of the horse, the unparalleled scenery all combined to sweep her away. She and Noah didn't talk as they rode up a broad, treeless slope. The horses' breath created clouds of mist, softening the landscape until it took on a dreamlike quality. At the very top of the slope, they stopped to look down over the farm, the untouched road, the lights twinkling in the houses along the lakeshore. Sophie relaxed forward over the mare's neck, just letting herself feel rather than worry and plan. "Thank you," she whispered, addressing both the horse and Noah. "This is beautiful."

"I figured you'd like it."

She wondered how far it was to town, having the wild idea of going to see Max and Daisy. On a horse. They would think she'd really lost it.

On the way back, Noah showed her the best sledding hill on the property, a grove of sugar maples Gayle tapped to make syrup, a small bridge over a completely frozen streambed. This was his world, the one he'd always known. It was a place she felt entirely safe, even in the aftermath of a record-breaking snowfall. She found that she liked being snowed in. Being forced by nature to slow down, to stay close to home, was not such a bad thing, particularly with Noah as company.

She shouldn't have waited so long to ride a horse again, but the lessons of the past had cut deep. As a girl, she'd given too much of herself to the bond with her horse—at least, that was her parents' view. They warned it was a distraction from more important matters, like school, sports, music and the kind of extracurriculars she could benefit from later on, when she was trying to get into college.

Over the years, she'd learned that there were different kinds of losses, and the worst were the ones she had brought about herself. Her fears, anxieties and ambition had eventually driven a wedge between her and her children.

Now she felt a sturdy sense of possibility. She was here for a purpose—to reclaim her family. This was her shot, her chance to rebuild her life. Meeting Noah was . . . an unexpected beginning. She had no idea if it would turn out to mean anything, but she felt curiously lighthearted as they groomed and put up the horses.

Then, as they walked to the house, she felt his hand at the small of her back. They went inside together, and she peeled off her boots and heavy jacket. The next thing she knew he had her backed up against the hall closet door and was kissing her into a state of willing submission. She didn't speak up, even when she had the chance. And in that instant, that brief heartbeat of hesitation, she was lost, and without her even saying anything, he knew it. He pulled her against him and imprinted her with another kiss that defeated every reservation she had. When they came up for air, she was obligated to whisper, "I didn't come here for this," echoing his words to her.

"But I'm not letting you leave without it," he said, and kissed her again.

• • •

The next day, Sophie awakened alone—no Noah, no warm puppy. She tensed, bracing herself for the left-over terror of nightmares. Then she opened her eyes with a soft gasp of disbelief. The nightmares weren't there. They didn't seem to be lingering like cobwebs she couldn't shake off. It might be an aberration, or maybe she'd turned a corner.

Hoping it was the latter, she got up and, almost without thinking, grabbed a plaid flannel shirt and slipped it on. She instantly felt better. The fabric, worn soft, held a hint of Noah's scent. Hugging the shirt around her, she went to the bathroom to put herself together. This was getting out of hand. She couldn't keep falling into bed with Noah Shepherd simply because they were snowed in. Simply because it was what every cell in her body wanted to do. It was impulsive, self-indulgent behavior, and she needed to exercise a little control. Yet she'd made some sort of decision, hadn't she? Perversely, that was the one element she loved surrendering to Noah—control. With him, she was able to live in the moment, to immerse herself in sensation the way she never had before. It was a kind of insanity, yet he acted as though it was the most natural thing in the world. Maybe for him, it was.

She scrubbed her face and vigorously brushed her hair, then went downstairs with a new sense of resolution. The snowfall had ended. Surely the road would be reopened today. Ordinary life needed to resume, and in ordinary life, she had to focus on her kids and how she was going to be their mother from now on.

She glanced at the small writing desk by the window. There was a stack of blank paper and a selection of pens, and she found herself remembering Dr. Maarten's advice to her. She was supposed to write things down in order to release them. The idea was simple. Take something festering inside, and let it out.

I don't have anything festering inside, she'd told the doctor. She had actually said so with a straight face. And to his credit, he hadn't burst out laughing. Now she really had found relief—in sex with a stranger. An insane act that was restoring her sanity. "Just write down something each day, large or small. Write down a conversation you wish you'd had with your captors. Write down something you wish you'd said with someone close to you, but never did."

Now that was an assignment. In a hundred years, there would never be enough time to cover that. She wished she'd been more forthright with her parents, back when she was young and too preoccupied with not disappointing them. She wished she'd had a thousand honest conversations with Greg, and maybe the derailment of their marriage could have been averted. She wished she'd managed to make her children understand why she had let a sense of mission keep her away from them. And her captors? Good God. She couldn't even begin to write down what she wished she had told them.

She decided to take a stab at some of these conversations. She took a piece of paper and started, "Dear Dad." And then nothing. Not because she had nothing to say but because she had too much. She faced the same dilemma with "Dear Greg." And then "Dear Daisy and Max . . ." She wondered what her children would think if they knew how she'd waited out the snowfall. She hoped they would never find out. Instead of writing a note, she made a list of momlike things she hoped to do. Go to Max's hockey games. Help Daisy make a baby book for Charlie. Sign a progress report. Learn to bake cookies.

It was a start. She folded the list and slipped it in her pocket. Following her nose to a pot of coffee in the kitchen, she found evidence of an early breakfast—a cereal bowl in the sink. Ugh, Cocoa Puffs. Judging by the tracks in the snow, she concluded that Noah had gone out with the dogs. She fixed herself a cup of coffee and hoped he would be back soon, so she could explain that this . . . whatever *this* was . . . probably wasn't a very good idea. Or was it?

A pity, she thought. Because as bad ideas went, this one felt completely wonderful. She sighed and hugged herself, took her coffee to the front room and added a few more items to her list. Through the window, she spotted a small group of parents and children at a roadside bus stop. The road appeared to have been plowed and sanded. *Yes,* she thought. *I finally get to see Max and Daisy.*

So life was going on. One mother was standing behind a little girl, braiding her hair, while others stood back and chatted while the kids chased each other around the bus shelter. A moment later a black-and-yellow school bus lumbered around a bend in the road and ground to a halt with a gnashing of air brakes. A surge of children in snowsuits and backpacks piled toward the open door of the bus. Watching the hugs being dispensed, Sophie felt a deep and elemental clutch of emotion. It was a simple, mundane moment, a mother seeing her child off to school, yet to Sophie the experience seemed rare and special.

Noah came into the room and hugged her from behind, nuzzling her neck until she practically melted. He smelled of the outdoors, fresh snow and wood. "That's the same bus I used to ride as a kid," he said.

She tried to imagine living in one place all her life. "Did your mother stand at the bus stop with you every day?"

"Nope. She was too busy working. But my grandmother was always there."

"I see—well." As she watched, the bus swung wide around a curve, its broad yellow flank looming ominously close to the guardrail. She tensed, her mind veering sickeningly to a moment in the van. She reeled her thoughts back in, then relaxed against him as the bus chugged away in a cloud of exhaust smoke.

She caught herself wondering if Noah liked kids, but asking him was way too personal, despite last night's intimacy. It was also date talk: *Do you like kids?* was obvious code for *Are you a decent prospect for settling down?*

It was not the sort of thing you asked a guy, even one who rescued you from ditches, brought you firewood, fixed you macaroni and cheese. Who gave you addictive, orgasmic sex, again and again.

"You're too quiet," he commented. "What are you thinking?"

Like she'd tell him that. Still, she felt like talking. "Seeing that—" she gestured outside, where the mothers were heading back to their houses "—makes me feel guilty. I never did that for my kids, never waited at the bus stop with them."

"Most serial killers would say the same thing."

"I'm serious, Noah. I've got a lot to answer for. This divorce—I've handled it poorly. Kids are supposed to go with their mother after a divorce, right?"

"There's no 'supposed to.' Every family's different. I'm sure you did what was best under the circumstances."

"That's interesting, because I'm not sure at all."

"How's the knee today?" he asked. "I hope you didn't overdo it last night."

It took her a moment to realize he was referring to the riding, not the sex. *All right,* she thought. He didn't want to talk about her kids. Of course he didn't. And she didn't blame him one bit.

"It's fine. I've got an appointment to see a doctor in town." She'd found Dr. Cheryl Petrowski in the phone book and, solely on the strength of her name, had made the call. Ordinarily Sophie would obsessively research a doctor before committing herself to her care. But being so new here, she had to take a leap of faith.

He nuzzled her neck again. “So we’ve got all morning . . .”

She was inches from succumbing. He made it seem completely natural to do so. “You’re turning me into a hussy,” she said.

“Being snowed in will do that to a person.”

With a groan of reluctance, she peeled herself away from him. “I need to get busy. I’m finally going to see my children today. And I have to get rid of my rental car and lease a different one. I was thinking of a minivan.” If she was going to start acting like a mom, she might as well drive a car that made her look like a mom.

“Make sure you get snow tires and all-wheel drive.”

“I will.” Just like that, the plan began to feel very real, and nervousness hummed through her. This was going to work, she promised herself. There were only a few hurdles to cross, like the fact that her kids were bound to be skeptical of this ever working out at all. Or the fact that she hadn’t exactly explained the plan to her ex-husband.

Thirteen

"You're doing what?" Greg Bellamy took Sophie's coat from her and frowned. "Come on, Soph. Back up a little. Let's go over this again."

Sophie tried not to feel defensive as she regarded her ex-husband in the vestibule of his house, a house where she was a stranger. He had every right to be suspicious of her motives and actions. She had done a spectacularly bad job of being a wife and mother. It was understandable that he would question her now.

"Can we sit down?" she asked evenly. "I'll try to explain." She doubted she could fumble through a reasonable-sounding explanation of why she'd come to Avalon, but she was going to try.

He gestured toward the old-fashioned parlor. "I'll hang up your coat. Go have a seat."

He didn't say, *Make yourself at home,* but she shouldn't have expected that, of course. Nor did she want the gesture. She and Greg were exes for a reason. For a lot of reasons. When they were married, they were so busy taking care of business that they forgot to take care of each other and had let the marriage die a slow death. They were not like wistful TV exes who got along beautifully, trading kids back and forth like keys to a mutually beloved car.

She took a seat in a Queen-Anne-style oval-backed armchair and regarded her surroundings with mild fascination. Greg had reinvented himself and rebuilt his life from the ground up, and every item in the room was unfamiliar to Sophie, from the overstuffed armchairs to the bowl of Jelly Bellies on the coffee table.

When Greg had first made his move, she'd thought he was nuts. He'd sold his Manhattan architecture firm and moved upstate, to the town where he'd spent all his boyhood summers. He'd bought a historic lakefront hotel, the Inn at Willow Lake, and had recently married a woman who seemed to be Sophie's polar opposite. They lived on the property in a tall, boxy house built in Carpenter Gothic style and furnished with a bright, eclectic mix of antiques and contemporary pieces.

The room was casual and comfortable in a way no room in their former home together had ever looked. There was a cushy, lived-in atmosphere here, and despite her differences with Greg, she was glad Max got to live here. There was an array of photos on a narrow table against one wall, showing Max and Daisy at various ages. There were also pictures of Sonnet Romano, Nina's daughter, who now attended American University.

Just like that, Greg had another child. Even though Sonnet was away, she was a permanent fixture in Max and Daisy's lives. So far, the three of them got along beautifully. Or so it seemed to Sophie. Suddenly, sitting here, it finally struck her how out of the loop she had been.

She recognized a couple of shots from last summer

when Greg's niece, Olivia Bellamy, had married in a big wedding at the Bellamys' Camp Kioga, a rustic wilderness camp on the north end of the lake.

There was a collage frame of brand-new images, too, and Sophie couldn't help herself. She was fascinated. The photos depicted Greg's wedding, which had taken place on Epiphany. Sophie now had two reasons she wished she could forget that night.

She felt an unexpected twist of pain. Yes, she'd known on an intellectual level that Greg had fallen in love with Nina Romano, a young single mother with a grown daughter. Yes, Sophie had known he'd remarried in a small oceanside ceremony on the island of St. Croix.

She thought she had processed this data and neutralized the pain. She thought she was all right with the turn of events. Now, looking at the smiling faces of her children, her ex-husband, her ex-in-laws whose name she still carried, she realized she was not okay. She was devastated. It was not that she wished she was still married to Greg, God, no. It was not even that she resented seeing him so happy. The thing that ripped into her heart was the knowledge that the Bellamys had once witnessed her own wedding. She felt entirely expendable. But she stopped herself from unraveling by keeping a stiff upper lip. She'd made a decision years ago, and she knew how to live with it.

She focused on a group shot of the Bellamys and Romanos, who were complete strangers to her. Everyone looked so happy, laughing and carefree against the bright white of the sand and the deep Caribbean blue of the water in the background.

Nina was a small-town girl, born and raised in Avalon, even serving a term as its mayor. Sophie, on the other hand, had grown up dividing her time between two large, vibrant cities—Seattle and Vancouver, British Columbia. Nina had some ungodly big family with members numbering in the double digits, while Sophie was an only child, with the entire weight of her parents' expectations on her shoulders. Nina was dark and intense, small and curvy, given to expressing every emotion in true Italian-American fashion. Sophie was fair and tall and slender, and so emotionally reserved that even her therapist got frustrated with her. Nina was casual and comfortable in her creamy, olive-toned skin; she'd actually gotten married in flip-flops. Sophie had never worn flip-flops in her life. Seeing these photos was proof in living color that she had been wrong for Greg in every possible way.

Hearing him return to the parlor, she turned away from the array of photos. "Congratulations on your marriage. I should have said so before."

"Thanks." He looked distinctly uncomfortable. Like Sophie, he clearly had no clue about the etiquette in this situation.

Studying him, she noticed for the first time that he still bore the faint shadow of a suntan from his Caribbean wedding trip, and it looked wonderful on him, enhancing his golden good looks. Her gaze was drawn to his hands. It was a curious fact that when you were truly intimate with a man, you knew every detail of his hands—their shape and texture, the nails and creases of the palms. She couldn't remember much about Greg's hands these days, which was a good sign. However, she became fixated on his wedding band. It was a wide chunk of gold, bluntly beautiful, nothing like the slender Tiffany band he'd worn while married to her. No, the two wedding bands were as different from one another as . . . Sophie and Nina.

Which, she conceded, was entirely appropriate and as it should be.

Focus, Sophie reminded herself. It was too easy to be distracted by things like the fact that her ex had remarried and was living a dream life, a life he never could have had while married to her.

"We've been worried as hell about you," he said. "It's not like you to just walk away from something. I read the published reports about what happened in The Hague. It was bad. Really bad."

"I won't lie to you. It was horrible. I'm sure it will haunt me for the rest of my life. But I wasn't hurt, and I'm ready to move on."

"Are you sure you're all right?"

Could anyone be "all right" after what she'd done? She looked him in the eye. "One hundred percent."

"Then why are you here, Sophie?" he asked.

Even though his voice was gentle, the question was a touch of fire to the base of her spine. Of course he would ask that. Of course he would assume that she'd come simply because she had no other options. He had no idea what she'd sacrificed to come to Avalon.

"I'm here for Max and Daisy and the baby," she said evenly. "And yes, the incident at the Peace Palace was a wake-up call, but my being here is about the kids, not about me." Good heavens, understatement there. Why else would she move to a town where the name of her ex-husband was uttered in reverential tones, and where Greg's new wife, the former mayor, was known and loved by all? Did he think this would be fun for her?

"That sounds reasonable," Greg said, "but for how long?"

Again, she reminded herself that he was looking out for his kids. "I can understand why you'd ask me that," she said. "Ever since our children were babies, I've been coming and going between them and work. It's different this time. Greg. I'm here for good."

He studied her for a long moment. There were things about her that Greg Bellamy knew better than any other living soul, and vice versa. Married at an absurdly young age, it was no shock that they'd wound up divorced. The shock was that they'd stayed married as long as they had. Sophie attributed this to their stubbornness and commitment to their kids.

She shifted uncomfortably under his scrutiny. "What?" she asked finally.

"You seem . . . different," he said at last. "A lot less uptight."

A night of wild sex will do that to a girl, she thought.

"I didn't mean to make you blush," Greg said.

She waved her hand nonchalantly and reminded herself not to get defensive. "It's not you." Another huge understatement. "Listen, we're going to have our moments, but I don't want it to be about us, either. My total focus is going to be the kids."

"From international lawyer to soccer mom, just like that."

"You don't buy it." She didn't trust herself, either, but the uncertainty wouldn't keep her from trying.

"It's hard to see you in that role. I don't want the kids getting hurt."

Then why didn't you work harder on our marriage? She almost asked. No, that wasn't fair. They had both worked on it, but eventually each had to concede defeat.

"I'm not here to hurt them."

"I know."

Even though he agreed with her, she heard what he didn't say aloud: You can't help hurting them.

As objectively as possible, she explained that she would take a hiatus from work. The Wilsons had invited her to stay as long as she wanted as they rarely used their lake house until the Fourth of July. Sophie planned to find more permanent living quarters well in advance of that. She was still licensed to practice law in the state of New York. Since her family was here, she had been diligent about keeping her license current. Eventually she might join a local firm as an "of counsel" associate, working two or three days a week.

That, of course, might be overly optimistic. Getting people in Avalon to put their trust in Greg Bellamy's ex-wife could be a bit of a stretch. Still, she was determined to make this happen. That meant carpooling, attending sports events, doctor appointments, teacher conferences. It meant hosting birthdays, laughing at Max's fart jokes, listening to Daisy's hopes and fears. It was a glaring contrast to her former life, with its excitement and high stakes. Yet in a different way, the stakes were even higher now.

To his credit, Greg listened without comment and kept his expression neutral. When she finished talking, he got up and went over to a corner desk, returning with a calendar covered in someone's unfamiliar handwriting. Nina's, she realized.

"Max's schedule," Greg said. Somewhere in the house, a phone started ringing. "You can take a look at it. I need to get that."

Sophie used to have a staff that took care of things like calendars and schedules. She was on her own now. This was all brand-new and the responsibility made her somewhat nervous. Forgetting something was not an option.

She took out her global PDA and studied the screen. She had to scroll through meetings, briefings and hearings, events at court she would miss. She couldn't help feeling a twinge.

Quit making comparisons, she admonished herself. You don't compare your son's hockey practice to a meeting with the president of the International Criminal Court. They're two different things. Two mutually exclusive things.

The calendar gave her a snapshot of a busy family functioning well. Max had plenty going on in his life—hockey practice, snowboarding on the weekend, an orthodontist appointment.

"Orthodontist?" she muttered aloud.

"He just started with Dr. Rencher," Greg said, returning to the room.

Her son was going to an orthodontist and she didn't even know about it. "Is he getting braces?" she asked.

"Soph. He's already got them."

"He didn't tell me. You didn't tell me. How is it that my own child gets braces and I don't even know?"

Greg must have recognized the raw pain in her voice. His expression was mild as he said, "That's a good sign. It means it's no big deal to Max, which is what we want. He's only had them a couple of weeks and he doesn't seem to mind. You can take him to next month's appointment and hear what Dr. Rencher has to say."

She nodded and entered it into her PDA. She was on her own now. In addition to the orthodontist and hockey practice, Max had a couple of birthday parties to go to, a weekly match with another team, a school trip to the Baseball Hall of Fame in Cooperstown and a Boy Scout outing to West Point.

"Drum lessons?" she asked, looking at Wednesday afternoon.

"He switched from piano."

"And you let him?" She could already feel herself starting to butt heads with Greg.

"It's his choice, Soph."

"He's only twelve years old. He doesn't get that he needs piano."

Years ago, she had read that music training was crucial to a child's intellectual development, and she'd enrolled Max and Daisy both in piano lessons. Max in particular had done well on piano, winning prizes in age-group competitions.

"Do you really want to argue about this?" Greg asked.

"I . . . no." She forced herself to let go and studied him. When she questioned a witness, she was able to figure out what his real agenda was. With Greg, she could discern nothing. She didn't know if he was challenging her because he resented the fact that she was an absentee mother, or if he simply understood that there were so many things for them to fight about, she was crazy to focus on an issue as minor as this.

Of course, she could argue that it wasn't minor at all. But she wouldn't let herself fall into the old patterns with Greg, when one dispute used to segue seamlessly into the next, and then the next, until they were both enmeshed in a tangled web of conflict.

She set aside the schedule. "I really do mean to do this," she told Greg. "I'm not going to bail in a few months."

"Just keep in mind that Max is my main concern. Not your sudden revelation about being a full-time mother."

"Of course." She clenched her jaw, forbidding herself to lash back at him. Why couldn't he see anything good in what she had done, or acknowledge she was driven by noble goals? "There's something I hope you'll keep in mind, too, Greg. Our children have been hurt enough by me—by both of us—and I'm going to dedicate myself to them now, and hope to God it's not too late."

A sound came from the kitchen and Sophie felt her whole being warm up with anticipation. Finally, Max was home. She turned toward the door, already hungry to feel her arms around him.

Instead of Max, a small, dark-haired whirlwind came bustling into the room. Sophie froze, rooted to the floor. "Nina."

She had a bright, spontaneous smile that lit her face as she plucked off a knitted wool hat. "Hello, Sophie."

Her smile seemed to light up Greg, too, as he went to take her parka, a shapeless red thing that was oddly flattering. Somehow, in taking her coat from her, he managed to give her a kiss and a shoulder squeeze all in the same motion.

Sophie wondered if he'd ever looked at her the way he was looking at Nina. Not likely, she decided. "I came to visit Max," she said. "Sorry about being early."

"He should be home any minute," Nina said. "He's going to be so excited to see you. Can I get you something to drink? Tea, or coffee?"

"No, thank you."

The three of them chatted a bit, mostly about Max. Greg and Nina were innkeepers. Hospitality experts. And Sophie was an experienced diplomat, so the conversation went well, though it didn't go deep. She and Greg had been as civilized as possible about the divorce. When it came to the kids, they had agreed not to get into any mutual pissing contest with one of them trying to outdo the other.

Greg excused himself to go hang up her jacket, leaving Sophie alone with Nina. Manners, she reminded herself. A diplomat's front line of defense. And honestly, it wasn't that difficult to be civil with Nina. She possessed the one quality Sophie needed to see in the woman who had become Max's stepmom. She genuinely cared about Max.

My son has a stepmother.

"Congratulations, Nina," Sophie said. "I just had a look at your wedding pictures."

"Thanks. It was a whirlwind, all planned and executed within a couple of weeks. St. Croix was beautiful." Nina seemed comfortable being who she was. Both Max and Daisy claimed they liked her. Sophie actually didn't blame them. She was supremely likable.

This was not a quality Sophie possessed in abundance. She knew it.

"Mom!" Max burst into the room.

She forgot everything as she went to hug her son. The feel of him in her arms brought tears to her eyes. She was always glad to see him, but after what she'd survived, she keenly sensed how precious he was. He smelled of the winter air, and his arms around her were strong. And he was . . . "Look at you." She stepped back. "You're so tall."

They stood nearly eye to eye. What was Nina feeding this boy?

He grinned, giving her a close-up of his new braces—bright bands across his upper teeth, accented with Day-Glo green. She didn't say anything, worried that he might be self-conscious.

He needn't be. Her son was incredibly good-looking, with his father's strong, regular features and the Nordic fairness of the Lindstroms.

"So I thought we could go see Daisy and Charlie," she said. "Would that be okay?"

"Sure." Max looked at Nina. "I have math and English homework. The English isn't due until Wednesday, though."

So very many ways to be awkward, Sophie thought. Nina was on homework patrol.

"I was going to take them to dinner," she added. "It won't be a late night, though." There. She had not asked permission. She was simply keeping Nina in the loop.

"Sounds good," Nina said easily.

"Hey, Dad," Max yelled. His voice was loud enough to make Sophie flinch. "We're going to Daisy's, okay?"

"See you later, buddy," Greg said, coming back into the room. "Sophie, be careful on the road."

"Always," she said, and had to remind herself not to run to the car.

Fourteen

Daisy liked having a home of her own. After she'd had the baby, she'd lived with her dad, but with the understanding that it was only temporary. She was desperate to live her own life, even though she knew it would be hard. And it was, but that only made her more determined to succeed. She was not without support. She did have a trust fund from her grandparents, something they'd set up for all their grandchildren. Daisy was given access to hers when the baby was born. This did not exactly make her Paris Hilton, but it gave Daisy the freedom to focus on her son and her education.

The house was nothing fancy, half of a duplex on the far side of town, with tree-lined sidewalks and a small public playground at the end of the street where Charlie could play when he got old enough. The rooms were small, but Daisy loved her house, because it was hers. However, her mother was coming over any minute, and Daisy was having a crisis of confidence. Suddenly the cozy rooms merely looked small and poky. The eclectic décor—mostly things left over from the renovation of the Inn at Willow Lake—reminded her of a garage sale. All she could see were the dishes in the sink, the dust bunnies on the floor, the pile of winter clothes and baby gear in the front hall. With one eye on the clock, she went flying around, fluffing pillows and shoving folded laundry into the linen closet.

Mom had said she would come over with Max after school, so her visit wasn't exactly a surprise. There had been plenty of advance notice. Then how was it that here she was, having run out of time, with the house still cluttered with baby toys and brochures and clippings of projects she was working on? How was it that she still hadn't changed out of her zip-front hoodie, the one with the frayed cuff on her left hand from drawing, and an apparently permanent yellowish spit-up stain on the shoulder? In childbirth class and in all the books Daisy had read, babies who were breast-fed didn't spit up, or if they did, it was a charming little hiccup of drool, easily expunged with a baby wipe. This was because breast milk was the perfect food for an infant. However, Charlie, it seemed, had a special gift. Even with nothing but a meal of mother's milk in his stomach, he could spew halfway across the room.

She peeked into the bedroom, where her son slept in his crib, which was set in an alcove just a few steps from Daisy's bed. Spying a big bag of diapers she'd left lying on the bed, she stuffed it into a dresser drawer. Charlie made a soft sighing noise but didn't wake up.

Daisy smoothed the bed—at least she'd made it already—and then threw some used towels into the hamper. Charlie chose that moment to wake up, calling out with a vaguely cranky moan.

"Hey, you," she said, going to the crib and leaning over, winning a smile that had more power over her than the rising sun.

He pumped his legs and reached for her. She scooped him up—soaking wet, of course—and got busy changing him. This involved peeling off his stretchy suit and leaden diaper, cleaning him stem to stern with baby wipes, putting on a fresh diaper and coverall. She picked the fluffy one her mom had given him for Christmas. Mom would like that. Maybe she'd like it enough that she wouldn't criticize anything.

Daisy's mom had always made her feel like a loser. She didn't do it on purpose. It wasn't like her mom called her a slob or told her she didn't measure up. It was just that Mom was so freakishly perfect.

She looked like an actress in an old black-and-white movie, the embodiment of class and elegance. She had been a perfect student and became the perfect lawyer. She had been a nationally ranked distance swimmer in college, and sometimes still competed at the masters level, always beating everyone else in her age group. In her career, Mom did things that made a difference in the world.

She made Daisy feel totally inadequate. And Mom didn't even have to say a word in order to do it.

Hearing the thud of car doors, Daisy rushed to let her mother in. There was a mirror over the hall table. She paused to check her hair—*whatever*—and answered the door with a just-awakened baby in the crook of her arm and a tentative smile on her face. "Mom!"

"Hello, sweetheart," Mom said, stepping into the house, Max following behind. The moment she set foot inside, the place seemed a bit dimmer and shabbier. Daisy hoped like hell it was just her imagination.

They hugged, with her Mom encircling both Daisy and the baby. For just a few seconds, Daisy felt nothing but warm contentment. "I've missed you, Mom," she said.

"Same here. I missed you and Max and Charlie so much I couldn't stand it."

"Mom, are you crying?" Daisy asked, amazed.

Her mother nodded, gazing down at Charlie's face. "It's just so good to be back with you all."

Daisy and Max traded a glance. Her brother looked clueless, as usual. Daisy stepped back, studying that film-star face. This was unexpected. Their mother never cried. "You're not all right. Mom—"

"Not now," she murmured.

Meaning, never. Daisy knew the ploy well. She decided not to push. "Right now, I'd like to hold my grandson." Mom reached for the warm, soft bundle. "Hello, you precious, precious little boy," she said in a singsong voice.

Charlie was just getting to the age where he had strong opinions about strangers. When he was really tiny, he'd pretty much go to anyone, with only a preference for Daisy, the source of all milk. Now he recognized certain people—Max, their dad, Nina. And

Logan. Those weekly visits were beginning to make an impression on Mr. C.

Now Daisy held her breath while Charlie fixed a solemn stare on Mom, trying to make up his mind about whether she was friend or foe. Was this what a parent did, stopped breathing until their kid decided to behave? When had she gotten so bound up in her son's behavior? Why would she feel as though, if Charlie blew it, Daisy was the failure?

He glanced at her, and she offered a smile of encouragement. The baby stared unabashedly up at Mom. He didn't fuss, so that was a good sign. At last, he offered a gummy smile and a fine string of drool.

Way to go, kiddo, Daisy thought, slowly expelling her breath. Mom held and cooed over Charlie for a long time. She cried a little more, and Daisy tried to figure out how to be with this new, heartbroken mother.

"Have a seat, Max," she said to her brother. "You can watch Charlie while I show Mom around."

"He certainly likes you," Mom said, carefully passing Charlie to Max. "What a smart baby."

"The smartest," Max agreed.

Daisy stood back, watching the three of them, and realized some of the tension of her mother's visit had defused. Mom was totally into the baby, not wrinkling her nose at the cluttered little house. It didn't take long to show her around the place and she didn't have one bad thing to say.

Another thing the baby classes and books didn't tell

you was that a baby had magical properties. Daisy had discovered this on her own. A teenage party girl who got pregnant was an object of gossip, judged for her lack of caution, her poor impulse control, maybe even her slutty tendencies. She was also an object of pity, especially later in the pregnancy when she turned fat and blotchy faced. The whole world pretty much liked to hate on a girl like that, a girl like Daisy had been.

Then, with the baby's birth, a miracle happened. Sure, there was the miracle of birth. Of life, and all that stuff. That was everything it was cracked up to be, but it came as no big surprise. The big surprise was that just by showing up, the baby transformed everything around him, starting with his mother. She was no longer a knocked-up teenage slut or a fat loser. People went from looking down on her to looking up to her. She was a Mother. With a capital *M* like Madonna. She was worthy of praise for giving the world the precious gift of her child. She was offered preferential treatment in grocery store lines and on trains. Suddenly, the world respected her.

And the baby's magic didn't stop there. It transformed a bratty kid, like Daisy's brother, into Uncle Max. And now as she watched her mother, Daisy saw the effect fall over her like a glowing veil.

"I need to feed him," she said. "Then we'll be ready to go."

"I'll be on the computer," Max said, heading for the spare room, where Daisy's equipment was set up. He was into some online virtual hockey game that had elaborate, ongoing storylines more convoluted than those of soap opera stars.

Daisy took a seat on the sofa and freed her breast one-handed. Charlie latched on like the old pro he was. It had taken Daisy almost no time at all to get over feeling self-conscious about nursing. A few minutes of listening to your newborn screaming with hunger until his voice rattled made modesty take a backseat to expediency. Before the baby, whipping out your boob was an audition for a "Girls Gone Wild" video. After the baby, it was a political statement, as well as an act of maternal compassion.

"You'll have to excuse the shirt," Daisy said. "I didn't want to change until after I fed him. He spews like a geyser. I asked the doctor about it, but supposedly it's normal for some babies, as long as they're gaining weight."

"You used to do that, too."

This was news. "You breast-fed?"

"Of course. You look surprised."

Daisy *was* surprised. It was hard—no, impossible—to picture her mom holding an infant to her breast. Had she experienced the same terror and wonder Daisy felt when she held her baby? Had she awakened in the middle of the night and rushed to the crib, just to make sure the baby was breathing? Her *mom?* "You don't seem the type."

"What's that supposed to mean?"

"Nothing. Never mind."

"No, I really want to hear this . . ."

"Fine. I'm just saying, it's hard to picture you whipping out your boob and nursing a baby."

"No offense," Mom said, "but until a few months ago, it was hard to picture *you* doing it."

"You'd think by now I'd know better than to argue with a lawyer."

"I'm not arguing and I'm not being a lawyer."

"Felt like arguing to me."

"Now we're arguing about arguing. Let's not do this, Daisy."

"Good plan."

They fell silent. Down the hall, the faint beeps and sound effects of Max's video game came from the study. The baby's gentle, rhythmic swallowing could be heard. After a few minutes, Daisy switched him from one side to the other.

"So I guess we're either arguing or we're not talking at all," Daisy said.

"Don't be silly. We talk all the time. I learned IMing and text messaging just for you. Talk to me, sweetheart. I want to catch up on your life and your plans."

Daisy felt a beat of caution. This could be dangerous territory for the two of them. Her mom was very opinionated about plans. About everything, but especially the importance of a good education. They had been arguing about that very thing the same weekend Daisy had gotten pregnant. She wondered if her mom had remembered that.

Her parents' divorce had just been finalized and her mom had given her a lecture about how she didn't need to allow it to change her plans, how it was more important than ever for Daisy to achieve great things in her education.

"Great things," of course, being code for "getting into Harvard."

Daisy had informed her mother that she didn't want to go to college at all. Of everything she could have said, she knew that one would get under her mom's skin most of all. To her mom, saying "I'm not going to college" was way worse than saying "I'm gay" or "I'm joining a cult." The funny thing was, Daisy wasn't even sure she meant it. But the fight had given her a reason to explode, storm out, and go crazy for a whole weekend, which included having sex with Logan multiple times. Protection optional.

So really, she owed her mom a debt of gratitude. Without that fight, Charlie might never have been born.

"Something funny?" Mom asked.

Daisy shook her head. "Just wondering if this little guy and I are going to give each other a hard time one day."

"Count on it," Mom said.

The tension eased a little. "I'm enrolled in a photography class at SUNY New Paltz," Daisy said. "Classes start Monday."

"That's fantastic. Daisy, I'm excited for you."

Was she? Daisy couldn't quite tell. Not so long ago, Mom had expected Daisy to go to some famous, competitive school. The state college didn't quite measure up to those standards.

"Do you think it's too soon? Sometimes I worry that I'm ditching him for selfish reasons, like—" She stopped, but too late.

"Like I did to you and Max?" her mom queried.

Daisy looked down at the whorls of red hair on Charlie's head. She used to stare at him for hours, watching the gentle pulse in his fontanel as though it was a measure of the moments of his life. Now she could barely see the soft spot, and somehow, it felt as if she'd missed something. "Mom, I'm sorry. It just came out."

"Don't apologize. I'm here now, all right?"

"Yes. All right. It's just . . . sometimes I'm so scared I'm going to screw up with him, and Mom, I love him so much."

"That's why you're so scared."

"Sometimes I think I should completely blow off school and be with Charlie."

"You could do that," Mom agreed. "Then again, you could try not to feel so guilty about wanting—needing—something that doesn't have anything to do directly with Charlie."

Oh, God. Why did that sound so . . . Momlike? And why did it make so much sense? "I can't help feeling guilty," Daisy said. "On the one hand, I want to be the best mother I can to Charlie. But on the other hand, that means making a better life for us both."

"I understand. And while I'm probably not the

highest authority on the subject, I can tell you that no one is able to do it all. You just have to do your best. To be the best person you can and to let Charlie see who you are. I wasn't perfect, Daisy. And I know you didn't always like what you saw in me. I left you for a job that sucked down a good sixty hours of my week. I wish I'd balanced things better. You didn't ask for my opinion, but I have one."

Daisy couldn't help smiling. "Yeah?"

"You get to have a life, Daisy. Don't let anyone tell you otherwise. I'm not saying the way I did it was perfect but somewhere in the middle, there's a balance between having your own life and being there for Charlie."

Daisy studied her for a few minutes without saying anything. "How come the older I get, the smarter you get?"

Mom smiled back. "We're both so very gifted."

Daisy hesitated. "I'm not even sure I'll be able to do the class after all. My daycare arrangement fell through." If her mom was here to stay, she might as well be brought into the loop, so Daisy explained about Irma. "I've got the rest of this week to figure something out. Dad and Nina said they'd watch him, but they're going to start getting really busy with the inn, what with Winter Carnival coming up, so I don't want to—"

"What am I, chopped liver?"

"Mom, I don't expect you to hire someone—"

"That's not what I'm suggesting. What I'm suggesting—from the bottom of my heart—is that I'll take care of him while you're at school."

"Mom, classes go through May."

"I'm planning to be around a lot longer than that."

This was completely out of the blue. "I didn't bring it up to get you to help."

"It's a sincere offer."

Despite her mom's words, Daisy felt a moment of distrust. "You just got here, Mom. Pretty soon you'll get bored and be ready to move on."

Mom looked down at her hands. "I deserved that."

"Mom—"

"Perhaps you could take two classes, back to back," Mom went on, looking incongruously excited. "I came here to be with you and Max and Charlie. So let me. Please."

Daisy frowned. In spite of her doubts, she got the feeling her mom really wanted to do this. To take care of Charlie regularly, week in and week out, so Daisy could pursue a dream. "Excuse me. Who are you, and what have you done with my mother?"

Sophie didn't know whether to feel insulted or amused by Daisy's shock at her proposition. Sophie felt certain she wanted to do this. She hadn't messed anything up with her grandson. Yet holding him, she felt a hint of apprehension. Her heart was as fragile and vulnerable as an object of blown glass, apt to be shattered by something as tiny as the doll-like fist curling itself around her finger. Could she really do this? Yes. She was determined to make good on her promise to Daisy, to support her daughter in this fundamental way, to be part of this family.

They drove to their first stop, a clothing shop called Zuzu's Petals. A sign in the window proclaimed, "Fun Fashions for the Whimsical Woman."

"Am I fun?" Sophie asked, eyeing a window display of drapey knits she could imagine a fortune-teller wearing.

Daisy said nothing. She didn't need to.

"How about whimsical?"

At that, Daisy laughed. "Not hardly. But you're fashionable and you look like you're freezing to death. Let's go."

Max and the baby went to wait at the nearby Sky River Bakery, an institution in the small town.

Sophie was not a shopping snob. However, because she used to be extremely busy, she'd grown accustomed to places that offered personalized service, like a few select establishments on Fifth Avenue in New York, or the Grand'Place in Brussels. When confronted with an entire shop full of boutique racks and rounders, she was a bit overwhelmed by all the choices.

The shopgirl offered some basic layers, including thermal underwear printed with little frogs wearing crowns and lipstick. And flannel pajamas printed with chickens who were not, thankfully, quite so anthropomorphic. Like it or not, Sophie was well on her way to becoming a flannel granny.

"I'm kind of drawn to solid colors," Sophie said to the girl.

Daisy grinned. "She means browns and blacks. Maybe the occasional charcoal-gray."

It was more fun than it should have been, sifting through the racks with her daughter, getting each other's opinion. Sophie caught herself wishing they had done more of this when Daisy was growing up. A girls' shopping day—wasn't that a rite of passage?

Stop it, she told herself. Regrets were a slow poison that had no antidote.

Daisy picked out a soft angora cardigan in powder-blue and held it up against Sophie. "Get this," she said. "It matches your eyes perfectly."

"It's too young for me."

"What do you mean, young? It's a sweater, Mom."

"This matches *your* eyes perfectly. I should get it for you."

"Mom—"

"Indulge me," Sophie said. "Come on, just try it." She pulled Daisy into the dressing room and made her put it on. The sweater was adorable on her, as Sophie had known it would be. And like all nursing mothers, Daisy looked incredibly womanly. Sophie wondered if boys ever called her daughter or if she felt like dating. She might ask, but not right away. Now that Sophie was here for good, there would be plenty of time to talk about such things. She insisted on getting the sweater for Daisy.

"It's beautiful, Mom, thanks. Now. What size jeans do you wear?"

"I don't know. I haven't bought jeans in forever."

"How could you not have jeans? That's just wrong. It's like not having breakfast in the morning."

"Fine, I'll get some jeans."

Daisy made her try on a few pairs, frowning in concentration as Sophie came out of the curtained changing area to model the selections.

"Well?" Sophie asked.

"You have a freakishly good figure for someone your age."

"I'm going to take that as a compliment," Sophie said. Could a remark with the words "for your age" tacked on ever truly be counted as a compliment? Sophie thought not, but she didn't let herself dwell on it. She and Daisy had been together a whole two hours and hadn't gotten into a spat yet.

She tried on a second pair. "These are too tight."

Daisy took a step back, subjected her to a frank once-over. "They're supposed to be formfitting," she said. "Just look at Jennifer Aniston."

"Jennifer who?"

"The actress. You're about the same age as she is. You're allowed to look sexy, Mom."

Good to know, thought Sophie, particularly given the way she had endured being snowed in.

"Is it the swimming?" Daisy asked.

The swimming. The very words caused Sophie's stomach to clench to the point of pain. Unexpectedly, the physical reaction came in a wave of nausea. Sophie ducked back into the dressing room as the shivers came over her. There was no way Daisy could know that this was one of her triggers—a memory of swimming. "Is *what* the swimming?" she asked sharply through the curtain of the dressing room.

"Jeez, take my head off, why don't you?" Daisy said. "I was just wondering if it's the swimming that keeps you in such good shape."

"Sorry. Yes, it was," Sophie said. She fought to quell the tightness in her chest. "I need to find a new sport." Although it seemed minor, swimming was another thing the terrorists had stolen from her. Swimming fast and far had been her sport ever since high school. After The Incident, she never wanted to go near the water again.

She glared at herself in the mirror, dabbed at the sweat that had broken out on her face. She'd been warned that certain prompts would be a trigger for her. She took a minute to shake off the memory and put on a smile. Within a short time, she had picked out cashmere sweaters in chocolate-brown, beige and deep heathered moss. Daisy insisted that Sophie needed a jacket called a fleece to wear under her ski parka.

"I don't have a ski parka."

"Not yet, you don't."

They went into an establishment a few doors down—the Sporthaus—and added mittens, a muffler, a parka, snow boots and a hat to her wardrobe.

"That was fun," Sophie said, stepping onto the sidewalk, laden with parcels, already wearing the new jacket and boots. "Thanks for the fashion advice, Daisy."

"You're welcome."

They loaded the parcels into the trunk. As they walked along the sidewalk, Sophie took a good look around. It was her first serious look at the place she had chosen to live. Avalon was a classic old-fashioned small town, with the main square formed by buildings of red brick and figured stone, a municipal park in the middle, tree-lined streets radiating outward and a quaint train station. Twilight was coming on, the sinking light painting the snow on the rooftops a deep, mysterious indigo. The shop fronts glowed with golden light. In addition to Zuzu's and the Sporthaus, there was a Christian Science reading room, an old-fashioned drugstore and soda fountain, a jewelry shop and toy store, and a five-and-dime. Above the Camelot Bookstore was an office with a name painted on the window behind horizontal blinds. M. L. Parkington, Attorney-at-Law.

Spotting the sign, Sophie felt a small thrum of possibility. Eventually, she was going to have to make a living. Her parents, when she called them in Seattle to explain her big move, had warned her that she would find small-town life horribly oppressive and stifling. They said she would smother beneath provincial attitudes and mundane details of small people living out their small, unimportant lives.

And fool that she was, Sophie had allowed doubts to creep in.

Now, looking around at the picture-book scenery, she regained a sense that this was the right thing to do. Avalon represented something she'd never had before—a hometown. And with that thought came a flood of doubts.

What in the world am I getting myself into?

She put on a bright smile as she and Daisy went into the bakery. It was warm and bright inside, the air rich with heady fragrance. The Sky River Bakery was a community hub, where people could sit down over a cup of coffee and read the paper, pick up a loaf of bread or a berry pie for dessert and probably run into a friend in the process. When Daisy had first moved to Avalon, she had an after-school job here. Some of her best prints—framed photos she had taken around the area—were on display, beautifully lit like the works of art they were and marked for sale. There were a few customers at the small round café tables by the window, and a woman picking out pastries from the curved front glass case.

Charlie was, predictably, the center of attention, being held by Laura Tuttle, the manager of the bakery, and admired by Philip Bellamy—Greg's brother. *Get a grip,* Sophie warned herself. *You knew this was a town of Bellamys. Get used to it.*

The eldest of the four Bellamy siblings, Philip was about a dozen years older than Greg. They shared the same clean-cut good looks, though. The same air of easy confidence.

Spying her, Philip stood up. "Sophie," he said with

just the right touch of friendliness. "It's good to see you."

Probably not, she conceded as they embraced oh so briefly, then stepped away from each other quickly, before awkwardness could set in.

"You remember Laura Tuttle," Philip said. "Bakery manager and first-class baby-holder."

Laura had a smile that eclipsed her unflattering haircut and dowdy outfit. "I was just admiring this incredible baby," Laura said.

It was exactly the right thing to say. Since Charlie had been born, Sophie had discovered a universal truth: A woman was a fool for her grandchild, every time. All someone had to do to fall into her good graces was compliment her grandchild, and Sophie considered that person a friend for life.

She went to order a cup of tea, and was startled to find Philip at her side. "You're all right," he said. "Right?"

"I am," she assured him. "I promise."

He grinned. "Why do I get the idea I'm the eighty-ninth person today to ask you that?"

The counter girl served the tea in a small white china pot. Sophie carefully measured a level teaspoon of sugar into her cup. "You're not. I'm just not used to—" She stopped. Not used to what? People caring what happened to her? That was simply pathetic. "I'm fine," she stated. "I've got a place at the lake, and I'll be looking for a permanent home soon."

"So you'll be practicing law?" he asked.

"Why, do you need a lawyer?"

To her surprise, he nodded. "No rush, but as you know, my circumstances have changed in the past couple of years."

A slight understatement there. Practically out of the blue, he had discovered the existence of a grown daughter—Jenny Majesky, the bakery owner. Unbeknownst to Philip, his former girlfriend, Mariska, had had his baby, never telling him.

She lowered her voice. "Is everything all right?"

"Oh, yeah. But both my daughters—Olivia and Jenny—are newlyweds now. And I'm about to become a member of that club myself."

She whipped a glance at Laura Tuttle. "Philip!"

He was grinning from ear to ear. "I'll call you, okay?"

She studied Laura more closely. She was about Philip's age, the sort of woman with a warm heart, a soft body and a ready smile who seemed completely comfortable in her skin. Sophie sipped her tea, wondering if she would ever feel that way about herself. She stood back and watched her son and daughter talking animatedly to their uncle and, apparently, to their aunt-to-be. This community seemed so tightly woven together that Sophie wondered if there was room for her to squeeze in.

She finished her tea and pulled on her new parka. "We should get going."

Max was leaning against the counter, devouring a frosted butterhorn.

"It'll spoil your dinner," she warned.
"Not even close," he assured her.

They went to the Apple Tree Inn for dinner. It was in a converted Victorian mansion by the river. At this time of year, the Schuyler River was almost completely frozen. The boulders and stones in the streambed were layered in a thick coating of ice, and there was a miserly trickle down the middle.

"Ms. Bellamy, welcome back," said the host, an elegant man named Miles, whom she remembered from past visits.

"Thank you," Sophie said, and then with a glow of pride showed off the baby. "This is my grandson Charlie, the newest Bellamy. I don't believe you've met him yet."

Miles had the usual startled reaction to the news that Sophie was a grandmother, gratifying as it was. And of course, he took one look at Charlie and was lost. "What a handsome little fellow. Congratulations."

"Thanks," Daisy said.

As they were shown to their table, Sophie spied someone out of the corner of her eye, a swift impression of a broad-shouldered form, thick dark hair, a ridiculously handsome face. *Noah Shepherd.* She did a double take, and froze in her tracks. It was indeed Noah, and he was smiling across a candlelit table at Tina Calloway, the girl with a wrecking ball of a crush on him. The girl who was barely old enough to be drinking that glass of white wine with him.

"Mom, is something wrong?" Daisy asked.

Let me count the ways, thought Sophie. She wanted to melt into the floor like the snow off her newly purchased boots. Even though she and Noah were nothing to each other, nothing but a couple of nights of amazing sex, she felt a sickening blow of disappointment. Like a fool, she'd let herself hope and believe in him. That he might be different. That he might not hurt her. That he might actually be someone trustworthy.

Then she reproached herself. This guy was a stranger; she'd stupidly fallen into bed with him, but that didn't mean it was the start of something.

Clearing her throat, she put on a good face for the kids. "I just spotted my neighbors at the lake." The place was too small to pretend she hadn't seen him. Might as well get it over with. "I'll introduce you." The strangeness of the situation did not escape her. She was about to introduce her children to . . . what was Noah to her? She hadn't even worked it out in her mind. They had made love, but that didn't mean she had to call him her lover, did it? They had only just met, so "friends" didn't work, either. What was amazing was that Noah Shepherd had become so many things to her in such a short time—rescuer, healer, neighbor, friend, lover . . . and now, apparently, liar.

Allowing none of this to show on her face, she introduced him to Max, Daisy and Charlie. "My neighbors at the lake," she stated, trying to appear as neutral as Switzerland.

"Your baby is so cute," Tina said to Daisy.

"I hope he stays quiet during dinner," Daisy said. "He's pretty sleepy. He might nap."

"If you need someone to watch him, I'm available," Tina volunteered. "I adore babies. I was just telling that to Noah."

Noah seemed distinctly uncomfortable as he stood and shook hands with Daisy and Max. In a way, he seemed as awkward and boyish as Max. Well, it *was* awkward, bumping into someone you'd just slept with when you were out with someone else.

"Our table's ready," Sophie said.

As they took a seat, Daisy parked the baby carrier on a window seat by their table, getting Charlie settled with a blanket and pacifier. Watching her brisk, loving gestures, Sophie wondered, where had she gotten that? Where had Daisy learned to be a mother?

Max was chattering away about Tina. "Her dad is Sockeye Calloway, you know, from the U.S. hockey team that won the gold medal a long time ago?"

Sophie did know. Noah had told her. What he'd neglected to tell her was that he was dating the Olympian's daughter. She tried to listen to Max, but she was distracted. It wasn't every day you had to introduce your children to a man you'd slept with.

More than once.

The kind of "sleeping with" that involved very little sleeping.

And to be honest, she thought, that wasn't even the

worst. The worst was that he was out to dinner with Tina Calloway, mere hours after sharing a bed with Sophie.

Sophie refused to be upset by what she'd seen at the restaurant tonight. Noah was just a guy, she thought. A guy who'd pulled her out of a ditch, stitched up her wound, brought her firewood. And all right, a guy with whom she'd had multiorgasmic sex. This was what you got for hooking up. For failing to look before you leaped.

Fine, she thought. *We're better off as neighbors.* She was here to focus on her family, anyway. And in that respect, the evening had gone well. Her children seemed excited to have her living so close to them. Charlie was a gift—no, a blessing—and she looked forward to watching him grow, to being part of his life.

It was enough, she told herself. After what she'd survived, her children and grandson were enough. Eventually, she would make friends here in Avalon. She'd make a life here. The interlude with Noah Shepherd would simply fade away.

She'd make certain of that. Picking up her phone, she checked the time and then scrolled to Brooks Fordham's number in New York.

"I hope it's not too late to call," she said.

"Absolutely not. I'm dying to see you, Sophie. We've got a lot to talk about."

"We do. But mostly, I want to see for myself how you're doing."

"I can take the train up any day you like," he said. "Name it."

"Let's get through this patch of bad weather." She paced as she spoke with him, flinched at one point at the sound of his voice. It wasn't him specifically, but memories darting in and out of her consciousness. It had started out such a special night, punctuated by rare snowfall as if to underscore the magic. The terror and violence that followed had imprinted themselves on her.

"All right," he said. "But in the interest of full disclosure, I have an ulterior motive. I'm doing a piece about what happened for the *New Yorker*, and I hope to expand it into a book."

Sophie was silent for a moment. He was a writer. It was what he did. Then she said, "I'll help you in any way I can, Brooks."

Fifteen

"Man, that's some nasty-ass shit," Bo Crutcher remarked helpfully as Noah wheeled a teetering barrow of horse manure past him in the barn.

"Yeah, thanks for pointing that out," Noah said over his shoulder. "I mean, otherwise I might not have noticed." He maneuvered the wheelbarrow down the ramp, out of the barn and along a much-traveled path to the heap at the edge of the paddock. In the cold air, the manure pile steamed like a geyser.

Bo stood watching from the doorway of the barn. He was clad like Nanook of the North in a down jacket, snow boots, insulated gloves and a plaid hat with earflaps that, amazingly, did not look dorky on him. Having grown up in the muggy climes of the Texas Gulf Coast, he made no secret of his unabashed horror for the cold and snow. As the star pitcher of Avalon's professional baseball team, he spent most winters on the beaches of Texas, working in the oil fields and partying like a just-released convict until his agent made him go to spring training.

This winter was different, though. Prior to spring training in Florida, he'd decided to spend some time in Avalon because, he'd explained, he needed to put some distance between himself and his ex-girlfriend. One of his exes. Crutcher had a lot of exes.

He blew a plume of smoke into the air from the skinny cigar he was smoking.

"Now that," Noah remarked, "is nasty."

Bo took a slender flat box out of his pocket. "Want one?"

"Right. I've always had a death wish."

"I don't inhale."

"Then you'll still be alive to see your mouth rot."

"Don't start sounding like my mother," Bo said, leaning back against the wall, his foot propped like the Marlboro man. "Not that I have a mother. And I only smoke in the off-season, anyway."

"Oh, that's right. Then you turn into a health nut and switch to chewing tobacco."

"Dip. It's called dip. As in dipshit."

"I'll remember that." Noah studied his friend. They had met three years ago after Bo had just signed on with the Hornets, a professional independent baseball team in the Can-Am League. Not long afterward, Bo joined Noah's garage band as bass player.

"Seriously, man," Bo said, standing well out of the way as Noah hosed down the barrow and the sloping concrete floor of the barn, "don't you have someone to do this shit for you?"

"Sometimes," said Noah. "Girl down the road, name of Chelsea, helps out in the clinic three days a week, but horse manure is kind of an everyday event."

"Wonder why," Bo muttered, pushing away from the wall.

"It's not so bad," Noah pointed out. "Back when my family had the dairy, I was dealing with cow manure, which was a lot nastier and there was a lot more of it." With practiced routine, he scooped feed from the bin, filling four pails.

"Take the bucket to that one, will you?" He handed Bo a galvanized pail of feed deeply scented with molasses.

Grumbling, Bo went to tend to the big roan quarter horse. Friendly as a Labrador retriever, it sidled right up to him. "Jesus, he's stampeding me," Bo said, nearly spilling the bucket as he plastered himself against the side of the stall.

"Nah, he's just glad to see you," Noah called, feeding Alice in the next stall. "Relax, buddy. I thought guys from Texas were all cowboys who liked horses."

"That's what everybody who's not from Texas thinks. Closest I ever got to a horse growing up was watching old *Bonanza* reruns on a TV I stole."

"Hang on a second while I take out my violin." Noah pantomimed drawing a bow dramatically across the strings.

"I'm just saying." Bo finished emptying his bucket and moved back as the horse went to the trough.

Noah knew Bo hated pity. He would rather be made fun of than pitied for the way he'd grown up, raised by his older brother. The Crutcher boys had lived in a trailer park in East Houston, with a yard that backed up to a ship channel so polluted with petroleum products that it regularly caught on fire.

"Anyway," Bo continued, "you're the one shoveling stalls while I'm fixing to head down to Florida to work on my tan."

Noah reeled in the hose and put up the equipment. "Okay, we're done here."

"Finally," Bo said. "Remind me next time to drop by after chores, not before."

"You sure complain a lot," Noah said as they crossed the compound, the twilight throwing long shadows across the snow-covered yard.

"I do, don't I, Tom Sawyer?" Sometimes Bo called him Tom Sawyer, because he was convinced that Noah's idyllic small-town boyhood was the kind of thing that only happened in fiction. Bo himself was more of a Huck Finn, unattached and rambling wherever he pleased. Self-educated, Bo had read more books than anyone Noah had ever met, and loved to sprinkle his conversation with both literary references and obscenities. "I reckon," he went on, "it's because I haven't been laid in a while. Tends to get a guy down, feeling sorry for himself. I reckon you know that."

Noah didn't say anything, which was a mistake. Even after slamming a couple of beers, Crutcher had a sensitive radar for that kind of thing.

"Son of a bitch," he said, slugging Noah on the shoulder. "You got yourself laid—finally."

Noah kept walking.

"Who is it?" Bo demanded. "Out with it. Come on. I just froze my nuts off keeping you company in the barn. Practically got stepped on by a horse. You owe me, man."

Noah found himself curiously reluctant to talk about Sophie Bellamy. At the same time, the thing that had happened with her was so . . . unexpected. And intense, like nothing else he'd ever experienced.

Crutcher, despite his flaws, was a good listener, so Noah slowed his step and said, "It was kind of a . . . spontaneous thing. Nobody you know."

And as far as he knew, it was over. When he stopped by Sophie's place, she was either gone or claiming to be busy. Just the other morning, he had dropped in to bring her more firewood and brought up the topic of Tina, telling Sophie that what she'd seen at the Apple Tree Inn wasn't a date. She had brushed off the explanation, telling him he didn't owe her one. To top it all off, some guy had shown up from the city, a visitor from her past, as far as Noah could tell. He'd seen them having coffee in the bookstore, and just seeing them made him feel like a complete stalker, so he'd been forcing himself to mind his own business.

It wasn't working. He couldn't stop thinking about her.

Bo regarded Noah with deep concentration. "Well, this is serious, then. I can tell by how quiet you are."

"I just said it was—"

"You seriously like this girl," Bo said with a laugh. "Come on, bud. Spill."

"There's nothing to spill." Yeah, sure. Noah took the path that forked downhill and to the right. "I need to finish up a couple of things in the clinic. Come on, you can give me a hand."

"So long as it's nothing gross."

Noah shouldered open the back door of the clinic. He currently had several patients staying over, dogs and cats crated in a darkened room with slow jazz playing on a radio.

"Now this is more like it," Bo remarked, carefully removing Samson the miniature dachshund from his cage. "But how the hell did a wiener dog break its leg?"

"It's not a fracture. Dew claw injury."

"I didn't forget that you got laid and haven't told me

about it," Bo reminded him. "Come on, man, give me something."

"I got nothing." Noah checked the chart of Mr. Tibbs, a big yellow Persian with a hernia.

"Then make something up. Or else I'll start a rumor about you and . . . let's see . . . Didn't you go out with Nina Romano last summer?"

One humiliatingly boring night, Noah recalled. In the aftermath of Noah's breakup with Daphne, he'd asked Nina out. She'd practically fallen asleep on the ride home. "Don't be a turd," he said to Crutcher. "Okay, it's someone I just met. It's still new and probably won't amount to anything." As he spoke, it struck him that he was hoping for more from Sophie Bellamy. But she was skittish as hell in a way he couldn't quite put his finger on. And now, Noah had a secret from her, too. He couldn't very well explain the real reason for the not-really-a-date with Tina Calloway, not if he wanted to respect Tina's privacy. Of course, she hadn't sworn him to secrecy. In fact, she'd asked him if he knew of any other "potential candidates."

Bo opened the fridge, scrutinizing the contents. "Got any more beers in here?"

"That fridge is for medicine. And don't even think about the horse tranquilizer."

Bo held the tiny dachshund in his big hands, looking like King Kong. "I'm only allowed to drink beer in the off-season," he pointed out. "I like to get a nice slow, enjoyable buzz, not knock myself out."

"You end up the same anyway," Noah pointed out.

"Okay, now you're starting to piss me off. Not only do you refuse to tell me anything about the momentous occasion of the end of your celibacy, you start ragging on me about my drinking."

"Tough job, but someone's got to do it."

Bo put the dachshund back and studied Duchess, a shih tzu with a chip on her shoulder. As he peered through the mesh of her crate, she rolled back her lips and showed her tiny, sharp teeth. "So is she a local girl or—"

"Jeez, enough already." Noah decided a diversionary tactic was in order. Sure, he had gotten laid, but that wasn't the only interesting thing that had happened to him. From a gossip standpoint, anyway. "This is strictly confidential but I've got to tell somebody."

"My lips are sealed," Bo promised.

"You know who Tina Calloway is?"

Bo gave a low whistle. "Are you kidding me? *She's* your new girlfriend? Of course I know who she is. Her old man and I are drinking buddies. Damn, Noah. Way to go. She's unbelievable. Is she legal age?"

"Screw you, Crutcher." Noah was already regretting his decision to confide in his friend.

"I thought she liked girls," said Bo.

"She did," Noah said. "Does."

"Son of a bitch. You mean she wanted a threesome—"

"I like the way your mind works, but that's not it." Noah was still a little shell shocked from Tina's request. "Okay, so she invited me to dinner at the Apple Tree Inn." Everyone in town knew what that represented. Candlelight, soft music. Seduction—that was generally the purpose of a date at a place like the Apple Tree. "So I figured she wanted something."

"A three-way. Son of a bitch."

Noah should his head. "Not that. I told you."

"Then what?"

Noah put aside the IV tubing. "Remember, not a word of this to anyone."

"I told you, man. We're in the confessional. Hell, what'd she do, propose?"

"Yeah, but not marriage. She and her partner want to have a baby."

Bo gave another whistle, this one loud enough to make the dogs yap at him. "You have got to be shittin' me."

Noah said nothing. The moment Tina made her request had been completely and utterly surreal for him. Even the memory of it felt surreal. It was a crazy, cosmic joke, even a cruel one, although Tina couldn't know that. One woman had left him because she didn't want kids. And here was another who wanted the kids, but not him.

"I swear, if it had been anyone but Tina, I would've started looking around for hidden cameras," Noah admitted. "It felt like either a joke or some social experiment."

Bo gave a laugh, shaking his head. "You the man," he said, then clapped Noah on the back. "You the man."

"Come on."

"I assume she wasn't proposing artificial insemination."

Tina had blushed furiously when she'd come to that part of her proposal. She and Paulette didn't have the money for artificial insemination.

When Noah didn't answer, Bo ripped off his hat and clutched at his hair with both fists. "Damn. *Damn.* Some guys get all the luck."

At that, Noah had to smile. "You don't think I agreed to do it."

"You turned her *down?* She's a goddess, man. A freaking goddess." Bo shook his head. "Of course you turned her down, you dumbass."

"The crazy thing wasn't that she asked me," Noah confessed. "The crazy thing was that I actually considered her proposal—just for a minute. Ultimately, though, I couldn't do it, couldn't hand over my DNA like that, no strings attached. I knew a few guys who earned tuition money in vet school by donating sperm samples, but I wasn't one of them." He shook his head. "So there you have it. I finally found a girl who wants to have my baby, but not with me." He hadn't thought of Daphne in a long time, but he did now. "What's up with all these women wanting to be childless, huh? Who are these women? Do they not have clocks? Are they not ticking? I thought women were supposed to be all worried about their biological clocks."

"You're serious. You really wouldn't do it?" Bo asked.

"Would you?"

"You know the answer to that. What's the expression? 'In a New York minute.' And you're an idiot."

"Maybe. Hell, I do want kids," Noah admitted. "But I need to work on getting a date, first. A relationship."

"That's sad for you, buddy. You deserve better."

"Yeah, but do people always get what they deserve?"

"You never know. I mean, look at you, Eagle Scout, member of the chamber of commerce, pillar of the community. You deserve nubile slaves peeling your grapes for you. They should legalize polygamy for guys like you, so there can be more of you walking around. And then look at me. Beer drinking, cigar smoking, never saw the point of doing an honest day's work. Lousy prospect for love and fatherhood. And I got . . ." His voice trailed off.

Noah watched a curious expression cross his friend's face. All right, so this was new. "You've got . . ." he prompted.

Bo looked off into the distance. "I got a kid in Texas."

"Holy crap. You never told me that."

Crutcher twirled the empty beer bottle between his hands. "Yeah, you did the right thing. Trust me, you don't want some woman having your kid unless you plan on sticking around to be the daddy."

This was news to Noah. "Boy or girl?" he asked.

"Boy. I've never seen him. Not once, not even a picture. His mother likes the color of my money, but she flat out refuses to let me meet him."

Few people would recognize the pain in Bo's voice. Noah did, though. Outwardly, Bo projected a devil-may-care image, but Noah knew him better than that.

"I'm sorry," Noah said.

Bo was quiet for a moment. "You're making a good call, even if it means turning down a goddess."

Noah and Tina had ended the evening on good terms. She had been braced for his refusal. Then, to cap off his very strange dinner conversation, he'd encountered Sophie Bellamy. He'd been hugely distracted by her arrival, with her kids in tow. Sophie Bellamy, Noah thought, *there* was a goddess.

"Now I'm depressed," Bo said. "I thought you got lucky."

Noah glanced away, but not quickly enough.

"You did, you son of a bitch. Come on, spill. Who is it?"

Busted. "No one you know," he hedged. "She's new around here." Because he knew Bo was relentless, he told him about Sophie Bellamy.

Bo regarded him knowingly. "She's special. I can tell."

"Then you know more about the situation than I do. We just met, okay? There might be . . . complications."

"Yeah? Like what? She married?"

"No. Jesus, Crutcher. She might be . . . older than me. I don't think she realizes that. I'm trying to figure out how to explain it to her without running her off."

"Just tell her. No big deal."

"She might not see it that way." Noah wasn't sure why he felt that way, but he was pretty sure she wouldn't like it, not one bit.

"If she finds out you're keeping it from her, you're fucked, if you'll pardon my French."

"That wasn't French."

"And here I thought I was bilingual." He held up his now-empty bottle. "I need another beer."

"I'll be finished here in a minute, and we can go over to the house." In the front of the clinic, a bell rang. Immediately, the dogs sounded off. Noah went to see who it was. Someone who couldn't read the Closed sign, obviously.

"Hey, Sophie," he said, his irritation washed away in a rush of gladness.

"Hello, Noah. I—" She broke off, focusing on something behind him.

"Ma'am, I'm Bo Crutcher." Bo crossed the room, arm extended, his trademark star-pitcher smile on his face. "I'm a buddy of Noah's."

"How do you do. Sophie Bellamy." She looked a little flustered. And even though it was probably impossible, she was ten times hotter than she'd been the last time he saw her, in the restaurant. She wore jeans and a sweater and ski parka with the zipper open, and her cheeks were bright red from the cold. "Sorry, Noah," she said. "I didn't realize you were busy."

"I'm not busy," said Noah.

"He's not busy," said Bo. They both spoke at the same time.

"Seriously, what can I do for you?" Noah shot a glare at Bo. He'd better not say a word about what Noah had just told him.

"The stitches," she said. "You know, the ones in my knee."

"Is everything all right?" Noah's stomach clenched. Damn. Had he blown it? Was there an infection? Was she going to sue his ass into the poorhouse?

"Fine," she said quickly. "In fact, the physician I saw for a follow-up said you did excellent work."

"You?" Bo jabbed him in the rib cage. "No way."

She favored him with a smile. "I hurt myself the night of the snowstorm, and Noah sewed me up."

"That Noah," Bo said. "Ya gotta love him."

"Anyway," she said, turning back to Noah, "the doctor told me they would be ready to come out today, but her assistant still can't get to the clinic because of the snow. So I tried doing it myself."

Noah felt his mouth twitch. "Bad idea."

"I found that out. I'm not quite as hardy as I thought, but I really need the use of my knee back. I was hoping maybe you could do it. That is, if you wouldn't mind . . ."

Mind? *Mind?*

She was blushing as she looked from him to Bo. "I'm sorry, asking you this after everything you've done," she said, full of apologies.

"I don't mind a bit," he said quickly.

"I feel a little sheepish, coming here . . ."

Noah made the mistake of looking at Bo. *Sheepish.*

Had she really said sheepish to a vet? Yes, she had. And Noah and Bo were twelve years old again. Noah could barely suppress a snicker.

"Ma'am," Bo said, all but helpless with laughter, "you came to the right place."

Sophie pressed her lips together, then gave in to a smile. "Let's get to it, then, shall we?" She paused in the clinic doorway.

"I don't mind if you come along," she said to Bo. "Maybe you could distract me."

"Ma'am, I'd be honored." He followed her like a gangly-limbed coon hound. He elbowed Noah. "You're a man of many talents. Fertility god, emergency tech, veterinarian."

Sophie frowned. "Fertility god?"

"His idea of a joke," Noah said. Hoping to create a diversion, he held the door to the exam room. "Right this way." He shot Bo a murderous look.

Sophie stepped into the room. "Where do you want me?"

He flashed on a memory of her beneath him, her small, delicate hands clutching the spooled wooden bed rails as she arched her body toward him.

"Noah?" She regarded him quizzically.

"Oh, right here will be fine." He indicated a vinyl chair by the exam table and flipped on a light. Then he rolled back his sleeves and took out a sterile pair of disposable gloves.

She had a seat and drew up the cuff of her jeans.

Bo watched with his mouth agape. Noah handed

him a stainless steel tray. "Hold that, will you?"

"Um . . . yeah, got it."

Noah had a seat on a rolling stool and put on his headgear with the light and the magnifying glasses. Using long-handled tweezers, he removed the dressing. He adjusted the light. "Hold still," he said. "This won't hurt, but you might feel a little pull." With his smallest pointed scissors and tweezers, he gently teased each suture free, pleased to see that the wound had healed decisively.

"So you're new around here," Bo said, as though approaching her in a singles' bar.

Noah concentrated, thinking maybe the chitchat would distract her.

"That's right," she said.

"Where are you from?"

"Lots of places. Most recently, the Netherlands. I used to work as a lawyer in The Hague, at the International Criminal Court."

Bo gave a low whistle. "Never heard of it, but it sounds mighty important." Only Bo Crutcher could make ignorance seem charming. Noah, on the other hand, felt provincial around her. She'd been all over the world, while he'd barely been out of Ulster County. He'd damn well better keep her entertained. Maybe she was already bored with him. Witness the guy he'd spotted her with in the bookstore.

"Looks good," Noah said, trying to banish his doubts as he finished up. "You're a quick healer."

She smiled at him. "So I've been told. Thank you,

Noah." She looked a bit self-conscious. He grabbed Bo by the arm and hauled him out of the room, giving Sophie privacy to readjust her jeans and put her boots back on.

Outside the exam room, Bo looked as though he was about to burst. "Man, is *that* the one—"

"All set," Sophie said, joining them in the reception area. "I'll just be on my way now—"

"Hold on, ma'am," Bo said in his best Texas drawl. "As Dr. Shepherd's last patient of the day, you get a bonus treat."

"He offered me a hairball remedy last time," she said, straight-faced as she flexed her knee. "I'll have to pass. Now that the stitches are out, I need to break in my new ice skates. My son's going to be with me this weekend and I'm sure I'm rusty."

"Not by yourself, you're not," Noah said. "I'll go with you."

She shook her head. "I couldn't ask that." She glanced at Bo. "And you've got company."

"Bo can come, too," Noah said, confident of his friend's reaction.

Bo didn't disappoint him. "Me? Ice skating? Yeah, I'd rather have a root canal. You two go on ahead. I'll go up to the house, make sure the beers are cold."

A few minutes later, they were alone on the lake. The late-afternoon light rendered the landscape in pink and gray, and the heavy coat of snowfall muffled the sound of their voices. Noah was not surprised to see that she was a fairly good skater, moving with unhurried, fluid grace. Noah had always thought there was something sexy about a woman on ice skates. Of course, he'd probably think Sophie was sexy on barrel slats.

"How's the knee?" he asked her.

"Feels good as new."

They glided along, side by side. "You're not rusty," he assured her.

"You sound disappointed."

"I was kind of hoping you'd need to lean on me more," he admitted. "I like holding you, Sophie."

"Uh-huh." Her tone was heavy with skepticism.

"Seriously, I want to talk to you about the other night."

She branched off from him, gliding away. "We don't need to discuss it. As I said, you don't owe me an explanation."

He grabbed her hand before she got too far. "Not that way. Thin ice." He kept hold of her hand. "It probably looked like a date, and I don't want you thinking it was."

"Noah, you don't owe me an explanation."

"Maybe not, but it bugs the crap out of me that you might think I'd go out with someone else after you and I had been together." He tried to imagine how weird it would sound if he explained what Tina really wanted.

Sophie wobbled a little, giving him a chance to slide

his arm around her. "I've got you," he said. "And you don't owe me an explanation, either."

She stiffened. "An explanation of what?"

"The guy in the bookstore. And no, I wasn't spying on you. I was picking up my mail at the post office, which is next to the bookstore."

"That was Brooks Fordham," she said. "He's a writer, and he lives in New York. And no, I don't owe you an explanation."

"But I'd listen, if you felt like explaining it," Noah said.

She laughed. "You're not going to give up on this, are you?"

He matched her rhythm so they were skating in tandem. "I'm just getting started." But the doubts crept in again. A writer from the city. Noah wondered if his world could ever be big enough or exciting enough for her.

"Look at the two lovebirds," Bo shouted from the lakeshore. "You're going to freeze your asses off. Come on in for a beer," he called.

"Good idea," Noah seconded. He still needed to figure out a way to tell her about Tina. "How about it?"

She hesitated.

"We can raise a toast to no more misunderstandings," he said.

Her hesitation eased into a smile. "I'll drink to that." She left her skates on the porch of the cottage, and the three of them hiked up to Noah's. At the house, Opal leaped into paroxysms of ecstasy when she recognized

Sophie. "I'm not used to having anyone act so delighted to see me," Sophie said.

In all honesty, the puppy was merely expressing the same feelings Noah had—total exuberance at seeing Sophie again. "Didn't you know?" he asked. "It's the reason we have puppies."

Bo took three Utica Clubs from the fridge and passed them around. "Ever had a Car Bomb?" Bo asked her.

Noah grimaced, "Come on, Crutcher—"

"I'm not a fan of car bombs," Sophie said. Her face paled visibly.

Noah didn't think Bo noticed but he sure as hell did. She had been living overseas. Maybe in a place where car bombs were no joke.

"I mean the kind made with beer and tequila. Come here, I'll show you." Bo paused to grab a bag of chips and a jar of salsa, two staples that could always be found in Noah's kitchen.

Everywhere Bo Crutcher went, a party ensued. It was a gift. His personality was as big as his potential as a baseball star, so when he opened up a bottle of tequila and dropped shots into their glasses of beer, Noah and Sophie drank up as obediently as children ordered to finish their milk.

"This is completely disgusting," Sophie declared, dabbing at her mouth with a napkin.

"I've been told worse." Bo poured a second round. "Trust me, it gets better."

"Cheers." Taking himself back to the days of Alpha Zeta at Cornell, Noah knocked back his refill.

"Cheers," echoed Sophie. *"Salut, proost, amandla."*

"Whoa, did you hear that?" Bo regarded her with awe. "She knows French."

"I recognized Dutch and . . ."

"Umojan," she said. "It's an African dialect." Sophie dispatched her drink with impressive panache, then emitted a lengthy belch.

Bo clutched at his chest. "Be still my heart."

Concentrating on not spilling, Noah set them up again. "Yeah, take a number, buddy."

Sophie burst out laughing. "You guys are better than my shrink."

"You have a shrink?" asked Bo.

She laughed again. "You don't?"

"I don't." Noah held up the bottle of Patrón. "Unless you count this."

"I've never met anyone who didn't have a shrink."

"Even I've got one," Bo said. "Lately. My agent's making me see somebody. He wants to be sure I got my head on straight before the new season."

"I've never known a baseball star before," Sophie said.

"Oh, I'm a treat," Bo said, refilling her glass and then Noah's. "No bout adoubt it. Or whatever."

"Drinking away my problems," she mused. "What a concept. Look, she's sound asleep," she added, indicating the puppy in her lap. "I feel such a sense of accomplishment."

"You mean you've never tried drinking away your problems?" asked Noah.

"You mean you have problems?" asked Bo. "You sure as hell don't look as if you've got problems."

She hiccuped, and gave him a little smile. "You have no idea." Despite her words, she spoke pleasantly, and turned the dazzling wattage of her smile on Noah. They clinked bottles.

"To your hidden talents," Sophie said. "And we'll add skating coach to the list, along with cosmetic surgery. My knee is going to be just fine."

"Cosmetic surgery," echoed Bo. "That's where the money is."

"Yeah, sure."

"Lots of women eventually go for a brow lift," Sophie said.

"Your brows are perfect," Noah told her. "Don't ever let anyone mess with your brows."

"That's sweet," she said. "But sooner or later, we all need a little help."

She was an amazing contrast of brains, self-confidence and insecurity. He found it incredibly attractive. But challenging.

"And stud service," Bo added. "Don't forget that. Dr. Noah Shepherd—Veterinary Medicine, Cosmetic Surgery, Emergency Medicine and Stud Service."

"Shut up." Noah glowered at him. Belatedly, he realized he shouldn't have said to shut up. It only egged Bo on.

"I don't get it," Sophie said. "Stud service? Are you breeding something?"

Bo slapped his thigh and guffawed. "Didn't he tell you?"

"That's enough," Noah said. "You turd, you said your lips were sealed."

Crutcher ignored him. "They were, but then I drank more beer." He turned back to Sophie. "Sockeye Calloway's daughter wants to have his baby."

Sophie didn't need a surgeon to give her an eyebrow lift. She did a great job on her own. "Good heavens."

"I swear, I'm not making this up," Bo said. "Tina and her partner, Paulette—they're a couple." He shrugged in bafflement. "Don't ask me why. That's just the way they roll."

"I see." Sophie took a prim sip of her beer.

"Yeah, it's a crying shame, if you ask me." Bo shook his head tragically, his lion's mane of hair shimmering with the movement.

"Nobody asked you," Noah said, but he knew it was already too late. The cat was out of the bag and would not be going back in any time soon. *I'm an idiot,* Noah thought. Stone-cold sober, Bo would take a secret to the grave. However, with a few beers in him, all bets were off.

"So you're saying these women want to have a baby together?" Sophie asked Bo.

"Yep."

"And they want Noah to . . ."

"Yep."

Sophie gazed at him with eyebrows raised sky-high.

He was quick to say, "Not going to happen, of course. Nothing against Tina and Paulette. I just . . . when I have kids, I want a little more involvement."

"It's amazing, the lengths some women will go to in order to be a mother," Sophie said, then turned to Bo. "I have two children and a grandson."

"Wait a second." Bo blinked like an idiot. "Two kids and a grand—what?"

"A grandson."

Bo gave one of his low whistles.

Noah sent him a look that promised dismemberment. If Bo mentioned the age difference now, he was dead meat. Fortunately for Bo he merely lifted his glass in a toast.

It *was* kind of mind-blowing, the idea of her being a grandmother. On some level, her situation appealed to Noah. She was at a place in her life that, to him, seemed like a distant, nearly unreachable future. Now he could look at Sophie and see the future as something real and possible. Although divorced and alone, she was the connective tissue in a family, whether she realized it or not.

She took another drink. "My kids and grandson are the whole reason I'm here. For the first time in my life, I'm going to be a full-time, stay-at-home mom. This is a second chance for me, and I'm going to be the best mom ever. I'm going to make the mom Hall of Fame. I'm going to be such a good mom, I'll be scary."

"The Mominatrix." Noah clinked glasses with her.

"I swear, I'm going to be supermom and supergrandma all rolled into one."

Bo took a thoughtful sip of his beer. "Yeah. Well, good luck with that."

Sixteen

On her first day of classes, Daisy kept feeling as though something vital was missing. And it was, of course. Charlie, and all that he entailed. Since the moment he was born, she hadn't even drawn a breath without taking him into account: Charlie. His diaper bag. His binky. His favorite cuddly toy. Teething gel, diaper cream, baby wipes, change of clothes. Was he awake or asleep? Hungry? Content? Crying? Doing something that made her dive for her camera? Studying his own hands as though they were the lost Ark of the Covenant?

It was amazing how one tiny being, approximately the size of a football, could consume her entire life.

And of course, thoughts of him caused her to have an inevitable physical reaction. She felt a tingling in her breasts, followed by the warm release of milk. Her boobs didn't distinguish between Charlie and the thought of Charlie. Fortunately, she was prepared with round disposable pads tucked into her bra.

A whole industry had grown up around the fact that mothers left their babies. There were monitors to transmit every sound they made. Web cams offered a glimpse of exactly what was going on at any given time. There were toys that would play back the sound of your voice for your baby, books to advise you to leave behind a blanket with your scent, a picture of your face. There was a whole support system and industry behind the phenomenon of leaving your baby.

Daisy made use of a lot of them, from the super-absorbent breast pads to a mobile phone with her mother's number on speed dial. Daisy had already called. Twice. Still, she walked around the campus feeling as though she had forgotten something.

And she felt lighter than air.

She had forgotten what it was like to go anywhere without Charlie and all his gear. Here on this campus, it was just her, a backpack and shoulder bag with her camera. She felt like the old Daisy, worrying only about herself. She hadn't liked that Daisy much but liking herself wasn't such a big priority anyway. She knew she was going to like school, yet that made her feel guilty. How could she like something that took her away from her baby? Did that make her a bad mom?

Looking at the other students, she felt like an observer. A misfit.

In high school, she'd been the popular one. The party girl. Everyone thought she partied because it was such fun. They didn't realize she did it to bug her parents. She didn't love having them pissed off but at least they were thinking of her. Otherwise, they were focused on other things, such as getting a divorce.

It had all ended predictably, with her parents' marriage over and everybody miserable. She'd moved with her dad from Manhattan to Avalon, a backwater town she'd been prepared to hate.

She didn't hate Avalon. Okay, she didn't exactly love it, but it was a safe place to live. Then she discovered she was pregnant, and then there was no question of leaving. This was a good place to raise her child.

And now Mom. How surreal was that?

So here she was, scoping out her new school, dealing with a kind of culture shock she hadn't anticipated. She did what she often did, viewed it through the lens of her camera. It was a cold day, but not a frostbite day. Students walked in groups, laughing and chattering, making Daisy conscious of her aloneness. There were couples, too. Tons of couples strolling with their arms around each other or holding hands. Some of them, in the new ecstasy of discovery, stopped every few steps to make out and then continued walking in a daze. And of course, there were the loners, plugged into their iPods, lost somewhere in the middle of a playlist. Daisy noticed girls on their cell phones. She figured some of them were having fake conversations just for the purpose of looking busy so people wouldn't think they had no friends.

Daisy wasn't sure where she would ultimately fit in here. This was a state college so it had all kinds, from fulltime students living in dorms or in the big boxy

Victorian houses along fraternity row to commuters who had jobs and families. Logan lived in the Chi Theta Sigma house. She had never visited him there. This part of his life was separate. Best to keep it that way.

She missed Charlie but, at the same time, knew these few hours away were an incredible gift. Maybe she should go to the student union, get a cup of coffee and talk to other girls about shopping, celebrity gossip, the day's headlines, last night's campus performance of *Antigone.*

Maybe she would do that after class today instead. Her mom had assured her that she would take good care of Charlie. Of that, Daisy had no doubt. One thing about her mom: she did everything—whether it was bringing down a foreign dictator or picking out a grapefruit—with complete competence. Daisy thought about her mother and what she'd endured. A security situation, she'd called it, and she had totally downplayed her role in the drama. She didn't like talking about it, though she implied she had merely been an observer. Daisy suspected her mom had been more than that, though. It must have been really bad to make her move to Avalon. For Daisy, the timing couldn't be better. A thought that made her feel totally selfish.

Daisy took a few pictures. She always liked the way the snow illuminated faces, stark but with a peculiar clarity that lent honesty to features and expressions.

She panned the camera around the quadrangle, an

oblong yard surrounded by tall, bare trees and stately brick buildings, one of the prettiest and most traditional of college campuses in the state college system. Her viewfinder touched on a boy with shoulder-length white-blond hair, walking with a stack of books propped against his hip.

She nearly dropped the camera in surprise. Could it be . . . ? Zach.

Daisy started to call his name but decided against it. If she was mistaken, she'd look like an idiot. She tucked her camera away and hurried toward him, passing some students putting up a banner for a rally and a professor surrounded by adoring protégés.

Maybe she was wrong. A whole year had passed. But no, she would know Zach Alger anywhere. She and Zach and Sonnet—her best friend, and now her stepsister—had been through so much. Some of the finest pictures Daisy had ever taken had been of him. Not model-ish shots or poses, just studies of his remarkable, oddly compelling face. The pictures had been taken last winter, studies in black and white of a striking young man hiding a world of pain. When she'd taken the photos, she hadn't known about the pain or its source, and perhaps that lent an air of mystery to the shots.

As she drew closer to him, there could be no mistake. Everyone had a unique way of carrying himself, and when you had viewed a person through a camera lens the way she had Zach, you recognized his particular posture and movement.

"Zach," she said when she was a few yards behind him. "Hey, Zach."

He stopped immediately as though someone had jerked an invisible chain, and turned to face her. It was the same Zach she had known . . . but different. Same remarkable face with its prominent bone structure, Nordic features, amazing cornflower-blue eyes beneath pale brows, hair so light that people asked him if he bleached it, or if he was an albino. And yet there was something different about him. A distance. A hard shell of wariness.

"It's me," she said. "Daisy."

He smiled briefly, a social reflex rather than a reaction. "Yeah, I can see that."

"So, how are you?" She felt totally awkward. They'd been friends once. Close enough to tell each other their secrets. Together with Sonnet Romano, they'd been the three musketeers, all for one and one for all. Inseparable.

Until, of course, they'd been ripped apart by scandal.

"I'm okay," Zach said. "You?"

"Fine," she said. "Great."

"That's good."

Uncomfortable silence. Crunching of snow underfoot, babble of voices around them.

Daisy didn't know where to began. "I'm sorry," she said, "this is weird. I didn't mean for this to be weird."

Her admission seemed to help a little. He glanced at the clock tower. "Are you on the way to class, or . . . ?"

"Not for about thirty minutes."

He indicated the student union, a blocky building with a figured concrete entryway. "Want to get a cup of coffee?"

"I'd love that."

They moved through the line side by side, getting coffee. Zach picked up a fat cellophane-wrapped cinnamon roll, then put it down again. "Just the coffee," he said. "Working at the Sky River Bakery turned me into a baked-goods snob."

His mention of the past broke through another section of ice between them.

"Me, too," she agreed. They had both worked at the bakery in Avalon last winter. Seeing so much of each other had made them fast friends. Zach and Sonnet had rescued Daisy from feeling like an outsider when she'd moved to Avalon.

They sat together at a Formica-topped table by the window. "It's good to see you," Daisy said. "I didn't know if I'd ever see you again, after what happened—"

"You don't have to dance around it," he said. "You mean, after my dad got caught ripping off the city of Avalon."

Zach's father, Matthew Alger, had been the city administrator under Nina when she was mayor. When funds mysteriously went missing from the city coffers, Nina was blamed but ultimately, the theft was traced to Matthew. Everything unraveled from there. It was discovered that Alger had a massive online gambling addiction. To make matters worse, Zach tried to cover it up by stealing from the cash register of the Sky River Bakery, where he worked. Now Matthew Alger was doing time. With no other family or ties to Avalon, Zach had left town. And even though Nina wasn't directly responsible for the loss to the city, her term in office had ended under a cloud of scandal.

"Yes," Daisy said. "After that. You quit school, quit the bakery and took off before I could even tell you I was sorry about everything that happened. Before Sonnet could say goodbye."

"You mean good riddance. My dad screwed over her mother. I didn't think she'd be too sad to see me go."

"We were both sad, Zach. What your dad did wasn't your fault, and I'm glad I found you again. And FYI, I'm telling Sonnet. I ought to text her right now."

He was finally relaxed enough to almost smile. "Still your same bossy self."

In the silence that followed, she could sense his unspoken curiosity. She folded her arms on the tabletop and looked at him. "It's all right to ask me about the baby," she said.

"Yeah, I was kind of wondering."

The last time Zach had seen her, she was just a few months pregnant and everything was up in the air.

"I didn't want to ask in case, you know, something happened," he added.

"I had a little boy in August," she said. "Emile Charles Bellamy. He's amazing." She pulled a photo out of her wallet. "We live in Avalon," she explained. "So I'm a commuter student here. Today is my first day."

"Wow." Like most guys, he didn't have much to say about the baby pictures. "I bet you're a great mom."

"I try." She asked Zach about his life. He was living near campus and working in a local bakery; unlike most people, the crazy hours suited him. Here at college he was studying, he admitted, accounting.

As she listened to him talk, it struck Daisy how much she liked Zach and how much she missed having him as a friend. She had so few friends these days. Most of those she'd known in high school had gone away to college or moved to the city for jobs. The ones who were left settled into an uncomfortable combination of preadulthood, getting unexciting jobs and going drinking on the weekends, drifting from day to day with nothing better to do. Daisy was desperate to avoid slipping into that kind of existence. It was why she insisted on having a home of her own instead of living under her father's roof. It was why she stayed up late working on her commercial photography and why she was in college right now. She didn't want her life to be something she endured. She wanted it to be something more.

She told Zach about the bit of progress she'd made with her fine art photography—her prints were on display at a few local businesses and she made the occasional sale. She had also found more steady work doing commercial photography for a local graphics firm, and posting her stock online.

"So my pictures pop up in surprising places," she told him. "Like in an ad for sliding glass doors. And gardening supplies and cold sore medicine." She finished her coffee, stuffed a napkin in her cup. "Some of the best pictures I've ever taken are of you," she told him.

"Yeah, well, I hope my face doesn't pop up in some ad or brochure."

"Number one, I would never do that. Number two, I can't without a signed model release." She handed him another picture from her wallet. This was one she had taken last winter with her shutter on timer. It showed the three of them—her, Sonnet and Zach—in the snowy woods, and it captured the friendship they'd once shared. None of them knew, in the picture, that just a short time later, Daisy would be taking pictures of something very different, something they'd discovered in an ice cave in the hills where they were hiking. They had set out that day to go snowshoeing, and they'd come across the remains of a woman who had been missing for twenty-five years. Not only had Zach's father known the victim. He'd been the last person to see her alive.

Everything changed after that, for all three of them.

"How is she doing?" he asked, no longer looking at the photo. There was a world of pain in the inquiry. Zach and Sonnet had grown up together, friends from kindergarten. Daisy knew that both of them had taken their falling-out hard.

"Sonnet's great. She graduated as class valedictorian and had a summer internship at NATO in Belgium. She's at American University now, in Washington, D.C. I think she wants to be a diplomat."

He nodded. "She'll do great, I'm sure."

Daisy was sure, too. Sonnet Romano was the kind of daughter every parent wished they had. She got good grades and had good manners. She did things for the community, like tutoring kindergartners and taking kids hiking in the summer. She had vowed never to have premarital sex and as far as Daisy could tell, Sonnet was sticking to that vow.

"Do me a favor and don't text her," Zach said. "I mean, I guess I can't stop you from telling her you saw me, but . . ."

"Fine, I won't," Daisy said. "But believe me, it's not that big a deal. So many other, bigger things have happened that this thing about your dad, well, it's just nuts to let it matter."

"Bigger things, like you having a baby?"

"Yes. And there's one other thing," Daisy said. "I have some other news. I hope it's good news."

"Try me."

"Sonnet's mom, Nina, got married a few weeks ago."

"Yeah?"

"To my dad. Nina Romano married my dad. So we're sisters now. Stepsisters, Sonnet and me."

He sat back, stared at her. "And you're still speaking to me?"

"Like I said, nothing that happened was your fault, Zach. Nobody blames you for anything."

He didn't reply but she could see it in his eyes—he blamed himself. She wondered if a person ever stopped needing his parents' approval. No, she thought, never. And right then and there, she vowed she would never make Charlie feel as though he had to somehow win her love. He would just have it, free and clear, no questions asked.

"So anyway, I hope we'll all get together again one of these days," she told him, then had an idea. "Winter Carnival would be perfect. Sonnet's coming home for it."

Winter Carnival was the biggest event of the season in Avalon. The event featured a gallery of ice sculptures, hockey matches on the lake, races of every kind—dogsled, toboggan, an "ice-man" triathlon involving snowshoeing, Nordic skiing and ice skating. The community festival was the brightest spot of winter.

"You should come, Zach," she said. "I'm serious."

"Yeah, Sonnet—not to mention your dad and his new wife—would love that."

"Zach—"

"It's almost time for class." He grabbed both their cups and threw them away. "I have to go."

Seventeen

Sophie had a vision of how her days with little Charlie would go. She pictured herself showing up at Daisy's house, being greeted by Charlie's happy gurgles and coos, her grateful daughter heading out the door, filled with confidence. Then, while the infant blissfully slept, she would study the library of child-care books she'd bought to brush up on her skills.

Instead, Sophie had arrived to chaos this morning—a stressed-out daughter, crying baby, messy house. Daisy had practically talked herself out of going at all.

"Don't be like that." Sophie raised her voice over the baby's cries. "You've thought this all out. You can do it."

"I can do it next year or the year after that," Daisy had wailed. "It doesn't have to be right this minute."

Pretending a confidence she didn't exactly feel, Sophie had taken the crying, damp baby into her arms. "Go. At least try it for this week. We can do this, Daisy. I promise we can."

Eventually, Daisy had flown out the door, leaving Sophie and Charlie by themselves. Charlie was still crying and Sophie was wondering if she was going to be able to make good on her promise.

She had planned her day with him practically down to the minute, scheduling meals, changing, playtime and a nap according to timetables recommended in childcare books.

The books were vague on what to do when the baby didn't cooperate with the schedule. She navigated a path across the cluttered living room and into the bedroom, where she changed his diaper. He was strong and angry, crying and squirming as she grappled with the diaper tapes and threaded his chubby, flailing legs into a clean stretchy suit. She pushed the soiled clothes to the floor, realizing how easy it was for the house to turn messy when you were alone with a fussy baby. She picked him up, pressing her lips to his forehead. He didn't feel hot. Jiggling him, humming, she went to the living room and put him in his swing while she hastened to warm a bottle. He didn't want the bottle, though. He didn't want his binky. Or the swing, or a toy. He didn't want Sophie.

She set him on a blanket on the floor and looked around for a toy to offer him. Finding none in range, she simply plunked herself down beside him. "Charlie, we need to talk," she said during a lull in his fussing. "I've already raised two children." She found that if she spoke to him as if he were an adult, he forgot to cry for a moment. "You don't scare me. But here's the thing. I never did it on my own before. When I first had Daisy, I hadn't married her father yet, but I wasn't really alone. I lived with my parents that summer. And, well, you have to know my parents."

Charlie formed his hands into fists, and he gnawed at his knuckles.

"You'll get to know them as you get older," she said. "They're still adjusting to being great-grandparents. Anyway, when I first had Daisy, they decided the solution was to surround me with help, twenty-four hours a day. I brought my baby home from the hospital and immediately surrendered her to a trained nanny. A few months later, after I married Greg, we kept the nanny on. Don't get me wrong—it was an incredibly supportive thing for my parents to do, and I'll always be grateful to them. But in essence, they were saying I couldn't do this on my own. I couldn't take care of a baby without help. Why shouldn't I believe that? To tell you the truth, I was grateful for Ammie and Della—the day nanny and the night nanny. Ammie was Lao and Della was from Queens. They both adored babies and Daisy was their life. It got to the point where I didn't have to lift a finger, not for Daisy or for Max when he came along. I simply got on with my life. I finished college and law school, and started a career while someone else looked after my babies."

Charlie made a crabby sound but didn't start crying again. She held out her hand, watched him grasp her finger and study it before putting it in his mouth, biting with his new teeth, but not hard enough to hurt.

"So what I'm saying is, you're my shot, young man," she said. "You're my chance to do this a different way, to make your life better because I'm here. Not that I'm putting pressure on you or anything, but I really want to be someone to you. Not just the nice lady who shows up occasionally to take you on play-dates."

Then she carefully took back her finger, gathered him into her arms. Her whole body shuddered with love for him, for this tiny creature who had arrived so unexpectedly, and whose very existence now defined Daisy's future.

He wasn't always regarded as a blessing. When the news of Daisy's pregnancy got out, some of the people Sophie had known in Manhattan, ambitious übermothers who mapped out their children's lives from womb to wedding, had offered their sympathy. They had acted as if someone had died rather than created a new life. *Oh, Sophie, I'm so sorry.* The platitudes had been murmured over tea at the St. Regis or drinks at the Oak Room. *This must be so hard on you. All your plans for Daisy, your hopes, just . . . gone.*

She set the baby down and went around the room, picking up toys, amassing a small collection of soft, squeaky things, bright knobby objects and squishy shapes. She offered him a plush doll, its flat face embroidered with a benign smile. He clutched it with both hands and carried it immediately to his mouth.

"Of course I had plans for Daisy," Sophie told him. "Of course I had dreams for her. Every mother does. She has them for you—trust me on that. But if she's smart, she'll keep them to herself and let you discover them on your own." Sophie hadn't been that smart. She had told Daisy what was expected of her—good grades, good schools, meaningful work, a marriage based on mutual love and respect. One or two planned-for children. In that order.

"She didn't listen," Sophie confessed.

The baby flung down the soft toy. She handed him a plastic ring hung with colorful objects. He grabbed it and brought it to his mouth, thus validating its existence.

"For that matter," she said, "I didn't listen, either. A mother rarely does. I mean, she listens with her heart and then ignores the things she doesn't want to hear. Like the fact that when a girl is mad at the world and in rebellion mode, she's likely to have careless sex with some guy. At least Daisy had the sense not to marry Logan O'Donnell. I'm sure there are those who claim any father is better than none at all. They could be right, but I trust Daisy's judgment on this one. It would never have worked out, and she was smart enough to realize that. She had a ringside seat at my marriage to Greg, and probably figured out that getting married for the wrong reasons won't make things right."

Charlie tossed the ring toy and sucked on his hands, gurgling as he regarded her owlishly.

"Once you stop bawling, you're a good listener," Sophie remarked. "You pay better attention than most adults I know." She found herself smiling at him, simply because he looked so wide-eyed and wise.

"You have green eyes and red hair," she told him. "Classic Irish looks. Are you sick of hearing that? I'm sure you're going to grow up with everyone constantly saying you look like your father. Daisy says Logan comes to see you every week, which is more than I would have expected of him, but then again, I don't really know him that well."

She offered a toy she had bought in Germany a few months ago, a caged ball that made a soft gonging sound when turned. "It's funny," she said, "Marian O'Donnell seemed like one of those perfect mothers to me. She was completely present in her kids' lives. She was always at the school, volunteering in the library or computer lab. She was a career mom, one of those who made me feel inadequate. But in the end, she couldn't save Logan any more than I could save Daisy."

Charlie dropped the toy from Germany. He squirmed a bit, screwed up his face. Sophie watched him for a few minutes. Bowel movement or boredom? Observing no sign of the former, she concluded it was boredom. She couldn't really blame him, sitting there, a captive audience while being talked at by his grandmother.

She gently gathered him up and walked from room to room, swaying rhythmically. Daisy was still a teenager; it showed in her housekeeping. Things were done haphazardly without much attention to detail. So what? thought Sophie. The world was not going to come to an end because there were piles of laundry that hadn't been folded yet. She stopped and looked out the window, angling her body so Charlie could see. The world was a winter wonderland, everything draped in pristine white. The sky was heavy and gray with a descending brow of clouds.

"Daisy told me you like going out in this," Sophie said. "Of course, you have to be dressed in nine layers of clothes, and zipped up like a pod person. I think we'll stay indoors today."

The afternoon stretched out, long and empty. Charlie showed absolutely no interest in taking a nap, not even after consuming two bottles and having two diaper changes. Sophie decided not to worry about the routine. This was part of the challenge she'd set for herself. The old Sophie would have already been frantically paging through the child-rearing books, looking up what to do when the baby wasn't willing to settle down for a nap. The new Sophie simply moved to his rhythm. It was an eye-opener to be with someone who lived so completely in the here and now. Someone for whom seeing his own hands float by his face was a revelation. Each passing moment was filled with discovery for him.

"You're very Zenlike," she told him. "I used to always think I needed to get up, go somewhere, do something. But you—you're just happy to be. It seems to be working well for you."

She discovered that it didn't bother her a bit that none of the things on her schedule had gotten done. Perhaps, she thought, raising a baby with no help from a spouse or nanny was more a matter of being rather than doing.

• • •

"How are things in Mayberry?" asked Tariq.

He had taken to calling her a few times a week. She knew he missed her, but it was more than that. He was worried about her.

"They're fine," she said. "I'm fine. Everything is fine. You should come and visit me and see for yourself."

"America is too scary," he said.

"Then you'll have to take my word for it. I don't know why it's so difficult for you to grasp that I could settle down in a small town and make a new life for myself."

"I think you can do anything you put your mind to. But—I know you're reluctant to hear this—you haven't even begun to sort out what happened that night."

"What, you're my shrink now?"

"Your friend, Sophie. Someone who loves you."

Holding the phone to her ear, she paced in front of the big picture window of the cottage. "I appreciate your concern, but I'm doing all right." She stopped pacing. "I saw Brooks Fordham."

"The reporter bloke."

"Yes. He's better. He's on a sabbatical from the paper, but he does plan to write about what happened."

"Of course he does. Is that the only reason he came calling?"

She considered this. "Hard to say."

"Still having nightmares?"

"Yes, except—" She knew of one occasion she hadn't. And that was when she had slept with Noah. "Lots of people have nightmares," she hastily pointed out. "It doesn't mean they're cracking up."

"But lots of people haven't been through what you went through."

She stood and glared out the window. It was another gray-and-white day, the lake dusted with more snow. Meager afternoon light lay flat against the snow. From the big picture window of the cottage she could see a bend in the road, a hairpin turn, more accurately, and the bank that dropped off abruptly into the lake. The road there was marked by caution signs and bordered by a laughably inadequate guardrail. When she saw the occasional car rounding the bend in the road, she felt herself tense up.

She turned away and focused on Willow Lake. Tina was out on her skates, doing her afternoon workout. It was impossible to see Tina and not remember what Bo Crutcher had told her—that Tina and her partner wanted to have a baby. That they wanted Noah to father it. Life in this small town was far more interesting than Sophie had ever anticipated.

"The Incident is completely behind me," she assured Tariq. "You don't believe that, but it's true. I've moved on."

"You've run off."

She smiled. "Charlie cut another tooth last week. Did I tell you?"

"Several times. And you e-mailed photos."

"And I'm driving hockey car pool this afternoon," she added.

"The fun never ends."

"I slept with the guy across the road," she blurted out. "More than once."

A beat of silence. Then Tariq said, "That's brilliant. Did you really?"

Sophie hugged her arm across her middle and paced some more as she explained. She skipped the bit about running her car into a ditch in a snowstorm, just saying she met him on her first night in Avalon. "He's your classic rugged outdoorsman variety, right down to the five o'clock shadow. He's a veterinarian."

"How very James Herriot of him."

"Don't be condescending. It was completely spontaneous," she said, and even the thought of Noah created a phantom warmth in her. "We're not dating. We barely know each other. But there's this thing between us—I don't even know what to call it. It's the sexual equivalent of dropping a lit match into a pool of kerosene."

"My, my. It sounds as if this move agrees with you after all."

"I have to say, it's one of the easier aspects of reinventing myself."

"And have you dealt with your ex?"

"I keep our interactions to a minimum. Truthfully, it hurts to see Greg and his new wife together. It hurts to see how much he adores her, and how happy they are.

It just hurts, and there's not a damn thing I can do about it."

"Except shag your neighbor."

"Well, there's that. Dr. Maarten would say I'm exploring new facets of myself. Or maybe expending my untapped sexual energy." That, she realized, pacing faster, was going to take more than two encounters.

She seized on the chance to change the subject and questioned him about court proceedings and the progress of cases he was working on. She found herself listening to him with interest that quickly intensified to an undeniable tug of yearning. A part of her still belonged in that world, where she was governed by a sense of mission, where the challenges were difficult but not impossible, where she experienced control and closure.

Yet another part remembered why she'd come here. Her journey had only just begun.

She hung up and patrolled the house, making sure it looked cheery and inviting. Today, Max was coming over after school. After hockey practice, she would fix him dinner—his favorite, sloppy joes—and then he'd stay the night.

A knock at the door startled her and her gaze flew to the clock. Too early for Max. She opened the door and saw that it was Gayle from down the road.

"I brought you some muffins," Gayle said, brushing back the hood of her parka. She held out a flat Tupperware box.

"Thank you so much," Sophie said, stepping back so she could come in. "That's incredibly nice of you."

"Don't get too excited. I'm a terrible baker. Cabin fever made me desperate enough to try something new."

"Can you stay?"

"Just for a second." Gayle looked around the cottage. "I've never been here before. Nice place."

"My son's coming over for the first time today. Max is twelve. I hope he likes it here as much as I do."

"It's lovely," Gayle said. "What's not to like?"

"Well, let's see. The fact that I don't have cable TV."

"Whoops," Gayle said. "Looks like you have a DVD player, though. Maybe you could rent some movies at Silver Screen in town."

"That's tempting, but I told myself I want this time with him. If we need a diversion, I can teach him cribbage or canasta. I'm nervous. And how depressing is that, to be nervous about a visit from my own son? He's lived with his dad since the divorce," she explained, bracing herself for the standard reaction—that questioning, judgmental stare.

"Then no wonder you're nervous." Gayle patted her on the arm. "A word to the wise, though. Be prepared for it not to be perfect. You've probably built up all these expectations in your mind for the way you want things to go."

She was relieved by Gayle's understanding. "That sounds like the voice of experience."

"Perfect example—after Adam's unit was called up, he had a short furlough before being sent overseas, and I planned this amazing day for the whole family. In my head, I was seeing one seamless stream of Hallmark moments, giving us memories to last through the entire deployment." She smiled ruefully. "We have memories, all right. Just not Hallmark memories."

"I take it things didn't go as planned."

"Starting with the baby's raging ear infection, a three-hour wait in the doctor's office and ending with us getting in a fight because he insisted on driving ten miles out of his way to fill a prescription, and—what do you know?—the pharmacist is his old girlfriend. So much for the sing-along around the campfire. And oh, the gourmet dinner, sitting on the dock at the Inn at Willow Lake and looking at the turning leaves? All that flew out the window."

Sophie could only imagine the stress. "I'm sorry."

"I remember screaming 'Get the hell out of my life' as his train was pulling out of the station. That's what I remember."

"Oh, boy. I'm sorry, Gayle."

"Fortunately, there's a happy ending. I was standing on the platform with the kids, devastated, when the train suddenly stopped, and Adam jumped out. He actually pulled an emergency lever to get it to stop, because he felt as bad as I did. So we had our goodbye after all, with a trainload of people cheering us on. Somebody got a picture, too, and a wire service picked it up and we were in I don't know how many newspapers."

"So you got your romantic farewell," Sophie said.

Gail nodded. "He even explained about the old girlfriend. She's a compounding pharmacist, which the doctor recommended. I didn't hear that over the screaming baby, and Adam was too mad to tell me."

"But you worked it out."

"Yes. He's just as gone, though. Gone is gone."

Sophie recognized that hurt in her voice. It was one thing to find yourself single because your marriage failed. But to be forcibly separated from her husband in this way . . . "I'm sorry," she said. "If there's anything I can do . . ."

"There might be." Gayle stuffed her hands into her pockets. "I need some advice. Noah said you're a lawyer."

Oh, dear. "I'm not practicing."

"But could you?"

"I still have my license for this state, but—" *You offered,* Sophie reminded herself. "What is it that you need?"

"I'm— Lord, this is awful. I don't want to bother Adam with it while he's overseas. It's just a minor thing having to do with our business license for the farm. I feel so clueless. Since he's been gone, everything seems to matter more."

A business license was nothing like the kind of law Sophie used to practice. Still, her heart went out to Gayle, so uncertain, her husband gone. "Absolutely. Tomorrow?"

"I'd love that." She glanced out the window. "I should get back."

"I'll walk you home and you can tell me what's up." Sophie offered a fleeting smile. "I have a bit of cabin fever myself, and I'm still adjusting to the fact that I have downtime."

Gayle's place was about a hundred yards down the road. "Your kids are one, three and five, right?" asked Sophie. Dear God, had Gayle left them alone?

Gayle correctly interpreted Sophie's alarm. "Don't worry, they're in good hands."

They stepped inside just as a small, laughing child flew up in the air. A second later she was caught by a pair of strong hands. The hands belonged to Noah Shepherd.

Gayle saw the way Sophie was watching Noah; Sophie saw her watching and blushed.

"Don't worry," Gayle said, "he has that effect on everyone."

Eighteen

Max felt totally out of place on the Lakeshore Road bus. He didn't know any of the kids on this route. He didn't have a usual seat. So once again, he was an outsider. A stranger, getting looks of suspicion as he approached the bus.

With his backpack and sports bag dragging at his shoulder like a load of granite, he climbed aboard, showing his permission slip to an indifferent driver, who simply nodded. The bus, like all buses that served

Avalon Middle School, was crowded with kids who represented a cross-section of the school population—girls who spoke only in either squeals or whispers, library geeks who tried to make themselves disappear into the pages of a fantasy novel, loud jocks whose mission it was to use as many cuss words as possible every time they opened their mouths, and a smattering of regular kids. Max considered himself one of these. A kid who is neither smart nor dumb, cool nor dorky, just somewhere in between.

He hesitated in the middle of the aisle, scanning for an empty seat and trying not to look too frantic about it. Every seat was taken, so he'd need to plunk down next to some other kid. But which kid? The one staring mesmerized at a handheld game probably wouldn't notice him at all. He headed for the empty spot.

"Taken," the kid said tonelessly, without looking up. "Sorry."

Max moved on. There were way too many girls on this bus. He found himself choosing between a space cadet named Kolby who was in his science class, and a fat girl with an angry look on her face.

Somebody shoved him from behind. "Sit down, will you?"

Max plopped down next to the fat girl. Maybe she wouldn't try to talk to him.

"Did I say you could sit there?"

"Nope," Max said. He pulled his backpack into his lap and shoved his sports bag under the seat. Then he pushed his knees against the back of the seat in front of him.

"Maybe I was saving it."

"Maybe you weren't."

"That pisses me off."

"Too bad."

"I'm Chelsea," the girl said.

So much for picking someone who didn't want to talk. "Max," he said, staring straight ahead.

"What are you doing on this bus?"

"Going to my mom's." He hated the sound of that. For most kids, going home and going to your mom's were the same thing. Not for Max. At least he didn't have to fly all night to see her, though, like he used to when she lived in Holland. So that was progress. Maybe.

"Where does she live?" Chelsea asked.

"Lakeshore Road."

"I live on that road, too," she said.

Ooh, let's be best friends.

"It's the last stop," she informed him. "End of the line. I'm always last to get home. That pisses me off."

Max took out his mobile phone. He didn't really need to get in touch with anyone, but he figured if he looked busy, maybe fat, pissed-off Chelsea would quit talking. For want of something better to do, he texted Dubois: *u on 4 practice 2day?* He kept his hand cupped around the screen so Chelsea wouldn't see. He already knew Dubois was going to hockey practice. So was his other friend, Altshuler. Their parents took turns. Today, Max's mom would be driving the car pool for the first time. She'd just leased an all-wheel-drive minivan, a real soccer-mom car, she called it.

Max shut his phone and stuck it in his pocket. His dad placed restrictions on his use of it and studied the bill each month to make sure Max was complying. If Dad had his way, Max wouldn't even have a phone. Its main purpose, Max knew, was for his mom to have a way to call him, and only him. She hated when she called the house and dad or Nina picked up. So Max got his own phone and Mom got her own ring tone—"I Go to Sleep" by the Pretenders.

The bus lurched and lumbered along its prescribed route, rumbling to a halt at each stop. Its brakes gnashed and hissed as it pulled over every few minutes to disgorge passengers. As soon as the geeky girl across the aisle vacated her seat, Max made a dive for it, dragging along his sports bag and backpack. He smashed himself against the window and gazed out, his breath fanning across the glass.

Unfortunately, being ditched didn't stop Chelsea from talking. Even though he gave the most minimal response he could without being completely rude, she kept yakking away. The list of things that pissed her off grew at every bend in the road—the fact that most of the snow days had been used up for the school year and it was only February. The fact that you couldn't get cable TV out on Lakeshore Road. The show "High School Musical," which she had to watch at a friend's house because she didn't get cable. The price of a lift ticket at Saddle Mountain, where she and her grandpa went skiing every weekend.

"Do you ski?" she asked Max, finally ending the litany.

"Snowboard," he said.

"That's awesome. I've been wanting to learn, but my grandparents don't want to get me new equipment. That pisses me off."

Of course it did. There were things that pissed Max off, too, although he didn't go around reciting them for anyone to hear. Flunking a test and then having to get it signed by his dad—that pissed him off. Having a bunch of new stepcousins he didn't know—that sucked, too. Not knowing what your mom's house looked like. Feeling torn between his mom and his dad. Knowing he had a totally boring weekend ahead of him. Now that he thought about it, there were a lot of things that pissed him off.

The route was starting to feel endless. At least the scenery was good. Willow Lake was pretty much Max's favorite thing about living in Avalon. His dad's property even had a dock, which in the summer was perfect for fishing off of, or getting a running start and diving into the lake. Even though the water was so cold it made your balls shrivel and your scalp scream, it was totally worth it to plunge in on a hot summer day.

In the winter, the whole lake froze. The city had an inspector who tested the ice on a regular basis to make sure it was at least four inches thick. Max's dad and stepmom didn't allow skating at the Inn at Willow Lake because they didn't want any of their guests getting hurt. He wondered if there was any skating to be done at his mom's house.

His mom now had a house in Avalon. He'd never expected her to move here.

"So where's your house again?" Chelsea asked, as if he'd already told her, which he hadn't.

"Across from the Shepherd Dairy," he said. His mom had told him to watch for a big barn—the only barn visible from the road. It had the dairy logo of a cow painted on the side. According to his mom, the place didn't operate as a dairy anymore. The guy they'd met in the restaurant that night had turned it into an animal hospital.

"That's my stop, too," Chelsea declared. "I work part time at Dr. Shepherd's, helping him take care of the animals."

To Max, that sounded semi-interesting, though he wasn't about to let on to this girl that he was curious.

"I'll show you where to get off," she said.

"Great." Like he couldn't find a barn on his own.

The bus swayed, causing his sports bag to slide. He grabbed it and stared out the window. Just for a moment, the sight shocked him. There was a high snowbank next to the road, then a sheer drop-off. Max's stomach clenched. He wasn't really afraid. It was just a reaction to looking out the window and seeing nothing but thin air. They wouldn't let a school bus go along a road that was unsafe. Plus, the driver was only crawling along, going probably twice as slow as necessary.

"There's an old story," Chelsea said, "that like, fifty years ago, a car went off the road right here and killed a man and woman who were headed to the Inn at Willow Lake for their honeymoon."

"Is it true?"

"My grandpa says yes, but I don't think he knows for sure. According to the story, the car and the bodies were never found because the lake's too deep here." She started gathering up her things. "Almost there."

The barn came into view just as his mom had described it. Finally.

Max could see about five houses crouched along the lakeshore. A thread of smoke came from the chimney of one cottage. Mom had said to find the mailbox colored in bright yellow smiley faces. He wondered if she was watching out the window, if she could see the bus coming around the bend in the road.

"Here we are," Chelsea announced.

Three other kids headed for the exit. Max murmured a thank-you to the driver and jumped down, taking care not to slip on the frozen ground.

The three other kids—two boys and a girl—hiked up the lane that branched off the main road. They paused in a tight cluster and lit up cigarettes.

"Eighth-graders," Chelsea said, her tone conveying clear disapproval. "I can't stand smoking. Pisses me off. Well. Guess I'll see you around."

Not if I see you first, Max thought. Eager to get

away, he headed across the road and found the designated landmark, the smiley-face mailbox. Someone had carefully dug the snow around it so that it was clearly visible. His mom had probably done that. She often acted as though he were an idiot. She had offered to hike up the driveway and meet the bus, but Max had declined. Mothers did that for kindergartners, not that his mom would know about that. As far as Max knew, she'd never met a school bus in her life.

From the moment she'd watched the bus round the bend in the road, Sophie had been holding her breath, catching herself and then holding it again. She wondered if there would ever be a time when she could look at something like this without tensing up and feeling assaulted by memories of that snowy night.

Was it warm enough in here? She checked the thermostat. Added a log to the fire. She was getting good at making fires in the wood-burning stove. Even though this was a borrowed house, it was her world and she desperately wanted Max to like it.

At the stomping sound of his footsteps on the porch, she opened the door. "There you are," she exclaimed. "I couldn't wait to see you."

"Hey."

He offered her a brief hug that held more tolerance than affection.

Sophie found herself babbling— "You can put your coat on a hook right there. Let me show you your room. How about a snack? Tell me about your day . . .

"Sorry," she concluded. "I don't mean to go on and on. I'm just excited to have you here."

"It's a nice place," he remarked, looking around at the vintage Adirondack-style furniture, the tattersall blankets, the crackling fire in the window of the stove.

She nodded. "I really love it, even if it's a bit out of the way. The Wilsons were so nice to lend it to me."

"Since they lent it to you, when do you have to give it back?"

Ah, she thought. *A test.* "Once I get my own place," she said. "In Avalon. I'm here to stay, Max."

"I don't get it."

"I know you don't. But you will, eventually. Are you ready for a snack? The neighbor brought over some muffins. And I'll make us some hot chocolate. You like hot chocolate, don't you?"

"Actually, I'm a coffee drinker myself."

It took her a moment to realize he was pulling her leg. "Coffee stunts your growth."

"Right."

While she put on a pan of milk, he explored the place. He was drawn to the sprawling view of the lake out the window, of course. That view was the whole point of the cottage, after all, the main window a frame for the wild beauty of the landscape. He seemed to like the Niagara Falls souvenir lamp with the animated shade. Like all kids—like Sophie herself—he stood on tiptoe to look down inside the shade to see how the waterfall worked.

"That's interesting, isn't it?" she remarked. "I mean,

it's just a color wheel going around and around, but it looks so realistic on the outside."

"Uh-huh." He acted noncommittal. "So I hear you don't get cable out here."

"The TV seems to get perhaps three or four stations. I haven't been watching much." She measured a scoop of Dutch cocoa into the pan. It was one of the few items she had brought back from Holland. It made the best hot chocolate by far. "What do you like to watch on TV?" she asked. "Do you have a favorite show?"

"I watch stuff on cable," he said bluntly.

Oh, boy.

When she'd visited him prior to this, each day together had been deemed "special" and TV-watching wasn't an issue. Now that she actually lived here, the visits would become more routine. Things like TV might start to matter. She hadn't thought about that.

"There's a DVD player," she said, "and I noticed a nice selection of movies in that cabinet. Some of my favorites."

"You have a favorite movie?"

"*Harold and Maude*," she said, without even thinking. Of course that was her favorite movie. She couldn't believe it wasn't everyone's favorite movie.

"Never seen it." He opened the cabinet and perused the selection. His expressive face clearly indicated that he didn't share the Wilsons' taste for imports and art films.

"We'll watch it together," Sophie suggested.

"What's it about?"

"A kid whose domineering mother drives him crazy."

"Sounds like a laugh a minute," Max said.

It was a strained afternoon, during which Max consumed four muffins, finished his homework, declined a game of cribbage and lasted through exactly seven minutes of *Judge Judy.* Sophie made things worse by insisting on leaving extra early to pick up his two friends for hockey practice, just in case the roads were bad. As a result, the friends weren't ready when they showed up and she had to sit there with the car idling while they threw together their gear. She'd hoped the boys' mothers might come out to the car to meet her, or even invite her in, but they didn't. She wanted to make friends here in Avalon, but perhaps car-pool pickup wasn't the best time to socialize.

The boys didn't have a lot to say during the drive to the hockey rink—not to her, anyway. Among themselves, they appeared to communicate in some private, incomprehensible language that involved elbowing and snickering.

At the rink, she introduced herself to the coach, who didn't look much older than Max himself, an apple-cheeked, eager man with a somewhat high-pitched voice. Once on the ice, though, the boys seemed to respect him as they went through warm-ups and drills.

Sophie joined a group of mothers who sat in the ringside bleachers behind a Plexiglas barrier, and felt the other women scrutinizing her. This, she knew, was going to be the hard part. She suddenly felt self-conscious about her bag from Italy, her designer belt and gloves. She was overdressed and clearly hadn't mastered the soccer-mom look. She wanted to. She wanted to look relaxed in sweats; she wanted to be comfortable in her own skin. She had a long way to go.

"I'm Max's mom, Sophie Bellamy," she said to the women, and then memorized their names as they introduced themselves. "Do you mind if I join you?"

The line of mothers shifted to make room for her.

"Ellie," said one woman. She was knitting something, a string of brightly colored yarn coming out of her bag.

"Max's mother." A woman named Gretchen lifted her eyebrows. She exchanged a look with the one beside her, who had pretty, olive-toned skin, glossy dark hair and unfriendly eyes. "Maria, it's Max's mother."

Maria folded her arms across her middle. "You don't say."

"It's nice to meet you at last," said the woman who had introduced herself as Gina. Either consciously or unconsciously, she emphasized the *at last.*

"You still go by the name Bellamy," Maria observed. "Wasn't that your married name?"

Sophie nodded, assimilating the reality that here in a small town, people knew each other's business. "In my profession—all my licenses and certifications are in that name. Everything I've published, too." As she explained, she watched their faces and realized she should have given them a simple, politically correct explanation—I wanted to keep the same name as my children. Too late. If she said that now, it would sound as though she had just thought of it.

"Aren't you the one who's been living in Europe?" the woman named Vickie asked.

Oh. So that's where this is going, thought Sophie. She could tell from the tone of the question and from the looks she was getting from the women that they were not okay with her choice. She decided to confront the issue head-on. In the year since she'd been apart from her kids, she had discovered that one of the most awkward aspects of the arrangement was actually explaining it.

People might think they had open minds about today's families, but that tolerance only went so far. *They live with their dad* ranked right up there with *They've never been to the doctor* or *They're allowed to smoke.* In the eyes of the world, Sophie knew what these women were thinking. She was a terrible person, a woman who had turned her back on her children in their time of greatest need, the aftermath of divorce. What kind of mother would do that?

"That's right," Sophie said. "In The Hague, Holland."

"Must've been so exciting for you."

"It was, sometimes." She cautioned herself not to get defensive. For Max's sake, she wanted to get along with his friends' moms. Yet among these women, she felt a distinct prickle of discomfort. She used to be defined by her career, prosecutor, diplomat. Now that she had no career, what would define her? Being a mom? Would that be enough to gain acceptance into this chilly tribe?

"We had this image of you as a jet-setter with a string of mysterious, foreign lovers," Ellie said.

"I'm sure you're joking," Sophie said. She wasn't sure, though.

"I always wanted to get away to Europe, but my family needs me," said Maria.

"Same here. I'll wait until mine are grown," Gretchen agreed.

"I flew to New York on a regular basis," Sophie explained, "to work at the UN and see my kids. And Max visited me in The Hague several times."

"Don't you have a daughter, too?" Gina asked. Their scrutiny burned like the glare of an interrogation light. "In high school?"

"Daisy," Sophie said. "She just started college in New Paltz."

"Daisy. Didn't she used to work at the bakery?" Vickie asked.

"Oh, that one," Gretchen said. "I'm so sorry about . . . what happened."

Sophie took a direct hit on that one. There would never be any definitive explanation as to why Daisy had been so rebellious, so angry and careless. Sophie could ask herself until the cows came home if it had happened due to the divorce, or if it would've happened anyway. She told herself not to take the bait of this woman's phony condolences. "Actually, I'm extremely proud of my daughter."

"What happened?" asked Ellie. "I didn't hear. Is she all right?"

"Daisy is fine," Sophie assured her.

"And the baby, too, right?" Gina said.

The others exchanged glances of surprise. "Your daughter has a baby?" Ellie asked.

"My grandson, Charles," Sophie informed them. "We all adore him."

Maria leaned over to one of the other women and said something in an undertone, but Sophie caught the tail end of it, ". . . out of wedlock."

Sophie was so surprised by the attack that she laughed. "Tell me you didn't just say 'out of wedlock.' "

Maria looked unrepentant. "You mean she's married?"

"No, but—"

"Ricky, watch out!" Maria was on her feet, yelling to a dark-haired boy on the ice. "Don't turn your back on number forty-seven."

That was Max's number.

"Your son plays rough," Maria said. "Didn't he have some kind of meltdown last summer and get kicked off his Little League team?" Maria persisted.

"He was invited to work for the Hornets," Sophie pointed out. She hoped she'd gotten the story right. Keeping stats for the Hornets—Avalon's independent baseball team—was a privilege. At least, that was how

Max had explained it to her. She reminded herself not to get defensive. She had dealt with international criminals. She could handle vindictive women, surely.

Vickie shook her head and added to the chorus of sympathy. "I suppose all kids deal with divorce in their own way."

"I guess you all have a pretty clear picture of my family," Sophie said. "I went jetting off to Europe to be with my foreign lover and left my poor kids to suffer and get in trouble. God, I don't believe you women. What century are you living in?"

"We're not trying to pick a fight," Gretchen said. "Just trying to understand the situation."

"The situation," Sophie said, "is none of your business."

"This is the kind of town where people care about one another."

Where people gossip and judge, Sophie realized. And she had chosen to move here. To live here. With women like this.

"Just to be clear," she said, struggling to keep her voice from shaking. In her profession she was used to confrontation and arguments. This was supposed to be second nature to her, but she was inches from losing it. "I lived in a furnished apartment within walking distance of the court building and I worked twelve-hour days on human rights cases. I missed my kids every damn minute but they couldn't be with both of us. And—news flash, ladies—we're not the first family that's gone through a divorce."

"Of course you're not," Ellie said. "Lots of families handle it just fine."

The condescending attitude grated on Sophie. She decided to bite her tongue. She *had* put her career first. The fact that these women were horrible didn't change that. She needed to move on from here.

A hockey puck cracked against the Plexiglas with a sound like a gunshot. Reflexively, Sophie raised her arms to shield her face. Then a whistle shrilled, signaling the end of practice. Thank God. Sophie leaped to her feet. It couldn't end soon enough for her.

"You ladies have a nice weekend," she said, garnering insincere smiles and assurances. As she walked out into the cold winter evening with her three charges, she wished she could get in the car and drive, and keep driving until she came to the end of the world.

No. That was the old Sophie's way of thinking. The new Sophie didn't run from trouble.

"How was practice?" she asked, reminding herself to drive slowly and calmly.

"Okay," the boys replied, predictably noncommittal. She knew better than to ask. She should, anyway.

"So you met Aunt Maria," Max said.

Sophie stopped, car keys in hands. "*Aunt* Maria?"

"She likes me to call her that," he explained. "You know, on account of her being Nina's sister."

"That woman is Nina's sister?" Sophie should have seen the family resemblance—the olive-toned skin, the glossy hair, the flashing dark eyes.

"Yep."

"She is the sister of Nina—your brand-new stepmother."

"Mom. That's what I just said."

She glared at him in the rearview mirror. "And you couldn't have perhaps given me a little clue about that? Maybe just a hint?"

He shrugged. "Didn't think it mattered."

It was, Sophie realized, one of the unknown hazards of small-town life. You never knew who you were going to run into.

When she got home, Noah called her while Max was in the shower. "I want to see you tonight."

Even the sound of his voice was a form of foreplay. She stepped into the bedroom for privacy. "Is this what's known as a booty call? I have to say, I've never been the recipient of a booty call before."

"There's a first time for everything."

"My son, Max, is spending the weekend with me."

A pause. "How's that going?" He sounded slightly chastened.

"He's so bored he can hardly see straight."

"Bring him over tomorrow. I'll show him around my place. You don't even have to call first. Just show up."

"Thanks, Noah, but I don't think so. For all I know, by tomorrow he'll be begging me to take him back to his dad's."

"My son finds me boring," Sophie said to Gayle Wright the next day. Sophie had adopted the habit of going on a morning run, exploring the splendor of the snowy lanes and trails along the lake. Noah had taken her to buy a special kind of trail shoe made for traction on snow and ice. At the end of her run, she often stopped to visit with Gayle when her neighbor was out playing with her children.

Gayle, presiding over the construction of a lopsided snowman, regarded her with concern. "He's twelve, right? What twelve-year-old ever finds his parents interesting? It's practically a law that he's supposed to find you either boring or embarrassing."

"I'm right on track, then." Sophie took a drink from her water bottle. "I had this whole grand vision of how this weekend was going to be so perfect. Instead, I got in a catfight with the other hockey moms—"

"No way."

"Oh, yes. Way. And he liked your muffins but hated my sloppy joes. They used to be his favorite. Now he's into Italian cuisine. Nina is Italian. She's probably a great cook."

"Don't make comparisons," Gale reminded her. "That way lies madness."

"He fell asleep during *Harold and Maude.*"

"Now that's a problem."

"I know. What kind of person hates *Harold and Maude*?" While Sophie had sat, transfixed and weeping over her favorite film, Max had fallen asleep on the sofa. She had to prod him awake just so he could shuffle off to bed. When she left him for her morning jog, he'd still been sound asleep. "I have no idea what I'm going to do with him today."

"Take him skating on the lake."

"Okay, that covers the first hour. Then what?"

"You don't have to *do* anything." Gayle bent down and fixed Mandy's mitten, which had come untucked from her sleeve. "Just be with him, the way you were when he was little."

Sophie swallowed hard. "I can't say for sure that I ever did that."

"Of course you did. You probably don't remember."

Sophie didn't argue, but neither did she agree. When Max was little, she'd been busy rushing off from one place to another.

"Take him to see Noah," Gayle suggested.

Just hearing Noah's name caused Sophie to have an unbidden reaction. She was glad for the cold air, which concealed her blush. "People take their Weimaraners to see Noah," she said. "Not their bored sons."

"Noah would like it. He's crazy about kids."

Sophie wondered if Gayle suspected . . . no, not possible. No one knew. No one would ever know. "He's probably too busy," she hedged. Even though Noah himself had extended an invitation last night, she suspected he'd done so out of politeness.

"Not on a Saturday," Gayle said. "He doesn't have clinic hours on Saturdays."

Sophie offered a noncommittal shrug. "I might, then."

"Mo-om," yelled Henry, her eldest. "Come and see my tunnel before Bear wrecks it."

Sophie stomped her feet on the ground to keep them from going numb. "I'd better go. I work up a sweat when I run, but I get too cold standing still."

"Give Noah a shot—I think he and Max would hit it off," Gayle said, never knowing—Sophie hoped—that her suggestion held an extra layer of meaning.

"So who is this guy again?" Max asked in a skeptical voice.

"Noah Shepherd. Dr. Noah Shepherd. You met him that one time at the Apple Tree Inn," Sophie said matter-of-factly. She checked herself in the hall tree mirror by the door. After a shower, she felt wonderful, but her fine straight hair had a mind of its own. She pulled on a wool beanie, then changed her mind and tried the black beret. No, too affected. She picked up a quilted cloche. That was a little better, casual and functional, very un-Bergdorf's.

She was taking great pains to make sure this appeared to be the most informal of visits. She wore makeup every day, didn't she? And the fact that the jeans and sweater were brand-new didn't mean anything. Half her wardrobe was new, acquired to help her adapt to the climate in Avalon. The fact that she looked good in the formfitting parka—all right. She had her vanity. Every woman did.

"And you, like, have a crush on him?" Max asked.

She whirled around to stare at him. Dear Lord. She wondered if this was just a stab in the dark on Max's part or if there was some kind of visible glow of attraction so obvious that even a young boy could see it. She felt compelled to play dumb. “Now you’re being silly,” she said. “Not to mention inappropriate. Why on earth would you say something like that?”

“Lipstick,” he said.

“I always wear lipstick.”

“I still don’t want to go see your neighbor. You sure you don’t—”

“I do not,” she said. “Heavens, are all boys your age so suspicious?”

Max shrugged.

“For the record, Noah was very helpful when I first got here in the middle of the last big snowfall. And he has a very interesting animal hospital and I simply think you’d enjoy seeing that.”

“Gosh, just like a field trip,” he said with phony enthusiasm. “I love field trips. It’ll be exactly like school, but on a Saturday.”

Sophie glared at him. “When did you turn into such a cynic?”

“When did you turn into robo-mom?”

“I have no idea what you’re talking about.”

“Robo-mom, with the hot chocolate, the car pool and sloppy joes and movie night.”

“I’m not a robot,” she told him, “because I have feelings.”

“And I’m not a cynic,” he shot back, “because I have feelings, too.”

They glared at each other for a long moment.

"If you hate it at Noah's, we'll come right back," she said, opening the negotiation.

"Too awkward," he countered. "Once I'm there, I'm trapped like a rat."

"He's got a puppy," she said.

That startled him. "What do you mean?"

"Noah. A puppy. As in, a tiny baby dog that wants to play and lick your face, and make you laugh for absolutely no reason."

"The guy has a puppy?" Max grabbed his boots, stuffing his feet into them as fast as he could. "Jeez, why didn't you say so?"

"I didn't want to have to play the puppy card." Sophie smiled as she followed him out into the bright winter morning. It was almost like cheating.

As Max loped up the driveway and crossed the road, she found herself wondering where the years had gone. Her son, whom she thought of as a little boy, was growing at a crazy rate. He was big and strong and athletic, and from behind, he looked almost manly.

He slowed down to wait for her at Noah's driveway. Someone had dug out around a painted wooden sign that read "Shepherd Animal Hospital."

Sophie wondered if she should have called first. Her gloved hand touched the phone in her pocket. No, if she called, that would seem too deliberate. Too calculated. And even though he'd extended an invitation the previous night, Noah might feel as though he had to treat them like company.

It was better to just casually drop by, she decided. Neighborly. She was learning to be neighborly.

She only hoped she could stand being in the same room with Noah and refrain from jumping his bones.

As she and Max approached the house, Sophie studied the way it crowned the brow of the hill, its largest windows oriented directly at the view of the lake. At one time, she guessed long ago, this had been the only house in the vicinity. Other than going to college and then vet school at Cornell, this was the only place Noah had ever lived. She wondered if he would always live here. If he would die here. She wondered if that gave him a feeling of satisfaction, of belonging and continuity . . . or if it felt impossibly stultifying and made him want to gnaw off a limb to escape.

"Hello," she called out when they reached the front porch. "Anybody home?"

This was no big deal, she reminded herself as she knocked at the door. He was a neighbor. She knocked again, and was immediately inundated with misgivings. She should have called first. It was bad form to just show up and—

"Just a second," she heard him call.

There was some barking from Rudy and high-pitched yaps from Opal.

"Dogs," said Max, his facing lighting up. "Those must be his dogs."

"Did you think I was making it up? Like I told you, he's a vet. Of course he has dogs."

Noah was half-naked when he answered the door.

He wore running shorts and shoes, a white towel around his neck. He was glistening with sweat and grinning at her. "Hey," he said, holding the door wide open to let her in.

"I should have called first," she said. "This is a bad time."

"This is a great time," he said, wiping his hand on the towel and holding it out. "You must be Max. I'm Noah."

Max shook hands with Noah, but all his attention was on the dogs behind the baby gate in the hallway. "Do you mind if I pet your dogs? I really like dogs, but we can't have one where we live."

Sophie hadn't realized that, but it made sense. The grounds and buildings of the Inn at Willow Lake were pristine, probably not the easiest place to keep a dog. Interesting, she thought. A chink in Greg's superdad armor.

"Sure you can pet them," said Noah. "They live for affection." He disengaged the baby gate. "This is Rudy, and the little one's Opal."

Max melted to the floor, trying to hug both dogs at once. They swirled around him, vying for his attention until he laughed aloud. It was, Sophie realized, the first spontaneous laughter she'd had from Max all weekend. Dogs could bring smiles from a stone—or from a boy who was determined to give his mother a hard time.

"I was downstairs, working out," Noah said. "I just need to turn the music off," he added. "Want to come check it out? You can bring Opal."

It was obvious Max was not going to let go of the little caramel-colored fluff ball. He and Sophie followed Noah down a flight of stairs to the basement.

"My gym," Noah said, picking up the remote control and turning down the volume. Sophie wasn't sorry to hear the end of that. It was music she'd never heard before and didn't care for, more noise than notes.

"T-Pain," Max said. "I like those guys."

"Word," said Noah.

The basement was outfitted like a professional gym—a treadmill, stair step machine, weights and pulleys, some sort of wall apparatus straight out of the Inquisition. The place was equipped with speakers, a fridge and a sink. There was a shelf crammed with water bottles, mugs and glasses, and a number of trophies shoved haphazardly away.

Max noticed them right away. "What are the trophies for?"

Noah was busy shutting down the equipment. "Some races," he said. "Mostly triathlons."

Heavens, thought Sophie. No wonder he was such a hunk.

"My mom swims. She was in a big swimming race last year, weren't you, Mom?" commented Max. He turned to Noah. "She swam the Zuider Zee. That's in Holland. Fifty kilometers, right, Mom?"

Sophie was surprised. "I didn't think you'd remember that, Max."

"*Hello?* When your mom swims across a sea, even a really little one, you kind of remember it." He turned back to Noah. "She finished in the top ten percent and probably would have done even better if it hadn't been for those East German women with hair on their chests."

Noah grinned. "I hate when that happens."

Max stood on tiptoe to check out one of the trophies. "This one's for an Ironman triathlon. What's that mean?"

"A two-mile swim, hundred-mile bike ride and a full twenty-six-mile marathon."

"You got first," Max said. "That's awesome."

"I'm training for a winter event now," Noah said. "It takes place during Winter Carnival. Speedskating, snowshoeing and cross-country skiing." He finished shutting down the equipment, pulled on a hooded sweatshirt and a pair of sweatpants, then led the way upstairs. Sophie was bemused by the way Noah and Max hit it off, buddies already. There was a peculiar eagerness in Noah as he showed Max around his place. Nothing like a little hero worship to perk a guy up.

Max was already intrigued by the overtly guylike features of the place—the foosball table in the middle of the living room. A full-size jukebox rescued from a local bar that went out of business. The giant TV and all its video games and accessories. A young boy's paradise.

"Is that the Wii?" Max asked.

"The latest model."

"What games do you have?"

"Super Smash Bros., Rayman. I also have a PlayStation with Guitar Hero III. . . ." Noah rattled them off, more foreign to Sophie's ears than an African dialect. "Tell you what. You can put something on while I run upstairs for a quick shower."

"That's okay. I'd rather play with the dogs."

"Fine by me." Noah turned to Sophie. "Be right back."

As Max sank to the floor to play tug-of-war with Opal, Sophie refrained from saying *I told you so.* Max wouldn't have cared, anyway. He was lost in laughter at the frisky pup.

She thought about the Ironman trophies. She thought about Noah's bare, glistening chest and powerful shoulders. She was attracted to the man, but her instinct was to conceal that from Max. It was nothing, she told herself. A temporary madness.

Could there be anything more awkward than dating in the presence of your children? How had Greg handled that? And had the kids been okay with him dating? Would they be okay with her doing so, even this soon after her arrival in Avalon?

Max let the puppy tackle him and lick his face. And Sophie couldn't help smiling at them both.

"She's an orphan," she told Max. "The puppy, I mean."

"Really?"

"Well, sort of. According to Noah, she comes from a very big litter. The mother couldn't take care of her, so Noah had to bottle-feed her."

"The mother rejected her?" Max held Opal up, brought his face to hers. "Poor thing."

"She needs a home," Noah said, coming down the stairs, his damp hair curling over his brow. He looked as sexy as ever in jeans and a haphazardly tucked-in plaid shirt, his feet bare.

Don't look at him, she warned herself. When she looked at him, she went brain-dead.

"Maybe you'd like to keep her," he said to Max, sitting down to put on clean socks and boots.

Max leaped to his feet, hugging the pup close. "Really?"

"If it's all right with your mom," Noah added.

"Oh, this is emotional blackmail," Sophie objected. "If I say no, that makes me the Wicked Witch of the West."

"Then don't say no," Noah advised her. "You mentioned before that it would be nice to get Max a dog. You said that first morning that you ought to get a dog. I'm doing this as a favor."

"I was speaking theoretically, not—"

"You said that, Mom?" Max was now regarding her with worshipful eyes.

"Yes, but maybe not so soon. I don't even have a place of my own. It's completely unacceptable to bring an animal into a house where I'm a guest."

"I talked to Bertie last night to make sure she didn't mind about the dog," Noah said. "She's totally on board with it."

"You did not," Sophie objected. "You said you didn't know her."

"I said I hadn't seen her in a long time. Do you

have your phone with you?" Noah asked.

Without thinking, she took it out of her pocket and handed it to him. He flipped it open and scrolled through her contacts, then hit Send and handed back the phone. "You can ask her yourself right now."

Sophie closed the phone before connecting. "I still can't do this. I don't have time. I have to watch my grandson three afternoons a week."

"The puppy can stay here while you're away," Noah said simply. "And when Max isn't in school, he'll take care of her."

"Mom, please." Max tucked the puppy against his chest. "She needs me now."

"Tell you what," Noah said, shrugging into a parka, "I'll show you around. The puppy can come."

Max and the dogs headed out the back door. Sophie started to follow, but Noah held her back, grabbing her hand and reeling her in to plant a kiss on her surprised mouth. It lasted all of two seconds, yet in that span of time, she relived all the ways he had touched her and the unexpected things he made her feel, and how, when she was with him, she never felt lonely.

She pulled away from him. "Stop that."

"Your boy doesn't know about us?"

"There is no *us*. There's nothing to know."

"Then what the hell are we doing, Sophie?"

"I don't believe you. Acting as though your feelings are hurt."

"Maybe they are," he said.

She tugged on her gloves as she walked out the back door. "You are in such trouble."

He followed her outside, his boots crunching on the snow. "What's that supposed to mean?"

"Not now." She marched ahead.

"He seems like a good kid," Noah said. "I'm going to show him around some more. Want to come?"

Like the pied piper, Noah led Max to the clinic. The puppy came paddling through the drifts behind. Sophie heaved a sigh, feeling confused and hopeful and out of sorts. Noah had overstepped a boundary, but the bottom line was, he had just given Max a reason to spend as much time as possible with her. She went to join them. After a brief tour of the facilities, which Max clearly found interesting, they went up to the barn. They checked out a room full of veterinary equipment and a stall for patients, currently vacant.

"Ever ride a horse?" Noah asked Max.

"Nope. Never had the chance."

"I'll show you how one of these days. There's a girl who comes a few times a week to work around here and exercise them. Chelsea Nash. Do you know her?"

Max looked uncomfortable. "Saw her on the school bus."

"Maybe she could teach you, too. And then there's your mom."

"My mom doesn't ride."

"I used to," Sophie said quickly. "I used to be sort of good at it. I had a horse of my own."

"No way." Max watched her stroking one of the horses.

"I got Misty when I was about your age. I rode her every day."

"You never told me you had a horse when you were a kid," Max said.

"I never told you I had the mumps when I was little, either."

"Yeah, but a horse. That's major."

"Mumps are major."

"So what happened to the horse?"

"She died and I was completely devastated."

Max scooped up Opal and hugged her against his chest. "Don't think that's going to talk me out of this puppy."

Nineteen

Noah hadn't been lying about having called Bertie Wilson. Sophie phoned her, and Bertie said yes, it was fine to adopt a puppy. "Little Noah Shepherd." She seemed amused. "It was great to get his call. I hadn't heard from him in years."

Little Noah Shepherd? Sophie had to smile. There was nothing little about him.

Max spent the afternoon rearranging his life—and Sophie's house—around the puppy. He brought the crate, bedding and food bowls from Noah's and set her up in his bedroom. Daisy and Charlie showed up at dusk, bringing a merry swirl of cold air. "I came as soon as I got your message," Daisy said. "A puppy?"

Sophie took the baby from her while Daisy hung up her coat. "It wasn't my idea."

"You should take credit for it, though. It's brilliant."

While Daisy went in search of Max and the puppy, Sophie gave her attention to the bundle in her arms. "Hello, you."

To her delight, Charlie offered her a funny grin, punctuated with a string of saliva.

"You know me now, don't you?" Feeling ridiculously pleased with herself, she joined Daisy and Max to find him transforming his closet into a puppy habitat. The crate fit on one side, and he'd created a play area with toys, a step stool and a fat, knobby log from the woodpile.

"I'm impressed," Sophie said. "For someone who's never had a dog before, you seem to know what you're doing."

"Mom. I've been planning this my whole life."

She stood back and watched him stroking the puppy, his face soft with adoration. She wondered what other dreams and plans he had. There was so much to learn about Max.

With the baby in her lap, she sat cross-legged on the floor. The puppy came to check out Charlie and was polite enough about sniffing him. Daisy applied herself diligently to helping Max. After a while, Sophie realized the entire afternoon had passed without Max complaining even once about the lack of cable TV or computer games.

As she sat there with her kids and grandson and the new dog, she felt an emotion she almost didn't recognize—happiness, pure and simple. A sense of peaceful contentment.

Life, for this moment, was good.

She was just starting to think about getting dinner when the phone rang.

"I ordered pizza. It'll be here in about forty-five minutes." Noah always seemed to have a smile in his voice.

"And this concerns me because . . ."

"Because I'm warning you now, there's no meat on the pizzas."

"I'll inform the media."

"Come over. We're going to be jamming."

"We?"

"Me and the guys in the band."

Band? "My daughter's here—"

"Bring her. Bring anyone you want."

Sophie reminded herself that she was mad at him about the dog. "Noah—"

"Be there," he said. "Aloha."

"What's up?" asked Daisy as Sophie put away her phone.

"How do you feel about an evening of culture?"

Her children regarded her skeptically.

"Continental cuisine and musical entertainment," she said.

The kids looked queasy, and she relented. "Pizza and Noah's garage band. We're all invited."

• • •

"Dude," Eddie Haven, the guitar player said, "lose the sweatshirt."

"What's wrong with this shirt?" Noah asked. "I just washed it."

"You reek of Bounce sheets."

Noah had stuffed a handful in the dryer with the last load he'd done. "So?"

"Chicks get suspicious when they smell Bounce sheets on a guy."

Noah frowned at him and went over to his drum set, tapping the snare to check the tuning. "I don't get it."

"When a shirt smells like dryer sheets, it can mean only one of two things. One, he's gay. Or two, he's got a girlfriend. Before today did you ever use it?"

"No. I had a box left over from when I was with Daphne."

"My point exactly."

"Sophie knows I'm single," Noah said. "And she knows I'm not gay."

Eddie adjusted the volume of his amp. "Yeah?"

"Definitely."

"Dude." He offered his fist and they touched knuckles. Of all the guys in the band, Eddie was the one with real talent. He could wail on the guitar like a young Stevie Ray Vaughan while belting out rock ballads that made grown men pine for their lost youth. The only reason he hadn't hit the big time was that he lived in Avalon—not by choice but by necessity. There was some convoluted story about a scuffle with the county prosecutor's nephew, a missed court date and a quarrel with a cranky judge. The upshot was, Eddie had been ordered to perform community service by serving the Heart of the Mountains Church as choir director. He did a remarkably good job at it, not surprisingly, given his background.

"About the laundry, I'm not kidding," Eddie concluded. "Bo said you're into this chick."

"I *am* into this chick," Noah admitted.

"And I'm just trying to be helpful."

Noah laughed. "Because you've been such a huge success with the ladies."

Eddie looked chagrined. "I've been unlucky in love." He had a long and complicated history with women—as well as the law.

"So you consider sleeping with the pastor's wife unlucky," Noah said.

"Nope, I consider getting caught unlucky," said Eddie.

Bo Crutcher arrived with two longneck bottles of beer stuck in his back pockets and a rebel yell on his lips. "Are you ready to rock 'n' roll, my brothers?"

"I was just giving our boy Noah a bit of advice for the lovelorn," Eddie said.

"He's not lovelorn," Bo said with a snort.

"How do you know?" Noah demanded. "I am too. I'm totally lorn."

"In lust, maybe. Not love, though."

"How the hell would you know that?"

"Because if you were lovelorn, you wouldn't be with us tonight. You'd be with her."

"I invited her over," Noah said.

"I mean, you'd fix things so it's just the two of you," Bo said.

"I can't. Not tonight," Noah admitted.

"Can't what?" Rayburn Tolley, their keyboard man, came in through the kitchen, his apple cheeks burned deep red by the cold, making him look more boyish than ever. Like Noah, he'd grown up in Avalon. He was a policeman under Chief McKnight. He was also Eddie's parole officer.

"Can't be alone with his new woman," said Eddie.

"Why not?" asked Ray.

"It's complicated," Noah said.

" 'It's complicated' covers a lot of ground. It can mean anything from 'I'm married' to 'I did time for involuntary manslaughter after my last boyfriend was killed.' "

"She's got her kids with her all weekend."

"Bummer," said Eddie. "So much for the booty call."

"And her grandson," Noah added, watching his friends closely for a reaction.

They took it in stride. "She's a grandmother?" Ray said.

"That's right," Noah confirmed. "And they're all coming over, and you guys are going to be cool."

"Nothing but cool," Bo agreed, opening a beer.

"You should never doubt our coolness." Ray stepped

up to the keyboard and switched on the power.

"Because she's kind of classy," Noah said.

"What kind of classy?" Ray demanded.

Just then, Sophie walked into the room. "Hello," she said. "I knocked at the door but I don't think anyone heard."

Noah felt a rush of happiness when he saw her. His friends were wrong about the lust. That was part of what he felt for Sophie, sure, but it was so much more than that. Or it was going to be, if he didn't blow it. While she took off her jacket, the others went silent. Under his breath, Eddie muttered, "Dude."

"Come in and meet the guys," Noah said. He hoped like hell she wasn't still mad about the dog.

"My crew is here, too." Sophie motioned them in from the vestibule, and there were introductions all around.

Noah wasn't surprised to see that her daughter, Daisy, looked a lot like Sophie—blond hair and blue eyes, a killer smile. Daisy's baby was a smiling, red-haired lump of a thing, his bright eyes moving watchfully around the room.

"How's it going with the puppy?" Noah asked Max.

"So far, so good. I found a perfect spot for her crate. She was sound asleep when we left the house. She was really tired."

"Puppies sleep a lot," Noah said.

The pizzas arrived in a stack of five boxes, five different combos. Everyone was quiet for a while, intent on eating. Noah found some sodas and a bottle of red wine in the pantry, and after a while, they got down to business. As a band, they didn't do much performing, but getting gigs wasn't that important. It was always good to have an audience, even a tiny one.

Noah put on his lucky baseball cap, brim turned backward, and took his seat. He offered Sophie a brief smile, feeling unusually self-conscious, which was not like him. They'd been practicing and, thanks to Eddie, they weren't half-bad.

Because of the little baby, they decided to stick with softer, acoustic numbers. They could rock and wail, but tonight they simply played some tunes they knew well, a mixture of new music from Eddie's talented pen, along with some classics from the dawn of time—"No Woman, No Cry," by Bob Marley and James Taylor's "Fire and Rain."

Sophie was an appreciative listener, at least she seemed to be, sitting thoughtfully on the couch. Maybe she was just being polite. Max—a baseball fan—regarded Bo Crutcher with the kind of hero worship Bo craved. When they finished with an Eric Clapton ballad, Sophie applauded and favored Noah with a smile that made him wish they were alone.

"Do any of you play?" Eddie asked at the break.

Max and Daisy both turned to their mother. She looked startled, but then admitted, "Piano. Not lately, though."

Turning on his trademark charm, Eddie took her hand and drew her to Ray's keyboard while Ray gamely moved aside. She stood there for a moment, looking bewildered. "I'm classically trained," she said.

"Don't worry, we won't hold that against you."

As she took a seat, she assumed a pianist's trained posture. Noah suspected he was seeing old habits kick in. She played a piece he didn't recognize, the sort of thing that aired on public radio on Sunday mornings. Ray jazzed it up with some electronic adjustments. Noah added an easy beat, and Bo underscored it with some bass. Finally, Eddie chimed in with a few guitar riffs, giving everyone just a small hint of his virtuosity. For the next few minutes, the bass-line melody, which had likely originated with some guy in a powdered wig, turned into something new.

Sophie's kids looked on with their jaws unhinged by surprise. At the end of the number, she laughed at their expressions. "I think I'm insulted by how amazed you are."

"Mom, that was really good," Max said.

"Daisy, why don't you give it a shot?" Sophie said. "You used to be a good piano student, too. And I understand you're a drummer these days, Max." She took the baby and traded places with her daughter. Noah motioned Max to the drum set. The kid was stiff and uncertain, but within a couple of minutes, they were having fun messing around with the guys.

Noah leaned over to Sophie. "Thirsty?"

"I could use some water," she said, and they went to the kitchen together.

Noah immediately kissed her, leaning across the baby she was holding. "Been dying to do that all evening. I've never been with a woman with a baby before," he said.

She gazed steadily up at him, then handed over the kid. "This is a grandbaby."

"That's a new one on me, too." If she thought it would faze him, she was totally wrong. The little one squirmed and squeaked at the notion of finding himself with a stranger, but didn't cry. Noah liked the soft, squishy feel of the baby he was holding, something he didn't get to do too often. He liked the way the baby smelled. He knew he'd like it even better when it turned into an actual kid. "I like this guy. And your kids."

"If you think you're off the hook about the dog," she said, "you're wrong. I can't believe you'd—"

"Mom," Max called from the other room.

She moved away from Noah as though he were poison, then marched back to the living room, apparently having forgotten the water.

"Play something else, Mom," Max said, taking the baby from Noah.

Ray, with his mouth full of pizza, waved in agreement. Sophie went to the keyboard and they tried some George Gershwin. Probably the person who was most surprised was Sophie herself. Noah got the feeling that simply playing music just for the fun of it was not a common occurrence in her life.

During a lull in the music, Noah saw Max lean over to his sister and say, "I'm *so* going to start taking piano lessons again."

Twenty

Sophie pulled her minivan into the well-plowed lane that led to the Inn at Willow Lake. In the backseat, Max was holding Opal in front of his face, rubbing noses with her and talking baby talk with a complete lack of self-consciousness. It was Sunday evening, the loneliest hour of the week for a certain type of person—the noncustodial single parent. All across the nation, every Sunday, people like her surrendered their kids to the other parent and drove away with only memories to keep them company until the next visit. Or, in Sophie's case, memories and a new puppy.

"How am I gonna make it through the week?" Max asked. "I wish Opal could live with me."

Welcome to my world, thought Sophie. Max would have to make do with after-school and weekend visits. Compromise was a bitch sometimes, she reflected. "I'll take good care of her."

"I know you will," Max said, "but it won't be the same."

"You'll have to have a little faith in me."

"I do, Mom. Jeez."

The inn was like the set of *Dr. Zhivago*, with its lawns and tennis courts blanketed in white, the gazebo and belvedere tower hung with glittering icicles. The historic main building looked warm and inviting, with lights glowing in the windows. The owners' residence was a tall, boxy house and, like everything else in her ex-husband's life, it looked nothing like the home they'd once shared in Manhattan.

Which, of course, was as it should be. They'd both set out, after the divorce, to lead different lives because the one they'd been living had stopped working.

"The place looks wonderful," Sophie observed. She made the comment to be supportive, but also because it was true.

"Dad and Nina are getting the inn ready for Winter Carnival. It's a big deal," Max said. "I think they're sold out, too." He kissed the puppy on the head, and Opal regarded him with an expression of comical adoration. "Come inside for a minute."

She bit back an automatic reply: *No, I need to get going.* For Max's sake, she would endure it. "I'll come in, just for a minute, so you can show your dad the puppy," she said, trudging up the walkway to the pretty, brightly lit house.

She was supremely uncomfortable in Greg's world, even for a few minutes. It didn't physically hurt to be near him anymore, not the way it once had. Now it was bizarrely possible to regard him with a kind of benign respect. Here was someone she'd once loved. Someone she'd made a life with for a lot of years. But they had both moved on.

That determination—on her part and on Greg's—to make the transition from married to single had saved her. Maybe it had saved them all, after putting the whole family through an emotional wringer. Ultimately, Sophie had stopped regarding her marriage as a failure. Rather than being a survivor of a failed marriage, she was focused on being successful in a new phase of her life. That meant surviving anything, from international terrorists to the momzillas at the hockey rink.

She followed Max up the porch steps. Sophie didn't really want these glimpses of the life he had made with Nina Romano. For Max's sake, though, Sophie drew on her training as a diplomat, putting on a pleasant expression as she walked through the door and waited in the vestibule, which was warm and inviting, fragrant with orange oil polish.

"Dad," called Max. "Hey, Nina and Dad! We're here. Come and check out my dog."

They arrived together, welcoming Sophie but clearly focused on the new arrival. Max was talking a mile a minute, full of stories about Opal as though she had been a part of his life forever. He carefully outlined her every habit and preference, from her affinity for the tattered fleece blanket in her crate to her playful habit of biting the snow as she ran.

"Now you've got a project," Greg said to Sophie.

She couldn't detect any sarcasm in his voice. "So it appears."

"No way am I waiting for next weekend," Max said. "I can take the bus after school to your place, right, Mom?"

Sophie glanced at Greg, who gave a barely perceptible nod.

Thank you. "That would be all right with me." She didn't pretend Max's comment had anything to do with her. Not even June Cleaver, in her high heels and apron, could compete with a puppy.

Then, to her surprise, Max said, "Mom played in a rock band. It was awesome."

Greg looked blank. "A rock band."

"Yeah, with the guy across the road, and guess who the bass player was? Bo Crutcher."

"I've heard them play," said Nina. "They call themselves Inner Child and they're pretty good. They'll be performing at Winter Carnival this year."

Sophie smiled, felt her cheeks start to glow. Then she remembered she still hadn't dealt with Noah about the dog. "Max can tell you everything. I'd better go." She took the puppy's leash.

Max gave the dog a final pat and then a kiss on the head. Then he offered Sophie a brief, spontaneous hug. "See you, Mom."

"I'll take good care of Opal," she said. "Promise."

She still felt warm from Max's hug. She now had a dog, for better or worse. She had to admit, having the puppy on the seat beside her made leaving Max just a shade less wrenching. Still, Noah had pulled a fast one on her, and she didn't intend to let the matter drop.

The next day, she got up and fed Opal, took her for a romp in the yard and then put her in the crate for a nap. A puppy, she realized, was a good deal less complicated than a baby. Still, that didn't make what Noah had done right. When her phone rang, she squinted at the caller ID, then stretched out her arm, but the name was still indistinct. In the past few months, she'd begun to suspect a growing need for reading glasses, but kept resisting. Reading glasses were for old people, weren't they?

"Sophie Bellamy," she said, still in the habit of using her crisp, professional voice.

"Sophie, it's your father."

"And your mother."

She was on speakerphone, which her parents used when they wanted to team up and convince her that she was making some huge mistake. "Hello," Sophie said, putting a smile into her voice. She summarized her weekend for them, noticing as she spoke that she felt tense with the pressure to perform, or to make her life seem important. This was always the case with her parents.

"It sounds as though you and Max had a marvelous weekend," her mother said.

Sophie immediately grew suspicious. "You didn't call to hear about our weekend."

"We were just saying this sabbatical is a good idea," her father added. "When you go back, you'll be even better equipped for the challenges of international law."

Sophie tightened her grip on the phone. "Dad, I meant what I said before. I'm not going back."

"Oh, sweetheart," her mother said, "you just need time. It won't be long before you're dying to be back in court, doing what you do best."

"Dying, Mom?"

"Sorry," her mother said. "Poor choice of words. Sophie, we can't imagine what you went through, but we know how strong you are."

"Mom, Dad. This is my life now, living in Avalon so I can be with Max and Daisy. I'm a hockey car-pool mom in a velour sweatsuit."

"Honestly, Sophie." Her mother gave a nervous laugh.

Sophie couldn't resist adding fuel to the fire. "And I've . . . met someone. His name's Noah and he lives across the way, on his family's former dairy farm." She paused, trying to hear past the vacuum of silence that ensued. "Hello? I need you both to respond, so I know no one's having heart failure."

"Sophie, you're not yourself. You shouldn't be making life decisions at a time like this."

"My decision's already made. I'm not going back."

"But your work is so important, Sophie," her mother said. "Our friends have all been asking about you—"

"I'm sorry, but I'm through being your trophy daughter," she said. "I'm through being the thing you get to talk about at cocktail parties. Find something else. Or go ahead and tell people the truth about me—that I'm putting my family first. I'm happy. Can you even comprehend that? In The Hague there were a hundred talented lawyers lining up for my job. I'm the only one who can do this one."

"Oh, sweetheart." Her mother's sigh traveled across the miles. "You don't sound like the Sophie I know. We wanted so much for you."

"Well, then. Congratulations. Mission accomplished. I have everything I need, right here." She took a deep breath. "I'm going to be fine. Be happy for me, please."

"We are," her father said. "We want to make sure *you're* happy." Despite his sincerity, his voice sounded strained, and after a few more minutes of small talk, Sophie hung up, feeling guilty.

A little later, she had an unexpected visitor. She let Noah in, refusing to acknowledge her very physical reaction to his presence, because she was still upset with him, her mood exacerbated by the conversation with her parents, though he couldn't know that.

"What, no pony?" she asked archly, pretending to search his jacket for one. "Or did you decide to build a bowling alley for me next?"

"You're mad?" He looked genuinely surprised. Uninvited, he peeled off his gloves and hat.

"Gosh, no," she said. "This is all just peachy. Damn it, Noah, you gave my son a puppy."

"You're welcome."

"Listen, I appreciate you wanting to do something nice, but a puppy. It's too much."

"Too much what?"

"It's just one more complication in an already-complicated situation." She paced back and forth. "A dog, Noah? You give my kid a dog, and you don't know why I have a problem with that? You didn't even ask me first."

"You would have said no."

"He doesn't know the first thing about raising a dog."

"It's no big deal. You help him raise the puppy and the whole family has a friend for life. It's just something else to love." He opened a beer for himself. "What's the worst that can happen?"

"God, Noah. Everything's so simple with you." Sophie realized what she'd said and gave a dry little laugh.

"That's me. Simple."

"I didn't mean—"

"I know what you meant. Look, the dog needed a home, and Max needed a dog."

"How do you know what Max needs?"

"He's a boy. Every boy needs a dog. He'll learn more about responsibility and compassion from that dog than you can ever imagine."

"And when Max isn't with me, then *I'm* going to be the one looking after the dog," she pointed out.

"So maybe you'll learn responsibility and compassion, too." He caught her glare and backed away with a grin, palms out. "Kidding."

"You don't do this to a person," she said. "You don't just hand over a commitment that lasts for years without thinking—"

"Oh, I thought about it," he said. "You said he wasn't happy spending time here."

"Yes, but—"

"Now he's got a reason to stay."

"That just makes me pathetic, having to bribe my own son with a puppy to get him to stay with me."

"You're overanalyzing this."

"Ha. I haven't even gotten started. A puppy," she repeated. "Noah, how could you? This is a live creature, not a toy."

"Yeah, the live ones are my favorite kind."

"Smart aleck. As a vet, you know better than anyone how horrible it is when the pet dies."

"Hell, yes, I know that. I also know what the other ten to fifteen years are like. It's terrible to lose a pet, yeah. But it's worse never to have owned it in the first place."

"It doesn't work that way for everybody."

"How about you give your boy a shot at it? A dog can teach him things about life. And about caring and tolerance and letting go, when it comes down to it."

She wanted to argue the point but found that she couldn't. Noah had given her the dog, which was a huge commitment. It was a mixed blessing. She hated that Max needed a reason to be with her, but she was coming to realize that a twelve-year-old boy tended to need things even the most perfect mother couldn't provide.

"You made the offer in front of Max. I was trapped." A cold feeling came over her. "I don't like being trapped."

"Are you mad about your son getting a dog or about the fact that I thought of it first?"

Opposing counsel makes an interesting point, she thought, but decided not to go there. "I just don't like what it implies—that I'm not enough for my son. That spending the weekend with me is so boring he needs a puppy and a damned rock concert to make him want to stay."

"So did he have a good weekend?" Noah asked.

"He got a puppy, hung out with a live band, met a baseball star and oh, I nearly forgot. He went skating with Tina Calloway, the daughter of an Olympic gold medalist. He had a *great* weekend."

"Then what's the problem?"

"Now you're being disingenuous."

"I'm not. I don't get it, Sophie."

"The problem is that *I* want to be his great weekend."

"Would you settle for being *my* great weekend?" Noah suggested. He shrugged out of his jacket and hung it on the hall tree.

"Now you're trying to change the subject."

"Hell, yeah, I'm trying to change the subject. You think this is fun for me, getting yelled at for doing you a favor?" He lowered his voice, stepping close to her, so close she could smell the outdoors on him. "Sophie. Are you really going to yell at me for giving your boy a dog?"

"Yes," she whispered, forgetting to yell.

He grazed her jawline with his knuckles. "It'll be

fine," he told her, taking her hand and heading to the living room. He took a seat on the couch and pulled her down next to him. "I swear, it will."

"It's a real blow to the ego to know I'm not enough for him."

"He's in middle school. If you were his whole world, I'd worry about the boy."

She couldn't argue with that. "The time when I got to be his whole world is long past."

"Be the mom he needs," Noah suggested. "Not the mom you think you need to be."

"God, Noah. Where do you come up with this stuff?"

"It's common sense, is all."

"I suppose it is. In my family—" She stopped herself, regarded him skeptically. "You can't be interested in this."

"I'm interested in everything about you."

For some reason, she found that statement incredibly sexy. She hugged a sofa pillow in her lap, keeping some distance between them. "Trust me, I'm not that interesting."

"Tell me about your family—your parents. Brothers and sisters?"

"I am an only child. My parents are good people. And I learned a lot from them, like how important it is to have a career you love. I only wish they'd taught me that something like a job is peripheral to what matters most." She was still discomfited by their phone call. Her parents believed they'd raised a perfect, high-achieving daughter. What they'd ended up with was an incomplete woman, someone who lived every day with regrets.

She regarded Noah thoughtfully. She was astonished to find herself talking this over with him. In such a short time, she had learned to count on him in a way she'd never counted on anyone before. She considered the conversation she'd had on the phone with her parents. The old Sophie would have kept it to herself, worrying the issue like a dog with a bone. But when it came to Noah, she wanted to let him into places she'd long kept private. Looking into his kind, caring eyes, she felt a kind of trust she'd never experienced before. She wanted him to know, absolutely, the true reason she was here in this town, having left a career fifteen years in the making. She wanted him to know she'd been searching for something else to hold on to, so much so that she had moved here to this strange town, a place where her ex-husband was a pillar of the community and where she was regarded as the cold, neglectful ex-wife.

She wished she could tell him the deepest things inside her—about that night, about the things that had happened to her, the way she had been taken apart by sheer terror and then put back together by an unexpected drive for survival. She wished she could tell him that, when everything was taken from her, when she believed her next breath would be her last, there was nothing inside her except thoughts of her family—all the ways she had failed them, the missed opportunities, the squandered chances.

"Do you think it's terrible?" she asked him. "What I just said about my folks?"

"Nah. At some point, everybody sees their parents as actual people."

"They still think my being here is only temporary. It's a kind of denial, I suppose. They always do this to me, make me have second thoughts about the choices I make. No matter how old I get, I still feel the need to please them." She took a deep breath, offering him a chance to interrupt, change the subject, run screaming into the hills. He did none of those things, just waited, listening.

There was something irresistible about the way Noah listened. She braided her fingers together and said, "When I found out I was pregnant with Daisy, I intended to raise her on my own. My parents questioned this decision until I started questioning it myself. They were very persuasive. They loved that Greg was a Bellamy. They loved that he would go far in his career. Ultimately, I was convinced that the right thing to do was tell Greg and marry him for the sake of the baby. So that's what we did. Through sheer force of will we made it work, but it was never right." She crushed the throw pillow more tightly against her.

"I had these two beautiful children who only wanted me to be there for them, and I wasn't. Even when I worked at the UN in Manhattan, I was always somewhere else—mentally if not physically. I keep wondering now how things would have worked out if I had been more present in their lives."

"You know," said Noah, "when I was a kid, I used to fantasize about my dad being an astronaut instead of a dairy farmer. I still think about how totally different my life would have been if my parents had worked in outer space."

She hurled the pillow at him. "Very funny."

"Just trying to make a point. With your family—with your whole life, really—you don't get to have a control group. You don't have any way of knowing how things would have turned out if you'd done something differently, made another choice, followed a different path. My advice? Not that you asked for it, but you ought to try dealing with the things that are. Quit trying to rewrite the way they were."

"Thank you, Dr. Freud."

"I'll send you a bill in the morning."

Strangely, talking to him did have a liberating effect on her. His way of looking at the situation was straightforward. Her own thought processes were more like a Venn diagram, with each decision leading to a perilous array of possibilities.

"Seriously," he said, "try not to second-guess yourself so much—not about the past, or the dog. Or me." He grinned.

She looked away, trying to figure out what it was about him. They were having a deeply personal conversation, and she kept thinking about what his kisses tasted like and how he looked without a shirt.

"Too much thinking," he said. "It can't be good for you."

"I could blame my training. In my job at the ICC, every single step I took, every decision had to be debated, every possible outcome projected. It's become second nature to me. Do you know, I once actually made a diagram to figure out a seating arrangement for a court dinner."

"It's not the only way to navigate through life," he said.

"Oh? And what's your way?"

"Just pick a horse and get on it."

"Again, so simple."

"It *is* simple if you let it be."

"Noah Shepherd—veterinary genius by day, Zen philosopher by night. All right. I'll try to take your advice."

He nodded gravely. "There is no *try,*" he said in a soft Yoda voice. "There is only *do,* or *not do.*"

"You're crazy," she said.

"I know." He moved closer to her on the sofa and kissed her softly on the mouth. Between kisses, he told her, "I missed you this weekend."

I missed you, too. She didn't let herself say it. Instead, she said, "We need to stop this."

"Why?"

"Because it's foolish to be so impulsive. We need to slow down, figure out where we're going. I thought we weren't going to do this anymore."

"Wrong," he said, unbuttoning her sweater with

slow deliberation. "We're going to do this every chance we get."

"I don't think it's a good idea."

"You're not supposed to be thinking at all. If you are, I'm falling down on the job."

"Oh," she said, her insides melting, "you're doing a fine job. Believe me, this is absolutely . . . fine."

He laughed with his mouth against hers. "Good. I like your family, Sophie. But now all I can think about is this. I *am* crazy. I can't keep my hands off you."

"I moved here for my family," she reminded him. "Being with you, like this—"

"Is not stealing anything from them," he said, sliding the sweater down over her shoulders, unfastening her bra. "You get to take off the hair shirt every once in a while."

Twenty-One

Daisy's life felt different lately. Ever since her mom had been helping her with Charlie, things seemed easier in a way that was hard to explain. Just knowing her mom was looking after Charlie made Daisy feel more rested, more relaxed. She still wasn't mother of the year. Her house was still pretty messy most of the time, and she always felt as though she was running late for something, but she no longer had the sensation of running just barely ahead of a steamroller, apt to get flattened if she slowed down even for a second.

She wasn't sure this was due to her mom being around for her, or if Daisy was simply getting better at dealing with her own life. It didn't really matter, and she wasn't going to dwell on it, especially not today. Winter Carnival was almost here, and Sonnet's train was due in any minute.

"This is a bad idea," Zach Alger said grimly to Daisy as they walked together toward the train station. "I shouldn't have come with you."

"Nonsense." She glanced over at him. His pale skin seemed more tightly drawn across his cheekbones than ever, adding to his air of tenseness. His straight blond hair fanned out behind him as he walked in long, quick paces. "You and Sonnet are bound to run into each other sooner or later, so you might as well make it sooner."

"She and I wouldn't be running into each other at all if I hadn't let you talk me into this. It's a bad idea," he said again.

Daisy tried not to feel annoyed. Her mom was watching Charlie for her, and Daisy was enjoying a rare sense of liberty. Plus, she was about to see Sonnet for the first time since their parents married each other in St. Croix. She didn't want Zach putting a damper on her excitement. "I think it would be sad if the two of you didn't work out your differences." She put her hand on his arm to slow him down. "You can't smoke inside," she reminded him.

He stopped walking beside a green-painted trash barrel and took a final drag on his cigarette. Daisy didn't judge him for smoking. *As if.* Before she got pregnant with Charlie, she had done worse than that.

"It'll be fine," she told him.

"Did you tell her I was going to be here?" he asked.

"I texted her. I'm sure she's fine with it." A white lie, that. Sonnet had texted her back: DONT U DARE.

They went through the salon and out onto the platform. Lots of people came to Avalon's Winter Carnival, tourists up from the city, mostly. Attracting tourists was the whole point of the festival, and the entire town pitched in. Daisy had been busy photographing the preparations all week long. The focal point of the festivities was a house-size ice sculpture in the form of a castle. There would be live music around the clock with a changing array of local talent, from grunge rock to a German oompah band; skating on the lake, a hockey tournament, a winter triathlon, booths for everything from face-painting to funnel cakes.

Tourists and locals mingled on the platform as the train pulled into the station. People poured out of the exits, and Daisy scanned each car, looking for Sonnet's trademark beaded cornrows, which made her stand out in any crowd. Sonnet was the first friend Daisy had made in Avalon, and now they were stepsisters. Daisy adored her. Even so, she knew there was a slender thread of tension between them. It was completely understandable. Sonnet, with her full scholarship and squeaky-clean reputation, was the all-American girl, even more impressive because she had been raised by a hardworking single mother—Nina Romano. On the other hand, there was Daisy, a product of the Upper Eastside, private school society, who had blown all her advantages and become a single mother herself. And now there was this—the fact that Daisy wanted to be friends with Zach again. She was determined to make Sonnet understand. Staying behind and making her life in a town like this, Daisy had to keep her friends close, because she needed all she could get. It wasn't like living on campus, where students could find friends behind every door in a dorm or sorority.

"I changed my mind," Zach said abruptly. "I'm leaving."

Daisy grabbed the sleeve of his army surplus jacket. "You used to be best friends," she reminded him. "You practically grew up together. That has to count for something."

"Maybe it did until my father ripped off the city when her mom was mayor."

Daisy flinched. When he put it so bluntly, she was forced to acknowledge that, yes, it was bound to be hard to get past that. Parents had such infinite power to hurt their kids. Every day, she promised Charlie she would never do anything to hurt him, but was she already doing that, raising him without a father?

Scanning the passengers, she spied Sonnet dragging a Pullman suitcase from one of the train cars. Daisy hurried down the platform. Sonnet saw her coming and let out a squeal of joy. They threw their arms around each other and held on tight. Daisy felt a surge of affection for Sonnet—her best friend. Her sister. So many good things had come from Dad marrying Nina.

Sonnet felt wiry and delicate in Daisy's arms. Then they stepped back, grinning at each other. Sonnet looked the same, but different. Same bright eyes and thousand-watt smile, same gleaming cornrows and beads. Different clothes—loose-fitting, more ethnic.

"I'm so glad you came home," Daisy said, "even for just a few days."

"Me, too. I miss it here. Where's Charlie?" she asked. "Does he know his favorite aunt has arrived?"

"He's with my mom."

"How's that working out?"

"It's working out, which comes as a total shock to me." Daisy took charge of the bag as they headed for the exit.

"Your mom was really good to me when I visited her in The Hague last summer," Sonnet reminded Daisy. "So I'm not shocked at all."

"It seems so strange—my mom, here in this little town. I fully expect her to flee to Manhattan as soon as the snow melts." Something else that was strange was seeing her mom act like . . . a mom. No, she didn't wear an apron and bake cookies, but she drove car pool and babysat Charlie and had conferences with Max's teachers. "Sometimes, I get the idea she likes it here. Might be wishful thinking, though."

"Maybe she'll find a job or something. How hard would it be?"

"For my mom? Working is, like, second nature to her. It's all she's ever done." Daisy considered this a moment. Maybe her mom needed more to do. "I want her to be happy here," she confessed. "I want her to stay."

"There's something about this town . . ." Sonnet said. "I get homesick a lot."

Daisy heard a wistful note in her voice, and looked closer at Sonnet's face. She had definitely lost her round, happy cheeks, and faint lines bracketed her mouth. "Is everything okay at school?"

"Everything's great at school." Sonnet perked up. "But I'm here for Winter Carnival, and—"

She stopped talking and stood still, as though flash frozen. Daisy held her breath, knowing Sonnet had just spotted Zach. He approached her on the crowded platform. His face was somber, an expression that brought out his strikingly pale beauty. For a moment, Sonnet's face turned soft with yearning. They used to be so close, and the estrangement was painful to them both. But very quickly, Sonnet's face hardened, her eyes narrowing to accusing slits.

"Hey," said Zach.

She thrust up her chin. "What part of 'I never want to see you again' did you not understand?" Then she jerked her suitcase away from Daisy. "I don't believe you."

"Sonnet, just listen—"

"Excuse me." She brushed past Zach and all but ran for the exit.

Zach's shoulders sagged as he tracked her progress through the milling crowd. "That went well," he said.

Part Six

Winter's edge

Congelation Ice

Congelation ice is frozen lake ice. It forms on cold, calm nights when the surface of the lake supercools and the ice spreads rapidly across the surface. When the light hits it just right, the secret world of ice is revealed. Individual crystals are exposed in a kaleidoscope of color and shape.

Dutch Hot Chocolate

1½ cups milk, or half and half, or light cream
2 heaping teaspoons of Droste cocoa powder
½ cup sugar (or to taste)
½ cup ground dark chocolate (use chocolate that has 60% or more cocoa content)
ground nutmeg or cinnamon to taste

Heat milk to just below boiling. Whisk in cocoa powder, sugar, ground chocolate and spices.

Twenty-Two

"Noah was right about the puppy," Sophie said to Charlie.

It wasn't her usual day to watch the baby. She had come because Daisy wanted to spend the afternoon with Sonnet, who was due in on the two-o'clock train.

The baby sat on a blanket in the middle of the floor, playing with a ball that had a bell inside it. He was a good listener. Sophie had taken to telling him everything about her life, from the smallest thing, like seeing a set of animal tracks across the lawn, to the big issues, like the fact that she still had nightmares about the incident in The Hague.

Charlie was simply a pleasant, benign presence, open to anything she had to say. He'd recently learned to clap his hands, and often did so at appropriate times during the conversation. Psychiatrists could learn a few things from babies, like the fact that sometimes a smattering of applause and a gummy grin did more for a person's mental health than hours of well-meaning advice.

Lately, most of her conversations had to do with Noah Shepherd.

"See, he gave me the puppy because he claimed it would be a huge incentive for Max to spend time with me. At first, I was insulted. I mean, a mother shouldn't have to use a puppy as bait, right?"

The ball rolled to the edge of the blanket, and she

rolled it back. "Turns out Noah's right," she reiterated. "He knows exactly how a twelve-year-old boy thinks. There is nothing—*nothing*—as powerful to a boy as a new puppy. Max can't stay away from Opal. She's a Max magnet."

Charlie offered a brief, insightful laugh.

"I know. It's so obvious, when you think about it. What's more fun to a kid than a puppy, right?" By now, Opal was crate trained and housebroken. Training a dog was a lot of work, but there was something to be said for being forced to get up every hour or so, stretch your legs, wander outside and smell the cold air and feel the snowflakes on your face.

Currently, Max was out in the neighborhood with Opal, taking her for a walk. He had probably taken her to the sledding hill at Avalon Meadows golf course, where the toboggan team racing was going on.

Charlie traded the ball for a squishy teething toy, which he mouthed like an ear of corn. Then he moved on to a sort of ugly clown weighted at the bottom, so that it sprang upright every time it was knocked down. Charlie pushed it over and watched it pop back up several times, gaping in fascination.

"You can't do the same thing over and over and expect different results," she told him.

"Bah."

She reached over and wiped his chin. "This—whatever—with Noah is the last thing I expected to find when I came here," she admitted, her thoughts drifting again. "Sometimes I wonder if I'm falling in love with him." She clapped her hand over her mouth and mumbled, "I can't believe I just said that."

Charlie imitated the gesture and laughed. Sophie swooped him up and rolled back on the blanket, holding him overhead as she savored the feeling that swept over her. Contentment. No, it was stronger than that. Happiness. *Joy.* Yes, that was it. She had nearly forgotten what it felt like.

It wasn't that she was a miserable person. And life had indeed given her moments of joy. But not like this. Never like this.

She found an oldies station on the radio and sang to Charlie as she warmed a bottle of milk for him. "Nights in White Satin" by the Moody Blues. "Mrs. Robinson" by Simon and Garfunkel. How did she know the words? She didn't remember ever studying them. Some things just stuck with you, lodging in memory through a secret door.

She fed the baby and, while he drowsed in her lap, she put the TV on low, flipping channels to see even just a flicker of international news. It was far easier to find an interview with a tattooed biker laying claim to a rich heiress's new baby than a report on national elections in Umoja. For the first time in decades, the Umojan people were going to the polls, yet here, it was a nonevent.

She clicked past a home-improvement show of a garage being transformed into a Qigong studio. Paused on a guy hawking a device that scrambled an egg right in its shell, which, inexplicably, she found herself craving. There seemed to be a hundred celebrity news stories to be watched at any given time. There was a talk-show host, apologizing for the umpteenth time for something he said. And here was the starlet du jour, radiantly showing off her new baby. And there was Ashton Kutcher, laughing off criticism that he was too young to be with Demi Moore.

In spite of herself, Sophie thought Ashton Kutcher was hot. Shaking off the lascivious thought, she changed the channel and glared at Headline News until they delivered thirty seconds of "international news," covering a polar bear in a German zoo. Still holding Charlie, she moved into the study and surfed the Web to a video report on the Umojan elections. The newsreader began, "In their first free elections in more than two decades . . ."

"I did that," Sophie whispered to Charlie. "I was on the justice team that made it happen." She expected to feel a surge of emotion, but instead merely felt distracted. The Web site was surrounded by blinking ads for nasal drip solutions and solicitations for matchmaking sites, which gave her a headache. She went back to the radio, which was now playing a song she didn't like to consider an oldie—"Jump" by Van Halen—because it made her feel . . . well, old.

"And yet I'm a grandmother," she said to Charlie. "Maybe I'm supposed to be old."

He finished his bottle and didn't look sleepy at all. He belched, then chortled as he emitted a small fountain of milk bubbles.

"Such talent," she said. "How did I wind up with such a talented grandchild?"

The doorbell sounded, startling her. She set the baby on his blanket and went to see who it was.

Oh, she thought when she opened the door. *Oh, dear.* And then, *oh, shit.*

"Logan," she said, moving aside to let him in, and then closing the door quickly behind him so the baby wouldn't be chilled by the cold air.

"Mrs. Bellamy," he said.

An awkward beat passed. Then Charlie squealed, breaking the ice.

"Hey, buddy." Logan turned as soft and sweet as a marshmallow as he greeted his son. Charlie desperately tried to reach for him like a man dying of thirst. There was an almost primal affinity between them, a clear recognition on Charlie's tiny face that this person was important.

Watching them, Sophie remembered perfectly why Greg had married her all those years ago.

Even so, she reminded herself, this was not Greg. This was Logan O'Donnell—a boy with a troubled past. He was ridiculously handsome and surprisingly tender with the baby.

He went to the kitchen and quickly washed his hands. Nice touch, thought Sophie. She hoped he did that every time, not just to show her how responsible he was. Charlie gave a cranky squawk, straining toward the kitchen.

"Coming," Logan called. "Hold your horses." He

hurried back to Charlie, sleeves rolled back, and scooped him up. “Did Daisy tell you I might stop by?”

“No, but it’s fine, of course.” What else could she say? “I’m going to fix myself a cup of tea,” she added, mainly to give them some privacy. “Would you like anything?”

“No, thank you.” Logan was grinning at the baby and didn’t look away.

Sophie took her time getting the tea. When she returned, Logan was in the upholstered swivel rocker, holding Charlie facedown across his knees, chortling as Logan spun the chair.

“Daisy tells me you’re in college now,” she said, taking a seat across from him.

“Yes, ma’am. I’m studying finance.”

“That’s good.” She had no idea what to say to this boy. This handsome boy, who had changed her daughter’s entire life.

“It’s all right,” Logan said. “You don’t need to make small talk. With all due respect, we can just cut to the chase. I have a pretty good idea about what you think of me.”

“Do you?”

“You’re thinking I was a dumb high-school jock. I was careless with your daughter. Not to mention an addict who went through rehab. I don’t blame you or anyone for being skeptical of me.”

Sophie was not about to insult him by denying it. “And now you’re trying to live down your past mistakes,” she said.

"I'm not sure what that means," he said, then flashed her a grin. "Must be the dumb jock in me."

She felt herself softening toward him. "It's impossible, anyway. Believe me, I've tried it."

"All I know is that I'm preparing for the future now," he said, "and Charlie is a part of that future."

"Fair enough," she said. "Can I ask you something personal?"

"Sure."

"Is your family supportive of this?"

"No," he said bluntly. "They haven't seen him. Not once."

Sophie never expected to like this boy. To empathize with his situation. She had never expected to regard him as anything more than a bad decision her daughter had once made, and the source of Charlie's red hair. Yet now, with his pained admission, Logan O'Donnell became someone to her. Someone whose parents took issue with the choices he'd made. And she finally understood why Daisy had liked him in the first place, and why she let him visit Charlie so often.

"I'm sorry to hear that," she said. "Perhaps they'll come around. In the meantime, giving yourself to Charlie is something you'll never regret." She stood abruptly. "Why don't you stay with him while I check my e-mail?" She gestured toward the small workroom where Daisy's computer was set up.

"Thanks, Mrs. Bellamy." His smile bore a remarkable resemblance to Charlie's. "I appreciate it."

"You can call me Sophie," she said. "That way I won't feel so old."

"You're not old, believe me," he said with flattering assurance. "I'll take care of the little guy."

While her e-mail loaded, she checked her PDA for the to-do list and upcoming appointments. In the past, the list had been endless, and even with a personal staff, she'd never been able to accomplish everything. That never kept her from trying, though, or from feeling the stress of her endeavor.

These days, the list revolved around her children and Charlie. She had signed up to volunteer for lunch duty at Max's school one day a week, and the hours spent in the overheated, oniony-smelling school cafeteria, listening in on the boys' fart jokes and girls' cliques offered an unvarnished glimpse at the workings of real kids' lives. She was fascinated by the range of humanity she observed, from acts of cold-blooded cruelty to heartrending kindness. She watched students being cut out of a group with the precision of a surgeon's scalpel, and others having their emotional wounds tended with unschooled compassion. She understood Max so much better now. She understood his need to be liked and admired and approved of—because those on the wrong side of their peers suffered the tortures of the damned.

Then there were the hockey practices and games. She enjoyed seeing Max play, but was no fan of the other moms in attendance. The mom squad. With Nina's older sister Maria as team mother, Sophie was not their favorite person. She refused to let herself care about that. She simply would not let it matter. During lunch duty, she'd observed that the outcast students who responded to their tormentors with cool dignity were most likely to be left alone, if they could survive that long.

Sophie knew she could outlast the women who regarded her with judgmental disapproval. It was a gift, this ability she had to make something fail to hurt her. Over the years, she'd built a shell of armor around her heart. It was simple survival. If she kept herself open, she was vulnerable. If she closed up and protected herself, she was a rock. But after the hostage situation, her protective armor had cracked open and she was vulnerable to the things she feared most—being hurt. Disappointing people. Failing to connect on the deepest, most important level to her own children.

Looking around the small, cluttered room, she studied the postcards pinned to a corkboard, probably from Daisy's friends who were now in college or traveling abroad. Sticky notes with lists seemed to be pasted everywhere; most were embellished with doodles or curlicue writing that reminded Sophie of how young Daisy was. A somewhat ominous quote she'd jotted down: "It is a fearful thing to love what death can touch." And another message from Rocky Horror—"Don't dream it, be it." An appointment card for the dentist. To Sophie's knowledge, Daisy had never voluntarily gone to the dentist in her life.

Her photographs were catalogued and labeled as

though by a trained archivist. On one shelf, a grouping of fat albums caught Sophie's eye, particularly one labeled *Family, until 2006.* The year of the divorce.

Sophie opened the album to find a chronicle of their life as a family. She viewed the pages with a painful combination of sorrow, accomplishment, regret and nostalgia. They had been like any family, their lives filled with genuinely happy moments—birthday celebrations and holidays, vacations and adventures. Many of the pictures brought on smiles and memories. Daisy had always loved climbing on the larger-than-life bronze Alice in Wonderland statue in Central Park. There were shots of her, and then of her and Max together, swarming over the well-worn structure amid the other children. There was page after page of holidays, school functions, trips and birthdays.

Compressed within the photographs, the years seemed to have flown by. There was Daisy as a tow-headed toddler, standing on a chair and bending forward to blow out two birthday candles. Pages later, there was a shot of her at Camp Kioga on Willow Lake, celebrating her grandparents' fiftieth wedding anniversary. Sophie was in many of the shots, but often hovered on the periphery of things. An observer rather than an active participant. Often she was dressed for work in a suit, her briefcase placed somewhere nearby. Because of the way she dressed—dark suits, tasteful pumps, pulled-back hair—she seemed to have changed little over the years. She'd always looked forty, even when she was twenty-five.

Seeing the photographs one after another, she could sense the gradual erosion of her marriage. Here was a pictorial chronicle of a relationship slowly and painfully wearing away. In the early shots, when the kids were little and she and Greg had tried so hard, the smiles had been bright with determination and hope. Bit by bit, the feeling had been lost, eroding so gradually they didn't notice its absence until it was gone and impossible to recapture. Eventually the strain of the effort showed; the smiles were less genuine, seldom reaching the eyes. There were fewer and fewer shots of the two of them in the same frame. Early on, they had used the camera's shutter timer, one of them leaping into the shot at the last second. As time went on, they didn't bother with that so often.

Some of the best—and most revealing—pictures had been taken by Daisy herself. Even with the first point-and-shoot camera she'd had as a little girl, she had shown talent and passion for her art. As a teenager, she'd observed the demise of her parents' marriage through the viewfinder of her camera. In the shots of Sophie and Greg together, they looked almost like any couple, but there was often some little telling detail in the shot, like a hand gripping a purse handle too tightly or shoulders that touched as they leaned toward each other for the shot, and then turned rigid on contact.

Eventually, Sophie and Greg as a couple all but disappeared from the pictures. Or, if they were together in a frame, they were separated by a gulf filled with relatives or friends in a group shot. Was there something they could have done, should have done? Or was the erosion inevitable, like the constant battering of waves against rock? There were things she would always miss about being a family. She'd miss looking around the dinner table at their faces, or skiing down a mountain together, or getting dressed up to attend a play. Yet she had to admit that there were things she didn't miss at all—the taut feeling in her chest when she woke up in the morning and tried to figure out how to leave the bed without waking Greg. The lines of unhappiness pulling at his mouth when he didn't know she was watching him. The way Max used to work too hard to act as though everything was fine, and the way Daisy used to act out just to get a response from someone.

Hearing a sound at the door, Sophie looked up. There stood Daisy, still dressed for outdoors in her parka and boots.

"Hey, Mom," she said, pushing back her hood.

"Hi." Sophie brushed at her cheeks. She hadn't even realized she'd been crying. "I came in here to check my e-mail and give Logan some time with Charlie. I didn't mean to go snooping around."

Daisy checked out the open photo album on the drafting table. "I've got nothing to hide. What are you looking at?"

"Your family album." Sophie studied the final images in the book. The second-to-last one showed the four of them on the dock at Camp Kioga two summers ago during the celebration of Charles and Jane Bellamy's fiftieth wedding anniversary. Greg and the kids had spent the entire summer there while Sophie traveled for work. The photograph was a portrait of a woman who simply didn't belong, who was uncomfortable in her own skin. Greg, Max and Daisy were grinning and tan, their hair sun-streaked and windblown, their feet bare. By contrast, Sophie was indoor-pale, wearing crisply ironed Bermuda shorts and a buttoned-down camp shirt.

There were shots taken a year after that, at another Bellamy family gathering—Olivia's wedding. All four of them, though dressed for the formal occasion, appeared to be on edge—for good reason, as it happened. Later that same day, Daisy had gone into labor. They had come together as a family for a brief time after Charlie's birth, but even that heady state of shared wonder was only temporary.

"What a day that was," Sophie murmured.

"For all of us." Daisy paused at a shot of herself, clasping hands with her father. The quality was more amateurish than Daisy's work, having been taken by Sophie herself. "Dad was a surprisingly good coach that day."

"I'm not surprised," Sophie admitted. Greg had dutifully attended a full round of childbirth classes with Daisy, determined to see his daughter through the most difficult transition of her young life. "Tell me something," she said. "Did you ever think about asking me to be your coach?"

Daisy frowned. “You were overseas. I knew you wouldn’t drop everything and attend six weeks of classes with me.”

“You knew?”

“I assumed. Would you, Mom? Would you have done that?”

Sophie stared out the window, watching a droplet of water form on the tip of an icicle, refusing to look away until the droplet fell. “I honestly don’t know,” she admitted, “but I wish you would have asked.” She studied the final shot of her and Greg standing awkwardly on either side of Daisy holding the baby. She was worried now that Daisy had never learned the most critical lesson a child gleaned from her parents—the sustaining power of love.

She closed the book with a gentle thud. “I wish these pictures had shown a different story. I didn’t realize . . . What I didn’t think about when it was happening was how observant you were, and what my troubles were doing to you. You saw it all, didn’t you? Every minute of it.”

“Well, yeah.”

“I’m sorry. I’m so sorry. I wanted better memories for you—”

“I wanted to remember, Mom. Everything, the good and the bad. Why wouldn’t I?”

Sophie hugged her daughter and shut her eyes. Although they were two adult women, holding each other, she felt herself being pulled back through the years. She could perfectly imagine Daisy at every age, from fragile newborn to laughing little girl to independent young woman. "I remember, too," Sophie whispered. "I remember every minute of it."

Daisy stepped back, then smiled. "I was just thinking about that today. This is the longest we've been together since I was in eighth grade."

It was all so bittersweet. "You kept track?"

"It's just something I noticed. But I was always proud of you. Max, too, even though we didn't always show it. We both know working for the ICC is a bigger deal than being on the band uniform auction committee."

"Still, I wasn't there."

"Max and I were surrounded by people. It's not like we were raised by wolves."

"I hate that I was gone so much. I wish I'd been there for you every single day. Maybe if I had, things would have been different for you."

"Mom. Listen, my mistakes are my own. Not yours or Dad's or anybody else's." She peeled off her jacket, draped it over the back of a chair. "You're not busy enough."

"I beg your pardon?"

"You need more to do, besides worry about stuff like this. You went from sixty to zero, moving back here."

"That's the point."

"It's possible to do something besides be around for Max and me. You're still a lawyer, right?"

"I'm not practicing."

"You could, though, if you wanted to."

"What are you suggesting?"

"I want you to be happy in Avalon. Because I want you to stay. Doing work you like—that makes you happy."

"I *am* happy—"

"When you're helping people, not just me. I don't want to be your full-time job. All kinds of people need help. Call Uncle Philip."

Philip—Greg's brother. "Why on earth would I call him?"

"He's a volunteer with the chamber of commerce, and he knows, like, everyone in town. He could introduce you to people. You know, other lawyers and stuff."

"You're an amazing daughter, Daisy."

"Yeah, that's me. Come on out and say hi to everybody." She lowered her voice. "Sonnet and Zach were weird with each other, you know. But I did a Sophie Bellamy."

"What's that?"

"Your peacemaker-diplomat thing. Sonnet said she didn't want to see Zach, but back at the train station I talked them into getting along, or at least acting like they do."

Sophie blotted her face with a tissue. She could hear voices from the living room. She took out a compact to check her makeup. Since she was wearing very little, there wasn't much damage from the crying. She snapped the compact shut, then went to join Daisy and her friends. Charlie was happily ensconced in Sonnet's lap.

“Hi, Sonnet,” she said, putting on her best smile. “It’s good to see you again.”

“Thank you. It’s good to see you, too.” Sonnet jiggled Charlie in her lap. He was a good prop, shielding them both from having to shake hands or embrace. Sophie did not dislike Sonnet. In fact, she admired the girl. She was brainy and ambitious, enrolled in a competitive college. The awkwardness came from the fact that Sonnet was Nina Romano’s daughter. Nina Romano *Bellamy*’s daughter. Stepsister to Daisy and Max. Charlie’s aunt. All of which made her someone who would be in Daisy’s life for a very long time, probably forever.

Sonnet had her mother’s vivid Italian-American features. Her father, a colonel in the army, was African-American. The girl had smooth, caramel-colored skin, deep brown eyes and abundant corkscrew curls. Was she too perfect? Thinner, maybe; her lovely skin seemed to be pulled more tautly across her cheekbones. To Sophie she looked older than her years, troubled, perhaps.

“How do you like being back in Avalon?” Sophie asked.

The troubled expression dissolved into a smile. “There’s no way I’d miss Winter Carnival. It’s a big deal in this town.”

“So I hear.”

“Mom, this is Zach Alger,” said Daisy, indicating the other boy in the room.

“I’m Sophie,” she said, holding her hand out to the quiet, extremely blond boy.

“Ma’am,” he said, getting to his feet. “It’s nice to meet you.”

He was a remarkable-looking boy, pale to the very tips of his eyelashes. Extremely serious looking. Daisy had told her a little about him. Zach’s dad, Matthew Alger, embezzled city funds in order to sustain his Internet gambling addiction. In turn, Zach had tried to cover up his father’s crime by stealing from the bakery where he worked. It was filial obligation taken to extremes. Zach had thrown himself under the proverbial bus in order to save his father. This was something Sophie understood so completely. It was something she herself had done, perhaps not so directly or recklessly. But she had sacrificed her own desires for the sake of her parents.

Sophie sensed a tension in the room but suspected it had nothing to do with her. “Well, I need to be going. I’m sure I’ll see everyone around.” She leaned down and took Charlie in her arms. She gave the baby a hug and kissed him on the cheek, then handed him back to Sonnet.

Daisy walked her to the door, and they went outside together.

“I was watching Logan and Charlie today,” Sophie said. “He’s very good with him.”

“I think so, too.” Daisy tugged her sweater around her. “How does Sonnet look to you, Mom?”

“She’s a beautiful girl.” Sophie was stating the obvious.

“I know that,” Daisy said. “But how does she look?”

"Thinner, maybe," Sophie said.

Daisy nodded, shivered again. "That's what I thought, too. Do you think she's okay, or is she scary-skinny?"

Sophie hesitated. On the one hand, here was a chance for her to be a mom, to offer advice to Daisy. On the other hand . . . "Sweetheart, she's Nina's daughter, and because of that, I have no business discussing her."

"Okay. I get it. I think I just answered my own question."

Sophie gave her a hug. "You know how to be a good friend, Daisy. And I'm glad we talked today."

"Call Uncle Philip. I want you to belong here, Mom. Really."

"How did you turn out so smart?"

Daisy went to the door, turned back with a smile. "Must be I get it from my mom."

Twenty-Three

Sophie knew her daughter was right. If she was in this for good, if she wanted Avalon to be her home, she was going to need to deepen her ties here. She had come to this town as some sort of penance, expecting to endure it for the sake of her children. Instead, she'd found the unexpected—a new chance to remake her life, to fill it with the rich textures of real connections. It was true that she'd grown closer to her children in the past weeks than she'd been in years. That alone was enough to hold her and make her grateful to be alive.

It was also true that whatever was going on with Noah Shepherd—she didn't want to label it—became more important to her with each passing day. She wasn't sure this was such a good thing, though. It had never been her aim to come here and meet someone special. Her children and grandson were special enough, thank you very much.

Still, as Daisy had pointed out, Sophie had room in her life for more. She used to be defined by her job; her identity revolved around the sense of purpose and validation of working for an ideal. She understood now that matters of justice existed on many levels. They could involve whole nations—or a lone military wife like Gayle Wright.

The prod from Daisy was all the motivation Sophie needed. Today she had a meeting with Philip Bellamy, her former brother-in-law. He wanted to introduce her to Melinda Lee Parkington, a local attorney who was about to go on maternity leave and needed a part-time associate.

Sophie arrived early at Blanchard Park, where Philip was working with a team of chamber of commerce volunteers. She passed a group of people installing a temporary stage for the upcoming Winter Carnival. Noah's band would be performing in one of the time slots. Sophie had become a fan of their music. They were better than they had to be, and hugely fun to hang out with. In the past, she'd never done much hanging out. Noah and his friends had shown her there was an art to it, a way of attending to rhythm and melody that was unexpectedly fulfilling. Did that make her a band groupie? How odd to think of herself in that way.

Philip was supervising a crew of college students in the construction of a life-size ice castle. This was the centerpiece of the upcoming festival. It was made of giant blocks of ice by people working around the clock to get everything ready.

"I'm amazed," she said, surveying the glittering walls. "I didn't quite know what to expect."

"It's a marvel of engineering." He took off his hard hat. "You ready to meet Melinda?"

"I really appreciate this," she said.

"It's no trouble." They started walking together toward the town center, a few blocks from the park. She could feel a peculiar tension pulsing between them. "Is this completely awkward?" she asked. "Because of Greg and me, I mean—"

"It's not awkward," he assured her. "I know what it's like after a divorce. It happened to me twenty years ago, and I still remember the pain and uncertainty. The sense of freedom, too."

She nodded. "Sounds very familiar. Just tell me it gets easier."

"You go on. And I hope like hell you do a better job of that than I did. For years—during and after my marriage to Pamela—I thought about a girl from my past, someone who didn't even exist."

He was referring to a local girl he'd known decades ago when he was in college. She had been his first love, but she'd abruptly disappeared from his life, never telling him that she had borne his child. "She existed for you, right?"

Philip stuck his hands in his pockets. "Yes, and when you're pining for someone who's long gone, you can turn her into anyone you want. No wonder I had no luck dating and moving on. I already had the perfect woman in my mind and no one else could measure up."

The conversation felt surreal to Sophie. Here she was talking to her former brother-in-law, whom she'd known for years, and this was probably the most honest conversation she'd ever had with him.

"Well. There's no danger of me pining away for some mystery man." There was nothing mysterious about Noah Shepherd. Except perhaps her desire to keep him secret.

"Everything's so good now," he said, "it's almost scary. Both my daughters are married, and Laura and I just set a date. First Saturday in May."

Sophie admired him for taking a leap of faith after so many years of being by himself, and for never giving up on love. "That's fantastic. I'm so happy for you, Philip."

He grinned. "She and I are proof that love takes its own time. Someone we've known for years suddenly becomes the center of our world."

They cut across the bustling town square. The law

office was located in an old brick building with three stories and a figured concrete facade, with a bookstore and coffee shop at street level. Sophie was surprised to feel a tug of apprehension. What if this M. L. Parkington was friends with the Romano sisters? As the thought tried to settle in, she realized it was the old-Sophie way of thinking—to assume the worst and run away. She wasn't that person anymore. All right, she was trying not to be that person anymore.

"You all right?" Philip asked. "You got quiet all of a sudden."

"Just taking it in. I know you and Laura are going to be great together."

"And you?"

"I'm going to be fine."

Melinda Parkington went by "Mel." She was Asian, with a law degree from a place Sophie had never heard of, a thousand-watt smile and an air of total confidence as she greeted her visitors. She was eight months pregnant with her third child. She had a law practice that, very soon, was going to have to do without her for a while.

"Don't get up," Sophie said, reaching across the desk to shake hands with her.

Mel smiled, propping a file folder on her protruding abdomen. "Thanks. I've been looking over your résumé," she told Sophie after Philip left. She indicated the file folder. "It's very impressive. I think I'm jealous."

Sophie scanned the wealth of children's artwork on one wall of the office—drawings in crayon, a clay impression of two little hands, plenty of snapshots. "Don't be. Your family is beautiful. Who takes care of your other children?"

"My mother-in-law. I'm very lucky to have her nearby, but I'm planning to stay home six months with the new one." Mel set aside the folder. "Is there some reason you're switching from international justice?"

She'd prepared for this question. She'd known it was bound to come up, and her prospective partner deserved to know what had happened. Yet even though she'd expected the question, she hadn't anticipated how hard it would be to answer. Even now, her mouth went dry.

"There was an incident in January, a . . . violent incident in The Hague, and I found myself caught in the middle of everything." She passed Melinda a dossier. "Here's the State Department's official report. You can read it and let me know if you have any questions."

Melinda scanned the document. Then she closed the folder, studied Sophie's face, long and hard.

"I can't afford to take a full-time family leave," she admitted. "I need to keep my practice going. Let me show you around."

The office consisted of Mel, another attorney named Wendell, who wore a bowtie and was so shy he could barely look at Sophie, and the office manager, Daphne, who had bright pink hair and a collection of anime figures on the shelf by her desk, alongside the reference and bookkeeping files.

"Don't be fooled by Daphne," Melinda said. "She's nearly thirty and smart as a whip, but part of her seems to be stuck in junior high."

"You say that like it's a bad thing," Daphne pointed out. She lifted the lid from a glass jar of licorice sticks on her desk. "Red vine?"

"No, thanks."

"This way," Mel said. "We're a little short on space, but this office has a view." The space for the new part-time associate was a tiny enclosure with only the basics—a desk, computer, bookcases and a pair of chairs for clients. A window with Law Office spelled out backward on the glass faced the main street of town which, at the moment, was being festooned with banners announcing the Winter Carnival.

Sophie could barely remember the view outside her window in the angular glass-and-concrete box of the International Criminal Court. Tidal flats, she supposed, wet pavement lined with buildings and the inevitable waterway. Fields of flowers in the springtime. And bridges in the distance, perhaps the very one she'd traveled that night.

"I won't waste your time," Mel was saying, and Sophie realized she had allowed her thoughts to drift.

"I'm sorry, what's that?"

"You're more than qualified, and I'd love to have you," Mel said. "I'll show you what we bill and what you can expect, and then you can let me know if—"

"I'm letting you know now," Sophie said. "This arrangement will work very well for me."

She understood Mel's expression. "In the interest of full disclosure, I should tell you—I consider myself a very good lawyer, but I've never worked in a small town. There's some . . . baggage, I guess you'd call it, that might affect clients' comfort level with me. Did Philip explain that I used to be married to his brother Greg?"

"Is that what you're concerned about?"

"In a place like this, it could have an impact on business."

Mel laughed. "In a place like this, *every*body is somebody's ex. Right, Daphne?" She addressed the office manager, who stepped in to deliver a dossier.

"Absolutely," Daphne said. "Mel used to date one of the county prosecutors."

"It never affected our job performance. Honestly, Sophie, don't worry about it." Together, Melinda and Sophie ironed out the details. Two days a week, Sophie looked after Charlie. The other three days, she would come in to the law office.

"We're not specialists," Melinda explained. "I take whatever comes through the door."

"I'm fine with that."

"Good. It keeps things interesting."

Rather quickly, Sophie found out how interesting. Her first case involved a man bringing suit against an exotic dancer in Lake Katrine. He claimed that, during a lap dance at a bachelor party, she kicked him in the head with a stiletto heel. Dancing in "a reckless and negligent manner," as Sophie was forced to write in a brief, was hardly a crime against humanity. But the man's injuries were real.

She also met with a woman, married for forty-seven years, who wanted to sue her husband for opening her mail, a poodle breeder seeking damages from a vet for docking a puppy's tail too short (she was relieved to know Noah Shepherd was not the culprit) and a boy who wanted to force a teacher to give him an A instead of a B+, to keep his perfect GPA intact.

All right, she thought, *so we're not saving the world here.* But then she'd come across someone like Mr. and Mrs. Fleischman, a long-married couple who became victims of a mortgage scam. Or a young couple whose insurance company was denying coverage of their baby, newly adopted from overseas.

There were several family law cases still pending when Mel left. Sophie found herself in the odd position of sitting across the desk from a man named Alfie Garner, who was divorcing his wife. The consultation felt odd to her, because the sense of déjà vu was jarring. She had nothing in common with this man. He drove a truck for a living and his wife was a stay-at-home mom, yet every word he spoke, the defeated expression on his face and the sadness in his eyes—it was all familiar to her. Familiar, but . . . distant. Yes, she'd been there to that dark place, but she was able to look Alfie in the eye and say with complete honesty, "It gets better."

She quickly realized that, to be good at family law, she had to have a solid understanding of family—how it worked and all the ways it could fail, and the very delicate balance between the two. She found herself flip-flopping between the former Sophie—sharp, judgmental, always in control, and the woman she was trying to be now—understanding, flexible, compassionate. Interestingly, she discovered some combination of the two styles seemed to benefit her clients. She still didn't trust the new Sophie, didn't like being that vulnerable.

Twenty-Four

Daisy pulled up in front of her cousin Olivia's house. She and her new husband, Connor Davis, had built the riverside haven together, and it was their dream house. The exterior was made of native timber and river rock, and it looked like a spread in a magazine. However, as she extracted Charlie from his carseat, she wasn't thinking much about the house. She was thinking about Julian Gastineaux.

He was Connor's younger brother—half brother—who had come to town for a visit. Everybody probably had a Julian buried deep in the past. The perfect boy, the one you think about even if you haven't seen him in months or even years. The one you wish you'd made a move on. That was Julian. He was the kind of guy parents worried about—dangerous and exciting, an adrenaline junkie who loved extreme sports, dizzying heights and edgy music. He had a sketchy home situation and bad-boy looks. He favored black T-shirts and low-slung jeans, and rode a motorcycle. All of which, of course, made him irresistible.

As she stood on the porch and knocked at the door, Daisy wondered if he'd changed much now that he went to an Ivy League college. Maybe his first semester at Cornell had turned him into a geek, or—

"Hey, Daisy." And there he stood, holding the door for her.

Cornell had most definitely not turned him into a geek. Cornell—or the passage of time, or all the extreme sports he did—had made him even more gorgeous than she remembered. He still had that crop of dreadlocks, the broad-shouldered physique of a star athlete and a smile that lit up his whole face.

"Hey, yourself." She grinned back at him. "It's really good to see you." Were they supposed to hug? Shake hands? With the baby on her hip, it was awkward. Charlie pushed his face into Daisy's shoulder as though to hide. In his hooded snowsuit, he looked like a fleecy teddy bear she'd won at a shooting gallery. "He's kind of shy around strangers," she explained.

"That's okay. I'm shy around babies."

The honest admission made her laugh. "Most guys are."

"Come on in. I was just about to load up the gear." They were going ice climbing with Sonnet and Zach in Deep Notch today. Julian, always up for doing something totally extreme, had organized the expedition, bringing equipment from the climbing club at Cornell.

"Let me get Charlie settled, and I'll give you a hand."

She left her boots at the door and headed down the hall, feeling a surge of excitement. Other than leaving Charlie with her mom for school, she didn't get out by herself very often.

She stepped into the kitchen to find not just Olivia, but Jenny Majesky and Nina. "Hi," she said, and turned to Nina. "I didn't know you were going to be here."

"Hi, yourself." Nina reached for the baby.

"I thought I was babysitting today," Olivia said.

Jenny laughed. "So young, and already he's got women fighting over him."

"We'll share," Nina promised, but she took charge of getting Charlie out of his snowsuit. He knew and adored her, and chortled with contentment as she unzipped him and held him out so Olivia could peel off the fleecy suit.

Daisy went to the fridge and unloaded the bottles. "So what's up?" she asked over her shoulder.

"Jenny has news," said Olivia.

Nina beamed at Jenny. "Does she ever."

"You're pregnant?" Daisy asked. That was sort of what she expected. Jenny had married Rourke McKnight a year ago, and she'd made no secret of wanting to start a family, ASAP.

Now she shook her head. "A different kind of news. You know I've been writing."

"Only all your life," Nina added. Jenny had a popular weekly food column in the local paper. She looked more excited than Jenny, as if she were about to bubble over. Nina and Jenny were true BFFs. They had met in grade school and had been best friends ever since. Daisy believed there was a special quality in that kind of relationship. The years, filled with shared good times and bad, gave a peculiar sturdiness to the bond.

Daisy didn't have a friend like that. In high school, she'd been too careless or maybe too preoccupied with keeping up her party-girl image. She and Sonnet were close, but they'd only been friends for a year and their lives had become so different that the bond didn't feel as safe and sure as it once had.

But Nina and Jenny, that was a different story. Daisy regarded the two of them as though through the camera's eye. They looked totally different—Nina dark and small and intense, a concentrated ball of energy. And then there was Jenny, who was quiet and beautiful, with delicate looks that made her seem as though she could easily break. Jenny had survived some terrible losses and tragedies in her life, but she had never let those things defeat her. Now she was lit up with some kind of happiness Daisy hoped she would find for herself one day.

"All right, so what's this news?" she asked. "Something about your writing?"

"Yep. My collection of memories and recipes from growing up at the Sky River Bakery is going to be published as a book."

Daisy knew Jenny had been working on it for years. It was incredible to know someone whose dreams were coming true right before your eyes. "Way to go, Jenny," she said. "Everybody loves the bakery so much. They're going to love your book, too."

"I hope so. And I have a request." She opened a big manila envelope and pulled out a collection of photos Daisy had taken at the bakery, back when she'd worked there part-time. "If it's all right with you," Jenny said, "I'd like to show these to the publisher. If they use them, you'll be paid for your work."

"Of course they'll use them," Nina said. "Those pictures are fantastic."

"I think so, too," Jenny said. "They want to include a few archival pictures of the bakery, but most of those were lost in the fire." She was referring to the fire that had burned her home to the ground the previous year. "I'd like to propose this image for the cover."

She indicated the photograph on the top of the stack. Charlie made a dive for it, but Nina held him in check. The picture was a shot of a woman's hands, dusted in flour and expertly kneading a mound of dough. The hands belonged to Laura Tuttle, who had worked at the bakery for, like, a zillion years, and all that experience and strength showed in the hands. It wasn't that they looked that old, but they looked sturdy and competent. The photograph, which Daisy had rendered in sepia tones, was filled with intimate detail. It had been a part of the portfolio that had gained her admission to her current photography class.

"I think that picture perfectly complements the book's title," Nina said. *"Food for Thought: Kitchen Wisdom from a Family Bakery."*

"So is it okay?" Jenny asked. "You'd be paid, of course."

"Wow, it's totally okay," Daisy assured her. "I just hope they're good enough."

"They're wonderful," Olivia said. "Everyone thinks so."

This news, Daisy decided, was proof that even after terrible things happened, dreams could come true. For Jenny, of course, but also for her. She couldn't wait to tell her mom. How cool that she finally felt that way.

Things were still tense between Sonnet and Zach, but at least they weren't openly fighting. Sonnet conceded that the real feud was between her mother and Zach's father, not between her and Zach. Daisy sensed they even kind of liked being together during Sonnet's week home. Julian borrowed his brother's four-wheel-drive Jeep to drive to West Kill, the closest town to the ice climb at Deep Notch.

As they hauled their gear up to the frozen waterfall, Daisy took some pictures—Julian, so intent as he led the way up through the forest. Sonnet looking dubious, Zach intrigued. Winter light filtered through high, thin clouds, and the shapes of the bare trees were etched against the snow.

"So, ice climbing," Sonnet said to Julian. "It's pretty much what it sounds like, right?"

"Depends," said Julian with a good-natured grin. "What does it sound like to you?"

"Challenging. Extreme. Lethal. How am I doing?"

"You'll be fine," he said. "I brought all the safety gear we'll need." He explained rope systems, tying in, belaying, leading, rappelling and lowering. She was familiar with the techniques from rock climbing, but when the vast wall of ice came into view, rows of icicles glinting like daggers of glass, she realized the ascent was going to be something entirely new.

Sonnet was in open rebellion even before they reached the base of the climb. "I am *so* not doing this."

"That's fine," said Zach. "You can hold the rope for me."

"You'd trust me to do that?"

"With my life," he stated.

She caught her breath, clearly not having expected such a statement. They shared a long look, and Daisy could see a softening in Sonnet's eyes. On his relentless quest to win back her friendship, he was clearly gaining ground.

They reached the base of the ice wall and put on their gear—rigid crampons on their feet, harnesses for belaying, belts for the ice axes and screws. Julian demonstrated the techniques that were not, Daisy observed, terribly elegant. Basically, scaling a wall of ice involved digging in a pair of handheld axes while holding steady with the points of your footgear, and using the occasional screw Julian had placed on the ascent. Julian, with his strength and grace, made it look easy—swing and then plant, methodically working his way up the rugged pillars of ice. It didn't take Daisy long to discover that it wasn't exactly as easy as that. Even the short practice ascent challenged muscles she didn't know she had.

"You're crazy, you know that?" she said, arriving in a crumpled heap at the top.

"You're the one who followed me here. What does that make you?"

Zach boosted himself up and then sat on a rock outcropping, his feet dangling over the edge. "Next," he yelled down to Sonnet.

"I already told you, I'm not going," she said.

Zach got up and took the rope from Julian. "I got this. We'll practice here for a while."

Julian motioned Daisy to a longer, steeper section of the ice wall. "You up for this?"

"Sure." Despite the fact that the sport was a monumental struggle, she loved the exhilarating sense of freedom she had out here in the wilderness. Just for a few hours, she wasn't thinking about anything but being with friends, looking at the scenery, having a good time. She couldn't remember the last time she'd done something like this. During the fleeting, perilous minutes of the climb, she was just Daisy, not a single mother who had made a lifelong commitment to a child she'd never planned on having.

"You're all smiles," Julian said when she joined him at the top of the icefall.

She took off her helmet and backpack and took the water bottle he offered. "I'm starting to get why you like doing this." Her smile faded. "I feel guilty, though. Every time I leave Charlie with somebody, I feel guilty."

"He was all smiles, too, when you left him at Olivia's."

"I guess." She took out her camera. The clouds had broken to reveal the kind of sky you only saw in winter—intense, eye-smarting blue, contrasted against the blinding white snow and shadowy mountains. She took some shots, then turned the lens toward Julian.

He sat still for a couple of frames, then jumped up. "I want to keep going."

She shaded her eyes and leaned back to study the ascent to the summit. The last bit was dizzying, the ice not just vertical but bowed out over a series of rocky cliffs. "It looks impossible."

He grinned. "That's why I want to keep going."

"I wish you wouldn't."

"My Spidey-sense tells me I can."

She glowered at him. "I'll make a photographic record of your last moments alive."

That made him laugh aloud. "You do that. It'll be good for your career." He put his helmet and goggles back on, checked his safety ropes and headed up the pillars of ice, moving with a determination she captured beautifully with her camera. Chunks and fine shavings of ice rained down beneath him. At one point, he was clinging to a sheet of ice so vast that he did resemble Spider-Man, suspended in midair. She zoomed in on him, the powerful lens giving her a detailed view of his struggle.

And of the extremely loose-looking screw he was perched on. The ice around it was cracking, crumbling.

"You're going to lose your footing," she yelled. "Julian, look out!"

Her warning came the same moment the ice gave way. He dug in with both ice axes and hung there while the screw fell in a hail of ice and rock. Daisy was transfixed, speechless with terror. Julian's feet swung free, and he seemed to be helpless. She rushed to the ascent rope, found her voice. "Julian, what should I do?" She sounded hollow, the words echoing off the walls of ice and rock.

"I'm good," he said. "Don't . . . worry."

She held her breath and watched. He gained a toehold and hugged the ice for a moment, and she could tell he was fatigued. Then he lifted one ax, moving upward. Upward? "Julian—"

"I can't go down from here," he said, correctly reading her thoughts. "Safer to go up."

She didn't want to watch, but she couldn't look away. The ascent seemed to take hours, though it was really only minutes. Her heart counted out the seconds, and she came to a stark understanding of the amazing fragility of life. Everything could change in an instant. In a single instant, a light could be switched on or off. A decision could be made. An egg could be fertilized. A climber could slip and fall.

Then it struck her—how very much she loved having Julian in the world. That was when she stopped breathing and simply held her breath. It felt like a kind of praying.

At long last, he reached the summit, disappearing over a glinting bulge of ice. Daisy slumped down, feeling weak and suddenly quite cold. A fat length of rope snaked down the wall of ice. A top rope? Was he kidding? Did he think she was going to follow him up?

Charlie, she thought. *I can't do stupid things anymore.* She looked at the rope again. This was Julian. He was crazy, but he knew how to keep her safe—didn't he?

She put away her camera, donned her backpack, helmet and goggles, double-checked her harness, secured the rope. "Belay on," she called, "and if I make it up there, you're dead meat."

She made the ascent with more caution—and more ice screws—than ever, picking the easiest route she could find. Even so, it was long and hard; her arms and legs were shaking, muscles screaming. She hadn't felt this physically challenged since giving birth. She was breathless and sweating when she finally hoisted herself to the summit. She stripped off the helmet and goggles, "That," she said, "was awesome."

He held out his hand, drawing her to her feet, and when she got up, he didn't let go. It was still there, the pulse of awareness she'd always felt when she was near him, the recognition, the wanting.

"Julian—"

He didn't let her finish but leaned down, framed her face between his hands and kissed her. He had never kissed her before, though she'd wanted him to. It wasn't a big, epic, Last of the Mohicans kind of kiss, but gentle and warm. Exploratory—a greeting. And in that way, completely devastating, because it made her heart ache with emotion.

He stopped kissing her and she pulled away, but her hands, still in their damp gloves, kept hold of his jacket. With an effort of will, she made herself let go and step back.

He didn't appear to take offense, but regarded her with solemn thoughtfulness. "I've been waiting a long time to do that."

"Yeah, join the club," she murmured, then felt embarrassed by the admission. "But, um, we probably shouldn't start anything." Oh, man. Had she really said that?

"Why not?"

"Because you and I, we're . . ." Her voice trailed off; she couldn't explain.

"What are we together, Daisy?" His voice was edgy with frustration. "Can you answer me that? Because I'd really like to know."

"You're one of my best friends," she said with

pained honesty. "I wish . . ." So much. There was just so much she wished. That she hadn't been such a wreck over her parents' divorce when she'd first met Julian. That the two of them weren't at such supremely different places in their lives now. That she could figure out how she felt about Logan. She thought about her mom, who hadn't followed her heart; she'd married the father of her child. It hadn't really worked out for Mom . . . or had it? Daisy remembered those photo albums, filled with images of a normal family through happy times and sad. One choice her mom had made had defined their family. It hadn't been so bad, had it?

She blinked fast and hoped he'd attribute her tears to the icy wind. "There's never been a good time for us." She smiled, even though she felt like crying. "What is it that you want, Julian? To date me? To be my boyfriend? To be with someone who lives miles and miles from you, who has a baby to raise? Because that's the way things are. We can go out and do crazy stuff for an hour or two, but then we come back to reality. You're heading back to Ithaca and I'm going back to Charlie."

"Sounds like you've already made up your mind about me."

Didn't he know? She didn't have that kind of choice, not anymore.

Twenty-Five

Juggling mail, paperwork from the law office and the dog's leash, Sophie let herself in and hurried to the wood-burning stove to heat up the cottage. Opal immediately wanted to play, so Sophie made the fire while accompanied by the nasally squeak of a dog toy.

This, then, was Sophie's life. She spent the day either with Charlie or at the law office. She picked up Opal from Noah's, where a girl named Chelsea looked after the dog along with the other animals after school. On some days, Max came for a visit; other days, Sophie went to a hockey practice or game. Gayle had introduced her to a few friends; Sophie discovered that not every woman in Avalon was allied with the Romanos. She was becoming a person she didn't recognize, someone who lived in a small town, creating a network of friends and family. Someone who had a puppy.

And . . . what *was* Noah, anyway? A boyfriend? Regardless of what she called him, he had a way of taking up a lot of room in a person's life, the human equivalent of having a giant, friendly dog in a tiny apartment. No, that wasn't fair. If Sophie was honest with herself, she wouldn't have him any other way. She loved his easy humor, unfeigned tenderness and huge appetite for sex, his absolute lack of concern over the fact that they were engaged in a whirlwind affair and his sturdy conviction that this was actually more than an affair.

He called at the usual time, just before dinner. Tonight's proposal—a hike through the woods with the dogs.

"It's freezing," she said.

"Wear an extra layer."

She met him on the snowy path that wound through the woods surrounding the old dairy farm. When he saw her, he broke into a grin, crossing the snowy expanse to grab her for a kiss. When had she ever felt this wanted? This important to someone—to anyone?

"How was your day?" he asked.

Or asked her about her day?

He took Opal's leash from her and they started walking. "Let's see. I vetted a real estate contract, wrote some letters in legalese, filed a brief with the superior court, consulted with a client. Atticus Finch I'm not."

"Nope, you wear lipstick, and you dress better."

Today's client had been Bo Crutcher, although Noah wouldn't hear that from Sophie. It was a well-known fact that Bo—whose legal name was, to his great humiliation, Bojangles—liked his beer, and while under its influence, tended to make promises he never meant to keep. His current dilemma was to make certain he was *not* the father of a local girl's baby, despite her assertion to the contrary.

The workday was over, though. Worries didn't stalk her home the way her job in the ICC had.

The path wound through the deep woods in the hills behind his farm. He pointed out some of the landmarks of his boyhood—a hickory tree where he'd once built a tree house, and a grove of sugar maples where he'd collected sap for maple syrup, winning a coveted 4-H club prize for his efforts. There was a rock he'd hit while tobogganing, splitting his head open, and the stream where he collected frogs' eggs in the spring to watch them turn into tadpoles. It was easy to imagine him in this setting, a boy at home in his world. No wonder he'd turned out to be such a well-adjusted adult.

"What's that look?" he asked her. "Did I say something wrong?"

"Lord, no. It just occurred to me that since we've met, I've been all take and no give."

He laughed. "I wouldn't say that."

"I would. I've been so focused on remaking my life that I've never asked you, never wondered . . . what do you want, Noah? What do you dream about?"

He thought for a moment. "A life that makes me happy. A life that makes sense."

"That's too simple."

"Maybe." He dismissed the topic with a wave of his hand. "Watch your step," he said, indicating a depression in the snow. "We're crossing a stream."

"I don't see the stream," she said.

"You just crossed it. Be really quiet, and you'll hear."

He was right. She held very still and listened,

detecting a faint trickle of water, invisible beneath the layers of snow.

"It's just starting to thaw," he said.

"And I'm starting to freeze. Let's head back." She looked around the quiet woods and smiled. "You can't imagine how different this is from what I used to do after work."

"Yeah?"

"In the first place, I almost never came home before dark. On the way back to my apartment, I used to stop at a deli for a rollmops."

"What's a rollmops?"

"My usual takeout dinner—pickled herring wrapped around a cucumber and served on a bun with onion."

He made a gagging sound.

"Hey, don't knock it. I found it convenient, something to munch on while I spent the evening working some more."

"Wait a minute, so you came home from work and then you worked at home?"

She tried not to cringe, remembering her lonely existence. "It filled the time for me."

"What did you do for fun?"

"Fun?"

"You know, partying, going out?"

"Tariq—my friend and colleague—liked going to clubs. Very old-school. I rarely went with him, though." She laughed. "Ever heard of a circle party?"

"You're not talking about the kind that takes place in a boys' locker room."

"Noah."

"Just checking. Is this a Dutch thing?" He made a hang-ten sign with his gloved hand. "Like, dude, circle party—"

"Well, they love inviting a *buitenlander*—a foreigner—to these things. But honestly, it's a bit like . . . I don't know. Watching paint dry. See, everyone sits in a circle in folding chairs, and we all shake hands, and have lukewarm tea or coffee and bad cake, meet the aunts and cousins, Oma and Opa and the little ones, and we tell each other everything is just *gezellig.*"

"Gezellig."

"It's sort of hard to translate. It means . . . nice. Cozy and cordial, I suppose. You know, *gezellig.* A circle party goes on for hours."

"I'd rather eat a rollmops."

"Exactly."

"But tonight, I'm making spaghetti."

"Is that an invitation?" she asked.

"Oh, yeah. So get your *gezellig* ass in gear."

When they returned to the house, he didn't even pretend to start dinner, but made love to her instead, and she didn't bother trying to resist. What she felt—desire, raw lust, whatever she wanted to call it—easily pushed past her customary caution. He was like the water under the snow, a secret spring, setting something free inside her. Like a couple of revved-up teenagers, they made out on the living-room sofa, eventually migrating to the bed and finally the deep, old-fashioned bathtub.

"Do you have any idea," he asked her much later, "how crazy I am about you?"

She was in his bedroom, in the middle of getting dressed in the semidark. "No idea," she said. "Remind me."

He took hold of the sweater she had just pulled on. "Crazy enough to do it all over again," he said, shimmying the soft cashmere up over her rib cage.

She was inches from going along with him. "Do you find it a little discomfiting, doing this in the same house where your parents—"

He stopped her with a kiss. "My mind doesn't go there. But I like the idea that there's love in this house." He laughed at the expression on her face. "And yes, I did say that. I said the *L*-word."

Love.

She tugged her sweater down. "You shouldn't use a word like that carelessly."

"Who said I'm being careless? I love you. It's simple."

"You can't know that," she said, folding her arms tightly in front of her.

"I know what I know. You're still trying to pretend we're nothing but a hookup, but you're wrong. We've both been around enough to know we've got something here. And yeah, it's new and unexpected and sudden and all that. Doesn't mean it's not real. This is turning into something. Trust me on that."

"It's . . . too soon." She was so startled she didn't know what else to say.

"It's right now. And right now, Sophie Bellamy, this very minute, I'm crazy in love with you."

It wasn't what she wanted to hear. And as declarations went, it was what some attorneys might call a squinting statement. It looked both ways, and gave itself a loophole. *Right now . . . this very minute.*

He laughed again. "You take the term *overthinking* to a new level."

"How would you know I'm overthinking this?"

"I can practically hear the gears grinding in your brain. But don't worry. There's a way to fix that." His hand slid smoothly up under her sweater. He had an assured—and now familiar—touch, yet she always got the sense that he was surprised and turned-on as though touching her for the first time.

This time, she didn't resist, and for the next hour, she didn't think at all. Moreover, she didn't have to continue the dialogue he'd opened with that one little word. Still, she couldn't stop the emotions from welling up when he touched her with such tenderness. Here was something she had been missing in her life and until Noah, she had not known precisely what it was. Now she did. There was a special grace and power in holding someone and being held, a feeling of both strength and vulnerability, a sense of safety. Sophie felt it now, unexpectedly and unmistakably, with Noah.

In The Hague, she had friends and colleagues, but they were not the sort of people who could fill her up with such sweetness, with the feelings Noah stirred.

The lack of a grand romance in her life had never been some huge issue or problem with her. Except in the sense that she didn't believe she had room for such a thing. She didn't want to wake up every morning thinking, *I need someone to hold me.*

But now, with Noah's arms around her, she knew a part of her needed this connection like air and water. He had the ability to see into her heart, and for the first time in a long time, maybe ever, she didn't feel so alone. She finally knew what love felt like, true romantic love, and its power was devastating. It scared her to need him so much. She was supposed to be making it on her own, wasn't she?

"Enough," she murmured, dragging herself back from the blissful edge of a postcoital nap. "You promised me dinner."

"Maybe it was a clever ploy to lure you to bed." He grinned and sat up, the sheet falling away to reveal a physique that nearly made her change her mind about getting up. There should be a law, she thought, requiring all men to train for Ironman triathlons.

With an effort of will, she left the bed and hurriedly dressed. Then she fixed her hair and put on fresh lipstick, pausing to study her image in the mirror.

"What's that look?" asked Noah.

"Shopping with Daisy was certainly fun, but I'm not so sure about this new wardrobe of jeans and skimpy sweaters."

"What's wrong with skimpy? I like skimpy."

"It looks ridiculous on a woman my age."

"You look hot. Don't knock it. Your daughter has good taste. I hope she picked out something dressy for you, too."

"Why is that?"

"There's a dance on Saturday night, at the fire hall. The whole town shows up for it."

She frowned at the mirror again. "It sounds . . . fun."

"Trust me, it's no Dutch circle party."

"Oh, Noah. It's just not really a good time for me to—" She stopped, took a deep breath. "Noah, I don't want my kids to know. About us." There, she'd said it, finally. She didn't let herself look at him in the mirror.

"Why not?"

"I came here for them. Not for . . . this. Not to meet someone, start something. They wouldn't understand." Finally she turned to look at him. "*I* don't understand."

"Quit worrying. I'm into you. I think you're into me. Any kid can understand that. What are you really afraid of, Sophie?"

Of how much it's going to hurt when it's over. "Noah, I don't—"

The doorbell rang, followed by the sound of stomping feet. "Yo, Noah!"

"Saved by the bell." He kissed her, briefly and hard, one last time. The bell rang again. "The guys are here."

"You knew they were coming?"

"Sure. I promised them spaghetti, and we're practicing afterward." He picked up a plaid flannel shirt, sniffed it.

"Nice of you to tell me. Now I'm trapped," she said. "They're going to know we're sleeping together . . ."

"I don't know about you, but I didn't sleep a wink. Don't worry, it's not like they're going to tell your kids or anything." Apparently deeming the shirt clean, he put it on.

"You know what I mean, and so will they."

"They're my friends. They like you. They'll be happy for us."

"I know. But it's just . . . I prefer to keep this—us—private." She spied a flash of hurt and anger in his eyes. "Because of me," she added hastily. "Not you. Because I'm new in town, and all people know about me is that I'm the ex-wife of the sainted Greg Bellamy, the woman who abandoned her children to live the high life in Europe. All I need is for people to find out I'm sleeping around."

"You're not sleeping around. You're sleeping with me." He found the cap he liked to wear, bill backward, when he played the drums.

"Yes, but—"

"Look, you didn't come back here to be a nun. You came back to be with your kids. And, I assume, to have a life. Besides, look at me. I'm a catch." He spread his arms in a comical pose. He had the fashion sense of John Deere and a smile that took her breath away. And there was something about him that warmed her heart and made her feel good about herself, as though she could face anything. As though she could take on the world.

Her evenings used to consist of sitting alone in front of the computer, going over cases. Now she spent her evenings with friends or family, or with a man who might have just said he loved her.

Twenty-Six

Sophie organized an afternoon at Mohonk Mountain House with Max and Daisy. Some of her fondest memories of being with them revolved around trips they'd taken over the years, when she'd shown them new places and introduced them to new experiences. She liked to remember that they had once been a happy family. She wanted to believe they could be happy together again. She wanted the two of them alone together, because she had some things to discuss.

She also had a surprise for them. Tariq was in New York on court business, and had arranged to meet them at the historic preserve. Sophie had been working hard at making a new life for herself, but part of her missed her other life desperately—missed Tariq, most of all.

The resort had been built by the Smiley family in the 1860s, and, to this day, still belonged to their heirs. While studying international law, Sophie had been an occasional guest at the resort. It was America's ultimate castle, with the grandest of salons and guest rooms, stables and a maze, an ice rink, formal gardens, a golf course, miles of trails through the Mohonk Preserve, and heart-stirring vistas through every window. Perched high atop the granite bluffs that towered over Lake Mohonk, it was a combination of Disney's Magic Kingdom, Mad Ludwig's castle and a vintage postcard, glittering with snow. She knew her children would have the same awed reaction to the place that she'd had.

As they surveyed the towering cluster of cut stones and spires, she watched their faces light with wonder. Daisy was grown, and Max nearly there, as well, but that Christmas-morning look reminded her that they would always be her children. She regarded them both, trying to see past Daisy's fragile beauty, past Max's studied nonchalance. Regrets washed over her in a wave. She wished she could turn back time, be there for them when they needed her, pay closer attention this time around. But regrets were a slow poison. She could only go forward. She focused on Charlie snuggled in his carrier, fast asleep from the drive. The chance to watch him grow up was such a gift.

"Mohonk means 'the lake in the sky,' " Sophie said. "Currier and Ives did a series of prints of this place. I've been dying to show you around."

In the vast library, amid soaring bookcases accessed by wheeled ladders, she showed them portraits of presidents and dignitaries who had stayed here. "The founders were two brothers," she explained. "Albert and Alfred Smiley. They were Quakers, dedicated to world justice and peace. About a hundred years ago, the Permanent Court of Arbitration was created right here, maybe even in this room."

Daisy regarded her suspiciously. "And we should care about this because. . . ."

"Because the PCA is now headquartered in The Hague," Sophie said. "I thought you'd be interested to know I was offered a position as an adjunct to that court." She looked around the enormous library, and imagined she could practically feel the old collections breathing with wisdom. "I turned it down, and the next day, I came back here to you two and Charlie."

"Do you wish you'd taken the job?" Max asked, visibly stiffening as though bracing himself for a blow.

"No, I don't. In fact, I'm incredibly glad I'm here now." She paused. "I'm going to be looking for my own place in Avalon."

There. She'd said it. Declared that she was no longer a visitor, but a full-time resident. A full-time mom. She was committed to this new life, to them.

"What kind of place?" asked Max.

She wasn't sure what he was asking. "I'm going to buy a home," she said.

"Where?"

"In Avalon."

"At the lake?"

"I don't know. I have an appointment with a real estate agent next week. Why, do you have a preference?"

"Yeah, I prefer where you are now."

"It's really nice there, Mom," Daisy said. She went

to the window, aimed her camera at the snowy scenery outside. "This is amazing."

"What about Opal? She stays at Noah's when you're not home. Where will she go if you move?" Max asked.

"Soon she'll be big enough to stay home by herself," Sophie told him. Truth be told, Sophie would miss living near Noah, too, but this was about her family. "If I get a place in town, you won't need to ride the school bus to come see me," she pointed out.

"I don't mind the bus."

This was new. Initially, Max had declared that he hated the bus. Maybe he'd made some friends on the route. "It'll be fine, Max," she reassured him. "Promise. Okay?"

"Okay." He went to study a ship in a bottle.

Sophie took a deep breath. The news about finding a house was the easy part. She spent several nervous moments working up to the topic. "I wanted to ask you something about your hockey game tomorrow."

"What about it?" Max asked.

"I'm bringing a friend to watch the game with me." She'd thought about it throughout the previous night and all day, and she'd come to the conclusion that Noah deserved public status. He'd never been less than wonderful to her, and she was through trying to hide their relationship. It was silly, juvenile and pointless.

Max kept his attention on the ship in a bottle, but Daisy lowered her camera and turned toward her mother. Sophie was nervous about explaining Noah to her kids. She told herself not to be silly, that she'd kept company with royalty, scoundrels, great men and criminals in conjunction with her job. She'd never had trouble before, yet the moment her heart was at stake, she choked. "Would that be okay, Max?"

"Depends. Who're you bringing?"

She glanced at Daisy, who looked intrigued. "Noah Shepherd. Do you mind?"

He shrugged. "Fine with me. He's told me before he likes hockey."

"Moron," Daisy said. "He likes *Mom.*"

Finally, Max straightened up. "So is he, like, your boyfriend or something?"

Or something. That was the standard term, though Sophie didn't have a word for what Noah was to her. But she couldn't deny he was important, and Max and Daisy were entitled to know it.

"I suppose you could say he's my, er, boyfriend." She stumbled over the word. It felt wrong, like trying on her daughter's jeans.

Neither of her children spoke. "Well?" she prodded when she couldn't stand it anymore. "Does that sound all right?"

"How do they get the ship in the bottle?" Max asked.

"The real question," Daisy said, "is what's the point of putting it there?"

"The point of a ship in the bottle," said a smooth, English voice, "is that there is no point." Tariq walked into the room, even more handsome and urbane than Sophie remembered.

With a cry of delight, she ran and threw her arms around him. "There you are," she said. "I was afraid you weren't coming."

"I'd never go back on a promise to you," he said.

"I can't believe you're here. Max and Daisy, you remember Tariq." Glowing with pride, she showed him Charlie, sweetly sleeping in his carrier. By any measure, he was the most beautiful of babies, with velvety pale skin and a bow-shaped mouth, a swirl of auburn hair.

Tariq was properly impressed. "Oh, well done," he said, beaming indulgently. "Well done indeed. Brilliant, in fact." Then he straightened up and faced Daisy and Max. "I miss your mother. I'm a selfish bastard and I wish we were still working together, but seeing her with you two and the little one, I understand. And I've brought you something," he said to Sophie. "I wanted to give it to you with your children present." He opened his briefcase and took out a flat, hinged box. "This was awarded to your mother the night of Epiphany," he said.

Cold tension gripped her. She'd never shared the details of that night with her children. "Tariq—"

"Mom, that's awesome," Max said, admiring the engraved medal on its multicolored ribbon.

With studied solemnity, Tariq placed the medal around her neck. This was just a tiny glimpse of her old life, but seeing her children's expressions now made Sophie glow with pride. Daisy insisted on taking pictures.

Sophie caught his eye and mouthed a thank-you. It was a moment she knew she would close into her heart, keeping it there forever.

The baby awoke, and while Daisy tended to him and Max went to explore the snowy gardens, Tariq ordered drinks. "It's glorious here," he said. "And you seem happy, Petal. I'm glad to see that. I wasn't sure you would be."

"I wasn't, either," she admitted. "I do miss you, Tariq. I can't say I want that life again, but I do miss the work."

"Come for a visit," he suggested. "Better yet, visit Umoja. I'm going there myself in a month."

She fingered the medal hanging from its colored ribbon. "That's tempting, but I'm needed here. It feels strange, saying that, but I am."

Twenty-Seven

Sophie sat in Noah's living room after dinner, trying to keep an open mind about the lighted beer clock that hung above the fireplace. Noah had promised that he would try to like her kind of films—a Fellini retrospective was playing in Kingston this weekend. Maybe she should try to like the clock. She certainly had no trouble liking many things about him, including his insistence on doing the dishes. He was in the kitchen now, finishing up.

How quickly they had fallen into certain habits. They'd taken to having dinner together more often than not. They were learning each other's taste in music—his was markedly different from hers, though she was beginning to appreciate the sound of groups with names like the Bad Pennies and Mastodon. They went jogging together with the dogs and sometimes rode horses. They were learning how to be in each other's lives.

She was starting to regret having to move somewhere else. It was lovely, having him so close. It was . . . *gezellig.*

Stepping over the sleeping puppy, who was always welcome at Noah's house, she straightened a stack of science fiction novels on the coffee table. He was a fan of Ben Bova, Theodore Sturgeon, Philip José Farmer. There was a sheaf of printouts from the Internet—articles by Brooks Fordham. The discovery sent a chill across her skin. Why was he reading Brooks's articles?

She heard him approaching, and quickly stacked the books on top of the printouts. She came across an ancient phone directory that should have been recycled three years ago. When he came into the room, she was about to scold him about the clutter. Instead, she flipped the phone directory open. "Adams, Anna," she read aloud. "Six forty-seven Mill St. 372-3858. Ammon, Bradley, 74 South Maple . . ."

"What are you doing?" asked Noah.

"Reading the phone book. You once said it would be interesting to hear me reading the phone book."

"Naked," he qualified. "Reading the phone book *naked* is what I meant."

"You didn't say that."

"I'm saying it now." He grabbed her, unbuttoning her shirt.

She batted his hand away and kept reading. "Anderson, Barbara. Twenty-one forty Lakeview Terrace, apartment 9-B. Archer—hey!"

She laughed helplessly, until the humor played out and heated into desire. Moments later, he was making love to her, right there on the sofa. His touch made her feel young again in a way she had never been young. When she was with him, she felt transformed. She was more full of hope and possibility than she'd been in . . . maybe ever.

Much later, she lay in his arms, quiet but teetering on the edge of something. "I need to ask a favor of you."

"Anything. I'd do anything for you." His matter-of-fact statement was more convincing than flowery promises. "What do you need me to do? Walk across hot coals? Follow you to the ends of the earth? Yeah, that'd be good. I've always wanted to travel."

"Worse. I need you to sit through a kids' hockey game."

"Ouch."

"As my date. I told Daisy and Max about—I told them I was seeing you. It was awkward, but they seem to understand. So will you?"

"It'll cost you." He whispered a suggestion in her ear that made her blush.

"I suppose I could accommodate that."

"I'll hold you to it."

While he made a fire in the grate, she went to the window and looked out at the glowing blue twilight, spreading darkness across the snow. A black silhouette was cut starkly against the landscape. It was a deer, browsing on strips of bark from the trees in the yard. She remembered the night they'd met. She liked to think the deer she'd hit had survived.

He finished making the fire, then circled his arms around her from behind. She turned in his embrace, feeling open and calm. "There's something I've been wanting to tell you," she said. "It's about what happened to me in The Hague . . ."

"Yeah? What about it, honey?" His voice was terribly gentle.

She told herself it was safe to trust him. She had never trusted anyone the way she did Noah, but then again, she had never loved anyone this way. *Tell him.*

"I haven't told this to anyone." She indicated the printouts on the coffee table. "Not even Brooks. You won't read about it in any of his accounts. I thought it wouldn't matter if I kept this to myself, but I was wrong. It matters, Noah. So much."

He opened his arms. "Would it help if I hold you?"

She nodded. "That always helps." She settled against him, feeling his warmth and the strong, steady rhythm of his breathing. "Remember when we first met, and I told you I'd survived worse than a cut knee?"

"You made some joke about being taken hostage at gunpoint and plunging off a bridge in a speeding van," he recalled. "And . . . you weren't joking after all, were you?"

"I was glad you thought so. It made it . . . less real. And that helped, for a while. But it did happen, and what you read about the incident is all true, every word of it. The lie was in what I left out." She stopped to catch her breath, knowing there was no going back now. "There's a part of that night I never told anyone, not even the doctors who treated me. It's the one thing I couldn't face. I still have nightmares, though. I still think about that night. When it was over, there was no diagnosis of PTSD, but I'm still at risk for it, and sometimes I worry so much about that. People depend on me here—"

"And people love you here, Sophie. Never forget that."

He wasn't letting her forget that. But just by shutting her eyes, she could take herself back to that night, to the scene inside the van, the chaos and rage, her desperation and determination to survive. "When the van went off the bridge, three of the men inside died."

"Ah, Sophie. I'm so sorry. I hate that you went through that—"

"Noah, listen." She turned to him, forced herself to look him in the eye. "It was my fault. I was the reason the van went off the bridge." She explained about how things had gone wrong for the terrorists that night, and how they'd been forced to abort their plan and flee, bringing her along as a hostage. She told him what was said in the van, and how her certainty that she would die led to her act of desperation. She was crying now, and shaking. "They died, and it's my fault, Noah. How do I live with that?"

"They died because they were murderers," he said, framing her face between his hands, catching her tears with his thumbs and wiping them away. "And you survived for the sake of your family, Sophie, and because you're brave, and you have a heart as big as the world."

After making her confession to Noah, she felt drained but, somehow, unknotted. Telling Noah about that night, about the terror and the trauma that had shot her life off in a different direction, had unfurled the tension inside her. He was a good listener, simply holding her, asking nothing but accepting everything she had to say. She told him about André and Fatou, and how helpless she'd felt. He didn't pretend to understand, he didn't try to offer advice on how to fix it, but by simply listening, he helped her. Outwardly, nothing had changed. Yet she felt like a new person. It was late, although she didn't feel tired in the least.

Noah held her cheek cradled against his chest, so that she could hear the beating of his heart. "I don't know what to say."

She smiled. "You're already saying it. The experience completely changed me. It's the whole reason I gave up my career at the ICC and came back to my kids."

"I don't blame you. I'd do exactly the same thing."

She hugged him tighter. "I wish just one of my colleagues in The Hague would have said that. I was so torn up about it."

"You need a glass of wine," he said.

"Maybe the whole bottle," she replied.

While he went to the kitchen, she switched on the TV. She found herself looking at a heart-tugging infomercial about orphans in Bolivia. Although she didn't consider herself vulnerable to such pitches, she found herself grabbing a pen from the coffee table. There was no paper, so she jotted the toll-free number on the back of her hand. For the price of a cup of coffee each day, she could save little Matteo from starvation. What she really wanted to do was scoop him up and hold him in her arms the way she held Charlie, making him feel safe in the world.

She muted the sound on the TV but it was too late. The inevitable guilt set in. It must've shown on her face.

"What's wrong?" Noah asked, returning with a bottle of wine and two glasses.

"Here I am, all warm and cozy, while children are suffering. I should do something—"

"You have. You spent your whole professional life doing something."

"But I could do more."

"You are. You're raising Max and Daisy. Charlie, too. You're teaching them to be like you—compassionate, dedicated. And I imagine one day they'll do their part." He handed her a glass of wine. "That's how you change the world, Sophie. One person can't do it all. Believe it."

He had a way of looking at things that struck Sophie as spectacularly sane. She couldn't change anything that had happened, but she could change from how she *was* in the past. She had been so locked into the idea that she had to be working directly on a problem or issue. Now here was Noah, telling her she could make a difference simply by being a good mother. No one had ever explained to her before that raising your family was the most important job in the world.

She set down her glass and wrapped her arms around his neck. "Noah. I love the way your mind works and the things you say." She paused, leaning back to look up at him. "I love you."

"Damn. You really mean that, don't you?"

"I do. I'm sorry, but it had to be said."

"Sorry." He laughed at her. "Sorry?"

"And I'm sorry I didn't tell you before."

"That's okay. That way, I'll always have something to lord over you—I said it first."

Always. He seemed to have no trouble making the assumption that they would have an *always.* When he pulled her close, kissed her as though sealing the deal, she wanted it to be so. And it amazed her to want such a thing. It amazed her even more to discover that she believed it was not only desirable, but possible.

He backed off a little, smiled down at her. "And here I thought you only ever wanted me for the sex."

"Is something the matter with the sex?" she asked.

"Lord, no. The sex is unbelievable."

No one had ever said such a thing about her before. Perhaps because no one had ever had that opinion of her, in bed, anyway.

He aimed the remote, clicked off the TV and slipped his arms around her. This night had set something free in her, igniting a new heat between them. There was an element of complete trust . . . and complete abandon. With Noah, she found herself doing things that would have made the old Sophie blush. With Noah, and her heart full of love, everything seemed exactly right.

Twenty-Eight

Chelsea, the girl who lived up the road from Max's mom, handed Max his phone. "Thanks for letting me borrow it," she said. "My grandparents won't let me get one, but they're always wanting me to check in. Pisses me off. If they expect me to call, they should get me a phone."

Max handed her Opal's leash while he stuck the phone in his pocket. No fan of hockey, she was going to watch the dog during the game. He shaded his eyes, scanning the parking lot of the sports complex by the lake. He and Chelsea had come with Max's mom, who was parking the car while they walked the dog. He kind of felt sorry for Chelsea, who didn't have many friends. It seemed she would rather spend the afternoon walking the dog than staying home with her grandparents.

"You looking for someone?" Chelsea asked, nosy as usual.

He took back the dog's leash and shrugged without looking at Chelsea. They weren't exactly friends, but they found themselves together quite a lot. For one thing, Max took the school bus to his mom's every day he didn't have something after school, and he often found himself talking to Chelsea during the ride. For another thing, she was really good with animals, and did chores in the clinic and around the barn. Max's mom said Noah's place, with all its video games, sports equipment and animals, was like a theme park for kids who didn't want to grow up.

"Sort of," he said. "Noah Shepherd. He's coming to watch the game with my mom."

"You mean, like a date?"

He nodded, glad he'd decided to level with her about this development. It was something new, and he was trying to figure out how he felt about it. He didn't want to bring it up with his dad or Nina—*no way*—and his other friends would just tell him it was no big deal.

"So is it weird for you?" asked Chelsea.

"Nah," he said, "it's not weird." This was what Max told himself, anyway. When married people split up, they dated other people. It happened, like it or not. "I don't mind Noah. He's cool."

"That's what I think, too."

The parking lot was fast filling up with players and spectators. This was going to be the biggest match of the season for Max's team. It was one of the first events of the Winter Carnival. The Inn at Willow Lake was completely full, and Max was staying at his mom's, which meant he got to spend lots of time with his dog—and with Chelsea. She wasn't that bad. Annoying maybe, but what girl wasn't?

He let Opal off her leash. She was getting really good off leash, although Max kept a constant eye on her. The dog scampered back and forth through the snow, plunging her muzzle in, then racing off in a zigzag pattern. "I suppose my mom could do a lot worse," he said. "Picking a boyfriend, I mean. She knows a bunch of boring lawyers and diplomats from her work. At least I'm not stuck with one of them."

"Noah's awesome, with all the animals and stuff. And him going out with your mother—I figured it was only a matter of time."

"What do you mean by that?"

"Well, it's so obvious he's into her. I could tell right from the start."

Max hadn't been able to tell a thing. "Did he say something to you?"

"No. I just work there, okay? But he was always

talking about her, you know, to his patients and friends who came by, saying how she just moved here from Europe and how smart she was and all. I heard him talking on the phone to his mother in Florida, and she asked him if he was seeing someone and he owned right up to it."

"You never told me that."

She stooped down, made a snowball and tossed it to Opal. The dog leaped up, detonating the snowball in midair. "It wasn't mine to tell."

Oh. Max was kind of glad to know she wasn't some big gossip like a lot of girls he knew. Chelsea was pretty okay. He didn't *like* like her, but she was okay to hang out with sometimes. She lived with her grandparents, and never talked about her family. Max never asked, because she tended to get all huffy and say how stuff pissed her off.

She nudged him with her elbow. "What're you looking at? And what's funny?"

"Nothing." He didn't really know how to explain it, but he felt better about stuff when he was around her, like it was okay to be mad and not pretend everything was fine all the time. "I'd better go. Time to get geared up for the game." He called to Opal, but she was either ignoring him or too far to hear. He tried whistling.

"You're a lame whistler," Chelsea pointed out. With practiced ease, she wedged two fingers into the sides of her mouth and blew a loud, shrill note. A moment later, Opal came bounding over a hedge and churned through the snow until she practically bowled them over.

"Not bad," Max said. "How did you do that?"

"Practice. You have to figure out how to make the air whistle through your mouth. See, I use these two fingers." She demonstrated. "Some people like to use their finger and thumb."

Max took off his glove and gave it a try, but only managed an airy, hollow sound. Opal stared at him, uncomprehending. Chelsea laughed. "Don't worry, it takes a lot of time, and you'll drool all over yourself. It took my dad about one minute to show me how, but I had to try for hours before I got it."

"Your dad taught you to whistle?"

"Yep, he . . ." She stuffed her hand back into her mitten. "It was a really long time ago." She hunched up her shoulders.

Max clipped on Opal's leash and caught up, but he didn't push her to talk more about her father. Some things you didn't talk about, like his mom and The Hague. And someone who was a true friend didn't make you. Max could see players heading toward the building, sticks and duffel bags over their shoulders.

"Hey, Bellamy, who's the hound?" yelled Altshuler.

Max patted the dog trotting by his side. "Opal. You've seen her before."

"No, I mean the hound, who's the hound?" Altshuler snickered.

Two perfectly round spots of humiliation appeared on Chelsea's cheeks. Max wished she would speak up, tell Altshuler to piss off, but she kept her eyes down.

For about a nanosecond, it occurred to Max to speak up, but all the words dried up in his mouth.

"Anyway, I'll see you after the game," she muttered, then took the dog's leash and scurried away.

Max felt a twist in his gut. He shot Altshuler a look. "Not cool," he said.

"Whoa, you're defending her? She's a freak, man. A hound. Nobody likes her."

I do. No way would Max own up to it, though. Not to Kurt Altshuler. He was one of the popular kids at school. Everybody wanted to be his friend. But you had to watch what you said around him. *That pisses me off.* He could hear Chelsea's voice in his head.

"Hey, Max." His mom came walking up to them. She looked bright and smiling, and Max flashed on Daisy. His mom and Daisy looked a lot alike.

"Hey, Mom."

She turned to Altshuler. "Hello, Kurt. Ready for the big game?"

"Um, yeah. Sure am." Altshuler was all phony politeness as he straightened up his posture and practically saluted her like a Boy Scout.

"Noah should be here soon," she said. "We'll be sitting by the bank sign in the usual spot."

We. Mom and Noah. Max felt a drumming in his chest. "Okay."

"Good luck, Max-a-megamillion. And I'm sorry to have to do this in front of your friend, but . . ." She gave him a quick hug and a kiss on his cheek. "Have a great game. You too, Kurt."

Altshuler stood with his mouth hanging open, watching her go. "Man, your mom is such a MILF."

"A what?" asked Max.

"A mother I'd like to—"

"Shut up," Max said, catching on, "or I'll have to hurt you. I swear to God, I will."

"Ooh, I'm so scared." Altshuler punctuated his speech by shoving Max's shoulder once, twice, three times. "Bring it, Bellamy. Let's see what you got."

Max shoved back, knowing he was about to start something but still unable to hold back. Somewhere, way deep in his brain, he knew it was a bad idea to get in a fight before a game. And with a teammate, too. But that knowledge was blotted out by a big red blotch of anger. He made a lunge for Altshuler.

Something held him back. A giant fist, clutching the fabric of his parka stopped him in midlunge and hauled him back.

"Hey, guys," Noah Shepherd said in a big, hearty voice. "It's about time to gear up."

Altshuler looked daggers at Max. "That's right, Dr. Shepherd." He scooped up his bag and stalked away.

"Good luck to you both," Noah said.

"Thanks," Max muttered, grabbing his gear and heading for the entrance.

"Hey," Noah called.

Max stopped and turned. He wondered if this guy thought the same way as Altshuler did about his mom. "Yeah?"

"Whatever it is, save it for the game, Max."

• • •

Sophie felt like a prom queen as she entered the arena with Noah Shepherd at her side. It was a bit juvenile to take such pleasure in swanning about on the arm of the best-looking guy in the place, but she couldn't help herself. She was buoyant with her decision to be in this relationship—to be in love.

They found seats in the bleachers with Daisy, Charlie and Daisy's friend, Julian Gastineaux. Sophie found herself wondering if there was something more to Daisy's friendship with Julian. The two of them seemed unusually attuned to each other, and Daisy's face was aglow. Sophie knew how hard it was to be a young mother and to be in a relationship at the same time. She hoped her daughter would find the balance.

Greg and Nina arrived, offering a polite wave and settling a diplomatic distance away. They were with Nina's sister Maria, who had been so charming to Sophie. She caught some of the other moms looking at her and Noah, and leaning toward each other to whisper.

"My ex," she murmured to Noah, indicating Greg.

The awkwardness was dispelled by the noise of the crowd and the fast action of the game. Noah merely nodded and turned his attention to the ice. Sophie found herself wishing she could be more like him, accepting things at face value and not caring so much about what anyone thought.

Max was a defenseman, working as a unit with his friend Kurt to protect their goaltender. Max looked so grown-up in his bulky gear, assuming the stance and posture of a professional. Each time an opposing player made a shot, he reacted with lightning reflexes. During the third period, with the score tied, he moved to block a shot, colliding with his teammate, Kurt. Instead of getting back into play, the collision escalated into a shoving match. Sophie jumped to her feet, not that it helped her see any better. Through his mask, Max's face seemed to be red with fury. The momentary distraction opened a window of opportunity for the opposing team. The puck slammed past the boys and slung into the goal. The crowd erupted, but Max and Kurt found themselves confined to the penalty box, their coach yelling at them.

"What on earth was that?" Sophie asked. "Should I check on him?"

Noah slid his arm around her. "No biggie. They're just being kids."

After the game, Max went home with his father, Greg promised to talk to him about the incident. Noah walked outside with Sophie. "Go get us some coffee at the concession stand. I'll go find Chelsea and Opal."

Feeling a bit unsettled, Sophie went to the concession stand, located in the skating house at the edge of the lake. People were skating, admiring the ice sculptures that graced the park. She joined the crowd milling around, and ordered two coffees. And there—

just my luck, she thought—was Kurt's mother. Ilsa Altshuler offered a tight smile of greeting.

"Well. It's a shame about the game, isn't it?" she commented.

"Definitely," Sophie agreed. "It's never fun to lose. I know the coach had plenty to say to Max and Kurt about their scuffle, and his father and I will both be talking to him, as well."

"Kurt will get more than a talking-to from us," Ilsa stated.

Sophie nodded. "Max will be grounded, too."

"He should be. He's got to learn to hold his temper."

Sophie bit the inside of her lower lip, forbidding herself to respond. From her vantage point, it had looked as though Kurt had instigated the scuffle, but the last thing Sophie wanted to do was quibble with this woman. She simply nodded. "Perhaps I'll see you at the festivities this weekend, Ilsa," she said.

Ilsa offered a sour look. "Maybe. We're planning to go to the dance on Saturday. I saw you with Noah Shepherd," she remarked. "Our dog, Sammy, is his patient."

Maybe she was going to play nice, Sophie thought hopefully.

"It's awfully brave of you, dating such a young guy," Ilsa continued. "I'd be far too self-conscious."

A young guy? It was true that Sophie didn't know Noah's exact age. The topic had never come up between them. She hadn't asked; she'd asked nothing beyond, *Do you have protection?* before falling into bed with him. Now, for the first time, a niggling doubt crept in through a back door of her mind.

"It never occurred to me to feel self-conscious," she said, determined not to let the comment derail her. "But thanks for your concern."

"Oh, it's not really a concern. I admire you, dating someone so much younger. I'd better be going." She brushed past Sophie and headed toward the parking lot.

Sophie took her time making her way to Noah. *So much younger . . .* The words echoed through her mind. Good Lord, *how* much younger?

He was waiting by the car, watching Opal dig in a snowbank. She handed a cup of coffee to Noah. "How old are you?" she asked bluntly.

He looked momentarily startled; then his eyes darted back and forth. "Why do you ask?"

"There are things I need to know if we're going to be . . . There are things I need to know. Like your age. Is it a secret?"

"Heck, no. How old do you think I am?"

"This isn't a guessing game. Just tell me."

"I turned twenty-nine in January."

She laughed, despite feeling a lurch of discomfort. "I mean it, Noah. I'm not playing games."

He dug his wallet from his back pocket, flipped it open. He was smiling in his driver's license photo. Who on earth smiled for a driver's license photo?

People who were born in 1979, that's who. She blanched, feeling the color drop from her cheeks as her heart sank into her shoes. Good Lord. It was true. He was a full ten years younger than Sophie. She'd thought—when she thought about it at all—he might be a year or two younger. Three, perhaps, or five, tops. Six was edging toward indecent. Seven and up—clearly forbidden. Out of the question.

But . . . ten. It was a hugely unpleasant discovery, like biting into a perfect, delicious apple and finding a worm. Half a worm.

Ten years.

Ten. Double digits. He was closer in age to Sophie's daughter than to Sophie. And how had she missed this? She used to pride herself on her analytical mind, on being a stickler for detail. She was shocked at her lapse in failing to find out every fact and nuance about Noah. Perhaps he was turning her brains to mush. Was that a side effect of the best sex she'd ever had?

She backed away from him, nearly slipping on the icy surface of the parking lot, not seeing the Noah she knew, but someone entirely different. Not a man she was falling in love with but a . . . a boy. A boy toy.

Oh, God. She felt like a fool for not figuring it out sooner. It explained so much. The Peter Pan lifestyle. The garage band. Maybe she hadn't wanted to see it and hadn't allowed her mind to go there, like the buyer who falls in love with a car but refuses to check under the hood. No wonder his appetite for sex was never ending, his taste in movies and music decidedly juvenile. No wonder he lived like an adolescent, with his house full of toys. He was one, practically. She was dating a child. A laughing, sexy man-child. She was Mrs. Robinson to his Graduate. Demi Moore to his Ashton Kutcher.

An urban cougar.

She was going to burn in hell.

"Hey, come on," he said. "It's no big deal."

"It's big to me. I can't believe you didn't tell me."

He paused. And in that pause, she realized he'd known this for some time.

"Unbelievable," she said. "You kept it from me."

"I didn't mention it because it doesn't matter. And because I knew you'd let it bug you."

"And that's a reason to keep this from me? Because you thought it would 'bug' me?"

"You're no picnic when you're like this, Sophie."

"It's not my job to be a picnic," she snapped.

He spread his hands, gloves out. "I got nothing to hide. You've been to my office. You've seen my diploma on the wall. You could have looked at the date."

"I did look. I saw the year you graduated, but I assumed you'd had some gap years. Most people do. I thought you must have had another career before vet school—"

"Yeah, I had a paper route." He grinned. "Kidding. There was no gap. And seriously, this is no big deal. Age is just a number."

"And those are just words. What about my kids? What are they supposed to think?"

He laughed. "You're making this too easy. You're

their mom. They want you to be happy. I want to make you happy. All you have to do is let me."

"But—"

"Maybe all this overthinking makes you a good lawyer, but you're making yourself crazy over a non-issue."

"I don't like this, Noah. It's . . . it feels wrong."

"Did it feel wrong five minutes ago, before somebody who can't mind her own business brought it up?"

She couldn't lie. "It seemed more right than anything I've felt in a long time."

"That's my girl."

"I'm not a girl. I'm a grandmother."

"And I totally love you. And you're nuts if you let somebody else's opinion influence the way we feel about one another."

Twenty-Nine

"I told him I needed time to think this over," Sophie told Gayle the next day, when she stopped in with the dog after her morning run. She considered Gayle her first true friend in Avalon. Her neighbor's household was always warm, cluttered and full of life. At the moment, the three kids were playing with Opal in a living room filled with more toys than furniture. She loved Gayle's generous heart and sturdy common sense, and knowing Gayle's situation helped Sophie put things into perspective. With her husband deployed, Gayle lived in the shadow of an anxiety only a military spouse could understand. It made Sophie feel silly, fretting over Noah, but Gayle claimed it kept her from focusing too much on her own worries.

"Is it just bizarre and terrible, being with a guy ten years younger than me?" Sophie asked her. "Does it make me look desperate? Pathetic? Desperate *and* pathetic?"

Gayle handed a sippy cup to her youngest and wiped his nose with the dexterity of long practice. "You're the one who needs to answer that. Not me. And not the hockey moms. You."

"I can't be objective about this."

Gayle laughed heartily. "Then there's your answer."

"You know, in some cultures, women often take younger men as their mates."

"Biologically, it makes sense," Gayle agreed.

"I talked to my daughter about it for a long time last night. Daisy says she has no problem with me dating anyone I want."

"Sophie, you don't have to justify anything to anyone."

What a concept—simply be with him. Simply be in love. Why did she have to do anything more?

Little George, who went by the name of Bear, toddled over to her, holding out his cup as an offering. "Ooh, delicious," she said, pretending to take a drink. "I'm a sucker for younger guys."

"How's it going with your daughter's baby? Are you liking the grandma role?"

"Loving it. Charlie's proof that I really can be a good mom."

"I can't imagine you were ever a bad mom."

"I was never the parent I wish I'd been."

Gayle laughed. "Is anybody? Some nights I go to bed, wondering what in the world I did that day besides yell at the kids, clean up messes, fold laundry and eat leftovers standing up."

"You were present—that's what's important. Now that I'm taking care of Charlie, I can see how ridiculously simple some things are. A lot of the time, trying hard isn't as important as being in the moment. Years ago, Max or Daisy would do something and I'd rush to the child-rearing books to figure out how to respond. What I really should have done was what my ex always did—be in the moment. Be present. Don't dash off to consult some authority. Greg didn't love them more, but he did a better job of simply being with them. Although he had his own firm in the city, and a lot of the time, he was busy, too, he managed to balance things better than I ever did. He wasn't perfect, either, though. There was one time I remember . . . when Max was eight or nine, Greg and I both forgot to pick him up from an after-school program. Max waited for a couple of hours, just sat there at the school trying our mobile phones. Finally he called Greg's parents, and they picked him up. Maybe that was it, the moment we both realized our lifestyle was toxic to our kids. But actually, there were a lot of little moments like that."

"Every parent makes mistakes."

Sophie nodded. "We both had different responses to the wake-up call. Greg wanted to retreat and circle the wagons. I wanted to run—as far and fast as I could."

"And now you're back, and everything's going to be all right," Gayle assured her.

Sophie wanted to believe it. With all her heart, she wanted to. She felt better every day about her children. This thing with Noah—it wasn't really a problem unless she decided to turn it into one. So she was involved with a younger man. Being involved with any man was fraught with peril. Maybe she ought to simply accept it and move forward.

The difference in their ages was something completely out of her control. Accepting it would be a major step for her. If she quit focusing on his age and instead let herself be in love, what would happen?

Her mobile phone rang. She was surprised to see the name "Fordham, Brooks" in the caller ID. "I should take this," she told Gayle.

"I need to get busy, anyway," Gayle said, walking her to the door.

When she stepped outside, Sophie flipped open her phone, wondering what on earth Brooks Fordham was calling for this time.

Thirty

Bo Crutcher was drunk again, Noah observed. It was his normal state for a Sunday night, when they headed up to Hilltop Tavern to shoot pool and drink beer. After the hockey game incident, Noah had decided to give Sophie a little space. He was surprised that she'd taken it so hard. Hell, that was why he hadn't said anything or admitted he'd been aware of the age difference from the start. He figured after she had a little time to think, she'd realize it was no big deal.

Apparently she hadn't come to that realization yet. Earlier in the evening, he'd called to say he wanted to see her. She'd seemed nervous when she said, "I've got something tonight."

Eventually, he'd pried it out of her. The "something" was dinner. With Brooks Fordham.

"It's business," she'd said, somewhat defensively.

"Whose business?"

"His." Noah had read some of the guy's archived articles for the *New York Times*. He was a foreign correspondent, reporting from places like Zanzibar, Portofino, The Hague. . . . The guy had been present the night of the hostage situation Sophie had told Noah about. Noah hated what she'd endured that night, and he figured he ought to be grateful she was in touch with others who had been there, so she wasn't alone with her memories. But . . . okay, Noah had never met the guy, and he already knew he didn't like him. Fordham had a bio as fancy as his fancy-sounding name, with an Ivy League education, list of awards, publications. And he had that silver-haired, distinguished-gentleman thing going. Successful. *Mature.* He looked, Noah realized, like the kind of guy Sophie Bellamy would date.

Too late, jerk-off, Noah thought. *She's taken.* He watched Bo aim for a shot and miss, losing his edge to his seventh or eighth beer.

"Come on, buddy," Noah said. "Let's take a break."

"Yeah, okay." Bo put up his pool cue and wiped his hands on his jeans. "Lemme order another round."

"In a minute." Noah motioned him to a booth. They slid in and kicked back to survey the mostly familiar crowd.

"So what's really bugging you, bro? Woman troubles?" Bo asked, cocking one eyebrow at him.

Noah explained what had happened after the hockey game. "She kind of hates the idea that she's ten years older than me."

"But does she hate you?"

He could still hear her earnest voice, soft with excitement. *I love you, Noah.* His mouth curved into a smile. "I don't think so."

"Then why are you hanging around here?"

"She might need some time to think."

"How much time? Is she waiting for you to grow up? That'll never happen."

"She's having dinner with a guy she knew when she lived in Holland."

Bo gave a low whistle.

"It's business," Noah stated.

"If you say so."

"She says so." Although he and Sophie were still new to each other, he trusted her. Didn't he?

"Then just go for it, man," Bo suggested. "Be with her, fall in love. It's not hard."

"No shit."

"I'll help you get rid of this guy, if—"

"Whoa." Noah held up his hands. "We're not getting rid of anybody. I don't want to mess this up. I want this to work out."

"Then work it out." Bo signaled the waitress for two more beers.

"Good plan," Noah agreed. "And I don't need another beer. I'm driving, remember?"

"Guess I'll have to drink yours, then."

Noah suppressed the urge to tell his friend to take it easy on the drinking. He'd mentioned it before, to no avail. Bo liked to get a buzz on, that was a fact.

The waitress set down two longnecks and a pair of frosted mugs. Bo made eyes at her, earning a wink, but then the young woman pivoted away and went about her business.

"I need to figure out my next move," Noah said. She'd asked him once what he wanted, what he dreamed about, and he hadn't been ready with the answer. He knew what it was now—Sophie herself.

He'd never known anyone quite like her. She was beautiful and vulnerable, yes, but more than that, she drew from him a tenderness he used to only wish he could show to a woman. Holding her, touching her, revealed things to Noah that he hadn't known before—that he could be with a woman like this and feel more than lust. That he had finally discovered a love deep enough to last forever.

He'd always pictured himself raising a family, here in the place he'd grown up, making a life filled with someone he could love forever. With every moment he spent with Sophie, he felt more and more confident that it could happen with her. Yet she made him think outside the box. Life was good here, but the world was a big place. Sophie—multilingual, a world traveler—could take him places he'd never dreamed of.

We've got a lot to talk about, he thought.

Apparently, he wasn't alone in his thinking. When he got home that night, he let Rudy out for a run and saw Sophie walking up the driveway. She wore the long, tailored coat she'd had on the first night he'd met her, along with the high-heeled boots.

"Hey," he said. "How was your evening?"

"It was . . . interesting. Brooks is following up on some things for his story."

"Okay, I have to say this. I'm insanely jealous of the guy."

She glanced away. "There's no need to be. Brooks suffered a lot, during and after the incident. He might be dealing with the brain injury for years—"

"That's not the part I'm jealous of. But I do wish I'd been there for you, Sophie, with you."

"No, you don't." She spoke low but forcefully, and when she looked up at him, he imagined he could see nightmare memories flickering in her eyes. "We talked about what happened, and it was surreal, as though I were talking about someone else." The yellowish glow of the porch light gave her face an ethereal cast. "He's planning to attend a national holiday celebration in Umoja, and was wondering if I was going."

"Are you?"

"I don't know. All of that seems so far away, and not just geographically."

Yet he saw it in her eyes, that unmistakable yearning. She had been a part of something big, so much bigger than anything Avalon had to offer. He couldn't blame her for missing that life.

"I didn't come to talk about that. Noah, about what happened—"

"Nothing happened," he said quickly.

"You're right. Nothing happened. I just *happen* to be ten years older than you." She shook her head. "I feel so foolish. When I phoned Bertie Wilson about the dog, she called you 'little' Noah Shepherd. I didn't even question that."

"She used to babysit me."

"Lovely. I'll keep that in mind when we're in bed together."

When we're in bed together. Thank God, he thought, practically staggering with relief.

"I won't pretend I'm not rattled by this," she said. Then she took a step toward him, pulling a set of DVDs from her pocket. *Star Wars,* the collector's edition, and a six-pack of beer. "But I'm willing to keep an open mind."

Thirty-One

Sophie hadn't dismissed Tariq's suggestion of a trip to Umoja out of hand. She had developed a true affinity for the people of the embattled nation. It was a hellishly long trip, but the closure of seeing the results of justice would be so satisfying. She thought about what she'd done that night, about the people who had died because of her. She needed to come to terms with that, too, with the breath-stealing moment of decision that had caused her to act. Seeing the liberated nation wouldn't erase the memory; she knew better than that. But its transformation would be a powerful reminder of the lives that had been saved because of the court's action.

Later, though. Maybe in the summer, she'd take Max, although that would mean missing the national week of celebration. For now, she planned to savor the new closeness she'd found with her family. There hadn't been one big dramatic moment of revelation. Simply by being there, moment by moment, she'd built a bridge between herself and her children. Instead of the temporary, truncated scheduled visits of the past, she was able to relax in the knowledge that she had all the time in the world.

Time. She was also coming to terms with being madly in love with a younger man. She was determined not to let the differences in their ages matter, and had come to believe that the more closely she knit herself into the life of this new community, the less preoccupied she would be with the idea that when she had been getting her law degree, he'd been earning a high-school freshman letter in baseball.

She had decided to go about the business of fitting into the community the way she did everything else—by making and executing a plan. She was actively looking at homes for sale. Another important component of that plan involved friendships. In her life, she had several close, cherished friendships—her girlfriends from college, who had been there for her when she'd found herself unexpectedly pregnant with Daisy. Tariq from The Hague, whose humor and caring had seen her through the lonely times without her children. But now everyone was so far away. Closer to home, she had only Gayle Wright. If Sophie was going to be in Avalon, she needed to expand her circle of friends. But how? She'd come to realize a planned siege was the old-Sophie way of thinking. The past few weeks had shown her that the rules were different now. Friends would ultimately seek each other out. Still, she was determined to make new connections here. She had to.

So far, she had bought a cup of coffee for Hattie

Crandall, owner of the bookstore that occupied the street-level space below the law office, and she'd taken in a movie with Becky Murray, the woman who had been Daisy's childbirth instructor. Today, she took Daphne McDaniel to lunch. The receptionist of the law office was young and hip. It wouldn't hurt for Sophie to hang out with someone like her.

They went to a trendy café on the main square, where all the menu selections were organic, vegetarian and named after characters in *Lord of the Rings.*

"I'll have the Boromir sandwich," Sophie told the girl at the counter.

"You didn't even read the description," Daphne pointed out.

"They had me at 'Boromir.' He's such a tragic character. He's the one who betrayed his friends, and then found redemption, but paid the ultimate price for it." The sandwich turned out to be not so dramatic—a whole-wheat pita stuffed with alfalfa sprouts and hummus.

"You sound like a Tolkein fan," Daphne commented.

"I need to reread those books," Sophie said, shocked to realize her copies were at least a quarter of a century old. "How about you? I noticed you're reading Robert Silverberg."

Daphne nodded. "I've been on a sci-fi kick for quite a while now. One of my ex-boyfriends introduced me to the classics of the genre, and I got hooked on Silverberg and Theodore Sturgeon."

Noah was a science fiction fanatic, too. Sophie decided she should give it a try.

"Ex-boyfriend?" she commented, focusing her attention on Daphne. "Are you seeing anyone now?"

Daphne shook her head. Her smile was a little wistful. She was a pretty girl, Sophie observed, though that was not immediately noticeable. The anime style—neon-pink highlights in her hair, uncomfortable-looking facial piercings and shiny black clothes—tended to overshadow her beauty. Sophie brought her thoughts up short. She was thinking like a mother, not a friend, a coworker. Someone to whom age was only a number.

"It's been a while," Daphne said. "I . . . my last boyfriend and I broke up a few months ago. Or no. God, it's been like, eight or nine months, and I haven't met anyone new. Guys worth dating, that is. Hazard of living in a small town, I guess." She added a dollop of honey to her rosehip tea. "Anyway, there are things I miss about him, so much."

"Like what?" asked Sophie.

"Like . . . pretty much everything."

"Maybe you shouldn't have split up."

"I think about that every day, believe me. But the reason for the split is a total deal-breaker."

Sophie waited, not wanting to pry but dying to hear more. So was this the lot of the small-town lawyer? To experience life vicariously through coworkers and clients?

"Simple, but there's really no work-around. He wanted kids and I didn't," she said, her eyes misty with regret. "It's one of those things you can't really compromise on. Well, I saw getting a dog as a compromise, but Noah didn't."

Sophie's blood froze. Was she talking about *the* Noah? Her Noah? Mr. Make-love-until-you-weep Noah? Mr. Storybook-woodsman-rescuer Noah?

She made herself ask. "Would that, um, be Noah Shepherd?"

"Yes. Do you know him?"

"Neighbor across the road." The words ached like ice cubes in her mouth.

"You do know him."

You have no idea, thought Sophie.

"So are you going to do like everyone else, tell me I'm crazy to let him go? Tell me I'm going to want kids one day and I'll never find a better man than Noah to do that with?"

"Sounds like you've already heard those objections." Sophie felt slightly dizzy, as though she'd been hit when she wasn't looking.

"I have, from everybody."

"And?"

"I miss him like crazy because he really is a great guy. Wait till you get to know him."

I didn't wait, Sophie thought. *I fell right into bed with him.*

"It would never work. I still don't want kids," Daphne said. "I never will. I'm the oldest of five, and

I raised my younger brothers and sisters after my mom got sick. So I'm done. That's it for me." She picked at her sandwich, taking out a pickle slice and setting it aside. "And Noah just couldn't get past that. If you ever meet his family, you'll understand."

"Understand what?"

"The Shepherds—they're one of those families that seems too good to be true, but they are, you know? They're just so good to each other and so good *for* each other. I mean, how many people do you know who live in the house they grew up in? Most of us can't wait to leave. Noah couldn't wait to fill the place with a family of his own."

Sophie's mouth was dry; she gulped down her water. The sudden cold caused a flare of pain in her chest. "But if you really loved him, couldn't you have worked something out? A compromise?"

Daphne offered a wistful smile. "You know what? That might have worked for me, but eventually, I figured something out about him." She took a knife and cut her sandwich down the middle. "He wanted babies more than he wanted me. It was a hard thing, accepting that and walking away, but ultimately, I saved myself a big fat heartache." She took a bite of her sandwich, chewed thoughtfully, then said, "A lot of my friends still think I was nuts to let him go."

"You want what you want," Sophie said. "Don't change your goals because of a guy." Then she forced herself to shut up. She didn't want to manipulate this situation.

"Is this the voice of experience talking?" Daphne asked.

"I wouldn't say that. I had my first child before I'd even considered the question of whether or not to have kids one day." But the information she had just learned kept pounding at her. Noah had broken up with a girl who did not want babies.

Sophie tried to finish her lunch, but the sandwich turned to cardboard in her mouth. Of course she and Noah hadn't talked about the idea of raising a family: it was too early for that. Now she considered what Daphne had told her, and it all made sense. He was a bighearted man with more love to give than anyone she'd ever met. *Of course* having a family was part of his dream. It was so obvious now that she forced herself to think about it.

She somehow managed to shift the conversation away from Noah, but couldn't pull her mind away from the things Daphne had said, the things Sophie knew in her heart to be true. Noah loved her, yes. But soon enough, the first glow of love would pale and he'd remember he wanted babies and not only would Sophie not give him that, she *could* not.

It snowed again, a fresh blast of winter, skirling across the lake. As soon as she got home from work, Sophie bundled up for the trek to Noah's house. He was just getting in from the clinic, and was still in his scrubs.

"Hey, you," he said, pulling her in for a kiss and then giving her a smile tinged with fatigue. "You're early."

"Sorry about that." She knew she had to address the situation right away. That night—before the usual sweet talk led to lovemaking. What she'd learned from Daphne was going to be a deal-breaker for them, and there was no point in putting it off. Still, she couldn't help noticing the sadness in his eyes. "What's the matter?" she asked.

He braced his arms on the counter, leaned back. "Nothing. Just didn't have time to shower off my day yet."

Sophie's heart lurched. He almost never complained. "What happened?"

"Nothing unusual, but I had to put a family's dog down today. It was definitely time, but it's never easy."

She felt horrible, not just about the loss but about her own blindness. He was a man with needs, but he almost never let them show. This whole winter had been about her needs, her issues. No wonder she hadn't bothered to find out his deepest dreams before falling in love with him.

"Oh, Noah," she said. "I'm so sorry."

"Thanks. I'll be all right. Comes with the territory." He turned to the sink and washed his hands. She went to the fridge, got a beer and opened it for him. He smiled. "Better already."

Sophie took a deep breath. Best to get on with it. The snowfall was coming fast and hard, much as it had been the night they'd met.

"I had an interesting talk with Daphne McDaniel today," Sophie said. "Your ex-girlfriend."

"Oh? I didn't realize you knew her." He seemed unconcerned.

"She works in my office."

"I didn't know that, either. We don't keep up, Sophie. I haven't seen her in months."

"She said the two of you split up because you want kids and she doesn't."

He hesitated, not for long, but it was noticeable. Then he said, "She told you that?"

"Tell me it's not true."

"Wait a minute. Tell me why you split up with Greg Bellamy."

"I beg your pardon?"

"Give me the reason you broke up with your ex."

"You're trying to change the subject."

"True, but I'm also trying to make a point. So what's the reason?"

"We've talked about this. Greg and I split up for a lot of reasons."

"Thank you. That's my point. People don't break up for *a* reason. There's always a lot of stuff."

"You can't compare a long-term marriage to dating."

"And you can't tell me why Daphne McDaniel dumped me," he shot back.

"I know why she says she did. I also know that we—you and I, Noah—we have the same issue. Maybe not today, but eventually it's bound to come up. And it's not something we can simply put aside, pretend it doesn't matter." She had underestimated how hard this was going to be. She hadn't anticipated the hurt and disappointment, the sense of loss. "The fact is, I'm not going to have babies. There was a complication with Max's birth and I can't have any more."

"It's not something we should be talking about right now. It's . . . we're too new. Let's just be together—"

"Why, so we can have this conversation weeks or months down the road, after we've invested even more in this relationship? There's no future for us, not one that works for us both." She turned to the window, watching the snowflakes falling fast and thick past the porch light. Noah had once insisted there was nothing scary about him, but he was wrong. The scary thing about Noah was how fast and hard she had fallen in love with him, and how much it hurt to let go of that.

She took a deep breath, tried to keep her voice from trembling. "You're twenty-nine, Noah, and you have every right to the life you want, including children of your own. The thing you want most of all is never going to happen, not with me."

Part Seven

Spring thaw

Comfort Food

Ouma's milk tart is a traditional southern African dish.

Pastry ingredients:

- 3 tablespoons butter
- 3 tablespoons castor sugar
- 1 egg
- 1 cup flour
- 2 teaspoons baking powder

Filling ingredients:

- 5 cups milk
- ½ cup white sugar
- 2 tablespoons cornmeal
- 6 eggs, separated
- 2 tablespoons flour
- 1 tablespoon butter
- 2 teaspoons vanilla essence
- ½ teaspoon salt
- cinnamon and nutmeg

Preheat the oven to 350°F. To make the pastry, cream the sugar and butter together, add the egg and beat, then add the flour and baking powder to form a soft dough. Press the dough into a large pie plate and set aside.

Then make the filling by mixing the sugar, egg yolks, flour, cornmeal, salt and vanilla essence. Melt the butter in a saucepan and add the flour. Whisk in the milk and heat gently until it thickens. Add the egg yolk mixture, whisking to avoid lumps. Remove from heat.

Beat the egg whites until glossy, stiff peaks form and fold into the custard mixture. Pour this into the pie crust. Bake in the lower third of the oven for about twenty-five minutes, or until the top is golden-brown. Sprinkle with cinnamon and nutmeg, and allow to cool completely. Serve with berries or other fruit.

Thirty-Two

Sophie moved away from the house on Lakeshore Road and there wasn't a damn thing Noah could do about it. He wouldn't beg her; that was just pathetic and would get him nowhere. Even his dog Rudy knew when you begged, people ignored you. Besides, what if she were right? What if he couldn't imagine a life without children? It was how he'd always seen himself, a guy with kids. Every choice of his adult life, from returning to Avalon to set up his practice, to buying the farmhouse, had been made with the idea that one day he'd have a family of his own. The dream was not going to go away overnight like a head cold, even if his heart was aching with love for Sophie.

He raced—and won—the winter triathlon, feeling no particular sense of triumph when he crossed the finish line. The victory felt hollow, because he was driven by a powerful frustration that desperately needed an outlet. He loved her, but if they stayed together, he couldn't have the things that mattered most to him. Children, a family, a house full of love.

He and the guys in the band performed for an appreciative—and probably too-forgiving—crowd. He attended the usual round of Winter Carnival activities, finding himself stupidly mesmerized by the sight of a guy dragging a load of kids on a toboggan, or a pregnant woman ordering hot chocolate at a concession stand.

"I'm just a fool for love, Clem," he said to Clementine, a big orange cat whose asthma was acting up. It was the end of a long day at the clinic, but Noah was in no hurry to get home, and he lingered over the final chores, telling his assistant he'd close up. "Or maybe I'm just a fool," he added. "Eddie would make a song out of that."

The cat buried his front claws in the scratching post in his crate, and ripped them down the length of it.

"A song out of what?" asked a voice from the doorway.

Noah turned, fixing a smile on his face. "Hey, Tina. Paulette."

"We brought you some cookies to cheer you up," Tina said, holding out a platter wrapped in plastic.

"Thanks," he said. "Those look good."

"But will they cheer you up?" Paulette asked. "We're really sorry about you and Sophie."

Hazard of living in a small town. It had only taken a few hours for the news about him and Sophie to reach his neighbors.

"Yeah, it sucks," Noah said.

"Is there anything we can do?" Tina asked.

"Just whatever the hell you do, don't tell me things will get better and that I'll find a nice girl who wants to settle down and have babies." He grimaced. Too many well-meaning people had told him that, and it was the same advice he'd been given after Daphne, and it flat out did not work that way.

“We wouldn’t do that,” Tina said. “Paulette and I still want to have a baby together, and sometimes, you’re right, it does suck.”

A part of him, perversely, had an insane urge to revisit Tina’s proposal that he father a child for her. “If you found out it wasn’t going to happen, what would that do to you?” he asked them.

The women shared a look. “We’ll figure out a way to make it happen. It’s one of my father’s favorite expressions, from his hockey days—‘Failure is not an option.’ ”

“Nice, but a baby is kind of an all-or-nothing proposition.” He helped himself to one of the cookies.

“So is love,” Paulette said, “now that you mention it.”

Noah kept waiting for the crushing feeling around his heart to ease. But no amount of cookies, no well-meaning advice from friends seemed to help. Several times, he picked up the phone and dialed her number, intending to ask her . . . what? Are you having as hard a time with this as I am?

She seemed to be doing okay, as far as he could tell. The reporter, Brooks Fordham, paid her another visit. Noah remembered that he was working on a book about the African nation called Umoja. So Noah told himself Fordham went to see Sophie strictly for research purposes.

Yeah, right. Catching a glimpse of them together at the bookstore or coffee shop in town disabused him of that notion. Finally, Noah got it; he understood how deluded he'd been about his real chances with Sophie. The well-traveled Fordham was clearly a much better fit, a distinguished type in tailored suits and Italian shoes, with an air of smart sophistication Noah lacked even on his best day. Not to mention all that shared history with her.

As though to probe a painful wound, Noah researched the situation in Umoja. Sophie had hardly spoken of her former life at all. He was haunted by her confession about the event that had caused her to end her career in The Hague. Had he been sympathetic enough? Understanding enough? Said all the right things?

Probably not. How could he? Her situation was so far out of his comfort zone they might as well be on different planets. He had never been out of the U.S. except when he'd driven to Canada the night he turned eighteen, so he could have a beer. His knowledge of corruption in the diamond trade was limited to repeat viewings of *Blood Diamond*, and even then, he'd fast-forwarded through the politics to get to the action sequences. His command of the geography of Africa came from a lifelong subscription to *National Geographic*, and from some primate disease studies he'd done in vet school.

Noah became a student of international politics. He combed the library and media for information about the changing fortunes in the southern African state of Umoja. Again and again, the name Sophie Bellamy came up, and gradually, he came to understand just what it was she had walked away from. Her legal team had brought about a peaceful restoration of power in a land where violence had raged for generations. Noah had always known she was extraordinary, but only now did he understand the depth of her commitment and the extent of her skill. She'd dubbed him the "deer whisperer" and called him a hero, but that was a joke compared to her own accomplishments. And then, in the middle of her life, Sophie Bellamy had done a one-eighty, heading off in a different direction. Noah wondered if she ever had regrets, if she ever looked at the path not taken and wished she'd done something else.

All of which left him questioning everything he believed about himself. He'd always seen his life in a certain way. Now his unwavering conviction that he was destined to create a life here in the place where he'd grown up, caring for animals and raising a family, didn't seem so immutable. Suddenly the world he'd built for himself felt very small. Restrictive, almost. Why hadn't he traveled more? Seen foreign lands? Learned another language? Sophie had been to Africa, for Chrissakes. He found himself wishing he'd been more of a traveler. Now he had his practice set up and couldn't leave. Or could he? He had a reciprocal agreement with a vet in Maplecrest; they covered for each other when the need arose. But hell, he didn't even have a passport.

The thought made him laugh at himself. Some problems, he conceded, flipping to the government pages of the phone book, were smaller than others.

Sophie failed to buy a house in Avalon after all, despite what she'd promised her kids. She was in too much of a hurry to move, and simply refused to wait for the right property to become available. She couldn't bear to live so close to Noah, seeing the places he'd shown her, remembering, with every beat of her heart, their time together.

She lived in a rental two blocks from Daisy's, and in good weather, it was walking distance from the law office. She rationalized that she hadn't found the perfect house to buy, and the rental was simply a stop-gap measure meant to end her reliance on the Wilsons' hospitality.

This was the story she told herself, anyway. God forbid she should admit to the real reason—that Noah Shepherd had broken through every barrier she'd surrounded herself with. That he had moved too close to her heart and, true to form, she had fled.

For good reason, she insisted. There was no point in lingering at the house on Lakeshore Road, where the time she'd spent with Noah seemed embedded into the very landscape. She couldn't stand to pass by the spot where they'd first met, bonding amid the worst snowfall on record. Now that roadside was a gully filled with filthy slush, the detritus of a long winter, insistently hanging on long past its prime. She didn't like looking out at the lake where they'd ice-skated together, lacking in form but more than making up for it in sheer romantic enthusiasm. She couldn't bear sleeping in the bed she'd once shared with him, or lingering in a place where she'd learned more about herself than she had in a lifetime. She simply couldn't bear anything that reminded her of Noah.

Which was, unfortunately, everything, down to each breath she took.

The house came furnished, and everything was bright and untouched. The rental agent admitted the house was a casualty in a sudden divorce. It had been built as a second home, but the couple split up before they ever had a chance to use it. Sophie claimed she didn't care, but sometimes, looking around at the carefully chosen fixtures and color schemes, she felt a melancholy lurch in her gut. Building a new house was such a hopeful exercise, yet this place was a reminder that things didn't always work out despite the best of intentions.

Most of the time, she managed to put aside such thoughts and focus instead on staying busy. This was not hard to do. Mel had her baby—an adorable little girl—and Sophie picked up more of the slack at the law office. Days with Charlie were filled with moments of hazy peace or silly joy or sometimes, tried patience, yet she loved it all. She continued to be an active hockey mom despite her differences with Mrs. Altshuler and the rest. By far, the moments of greatest happiness were those she spent with her family—Max, Daisy and Charlie. In those moments, she truly believed the life she had was enough.

And then spring break arrived, and she found herself all alone. Max went with his father and Nina to a Romano family reunion in Miramar. His *other* family. In his absence, his friend Chelsea was keeping Opal, and Sophie was surprised at how empty the house seemed without the dog. Daisy took Charlie to meet his paternal grandparents—the O'Donnells—on Long Island. They had finally asked to see their grandson. He, too, had another family. Better late than never, Sophie thought.

She had only been fooling herself that she was needed here. She wasn't needed, not in the way she'd expected. She wasn't the heart of a family; she'd given away that role years ago. It was tempting—oh, so tempting—to flee again, return to a world where she fit in and a life she knew. She wouldn't, though. She was determined to keep the promises she had made. She still had a vital role to play and could still make a difference in the lives of her family.

Her children's needs changed as they grew—it was such a simple concept. They didn't consume all of her time, her talent, her capacity for love. She'd made many unexpected discoveries, coming here in the dead of winter. She now realized that she could give everything to her children and grandson, yet instead of being diminished, her capacity for love expanded. It was, of course, a mixed blessing. She felt things in the deepest, most tender places of her heart—the bittersweet ache of knowing Daisy and Charlie were, at this very moment, opening themselves to a brand-new family, the O'Donnells. And pride in Max, who was already pulling away in anticipation of adolescence, and happily exploring his dozens of stepfamily members in the Florida sunshine.

And then there was the searing swath of hurt left by Noah Shepherd. If ever she needed proof that letting go of control was a perilous thing, she had it. With Noah, she had surrendered to impulse and desire. Now her heart was paying the price.

She sat looking out the window of her nondescript house. The weather report had been delivering rumors of spring, but here in Avalon, the only evidence was that the mounds of snow lining the streets had sunk into dirt-crusted piles, and the ice on the lake was now a floe of shifting slush. There was probably a name for the color of the sky, but it was too depressing to think of.

Awash in memories, she checked the scar on her knee, a fading crescent shape. It was still visible but it didn't hurt. That was the important thing.

So, she thought. So. She had survived everything life had thrown her way. She would survive this.

Picking up the phone, she dialed Brooks's number. He had made no secret of his interest in her, and they talked often. She tried to appreciate his attention, but the moments between them fell flat, though they were both too polite to point out the obvious. Still, they'd become friends, and she'd found she could talk to him.

“I need a diversion,” she told Brooks when he picked up.

“I can be very diverting,” he suggested.

There was no mistaking his tone. “You’ll do nothing of the sort. Just . . . keep me company. I’ve hit a rough patch. Not that I’m complaining. I never expected this to be easy all the time.”

“Maybe you’re in the wrong place,” he suggested. “Move to the city. You can work at the UN and live among civilization, in a world you already know, the international courts where just the right strategy can save a child’s life. Yet you’d still be close enough to your family to be part of their lives.”

“I’ve tried that, Brooks. It’s not the same. I made a promise and I mean to keep it.”

“Fine, but do your kids want a martyr or a mother?”

“I thought I called you for a diversion.”

“You called me,” he said, “because you’re having second thoughts about the choice you’ve made.”

Restless, she cleaned the house, though it was hardly messy, since she was the only one here. Still, the mindless rhythm of dusting furniture and scrubbing the kitchen was oddly soothing—at least for a few minutes. Then, while running the vacuum, she came across one of Charlie’s favorite toys. It was a brightly colored clown, weighted at the bottom so that it would pop up every time it was knocked down. The toy never failed to make him laugh. Even the memory of the baby’s laughter made her smile and, at the same time, pervaded her heart with wistfulness. She caught herself wondering what her life would be like with another child again. Could she do it? Go down that road with Noah? Even if she was willing, she couldn't have another baby, so it was pointless to imagine it. Frustrated, she slapped down the toy again. Up it popped, goofy smile in place, mocking her.

She grabbed the toy and put it in a cupboard, then looked around the spotless house. Eerily, it seemed to have the same impersonal air as her flat in The Hague. Maybe—

The phone rang and she snatched it up like a lifeline.

"Mom!" Daisy's voice sang in her ear.

"Hi there. How's Long Island?" Sophie asked. "How's my grandson?"

"Both excellent. Seriously, Mom, the O'Donnells are being pretty great. They've got this incredible house in Montauk. I'm glad we came."

"That's good."

"We miss you, though," Daisy said, her haste making Sophie smile. Since Sophie's arrival in Avalon, they had become best friends. Confidantes. Daisy was wise beyond her years, and Sophie trusted her completely.

"Same here. Seems like winter will never end."

"That's kind of why I called. When I was on the train, coming down here, I got to thinking . . . maybe you should get away, too," Daisy suggested. "I mean it, Mom. And I know just where you should go."

Thirty-Three

Umoja, southern Africa

The fine red dust of the Umojan plains swirled in small funnel clouds, coating everything it touched. Shading her eyes, Sophie could just make out the rain-drenched highlands, so rich with wildlife and pristine wilderness that it was now protected by an edict of the United Nations. There would be no more plundering this land, no more violence done in the name of greed. The goal was probably too idealistic, but over the course of her long career, Sophie had learned that ideals were a powerful thing.

Bibi Lateef, a jurist Sophie had last seen in The Hague, was now the minister of social welfare in the capital of Nossob. In honor of Sophie's visit, Madame Lateef had given her a tour of the city, where people were rebuilding their lives. Sophie was moved by the sight of broken families trying to mend, with aid workers on hand to help with medical issues, schools and farming. The orphanage, called the Children's Village, was heartbreakingly crowded with children who had lost everything in the war. Some had been orphaned at a preverbal age, and couldn't even tell their rescuers their names. There were so many displaced children that adoptions had been expedited under emergency provisions. Yet the staff and children sang as they went about their chores. Their high, clear voices had reminded Sophie of that night in The Hague, but here in the bright African sunshine, the nightmares kept their distance. There had been a small ceremony of thanks, and Sophie was given a booklet of photographs, a woven wall hanging and a necklace of colorful beads. One visit wasn't nearly enough. She'd promised to return that evening to have dinner in the dining hall.

At the end of the day, a spectacular sunset spread its intense colors across the landscape, lending an odd beauty to the broken buildings and monuments that made up the town center. Three-wheeled green-and-white taxis darted through the streets, kicking up dust that glittered in the sunlight like a storm of gold. Sophie's driver took her to the Hotel Paradeis, where the accommodations were simple, but clean and safe. There would be just enough time for a shower before dinner.

With her hair still damp and her arms laden with supplies from the airport commissary, she stepped out and stood on the brickwork pavement to wait for the driver. The airport bus lumbered into town as it did each evening, bringing aid workers and the occasional reporter. Every once in a while, Sophie encountered someone she had met while preparing the case.

Despite its air of poverty, the capital city still retained a timeless majesty in its tufa-stone buildings and network of streets and alleyways. The round, thatch-roofed towers of the Narina's palace overlooked stone-lined pits and livestock *kraals* and grassy upland fields beyond the city. She wanted to bring Max and Daisy and Charlie here one day, to show them this world, so distant from their own.

She had three more days before she had to leave. For her, the prospect of returning to Avalon was bitter-sweet. She felt a tug of yearning for her family, but also a sense of futility. Now she had two exes in Avalon. Two failed relationships. But the richness she'd found with her children superseded that, she reminded herself.

A group of scruffy dogs erupted in a sudden fight, grabbing her attention. A thick swirl of dust rose around the dogs, which were squabbling over some scrap of food or turf. Through the dust, a tall, broad-shouldered man approached, backlit by the setting sun. Another aid worker, probably. He had a duffel bag slung over one shoulder and a distinctive long-limbed gait that was somehow . . . familiar.

Sophie stood riveted as he ambled across the dusty plaza toward her. Dear Lord, could it be . . . ? She pressed her hand over her mouth to hold in a gasp of surprise.

"I once told you I'd follow you to the ends of the earth," Noah said, setting down his bag. In the same motion, he pulled her into his arms. "Does this count as the ends of the earth?"

"You are," she said, her voice breaking, "so completely insane."

And then he kissed her, and she couldn't help herself—she pulled back, still hanging on to him, laughed aloud in a way she hadn't since she'd last seen him, and said exactly what she felt in her heart. "I adore you, so I suppose that makes me insane, too."

"I was counting on it. Sophie, I screwed up so bad. I can't begin to tell you how bad. I should never have let you walk away."

"Then we both screwed up, because I should have stayed and found a way to . . ." She grew serious, gazed up at him. "To make this work," she concluded. "Oh, Noah. Can we?"

"After making this trip, I'd say anything is possible." He stepped back, combed his fingers through his hair as he looked around the plaza. "Seriously, until now, I've never been anywhere."

She took his hand, brought it to her cheek, turned her head and kissed his palm. "That's probably because you have everything you need back in Avalon."

"Not anymore. I mean that, Sophie. I love you, and where I need to be is with you, wherever that is."

Here was a man she loved, telling her things that made her heart soar. Yet at the same time, it had to be said. "The age difference between us—it can't be changed, Noah. It will always be there."

"Your age is one of my favorite things about you." He grinned. "It's nice to make out with somebody and not have to worry about a tongue stud."

"Yet another virtue of maturity." Still holding his hands, she stepped back. "But I know you, Noah.

You're a born family man. You want to be a father, and I can't give you kids."

"I want a wife, not a broodmare. You said the thing that I want most of all is a family. Kids. And you're wrong. The thing I want most of all is *you*."

Two taxis started jousting in the plaza, threatening each other with their nasally beeps. Sophie had to raise her voice to be heard. "I want to believe that, but you can't just go from wanting a family to settling for something less."

He touched his finger to her lips. At the same time, the taxis sped past one another. "No, wait a minute. Let me finish. I've had an extremely long flight to think about all of this. Giving you up, that would be settling for something less, because when I met you, everything changed. My priorities, my life. Look at me. I've never left the country before, and here I am halfway around the world. With a passport. I want to marry you. Please." Then he did something she had never dared to imagine. Keeping hold of her hands, he sank down on one knee, there in front of the busy hotel. "I'm begging you, Sophie. I'm dying to marry you."

Marry Noah? Spend the rest of her life with him? A part of her leaped up with a huge—but silent—*yes*. Then reason dampened the jubilant fantasy. Never taking her eyes off him, she tugged at his hands until he was standing again. "You say that now, but what about down the road? In ten years, I'll be nearly fifty."

"I'll be forty. And how old will we be in ten years if

we don't get married?" He took her by the shoulders and held his face level with hers. "Do you love me?" he asked bluntly.

She tried to escape his frank stare. Did she love him? *Oh, my,* she thought. Did she ever, in a way she'd never felt before and never expected to feel again. "Yes, but—"

"A simple yes will do." He framed her face between his hands and kissed her again. "Look at you. You're perfect. You speak all kinds of languages. You've got two great kids and Charlie. And me—I'm a country vet, rattling around in an old farmhouse. You loving me—that's a miracle."

She felt close to tears, but his words drew a soft laugh from her. "Believe me, it's not a stretch. You are incredibly easy to love."

He pulled her against him and kissed her. "I can't promise I'll always be so easy, but I promise I'll always love you—including your age and your family and anything else you want to throw at me. So come on, Sophie. What do you say?"

She hesitated, and he held her even closer.

"Don't think," he whispered in her ear. "You do a lot better when you don't think so much. Just tell me from the heart what you want."

"I want you, Noah Shepherd. Yes," she said, and didn't bother trying to hold her emotions in check any longer. She loved the tears because they were all about loving him. "Yes, I'll marry you."

"Yes," he said, shutting his eyes briefly. Then he

opened them and said, "When? As far as I'm concerned, the sooner the better. What about here? Now? Today—would it be legal?"

"It might be, but I'm not about to do something this big without Daisy and Max." Her eyes misted. "Too much of my life has excluded them, and I don't want to do that anymore." She looked up at Noah, studied his smiling face, shaded golden by the setting sun. "I hope you understand."

He nodded. "More than you know, Sophie. More than you know."

She clasped his hand in hers. "What are you doing for dinner tonight?"

"I had no plans. Did you have something in mind?"

"I thought you might like to meet some friends of mine."

Epilogue

Ulster County, New York
Summertime

Noah and Sophie got off the plane at the tiny regional airport in the sunny heart of the Catskills in summer. Each held a small child in their arms—their new son and daughter. Uba and Aissa were brother and sister, orphaned in the troubles in Umoja. The four of them had cleared immigration at JFK, and their long journey was finally at an end.

They had met their new son and daughter on Noah's first surprise trip to Umoja. The little boy and girl had been staying at the Children's Village, amid a sea of waifs with cardboard identification tags around their necks, desperate for a family. Madame Lateef had lent her considerable influence to expediting the adoption, and within a matter of months, Dr. and Mrs. Noah Shepherd became the proud, elated parents of an adorable brother and sister. At age three and six, they were undersized and bashful, but already clung to Sophie and Noah, recognizing them to be a safe haven in this strange new world.

Daisy and Max were at the county airport, waiting to greet them. They had been part of the decision to adopt, and to Sophie's eternal gratitude, her older children were as excited about it as she and Noah. Max and Daisy understood that their mother wasn't trying to replace them, but to add more love to all their lives.

Daisy went down on one knee and hugged each child briefly, showing a keen sensitivity to their fatigue and apprehension, and then Max followed suit. Daisy presented Charlie, who was napping in his stroller. She took out her camera, snapped a few pictures. She already had big plans to do a photo essay on the children.

"I'm very proud of you," Sophie said to her new son and daughter, speaking in Umojan. "You are very brave." She had given Noah a crash course in their language, memorizing phrases like "I love you" and "Do you need to go to the toilet?" During the adoption visits, she had shown them pictures of their new home and family—Daisy, Max and Charlie, Opal and Rudy and the horses in the barn, and the big painted farmhouse where they would be living, on the brow of a hill overlooking Willow Lake.

Now the children were seeing their new family for the first time. Uba was quiet. Aissa clung to Noah's pant leg, but the little girl's eyes danced with interest as she looked around.

"You guys are awesome," Daisy said. "I can't believe you're doing this. And so soon after getting married. You're the only people I know to bring two kids home from your honeymoon."

"They need us now," Noah said simply. "It's not too soon."

Sophie looked down at her youngest children, and her heart was so full of love she couldn't speak for a moment. Already these two, lost in a world of flame and then given to her like a gift from heaven, were so beloved that she sometimes wept at the mere sight of them.

Max sat down right on the floor of the airport lobby and took out his Hornets baseball cap, putting it on his head. Then he handed one to each of the others. "It goes on like this, see?"

Uba took the cap, soberly inspected it, and put it on his head with a gap-toothed grin. Aissa handed hers back to Max, silently requesting that he do the honors, which he did with a tenderness that caught at Sophie's heart.

Sophie noticed Daisy wiping her eyes. "Just like Brad and Angelina," she said.

"Not funny," Sophie told her, though she couldn't help laughing.

"I'm going to have to give you a celeb couple's name," Daisy insisted, mimicking the paparazzi with the camera to her eye. "Let's see . . . Soph-Noah? Snophie? Sofa?"

"Ha-ha," Noah said, lifting Aissa and settling her on his hip. "Let's take your baby brother and sister home."

Center Point Publishing
600 Brooks Road • PO Box 1
Thorndike ME 04986-0001 USA

(207) 568-3717

US & Canada:
1 800 929-9108
www.centerpointlargeprint.com